Laura

PENGUIN CRIME FICTION

THE QUEEN IS DEAD

Jane Dentinger is the author of *Murder On Cue,*
First Hit of the Season, Death Mask, and *Dead Pan.*
She lives in New York City, where she is also an
actor, director, and teacher. She is currently at
work on the next Jocelyn O'Roarke mystery.

THE QUEEN IS DEAD

A Jocelyn O'Roarke Mystery

Jane Dentinger

PENGUIN BOOKS

PENGUIN BOOKS

Published by the Penguin Group

Penguin Books USA Inc., 375 Hudson Street, New York, New York 10014, U.S.A.

Penguin Books Ltd, 27 Wrights Lane, London W8 5TZ, England

Penguin Books Australia Ltd, Ringwood, Victoria, Australia

Penguin Books Canada Ltd, 10 Alcorn Avenue,
Toronto, Ontario, Canada M4V 3B2

Penguin Books (N.Z.) Ltd, 182–190 Wairau Road, Auckland 10, New Zealand

Penguin Books Ltd, Registered Offices: Harmondsworth, Middlesex, England

First published in the United States of America by Viking Penguin,
a division of Penguin Books USA Inc., 1994
Published in Penguin Books 1995

1 3 5 7 9 10 8 6 4 2

PUBLISHER'S NOTE

This is a work of fiction. Names, characters, places, and incidents either are the product
of the author's imagination or are used fictitiously, and any resemblance to actual
persons, living or dead, events, or locales is entirely coincidental.

THE LIBRARY OF CONGRESS HAS CATALOGUED THE HARDCOVER AS FOLLOWS:
Dentinger, Jane.
The queen is dead: a Jocelyn O'Roarke mystery/by Jane Dentinger.
p. cm.
ISBN 0-670-84109-9 (hc.)
ISBN 0 14 01.5835 9 (pbk.)
1. O'Roarke, Jocelyn (Fictitious character)—Fiction. 2. Women detectives—United
States—Fiction. 3. Actresses—United States—Fiction. I. Title.
PS3554.E587Q43 1994
813'.54—dc20 94–7598

Printed in the United States of America
Set in Minion
Designed by Virginia Norey

For my mother,
MARY PETERS DENTINGER,
who has taught me, by word and deed,
that a real lady always makes up her own mind

ACKNOWLEDGMENTS

As always, many thanks to my medical team—Dr. Russell Menkes and Dr. Mark Dentinger. Blessings on Gene Wolsk and Laura Stein, true patrons of the arts; also Jeff Duchen and all the great folks at GRQ Productions. And a special nod to both Lori Lipsky and Nicole Guisto. Last but not least, my fond regards and gratitude to Georgianna Kennedy.

THE
QUEEN
IS DEAD

1

There are three things every true New Yorker knows as surely as his or her own name and address: water-main breaks always occur at either nine A.M. or five P.M. so as to flood the subways during peak travel hours, leaving the greatest possible number of commuters stranded; after unusually mild winters, a sudden cold front will invariably blow in for the first day of baseball and turn Shea Stadium into a frozen tundra; and one can never, *ever* find a cab when it's raining. These are the Murphy's Laws of Manhattan, and Lieutenant Phillip Gerrard of the N.Y.P.D. knew them as well as anyone. And he accepted them, normally, with the stoic grace of a man somewhat fatalistic by nature.

However, when all three laws conspired to go into effect at once, in this case on a Monday in late April that had begun with deceptively balmy skies, even the most philosophical of men might feel a bit aggrieved. Actually Gerrard was way past aggrieved; he was pissed as hell as rain trickled down the collar of his coat as he pounded the pavement on East Eighty-fifth Street, heading for the entrance to Central Park. Not only were there no cabs in sight, but the transverses at Seventy-ninth and Eighty-sixth streets were both so flooded that even the buses couldn't get across the park. Running hard now, he saw his breath misting in front of him and felt his lungs starting to ache from sucking in cold, damp air as he splashed through dirty puddles that were quickly soaking into his brand new cordovan loafers.

"Son of a bitch! This is so stupid," he cursed to himself. "I feel like a damn . . . rabbit By which he meant the White Rabbit from *Alice in Wonderland* since, for the last few blocks, his footsteps had seemed to be keeping tempo with the silly refrain in his head: "I'm late, I'm late—for a very important date."

Only it wasn't a date, he admitted to himself. Technically it takes two consenting people to make a date; so this had to be classified as a "surprise visit." And he'd intended it to be a great, classy surprise, but all his careful plans had gone awfully awry. He regretted this bitterly because, as he knew from hard experience, when trying to get back in Jocelyn O'Roarke's good graces, having the element of surprise on one's side was crucial.

And Phillip had been trying for several months. But it was no easy thing to woo a woman who was five thousand miles away. Especially when said woman, after their two-year love affair and a stormy falling-out, had left town shortly after he'd gotten engaged to *another* woman. By the time Gerrard realized that he'd made a big mistake—which, fortunately, his fiancée had realized as well when he'd called her "Josh" for the third time in as many days— O'Roarke had already begun a new acting career in L.A. and, worse yet, a new relationship with some jerk hairdresser who owned a horse farm. But the hardest pill to swallow was the fact that she'd gotten involved in the Buddy Banks murder case and cracked it, all on her own with no help from him, thank you very much. Irrational as he knew it was, Phillip couldn't help but feel mightily betrayed by this. It was like watching your old flame dance with another man to a tune that had once been "our song." Solving murders together had been *their* song.

God, that's so twisted, he thought. I must have a macabre sense of romance . . . No wonder she didn't want to get married.

That had been the reason for their initial rift: Gerrard's desire to get hitched as opposed to Jocelyn's need to remain untethered. But it didn't matter now. The important thing was she'd come back to New York, though Phillip had no idea what part he'd played in that decision, if any. He'd first called her right after the Banks case, ostensibly to congratulate her on a job well done, though he'd managed to work in the fact that he was no longer betrothed. O'Roarke had been supremely neutral on this point, replying with a bland, "Sorry it didn't work out. Better luck next time."

It hadn't been much to go on but he had gone on, in slow, careful stages, like a general hunkering down for a long siege. A forthright man by nature, he'd amazed himself by the trickery and subterfuge he'd resorted to: wriggling her new address and phone number out of her writer friend, Austin Frost, so he could send oh-so-casual notes with some news clipping about a pal of hers opening in a new play. His last letter was, he felt, the pièce de résistance; he'd attended the Equity Fights AIDS Easter Hat Parade, the Broadway community's finest shining hour, often the best show of the year and one that Josh had never missed, and the letter he'd written her about it had, hopefully, made her green with envy and awash with homesickness.

Yet she hadn't even let him know that she was coming back. He'd bribed that bit of news out of their mutual friend, the renowned actor Frederick Revere, with a bottle of vintage Napoleon brandy that had cost him half a week's salary.

"This *is* the nectar of the gods," Revere had said after a moment's blissful savoring. "And so kind of you to give me a bottle that's actually older than I am."

"Aw, c'mon, Freddie. Josh always says that you're beyond age, and she's right . . . By the way, heard from her lately?"

"Oh, dear boy," Freddie had *tsk*'d sadly, "such a good brandy . . . such a *bad* segue. Not like you at all. Since I've already accepted your lovely bribe, spare us both the shoddy subterfuge and out with it, man!"

"All right, all right! I called her the other night and got some ditzy girl on the phone who said she was out of town. So where the hell *is* she?"

"That's better." Revere, after taking another languorous sip, had added, "She's in Washington."

"Huh? The state or—"

"D.C., of course. And I'm sure, if you put your excellent mind to it for a moment, you won't need me to tell you why."

"Let's see. Can't be an acting job, I would've read—"

"Aha! Subscribed to the *Theatrical Index,* have you?" Referring astutely to the monthly industry publication that lists all upcoming productions and their slated casts, Freddie had given him an approving wink. "Clever move. And you're absolutely right . . . Now what else would prompt our Josh to leave such sunny climes and—"

"Got it! The Pro-Choice rally. But that's today!"

"That's right. And she'll be here tomorrow. She's coming in on the Metroliner at two-thirty."

"Is she back for good?"

"I wouldn't presume to guess. But she'll be here for a bit anyway. You know I've been house-sitting for her—well, cat-sitting, really."

"Yes. And how is ol' antsy Angus?"

"Oh, a holy terror, a furred fiend incarnate," Revere had said with a Shakespearean moan. "He's shredded six pairs of my best socks. Why she sets such store by that creature, I'll never . . . Well, that's neither here nor there. Fact is, as fate would have it, I've been asked to do a small part in the new Merchant/Ivory film and—"

"Freddie, hot damn! That's fantastic. Congratula—"

"A minor, minor role, really," the old actor had demurred though his face had suffused with keen anticipation. "And it's shooting in Cornwall, so I'm off next week for the Merry Ol' Motherland. And Jocelyn is returning for a tender reunion with that feline shredding machine. But what her future plans are after that, I've no idea."

That was when Phillip had started making plans of his own The initial idea was to surprise her at Penn Station with champagne and flowers, then whisk her uptown for the tender reunion with ol' Angus and, hopefully, one of their own. It had all the right ingredients—surprise, flair, and romance—designed to appeal to her love of well-orchestrated theatrics and, more importantly, make that hairdressing horse farmer look like a rube.

Unfortunately, an assistant D.A. named Bernard Saperstein had a different agenda.

Bernie the Sap, as he was known at the precinct, was a greenhorn prosecutor with delusions of grandeur and designs on running for office someday. If Gerrard had his way, that day would never come, since Bernie was already exhibiting every sign of becoming a law enforcement liability of the first order, the kind of gung ho prosecutor so hot to get a conviction that he'd ride roughshod over due process and let the perps slip through legal loopholes almost as soon as they'd been indicted.

That morning the Sap had issued a search warrant for the home of a suspect in a rape-murder case that Phillip had been investigating. Badly as he wanted to nail this goon, Gerrard knew there wasn't sufficient evidence to justify the warrant yet and it was sure to be overturned later—unless the goon's lawyer was even stupider than Saperstein, and the chances of that were infinitesimal. So he'd had to go over the little twerp's head and that had taken hours, first waiting outside the D.A.'s office, then, once inside, arguing against Bernie's lame whines about "demonstrating our potency to the public" and "striking while the iron's hot!" When, at around two o'clock, he'd made a last-stand assault on Gerrard's "A.C.L.U.-ish overconcern for the felon," Phillip had reached over and yanked him up by his Givenchy tie.

"Listen, dickhead, I was *there*. You weren't. I saw the body and what he did to her. You—you just want to make a splash and see your name in print. I want him inside and I want him to *stay* there—which we've actually got a shot at this time 'cause he's got priors. Now, I'm twenty-four hours away from nailing down a witness who can place him at her building just before *and* after the attack. You blow this for me on a flimsy warrant and I'll make damn sure you get more press than you ever dreamed of . . . and all of it *bad*. And *then* I'm gonna come over to your house and break your little pinhead."

Saperstein had threatened a lawsuit and demanded a new tie, but the D.A. had overridden him and agreed to do it Phillip's way. But by then it was three-thirty and it was pouring.

Coming out of the park at Mariners' Gate on West Eighty-fifth Street, a sodden Gerrard made a supreme mental effort to buck himself up for the task at hand.

"Okay, just take a different tack. Like I just heard she got back and ran pell-mell over to see her. So I show up looking like a drowned rat, so what? Looks impetuous—dramatic. No, comical. What the hell. Josh always liked a good laugh at my expense."

When he rang her buzzer, he was surprised at being buzzed in immediately. Could she be expecting him? Or had her months in

L.A. just made her lax? Whatever the reason, he took the stairs up to her apartment two at a time. No champagne, no flowers, still—it would be quite an entrance.

Even before he knocked, the door swung open and he found himself face-to-face with . . . Freddie.

"Phillip! You look quite drowned."

"Yeah, couldn't get a cab."

"Well, of course not. It's raining."

"I *know* . . . Where's Josh?" He was dripping and panting, leaning forward with both hands on his knees as he scanned the familiar brownstone apartment that he hadn't seen in so long, that had once been his second home. Did she still have his old dressing gown in the bathroom? "Where is she, Freddie?"

Even before Revere spoke he knew something was wrong—something intrinsic was missing. No Angus, that was it. That cat had never once failed to greet Phillip at the door by running his claws down his legs, using him as a human scratching post.

"And where's Angus?"

"Gone." Frederick pointed to the loft space where the cat carrier was usually stored. "The both of them, I'm afraid. Dear boy, I *am* sorry. It was all very sudden."

"What was? You mean she's already been here and *left?!*"

"Well, yes. You see, this arrived at noon." The old actor handed him a rumpled telegram. "Josh took one look at it, packed her feline baggage, and bolted. You'll see, it was rather urgent."

Phillip, feeling like he'd just been struck with a poleax, allowed Frederick to peel off his sodden coat and deposit him in the bentwood rocker by the fireplace. It was hard to focus on the telegram while rocking, but the kindhearted old actor handed him a glass of the Napoleon brandy and, after a moment or two, the print came into focus. It read:

CORINTH NY

TESSA GRANT DIED UNEXPECTEDLY SAT STOP GREAT LOSS STOP
FUNERAL IS TOMORROW STOP NEED YOU HERE DESPERATELY STOP
PLEASE COME ASAP TO FILL IN AS HERMIONE

ALL LOVE
RYSON

Using the towel Freddie had gotten him, Phillip mopped his head and wondered vaguely, "Who sends telegrams anymore?"

"People in desperate straits, I'd say."

"And who the hell is Tessa Grant?"

"You don't *know?*"

"I'm not certain. The name's vaguely familiar. I dunno, maybe Josh mentioned her once."

"More than once, I'd guess," Revere said, a quiet severity in his voice. "If you'd been paying attention, you'd know."

"Know what? Was she a good friend of Jocelyn's?"

"Not exactly. But she was something more. She was the reason Josh became, as a professional at any rate, what she is today."

"And she's dead? . . . Oh, shit."

"Precisely."

2

"And, finally, to paraphrase Shakespeare—which I think, in this case, is only fitting, since dear Tess was prone to rearrange the Bard's words from time to time—"

A faint but appreciative chuckle rose from the crowd and rippled through the small chapel, which was filled to capacity, as the diminutive old gentleman on the dais beamed down at them with moist eyes and cleared his throat.

"When she shall die,/Take her and cut her out in little stars,/And she will make the face of heaven so fine/That all the world will be in love with night,/And pay no worship to the garish sun." Professor A. J. Hargreaves put a hand on the podium to steady himself before finishing. "Apt words, indeed, for Tessa Grant shone like a star all her life as she will continue to, I trust, in all our memories and in the great hereafter." His voice a mere whisper now, he raised his eyes upward and said, "Shine on, Tessy."

If there was a dry eye in the house, Jocelyn O'Roarke couldn't spot it. But then she could barely see the pew in front of her since waterproof mascara isn't all it's cracked up to be and hers, after a steady onslaught of tears, had run into her eyes and down her face. Raising a sleeve to wipe her cheek, she was checked by a soothing Southern voice.

"Don't, darlin'. You'll ruin that pretty blouse. Here, take this."

She nodded gratefully and dabbed at her eyes, leaving oily black streaks on the snow-white hankie with the initials *RC* stitched in one corner.

"Thanks, Ry. Oh, lord, I've ruined it . . . I'll get you another."

"Nonsense. I got a drawerful. My Aunt Mamie sends me a box of 'em every Christmas. I could wallpaper a room with 'em," Ryson Curtis said with a soft, silky laugh as he ushered her out of the pew and down the chapel aisle. "Besides, it brings back fond memories. Like that time I found you caterwauling in the hallway after you blew your audition at the Public."

"Oh, right. You gave me your hankie then," Josh said with a ghost of a smile. "I remember . . . God, I'm just like Scarlett, huh?"

"Exactly." Curtis put a comforting arm around her shoulder as he lowered his voice to a bass growl. " 'Never at any crisis of your life have I known you to have a handkerchief.' And a lucky thing, too, or we never would've met."

"Lucky for me anyway," she sniffed as Ryson opened the door of his BMW for her and she slid in. Josh knew exactly what her old friend was up to: distracting her from her misery by leading her down memory lane. But she was more than willing to be led after the emotional roller-coaster ride she'd been on for the last forty-eight hours.

First there'd been the incredible high of being at the rally in Washington; hearing Faye Wattleton, Ron Silver, and Gloria Steinem speak, among others; marching alongside a tiny girl in a stroller who'd raised a chubby fist in the air and caroled out, "Choice! Now!" Then there were the Gorilla Girls, the supremely enraged Carolyn Findley, and the signs and banners everywhere you looked that ranged from the profound (IF YOU DON'T BELIEVE IN ABORTION, DON'T HAVE ONE) to the sublimely silly (LEGGO MY EGGO). Seeing the masses of young college women there, she'd been filled with pride and, at the same time, heartsick that they *had* to be there to fight this battle yet again.

After a night of celebratory carousing with some friends from the Arena Stage, she'd tried to get some sleep on the Metroliner, but the prospect of coming home after so long an absence and wondering what (and whom) she'd find waiting for her had put her adrenal system into overdrive.

What she'd found, of course, had been the telegram from Ryson, which had sent her over the top and crashing down into the abyss. Thank God Frederick had been there to help pull her back together. With his typical aplomb, he'd sent her off to shower and change, and, by the time she'd emerged from the bathroom, he'd had coffee on the stove, Angus ensconced in the cat carrier, and a car and driver waiting downstairs to take her back to her alma mater, Corinth College.

All Josh had had to do was repack her bags, her L.A. wardrobe not being suitable for upstate weather. Tearing about the apartment, she'd offered a feeble protest. "A car *and* driver! Freddie, that costs a fortune. I could drive myself."

"Not in the state you're in. Your pupils are the size of saucers and you have artesian wells under your eyes, my dear. It's a six-hour drive. Can't risk you drifting off the road and doing yourself and that *dear* puss some harm."

"Aw, that's sweet. See, I told you you'd get fond of the ol' var-mint," she'd said while her back was to Revere, who'd gleefully bared his teeth at Angus. "But it's still too much money to—"

"Tut, tut. There are times, like now, when you don't stop to count farthings. Besides, those lovely Merchant/Ivory people are paying me quite handsomely. So off you go."

And off she'd gone, for the first time since graduation, back to Corinth for the funeral of a woman who had been instrumental in shaping the course of her life; a woman Jocelyn had always felt was invincible.

Tessa Grant, ten years her senior, had also been a Corinth alum-nus, one that the college, and the drama department especially, had been proud to call its own. During her first year in New York, she'd made her debut Off-Broadway as Cecily Cardew in *The Importance of Being Earnest* and knocked the socks off critics and audiences alike. She'd gone on to Broadway and even greater acclaim. Then, unexpectedly, Grant had veered off to regional theatre because she'd wanted to try her hand at directing. O'Roarke had met Tessa during her junior year when Grant had come back to Corinth for one semester to give a special seminar on Shakespearean acting, which had become her special province. And that was when Jocelyn's whole world had changed.

But she didn't want to think about that now; she couldn't risk it.

Ryson was revving the engine, checking the rearview mirror as he carefully backed out of the parking space. O'Roarke's arrival the night before was all a blur in her mind and she took the time now to study the face that she hadn't seen for the last five years. It had changed very little, but that wasn't really surprising; Ryson Curtis, son of Amelia Ryson, one of the last of the real southern belles, and Percy Curtis, a West Virginia lawyer from a wealthy family, was one of those odd men who seemed to have sprung from the womb middle-aged. So now that he *was* middle-aged, after a lifetime of looking older than his contemporaries, he was starting to look younger than the rest. He still had those pudgy, cherubic cheeks and that wispy, curly brown hair, which, having receded some, looked even more halolike. But the angelic motif stopped short at the crinkly little lines around those knowing gray eyes, eyes that caught everything and saw the humor in all things. But it was a wicked humor that most people, lulled by his impeccable southern manners, often missed.

Curtis was also a Corinth grad in the same class as Tessa's. But O'Roarke hadn't met him until she'd moved to New York . . . until she'd blown that audition at the Public Theatre, in fact. He'd been working there as an assistant to the casting director and so had witnessed Jocelyn's disastrous callback for the part of Portia in *Julius Caesar;* a part she'd read brilliantly for on the first go-round, only to cave in when the stakes got high.

"You know, I've never asked—why *did* you come out to find me after that debacle, Ry?"

"Well, one thing, I saw on your résumé that you'd gone to Corinth. But I was also there when you first read. You know, you were really too young for the role, but you were so superb Rosemary *had* to call you back. And you weren't *that* bad the second time but you'd lost your fire—it was the pressure, I know. But I remember thinking, How could such a young pup get such a handle on Shakespeare? Then I guessed you must've studied . . . with Tessa."

"But you didn't say that then!"

"Shoot, no. When we were in school together, well, Tessa cast a very big shadow, you know? I mean, think of all those poor S.O.B.s who went to Yale with Meryl Streep. It makes it hard to find your own place in the sun."

"Well, you did all right, didn't you? *Mister* Chairman." For that was Ryson's current position, head of the Corinth Drama Department. He'd risen from casting assistant to producer and director of several respectable repertory companies before coming back a year ago to helm the drama school, and just in time to direct Shakespeare's *The Winter's Tale* for the college's centennial celebration with a cast comprised of students, faculty, and star alumnus Tessa Grant in the role of Hermione; the part that Jocelyn would now be playing, though not for the first time. In her undergraduate days, she had played the role in a student production directed by none other than the late Tessa.

Of course, she'd been far too young for the part then, but it had been a seminal experience thanks to Tessa. Even now she could remember each rehearsal vividly; like the one where she'd finally gotten a handle on Hermione's difficult courtroom speech and Grant had congratulated her when giving notes, adding in that distinctively deep velvet voice of hers, "Just make sure you play this part again—when you're older. Right now you're quite touching in that scene. Later on you'll be able to really rip their hearts out." And Jocelyn had always longed to return to Hermione, but now she felt only misery and dread at the prospect of stepping into her old mentor's shoes. As Ryson said, Tessa had cast a *very* big shadow.

"Yes, I guess I did all right." Curtis broke in on her reverie. Intuitively he patted her knee lightly and added, "You did all right, too. And you *will* do just fine. Don't you worry, darlin'."

"God, I don't know, Ry. For the last six months I've done nothing but commercial auditions and one dismal sitcom pilot. And I haven't done any Shakespeare in *ages*. Frankly, I'm not sure I've still got the chops."

"Fiddlesticks. It'll all come back to you, just like riding a bike—you'll see." Curtis spoke reassuringly, with an air of supreme confidence.

But this was one of his special gifts and a key to his success: the ability to project a blithe demeanor in desperate circumstances. The fact was, Grant's death was not only a tragedy, it was a potential disaster of the first order. The purpose of Corinth's centennial was not merely commemorative, it was fiscal as well; a fund raising tool for the college, and *The Winter's Tale* was intended to be *the* big draw. With Tessa in the cast, Ryson had assured the board, it was a sure thing. In return he'd gotten an unusually generous budget for the gala production, which meant that not only his reputation but his job was riding on the show's success. To lose his star two weeks into rehearsal was a devastating blow, but Curtis was not a man easily devastated.

Even in the midst of making funeral arrangements, he'd been scurrying through his mental Rolodex for an adequate replacement, and O'Roarke had quickly come to mind. Not only was she an alumnus of some repute—though not of Grant's stature, of course—but she *had* done the role under Tessa's tutelage and was known to be a quick study. More importantly, he knew Josh could take the heat. He'd seen her once in a showcase production of Molière's *The Imaginary Invalid* where every conceivable thing that could go wrong *had:* missed light cues, actors drying up, and props falling apart on stage. The worse things got, the better O'Roarke got, incorporating each fresh disaster as if it were Molière's sly way of saying, "Isn't life a cocked-up mess?" And she'd managed it without ever once breaking character. That was the kind of intestinal fortitude he needed now to save his show—and his bacon.

What he hadn't counted on was how keenly she felt Grant's death. He'd expected the shock and regret at losing a highly re-spected talent. But clearly, for Jocelyn, there was something deeply personal about the loss, which surprised him, considering she'd had virtually no contact with Tessa since her college days. However, now was not the time to probe. They were almost at the Barnes' home, where all eyes would anxiously be on the new leading lady.

He was searching for a delicate way to prepare her for what was in store as they pulled into the wide circular driveway but, merci-fully, there was no need. After briskly dabbing her eyes with his hankie, Josh pulled out her compact, mascara, and lipstick to make some swift repairs as she muttered, "As Billy Crystal says—'It's

more important to look *mah*velous than to feel *mah*velous.' Right?
I feel like holy hell, but we can't let these poor schnooks know that.
They're upset enough . . . By the way, will I *know* any of these
people?"

"Hmm, I'm not sure," Ryson said as he watched, fascinated as
always by the female craft of cosmetics, as she transformed herself
with a few adroit pats and dabs from a watery wreck to the semblance of chic. "You might. Do you know Hank Barnes? This is his
place."

"Wait. This is the Lake House, isn't it?" Josh looked around with
dawning recognition. "I thought the college owned this place."

"It does. But Hank and his family live here as caretakers—rent-
free, of course. That's how they wooed him away from Carnegie
Mellon. He teaches theatre history, and he's a fair actor to boot.
That's why he's playing your husband, Leontes . . . Uh, did I mention that you'll be staying here?"

"No! God, I hadn't thought about that," she said, having spent
the previous night at Ryson's cozy but small apartment. Trying to
cover her dismay, she asked, "You mean, I'll be living *with* them?"

"Not exactly. You'll be at the guest house," Curtis answered
hurriedly, jerking a thumb over his shoulder to the left of the
main house. "It's quite comfortable . . . It's, uh, where Tessa was
stay—"

"Yeah, fine," Josh replied through gritted teeth. It was far pref-
erable to being housed in a dorm or motel and she would have the
privacy she required. But it would, she felt sure, be permeated with
Tessa's aura. Well, she was going to have to deal with that every
step of the way. "Might as well take the bull by the horns, huh?
Let's go, Ry." O'Roarke yanked the car door open and walked purposefully up the cobblestone path to the Lake House.

Lake House was a slightly grandiose description, as the "lake" in
back was really more of a pond. In her day the house had been
unoccupied and, thanks to the circular driveway that swung round
to the back of the house, near the pond, a favorite make-out place,
where Josh had had a sweaty tryst or two with her old steady. A
wave of erotic remembrance washed over her and she didn't dare
look over her shoulder toward the pond for fear that she'd be en-

gulfed by those images. Geez, I feel like Scrooge with the Ghost of Coitus Past, she thought, as she stepped onto the back patio and saw the French doors swing open.

A diminutive woman in a light wool suit and pearls rushed through the doors to clasp her hand.

"Oh, you're Jocelyn, aren't you? I'm so glad you're here. We all are. It was so good of you—"

"Josh, this is Miriam Barnes, Hank's wife," Ryson said smoothly, coming up the steps behind her. "And the crowning jewel of our Ladies' Auxiliary Committee. Also, mother of your daughter."

"Beg pardon?"

"Ryson! Don't confuse her. This is not the time to be droll," Miriam said with some severity as she smoothed back a tendril of light brown hair. "What he means is my daughter, Belinda—she's a sophomore at Corinth—is playing Perdita."

"Oh, I see . . . Well, I'd like to meet her."

"Yes, yes, of course . . . Only, well, be a little patient with her." Putting her back to Curtis, Miriam tugged Jocelyn to one side of the patio to murmur sotto voce, "Bellie was enormously fond of Tessa, you see. Well, we *all* were. But she's young—it might take her a little time to, uh, readjust."

"Sure. I know the feeling," Josh said dryly. "We'll just take it one step at a time."

"Oh, that's wise, so wise," Miriam gushed gratefully as she put her arm through O'Roarke's and drew her through the French doors into the room. "Now let me introduce you."

Josh shot Ryson a beseeching look over her shoulder. But he merely raised his hands in a helpless what-can-I-do? gesture. Miriam Barnes appeared to be one of those women whom O'Roarke classified as a "professional wife"; the type who saw it as their bound duty to bridge all troubled waters at all times. And there was no question that she was going to take charge of running Jocelyn through this social gauntlet.

Knowing that resistance was futile, O'Roarke let Miriam lead her around the room, introducing her first to her husband, Hank, a tall, strapping, sandy-haired fellow with green eyes that, she guessed, were normally sparkling but now looked dulled and grim. Next came Belinda/Perdita, a very pretty blonde who bore scant resemblance to either parent and who wrenched Jocelyn's heart as she was so clearly stunned with grief.

Shaking Belinda's listless hand, Josh applied a soft pressure to catch her attention and whispered, "I miss her, too. She opened a big door for me. Maybe she did the same for you? Just don't think that it's shut now, okay?"

She hadn't planned to say it and she saw Miriam's eyebrows fly up in alarm, but something came alive in Belinda's face and the girl hung on to her hand for a moment as her eyes moistened and she mumbled, "Yeah, I know what you mean. She, uh—she really had the larger picture in her head, huh? . . . And she knew who she *was*."

"Yeah, I always thought so. Tessa was tough in the best sense of the word—and before it was fashionable . . . She taught me a lot."

Belinda's gaze drifted to the lapel of Jocelyn's linen jacket, the same one she'd been wearing since the rally in Washington, with the button that read: JUST SAY ROE. "Hey, were you in D.C. for the Pro-Choice rally?!"

"Uh-huh. It was great. Lots of college girls down there, too."

"I bet. We had busloads going down. I really wanted to go but we were in rehearsal and—"

"Jocelyn! Come meet your Polixenes," Miriam urged softly, drawing her toward a raven-haired man standing next to a tall, broad-shouldered woman with her back to Josh. "This is Michael Mauro. He teaches Acting 101."

Mauro spun round with a flash of pearly white teeth to grasp her hand. "Goddamn! Great to meet you, Ms O'Roarke. I'll tell you flat out, we'd be screwed if you hadn't come. Isn't that right, honey?"

The tall buxom woman at his side turned slowly around and said, "No, Michael, *I* said we'd be screwed if she didn't come . . . And I said we'd also be screwed if she *did* come. 'Cause, next to me, Josh O'Roarke's the biggest goddamn troublemaker I ever met. Right, J.O.?"

Ryson Curtis was astounded at the transformation that came over Jocelyn when she caught sight of the other woman's face. Her artful touch-up job in the car hadn't succeeded in erasing the signs of fatigue and strain in her face. But now all those lines and shadows melted away as a sudden, startled joy filled her face, then radiated through her whole body until she was bouncing on her toes like a kid on Christmas morning.

"Christ on a crutch! I can't believe it!" The subdued buzz of conversation in the room stopped abruptly as O'Roarke threw both arms around the neck of the woman who towered over her. "Frances Mary Findley! Where the hell have you *been?!*"

3

"Hot damn, Frankie! I didn't think I'd ever see you again!" The whole room was riveted on this unexpected spectacle, but O'Roarke, standing on tiptoe to place a big wet kiss on the other woman's forehead, was for once, entirely oblivious. Frances laughed and gave her a playful shove that nearly sent her reeling. Giddy with delight, Josh bounded back to give her another peck on the cheek. "What a rush!"

"Now just you get ahold of yourself, missy," Frankie chided in a mock-schoolmarm voice, then added in a stage whisper, "You're in the heart of academia now—a hotbed of intrigue and scandal. You want them to start saying we're lesbos?"

"So what? Worse things have been said of us in the past."

"Hell, yes . . . *much* worse." The two women burst into peals of laughter, causing eyes to widen all around. Then Frankie draped an arm over Jocelyn's shoulder and headed her toward the kitchen. "Come on, let's get some food in you. Then we'll have a drink."

"Let's have several."

"Aces . . . I think I feel an Irish wake coming on."

As soon as they went out the door, a flurry of whispered speculation filled the room as Curtis, nearly writhing with curiosity, immediately buttonholed Michael Mauro.

"What, pray tell, was that all about?! Are they long-lost cousins or something?"

"Nope. Long-lost roommates—for two years—until Frankie dropped out of college and went to India. Haven't seen each other since."

"Amazin', just amazin'." Despite all the heavy concerns hanging over his head, Ryson was never one to pass up a good human interest story and, knowing neither woman was normally given to such overt displays of affection, his interest in this one was mightily piqued. "Frankie never mentioned it to me."

"Me, either. Until we got the news that O'Roarke was stepping in for Tess. You know, Frankie's the type that doesn't much care what she throws on her back—and she changed her dress *three* times this morning!"

Well aware of her sartorial disdain, Curtis was deeply impressed. "You don't say. Then why have they been out of touch for so long?"

"That I don't know. But my guess is—well, Frankie's always been funny about stuff like that. The past is the past and she doesn't like to look back much or even talk about it. Until now. She talked a blue streak about O'Roarke. Seems those two cut quite a swath through Corinth in their time. They were *assigned* roommates and it just turned out to be one of those odd matches made in heaven. Frank was a freshman music major who *only* listened to classical stuff and Jocelyn was a sophomore drama student who *only* liked rock 'n' roll, but there was just one stereo in their room. So at first they fought a lot, then they kinda educated each other. Frankie got her listening to Stravinsky, Mahler, and Wagner, and Josh got Frankie into Spirit and Elton John."

"Oh, yes, I see. Makes perfect sense, really." Ryson paused a moment as his agile imagination filled in the pieces. "Two highly intelligent young women with a passion for their craft, both from Catholic parochial schools with a shared ethnic background. And both—"

"Born to raise hell together. Frankie calls it the 'nympho or nun syndrome.' When Catholic girls get out in the world for the first time, they either cling closer to their virtue or they rush to discard it . . . Jocelyn and Frank were the first girls in their dorm to own a vibrator."

"Fascinating," Curtis said with a beatific smile. "Is there any bond so strong or sweet as shared rebellion in youth?"

"Uh, I think it was more than that," Mauro said cautiously. "They went through some hard times together, too. Frank's father dropped dead from a heart attack during her sophomore year. It was totally out of the blue and O'Roarke helped glue her back together. Then Jocelyn had some serious trouble—Frankie wouldn't say what—but she helped bail her out of it, I guess. They were tighter than tight . . . they were family."

Miriam Barnes, still looking a little nonplussed after the raucous reunion scene, wafted by with a tray of canapés and Ryson reached out to grab a celery stalk stuffed with cream cheese and crabmeat, which he took a ruminative bite of before asking, "Then doesn't it seem doubly strange, given how overjoyed they were to see each other—I mean, shoot, I saw Josh when she got her first part at the Public and she wasn't *this* thrilled. Why haven't they been in touch?"

Michael took a sip of his drink and shifted from foot to foot; he wasn't entirely comfortable with this line of inquiry but was too polite to say so to the chairman of his department. Finally he offered: "I think—and I'm filling in some blanks here—but I think there was a rift when Frankie dropped out of school to follow her old boyfriend to India. He was in the Peace Corps there and Frankie was in love with him, plus she'd gotten heavily into Eastern mysticism by then. And she just wanted to *go* . . . and Josh felt it was a bad move. Didn't want to see her give up her degree and her shot at first-chair cello in the orchestra. So the relationship sort of fell apart. Frankie—well, hell, she hates to admit when she's screwed up. I don't think she could face Josh after that."

"Why? Jocelyn isn't particularly the I-told-you-so type."

Feeling more than a little out of his depth, Mauro ran a hand through his raven locks and shook his head. "I dunno, I dunno. I know I *should*, but I don't. I met Frankie when she was coaching cello players at Carnegie Mellon—which was pathetic really 'cause she was better than the lot of 'em put together. Then we got married and had the kids and . . . she's hardly touched the cello in years, okay? 'Cause she's taking care of them and she's taking care of *me*.

And, meanwhile, O'Roarke's been taking care of business, you know? I, uh, I think Frankie feels like . . . like maybe she failed her somehow."

"Hmm, interesting, very interesting," Ryson said with as non-committal a tone as he could muster.

He was doubly intrigued now, not just by Frankie's past history with Jocelyn but by the palpable signs of Mauro's discomfort laced with undertones of a vague guiltiness; interesting in a man who he had heretofore assumed took both his wife and his marriage entirely for granted. Michael was one of those teachers, popular with both students and faculty, who had endless time and enthusiasm for his work, leaving his wife to shore up the home front.

The Mauros had three children, two girls and a boy, and, by Ryson's reckoning, this was the first time he'd ever seen Frankie without one or all of them in tow. She was also one of the few faculty wives that Miriam hadn't bullied into joining the Ladies' Auxiliary. Now he had a dim memory of Miriam complaining to him that Frankie had told her: "I'm sure you gals do a bang-up job, but, shit, I hardly have enough time to *read* as it is. And besides, I just wouldn't know what to *wear*, you know?"

It dawned on him that Frankie Mauro had always been a renegade wife by academia standards. He wished that he'd given her more consideration before now, almost as much as he wished he could be privy to her conversation with O'Roarke at that moment.

What he was missing at that moment was: "Remember the day we dropped that purple mesc and went up to Truman Falls?"

"Shit, yes! And when we got back to campus at night, we hopped the fence to swim in the pool," Jocelyn answered. "And, damn you, you dared me to go off the high board and I did."

"Yeah, that was *very* funny."

"Not for me. Going down was okay, but coming back up—given drug/time warp distortion—took about fifteen friggin' light-years! And I was totally freaked," Jocelyn said, using vernacular she hadn't touched in years.

"I know," Frankie said with a broad grin. "That was what was so great about you. You just could *not* pass up a dare 'cause of your brothers."

"Yeah, you knew all that stuff—about them being older and bigger, and me always hot to catch up—and you *used* it to sucker me into shit!"

"Ah, it was so easy, I couldn't resist. Besides, it was just tit for tat. You used to do crazy actor-crap to scare me when we were stoned."

"Nah . . . well, just that one time."

"Oh, right. One time that took five years off my life. You won't wake up before dinner and I draw the covers back to find your face a bloody pulp."

"Hey, it was Halloween and I was getting ready for a test in stage makeup. You should've seen that one coming."

"Nah, I never did. That was my most salient characteristic back then—I never saw *anything* coming." Frank smiled wryly at her old friend. "That was *your* department."

Josh raised a questioning eyebrow as she popped a cheese puff in her mouth and reached for another. Her stomach had been in a tight knot all morning, but now she found herself suddenly ravenous. "Hmm? Wha'd you mean?" she mumbled through the pastry. "Wha' was my department?"

"This." Findley made her hands right angles to her arms, which she extended full length. Then she dropped her voice to a deep bass. "The B-*iiig* Picture. Figuring all the angles like a pool player. Always looking ahead to see what might be looming on the horizon . . . or lurking around a dark corner."

"Aw, you're full of it!" O'Roarke shook her head vigorously as she brushed crumbs off the lapels of her jacket. By her recollection, she'd spent most of her four years at Corinth struggling vainly to figure out which way was up. Frankie had always been the one to come up with the big plans, the capers that she could almost always finagle Josh into. "I was a wuss—just following your evil lead. Whereas *you*—God, you were outrageous! Like when a guy some girl was trying to duck would call the dorm, you'd pick up the phone and yell, 'She no wanna see you, pig boy!'" Apoplectic with mirth, Josh nearly choked on the cheese puff, then gasped, "You had *major* balls, Frank."

Findley turned away from her ex-roomie's adoring gaze to fill two coffee mugs from a single beer bottle. Handing one to Josh, she said dryly, "That wasn't balls—that was bravado. There's a difference."

There are those rare connections between two people that, even after a long hiatus, can be resoldered in seconds, so we like to think. So Jocelyn, still in the rosy glow of reunion, thought. She and Frankie had always loved to argue semantics in days past, so she took a sip of beer to wash down the cheese puff before answering lightly, "Okay, I take your point, F. F. Bravado is what we rely on before we have real self-confidence—which nearly no one does at that age. Balls come later . . . Screw it, I still say you had, well— incredible chutzpah. Plus, you were impulsive and spontaneous. Qualities I was entirely devoid of, at the time. And you taught me a *lot* . . . This is getting too soppy for you, huh?"

"No, no, it's okay," Frankie said as she rummaged through her purse for a pack of Winstons while Josh silently noted that she hadn't changed her brand. It took three flicks of her Bic to get the cigarette lighted. "It's just so . . . damn *weird!*" Smacking her lighter down on the Formica counter, she turned to Josh, half laughing, half exasperated. "You're so different. Look at you—your clothes, your A-1 haircut, the way you carry yourself. I mean, last time I saw you, you were still a *shlubb!* And then, you're just the same. You *still* won't cop to yourself."

"About what?!"

"You always were—probably from birth—and still are the most *circumspect* creature I have ever known."

"Oh, thanks a fucking heap! I'm still the cautious little worm I—"

"Nah-nah-nah!" Frankie raised her long index finger didactically, flashing Josh back to their old dorm-room fights. "The first definition in *Webster's* is 'Being aware of all circumstances.' At all times. That's what I meant about the Big Picture. My theory is it came from being the youngest child—watching your sibs mess up, then planning how to avoid their mistakes. See, what you don't seem to remember, Josh, is I was the one who got us into shit and you were the one who got us *out.*"

"Well, yeah, maybe . . . a couple times. Like when the campus cops caught us—"

"No, *every* damn time. You always had an escape route."

"So I was the better liar, that's all."

"Unh-uh. You could think ahead." Frank gave O'Roarke a teasing smile, but there was something else behind the smile that wasn't the least bit in jest. "And you never got freaked-out by stuff. Least not so it showed."

"Oh, puh-*leese!* Let me refresh your selective little memory. What about the time you got us those strawberry barrels? Remember, we dropped the tabs down at that little park in town and started walking back to the dorm? By the time we got to that real busy intersection where I-90 and I-70 cross Main Street, I was so gone I couldn't make out the signal lights—they *all* looked paisley—and I was totally panicked."

As soon as Jocelyn mentioned strawberry barrels, a type of LSD that had been popular at the time, Frankie had started to chuckle and make small snorting sounds. But still she shook her head and said, "No, see, that's *your* selective little memory, Joey . . . God, we must've looked like such basket cases standing at that crosswalk! Then you finally went, 'It's cool. Green's always on the bottom, yellow's in the middle. We just wait for the top light.' "

"I *did?!* Are you sure?"

"Positive." Staring down at the counter, Frankie ground out her cigarette, then added, "It used to scare me some, the way you could do that—be hallucinating and still be so . . . logical. Guess that's why you never had a bad trip."

"No, that's not why. It's because I only did that stuff with you. You made me feel safe."

Findley looked up in surprise. "You really mean that?"

Trying to keep the soppy quotient down, Josh just nodded once, then placed a hand over her heart to give their old solemn oath: "Or may I never get laid again."

Then it was there, finally, the look she'd been waiting to see. Frankie's face broke into an ear-to-ear grin as her eyes lit up and danced with the old infectious glee that O'Roarke remembered so well. She threw back her head and chortled, "I made you feel *safe?* Shit—I guess you weren't so smart after all."

"Guess not," Jocelyn said dryly, though she really didn't mind the joke being on her. "I mean, would a truly—to use your phrase—*circumspect* person have let you sucker them into opening a can of Hormel chili just as they were peaking?"

Sticking a thumb in each ear, Findley waggled her fingers as she crossed her eyes and crowed, "Yudda, yudda!" It was Frankie's old clarion call, the battle cry she'd used whenever she was about to go on the party-hard warpath. And it struck such a fierce chord in Josh that she didn't know whether she was going to laugh or cry. What came out was a kind of hiccuping guffaw that choked and then spluttered to a halt as Miriam Barnes' anxious face appeared in the doorway.

"Is everything all right in here?" she asked in a politely hushed voice that was, by its very demureness, a kind of reprimand. "I was just wondering if . . . there was anything I could get you?"

Realizing that the walls of the old house were thick but probably not thick enough to keep their boisterousness from trickling into the other room, O'Roarke was instantly abashed. But not Frankie.

"Nope, we're just fine and dandy. Right as rain—A-okay," she said as she breezed up to casually lean an arm against the doorjamb, blocking any further interloping on Miriam's part. "But thanks for the thought . . . Did I tell you I just *love* that dress?"

"Do you?" Miriam said, looking skeptical, then she returned the spurious compliment in kind with, "Well, I like yours, too. You always look so nice . . . when you make the effort."

Ignoring the insinuation that it was an effort rarely made, Frankie gushed, "You're too kind," as she slid a plate of pigs-in-a-blanket off the counter into Miriam's hands. "Here. You know, Mike's just crazy about these little suckers—damned if I know how to make 'em. Why don't you be a doll and trot some his way, huh?"

Miriam barely got the plate through the door before Frankie let it swing shut. Then she pirouetted around to the state-of-the-art refrigerator, the kind with the ice-water tap and cube dispenser in the door, and yanked out another beer. Popping it open, she chuckled evilly, "I gotta admit, I do enjoy putting that woman's nose out of joint."

"Gee, I'd *never* guess," O'Roarke said, pouring on the sarcasm. "Here I thought you two were best buddies . . . What've you got against her?"

"Aw, nothing and everything, I guess." Frankie shrugged as she swung the fridge door shut with her behind. "Miriam's like—like Rebecca of Sunnybrook Campus, you know? Look up 'faculty wife' in the dictionary and you'll find her picture."

"Careful. Remember you're a faculty wife, too, pal."

"Nooo! Not by Miriam's standards, anyhoo. I think she thinks I was a biker chick before I married Mike . . . So I do my best to keep that dream alive for her, see?"

"Oh, I get it. You're just trying to live *down* to her expectations. Noble of you." Jocelyn's eyes wandered around Miriam's immaculate, ordered kitchen as she added, "She's a little like Amy Danforth, isn't she?"

"Christ, you're right! I haven't thought about her in years. She went out with that Cro-Magnon linebacker. And we could always tell when they'd had sex 'cause—"

" 'Cause Amy would bolt out of the room with her bed sheets afterward and make a beeline for the laundry room," Jocelyn said, though her voice had lost its earlier zest.

And Frankie caught it instantly. "Whoa, Nellie! You're not about to have an attack of good breeding, are you?"

"Yeah, maybe," Josh admitted with some embarrassment. "Now, look, spare me the 'it's just the nuns' crap, okay? We *are* at a wake after all. Our carrying on like this could look pretty disrespectful."

"To whom? To Tessa? Would she think so?"

"Hell, no! She'd want a party, not a dirge."

"Then why're you getting the guilts?".

"Because there are people out there who're upset and worried about the show. And most of them don't know me from Adam. So I should probably be, you know, mingling and, uh, trying to reassure them somehow . . ."

"I'm sure you're right. That would be the tasteful and appropriate thing to do," Frankie said with supreme insincerity as she refilled Josh's mug.

"Aw, screw you, Fran!" She had always been able to do this— make O'Roarke feel like a jackass when she was trying to do the mature thing. Frankie had a genius for making "the mature thing" seem ludicrous.

"No, really, you should either march right out there and

make small talk with small people who're gonna bore you to tears . . . *Or—*"

"Or what?" She cursed herself for even asking because she knew she'd just cave in as she always had.

"Or we could take a walk out by the pond to see if the lean-to's still there."

"You are a pernicious influence. You know that?"

"Yeah, but I'm a *safe* one. Grab another beer, will ya?"

4

"Jesus Christ! It's still here, Frankie."

Squatting inside the dilapidated lean-to, Josh used a thumbnail to scrape away the moss that had grown over the carved letters as Frankie bent down, squinting until she could make out the inscription they'd etched into the wood years ago.

> *Doesn't one always think of the past, in a garden with men and women lying under the trees? Aren't they one's past, all that remains of it, those men and women, those ghosts lying under the trees . . . one's happiness, one's reality.*
>
> —*V. Woolf*

"Damn, Josh, that's spooky," Frankie said, rubbing her arms with both hands against a sudden chill. "I mean, how'd we ever pick that quote? We weren't *that* deep."

"I dunno." Jocelyn gently traced a finger over the carved words. "Call it precognition, I guess. I remember we came out here with a bottle of Jose Cuervo and the Virginia Woolf compendium, that's all."

"Yeah, the bottle was mine, the book was yours. You were all fired up over *A Room of One's Own.*"

"Uh-huh. But this isn't from that. Damned if I know how we hit on it."

"Too spooky," Frankie said as she straightened up and headed out the narrow opening of the lean-to. "I need a smoke."

Following her out, Jocelyn lit a cigarette off her friend's and they both stood a moment in silent reverie. Finally O'Roarke ventured, "What happened with you and Charlie? After you got back from India?"

"It wasn't after, really. It happened while we were still there. He got more into the Eastern mystical thing—which had been my bag at first—karmic influences and all that. Then I just got more and more disenchanted by the poverty, the illness . . . the waste of life. It's funny, 'cause I was the one who went to the ashrams in the beginning. But Charlie was the one who ended up really embracing the whole gestalt. Then I just couldn't hack it any longer. I got like—screw these sacred cows, just feed a child. I couldn't manage serenity around all those distended bellies, you know?"

"But Charlie could?" Jocelyn was more than a little surprised. She remembered Charles Halloran as a tall, stoop-shouldered fellow whose unassuming demeanor had masked the soul of a high-principled, die-hard dissident. For some guys, the antiwar rallies had been as much about hell-raising as making a political statement. But Charlie hadn't been like that, and joining the Peace Corps after graduation had been his way of putting his money where his mouth was.

"Yup, got to the point where he was meditating five, six hours a day . . . and smoking hashish the rest of it. I think it just got too heavy for him. If you haven't seen it, it's hard to imagine, Josh, that kind of massive deprivation. You want to make it better, but there's so little you can do and so many who need help. It's easy to get overwhelmed and hopeless. Their religion tells you that *none* of this matters," Frankie said throwing her arms wide open, "that it's just to be used as a path to enlightenment, so screw the corporeal world and just get into your head, my friend. Well, that's awfully seductive, 'cause it's exactly what you want to do. Just run away. That's what we both did. Only Charlie ran inside his brain and I hopped on a plane . . . 'Course, this is all hindsight talking. Back then I was too young and too freaked to know what the hell was happening to us. I just knew that we'd somehow gone smash and I had to split."

"Is he still there?" O'Roarke had a vision of Charlie, gaunt and bearded, wearing nothing but a loincloth, petrified in a permanent lotus position.

"Nah, he left about a year after I did, though I didn't know till much later. He went back to Pennsylvania and went into his dad's hardware business. Weird, huh?"

"Mind-boggling. Have you seen him since?"

"Shit, no. When I left, I, uh . . . I did *not* handle it well. And I've always wished I could tell him how sorry I was about that. But I'm too gutless, I guess."

They'd started walking around the edge of the pond. Frankie stopped to pick up a piece of shale. With a flick of her wrist, she sent it scudding along the water's surface, skipping nearly to the opposite side.

"Seven skips." Josh whistled in admiration. "You haven't lost your touch."

"Can't afford to. It impresses the hell out of my kid Shane. Some days, it's the only thing that gets me any respect," she said lightly, trying to dispel some of the vain regret still hanging in the air. There was a question Jocelyn wanted very much to ask, a question she'd wanted to ask for years, but she took her cue from Findley and, instead, asked the question that was expected of her.

"So, how many kids have you got?"

"Three, God help me, two girls and a boy. Shane's the youngest—just turned five. Jennie's nine and Terry's seven. They're both distaff versions of their dad. But Shane's like me—only better. He's a little devil, but smart as a whip."

"Got any pictures?" O'Roarke asked dutifully, well drilled in the routine.

"Nope. Mike's the one with the snapshots. Me, I like people to see 'em in 3-D. It's scarier that way." She waggled her eyebrows, grinning at Josh.

"You like being a mom?"

"Yes and no. I like *them*. They can be a lot of fun and they're always surprising the hell out of me. So, yeah, I like being their mother. But I don't dig being seen as just a 'mom.' I don't like the way it makes people slot you, you know?"

"Well, they're gonna do that anyway—whatever or whoever you are—if you're a woman."

"Oh, come on! I bet people don't do that to *you*."

"Sure they do." Josh looked down at her feet, abstractly noting that the wet grass wasn't doing her suede pumps any good but what the heck. "The world is filled with would-be casting agents."

"What're you saying? Life's like show biz? Christ, what a thought!"

"But it *is*. Casting agents see actors and they don't wanna know about your stretch—your range. They just want to know which pigeonhole you fit in. You're either an ingenue or a comedienne, a character type or a leading lady. Their job is to categorize people, and they really don't like it when you try to break out of the mold. It was a nasty shock when I first went to New York. See, I'd been here for four years, learning how to run the gamut, doing everything from Shakespeare to Neil Simon. Then I found out that being a good actor and being a good 'commercial type' are two completely different things. Which sucks, if you ask me, and it sucks more for women than men because there are fewer *acceptable* types for us . . . in show biz and in life."

"So how do they type you?"

"In the business, I'm a 'character woman.' In life, I'm a 'single woman'—worse yet, I'm a 'single woman of a certain age.' Never married. That automatically makes me suspect. Maybe I'm bright, maybe I'm accomplished, but still there has *got* to be something wrong with me because I couldn't get a man."

"Or maybe you're a dyke." Frankie shook her head with a dry chuckle. "Yeah, you're right. And I'm suspect 'cause I don't bake cookies, get my hair done, or . . . join the Ladies' Auxiliary. Which means I'm an unfit mother and a derelict wife."

"It's an interesting phenomenon because—when you really look at most women's lives these days—very few of us fit the slots. But the myths and the stereotyping go on because people get so spooked by the atypical."

They were on a roll now. Frankie nodded her agreement eagerly.

"Right, right. And the big irony to me is this is a country that got founded because some folks wanted to find a place where it was cool to do your own thing. But a lot of people can't handle the diversity that's our national birthright. So instead of *chacun à son goût*, it's like, like—choke on some glue!"

O'Roarke laughed so hard she nearly tripped over a tree root. Frankie grabbed her arm to keep her from falling. When Jocelyn regained her balance and her composure, Findley shot her a side-long glance and said, "Let me ask you something—and if I'm outta line just say so—your staying single, does that have anything to do with, uh, with you and Harry . . . and the abortion?"

O'Roarke stood stock-still as images of Harry Stein, her old college sweetheart, flooded her memory; foremost in her mind was the expression on Harry's face when she'd told him the rabbit had died. "Poor Harry, he was so sweet about it—'Whatever you want, babe. We'll do whatever you want,' he kept saying. But he must've been scared to death."

"Yeah. And with good reason. His folks would've *plotz*ed if he'd married a shiksa," Frankie interjected.

"True, but he offered, and that was brave of him—and dear."

"Sure. But I bet he knew deep down you'd never take him up on it," Frankie countered; she had liked Harry Stein but never felt him quite worthy of Josh's affections.

"Well, there you go then—there's your answer," O'Roarke said briskly as she resumed walking.

"Uh, I don't follow," Frankie said as she did just that, loping to catch up with Jocelyn.

"Honey, if *you* knew that *he* knew I wouldn't take him up on it—and you were my closest friend and he was the guy I was in love with—well, that says something, doesn't it? Something about me."

"Says what? That you were *never* meant to marry? Hell, Jo, you were just a kid."

"No, I wasn't," O'Roarke shot back instantly. "I was twenty, and old for my years at that. And I'd made up my mind what I was going to do before I told Harry or you I was pregnant . . . I only discussed it with one other person." Her face clouded over but she kept it hidden from Frankie and quickly went on. "Anyway, frightened as I was, I still had a gut *certainty*—I was luckier than most in that."

"And you still feel that way—in your gut?"

"Yeah, I do." The two women regarded each other solemnly, then Frankie laid a hand on Josh's arm and gave one short nod. O'Roarke grinned and broke into broad Long Island–ese. "Listen, dahling, it's not as if I haven't had offers, let me tell you."

Frankie followed suit by raising her eyebrows and whining inquisitively, "Really? *So*, tell—are you seeing anyone? A nice dentist, maybe? Or an accountant?"

"Gawd! Don't I wish. You know any nice, single, professional men?" Josh whined back in kind.

Rounding the end of the pond, they came to a stand of trees on a freshly mowed lawn. Frankie's arm shot out, pointing to a figure some yards away, as she exclaimed, "Oy! From your lips to God's ear, *bubeleh*. There's one now. A yellow-breasted bachelor." Then she put two fingers between her teeth and gave a short, piercing whistle. "Hey, Will! Come on over."

Despite her orders, the compact, redheaded man was slow to drag his gaze away from the ground beneath his feet. But eventually he ambled toward them with his hands shoved deep in the pockets of his jeans and a slightly peeved look on his square-jawed face.

"Hallo, Frankie. I see you made your escape early," he said witn a British accent Jocelyn couldn't quite place.

"I'm not escaping. Just taking a little stroll down memory lane with an old friend. Josh, this is Will Coltrane. Will, meet Jocelyn O'Roarke."

"Oh, gosh, yes—I almost forgot." Coltrane wiped one hand hastily on the seat of his jeans before extending it for a brief but firm handshake. "She without whom the show cannot go on, right? Awfully nice to meet you, Miss O'Roarke."

"You'd better make it 'Josh,'" Frankie suggested. "Since you're going to be neighbors and all."

"We are? How nice," Jocelyn said vaguely while her actor's ear tried to dissect his accent. On the surface, it had the clipped tones of the Upper Crust, but the vowel sounds weren't quite right. It was the voice, she decided, of someone well educated but not to the manner born; though Coltrane's bearing and the cool assessing look in his dark brown eyes bespoke someone who aspired to the aristocratic.

"Yes, I'm at the gate house, you see." He jerked his head in the direction of the small, cobblestone house that stood at the north end of the property, near the front of the driveway. "The college has very kindly put me up there for the duration."

"Will's over here on a grant from Cambridge. He's a limnologist."

"Really? That sounds very impressive . . . uh, what the hell is it?"

"Limnology's the study of freshwater bodies—ponds, lakes, and so on—and their surrounding biological environment." Coltrane managed to give this definition without making her feel like a huge ninny, just a very little ninny. "That's why I'm staying here. This pond's a great habitat because the college has maintained it in its natural state for so long. It's just rife with specimens . . . well, it *was*." He ended on a sour note as his gaze drifted down to the ground again.

"Uh-oh, me thinks Willie sounds a tad pissed off," Frankie kidded as she offered him a cigarette. "Somebody been stealing your weeds, precious?"

"Well, look!" In no mood to banter, Coltrane waved an accusatory arm at the lawn they were standing on. "They've *mowed* it, haven't they?! After I asked Hank not to. And, really, he had no right. They're just tenants, after all."

"Aw, bummer, Will." Frankie patted his back consolingly. "I bet Miriam put him up to it. She probably wants to have the next Ladies' Tea out here."

"No, no, it was Hank. Just being spiteful . . . Well, just being incredibly thick, I suppose."

"As a brick. That's our Henry," Frankie concurred. But Jocelyn felt sure that Will thought it was an intentional act and was being tight-lipped, or just "veddy" British, about Barnes' real motive.

Despite his reticence, he still looked mightily peeved, so Josh offered hopefully, "Won't it all grow back?"

The weary look he gave her made it abundantly clear that she'd just entered the big-ninny class, though his voice remained gallingly polite. "'Fraid not. Not this spring, anyway. Fortunately, I've already taken some cuttings. And, thank God, they've left the west end alone—so far. I should be able to get some more specimens there."

"Sure you will, doll. Hey, want me to screw up his Lawn Boy?" Frankie flashed him her evil grin and was rewarded with the driest of chuckles. It occurred to O'Roarke that her friend was fond of Will Coltrane, which came as something of a surprise since the guy clearly was not a party waiting to happen. "You gotta see, Josh, Will's turned his porch into a greenhouse. He's got amazing stuff in there. You'll show it to Josh, won't you?"

"Of course. It'd be my pleasure," he said with that brand of British civility that is just shy of the supercilious. "Though I don't think now is the time, eh?"

At least he didn't say "eh, what," Jocelyn told herself. The guy was really beginning to burn her butt. Maybe she was just a bit jealous of the attention Frankie was lavishing on him, but she dearly wanted to tell Coltrane where he could put his specimens. Instead she said, "You're right. Besides, I have a chalk thumb—as opposed to a green one. Plants see me coming and wither on the spot. Anyway—I should be heading back."

"God, me too. Mike's gonna be steamed," Frankie said, adding, "if he's even noticed I'm gone, that is." Jocelyn saw the two of them share a look of mutual long suffering and didn't like it. Yeah, she was definitely jealous. "But let's stop by the guest house first, so you can see your home away from home."

"Uh, I dunno, Frank." Jocelyn was in no hurry to take possession of Tessa's abode. Clearly Coltrane had no wish to accompany them either as he mumbled something about getting back to his greenhouse before beating a hasty retreat.

Still Frankie insisted, "No, you gotta see it. There are some great pieces—genuine antiques. Of course, *La* Grant rearranged things as soon as she got here. Still, the place has got real character."

A distinct coldness had come into Frankie's voice when she mentioned Tessa, but Josh was scurrying to keep up with her friend's long strides and hadn't the wind to ask why.

When they reached the gravel path leading up to the cottage, she shoved Josh in front of her, saying, "You first. Age before beauty."

O'Roarke came back with the expected Dorothy Parker rejoinder, "Pearls before swine." But her steps were listless as she drew near the front door. Just as she was reaching for the knob, the door swung open and she was face-to-face with a tall, bull-necked man in a navy windbreaker.

He'd aged, grown gray and heavier since she'd last seen him. But this wasn't a face she was likely to forget.

Antipathy can be a wonderfully rejuvenating influence at times; so thought Frankie as she watched her friend's spine snap straight as she drew her shoulders back. And when she spoke, her voice had that old feisty edge to it.

"Well, as I live and breathe, if it isn't Officer Calvin Kowaleski! And here I thought you'd died."

"You wish," the huge man grunted back. "And it's Sheriff Kowaleski now, O'Roarke."

"Aw, you remembered my name. Frankie, Officer Cal remembered my name! Isn't that just the sweetest?"

" 'Course I remember. I remember the name of every punk I ever arrested—in case they come back . . . So welcome home, O'Roarke."

5

Officer Kowaleski, we're down on our knees
'Cause you look like a fella with a social disease.
Officer Kowaleski, we're going to sue.
So, Officer Kowaleski, screw you.

Frankie was singing softly as she followed O'Roarke, who was following Sheriff Cal down a narrow hallway to the living room. Even
though she was fairly sure he couldn't hear the song, Jocelyn made
shushing motions behind her back, hoping to stop Frankie before
they both dissolved into giggles. The tune was "Officer Krupke"
from *West Side Story*, but the lyrics were Frankie's; something she'd
come up with in the back of a patrol car as she and Josh were being
hauled down to the police station after yet another student demonstration. Kowaleski, of course, had been at the wheel, and the
girls had gleefully serenaded him all the way downtown.

Shakespeare said, "Some men are born great, some achieve greatness, others have greatness thrust upon them." Calvin Kowaleski
fell into none of these groups. He belonged to a fourth category:
men who aspired to greatness out of sheer will, without having
either the mental acuity or moral vision to justify such aspirations.
This had always been O'Roarke's assessment of his character, and
the fact that he had achieved the rank of sheriff did nothing to alter

her opinion. It was, she felt, just another example of the Peter Principle at work.

Ol' Calvin has finally risen to the level of his greatest incompetence, O'Roarke thought. Unless he decides to run for office someday.

She was so caught up in memories of her old nemesis and the battles they'd fought that she hadn't had time to wonder, as at any other time and in any other place but Corinth she would have, just what Kowaleski was doing there. So she was thrown for a loop when she stepped into the sunny, antique-filled living room to find Ryson Curtis sitting on a chintz-covered sofa with a cup of tea balanced on one knee and an anxious expression on his face. But the teacup and the sorry face were whisked away as he rose to his feet to greet them.

"Ah, Jocelyn—Frankie! I was wondering where y'all had gotten to. Been jawin' about old times, I bet."

Looking askance, Frankie wrinkled her nose and said, "Excuse me? 'Jawing?' I don't *think*— Ow!"

"That's right," O'Roarke put in quickly after purposely stepping on Findley's big toe. She knew that Ryson only used such folksy Southernisms under stress. "We've chewed the fat until our gums bled. Then Frankie thought I might like to see the place, so—"

"Oh yeah?" Kowaleski broke in, lowering himself onto a spindly love seat that groaned under his weight. "And how did you plan to gain access, Mrs. Mauro?"

"Huh? Gain access? What do you mean?"

"I mean, do you have, like, a key to this house?"

"Of course not! Why would I need a key? It's never locked."

"Really?! You know that for a fact? You used to popping in and outta here a lot?"

"Of course not! Don't be ridiculous," Frankie shot back with some asperity, but Josh, trying to gauge how close she was to blowing a gasket, was surprised to find her friend more discomfited than irate. "But lots of people did—all the time."

"She's right, Sheriff," Curtis interjected. "Ms Grant was a very *mi casa es su casa* sort."

"*Me* what?" Kowaleski swung round to give him a dangerous

look; clearly the use of foreign phrases was, in itself, enough to raise his darkest suspicions.

"It means 'my home is your home,' Kowaleski," Jocelyn said, anxious to get to the reason for this impromptu grilling session. "It means Tessa had an open-door policy. That's not too unusual in a small town, now is it?"

"No, it ain't," he grunted back, then added, "What's not usual is when somebody changes their policy."

Swiftly O'Roarke slid an ottoman over with one foot and plunked herself down opposite Calvin, fixing her eyes on his, "How do you know she did?"

Enjoying the spotlight, he locked both hands behind his beefy neck and said smugly, "Easy. Somebody who's happy to have folks come and go as they please don't go out and buy an extra lock—which she did 'bout a week back . . . Plus the front door was double-bolted the day the body was discovered. Hank Barnes had to break the kitchen window to get in. Now that don't sound like 'drop in anytime' to me."

"What *does* it sound like to you?" Jocelyn asked, feigning a respectful interest. Actually the interest was real, very real indeed; the respectful bit was just a sop to help Cal forget that she'd always treated him like shit.

"I'd say somebody was making the lady nervous."

"Not necessarily. She might've always locked up at *night* for all we know. And maybe the old lock was broken," she said carefully. "So really, you're just speculating here."

Happily, vanity vanquished long-term memory and what little professional discretion Kowaleski possessed. "The hell I am! Grant reported a break-in three days ago. Said it wasn't the first, neither."

"Why—but that's not possible!" Ryson strode around the love seat to face Kowaleski. "She never said a word about it to me . . . What was taken?"

"Nothin'. That's why she didn't report the first one. Said she could tell somebody'd been going through her things. Even the second time, she couldn't find anything missing. So we didn't bother—"

Calvin tried to bite his tongue, but his foot was already in the way.

"You didn't bother to *investigate?!*" Ryson's eyes were bulging, but then his acquaintance with Kowaleski was relatively brief. Frankie and Josh, on the other hand, merely exchanged a look that said: Once a *putz* always a *putz*. "My God, man, even if there was no actual theft, you should've at least—the very least—let the college know!"

"Hey, take it easy now, Mr. Curtis." Calvin waved one ham-fisted hand above his head. "The lady said she didn't want us to make a big stink about it."

"Well, that damn dog won't hunt, Sheriff, and you know it," Ryson said with a strong twang. "Whatever Ms Grant's wishes were, you had a *duty* to let us know about the break-in. This is, after all, college property."

"Uh, yeah, I guess, only it didn't seem like much at the time, see?" Cal was sweating bullets now, and Frankie was clearly enjoying every drop. But Jocelyn wasn't.

She felt like she'd been dropped into the second act of a play without knowing the exposition. What were the two men doing here in the first place? If, as she'd been told, Tessa had died of a heart attack, what was Calvin up to?

Getting to her feet so she could position herself between Ryson and the object of his wrath, she asked, "If it wasn't a big deal then, why is it now? Why the Q and A? Are you just trying to cover your tracks or—"

"A little late for that, I'd say," Curtis got in, but she cut him off with a sharp look.

"Are you just on a fishing expedition? Or did something turn up in the autopsy?"

"Who said anything about an autopsy?" he muttered.

"Christ—spare me, Kowaleski. In cases of sudden death, there's *always* an autopsy . . . even in Corinth. So what did the M.E. say?"

If she had just sprouted a third eye, Kowaleski couldn't have been more stunned. It wasn't just her assertiveness that threw him; O'Roarke had always been a ball-buster. It was the terminology she used and the way she used it; it indicated a degree of insider knowledge that put him at an extreme disadvantage. Maybe she was just faking it, throwing around phrases she might have picked up from playing some lady P.I. The problem was, even if she were bluffing, so was he. Her crack about a fishing expedition was pretty close to the mark, too close for comfort.

The love seat made threatening noises as he shifted his weight and tried to throw her off stride with: "This ain't the big, bad city, O'Roarke. We don't have a medical examiner—just ol' Doc Morgan down at Tompkins Memorial is all."

Undeterred by this feeble feint, Jocelyn asked, "And what did old Doc Morgan have to say about his findings?"

The trouble was Kowaleski was having a hard time remembering exactly what the doctor had said. The old coot always mumbled, had a voice that sounded like dry leaves rustling, and used so much medical jargon it was tough to tell what he was driving at. What little Cal did remember seemed pathetically thin at the moment, but it would never do to admit it.

Instead he growled, "I'm, uh, not at liberty to disclose that information at present." A phrase that he had, in fact, picked up from watching "Hawaii Five-O" reruns.

"Well, was there *any* forensic evidence that would rule out a normal heart attack?" O'Roarke took the edge off the question with a cajoling smile. "You can tell us that much, can't you?"

"All I can say—all I'm *willin'* to say right now," he amended with a huffy sniff, then faltered, "is, well . . . officially, the deceased's, uh, cause of death was a heart attack. No question there—her ticker just stopped."

Standing behind Kowaleski, Frankie winked broadly at Josh as she tapped a finger against her forehead and mouthed one word: *Brilliant!* To her surprise, O'Roarke ignored her little pantomime. Instead, she kept her eyes locked on Calvin as if she were trying to stare through that thick skull of his.

"Okay, that's your official position. Fine." She kept her voice carefully neutral. It was clear that Calvin was mainly blowing smoke. He didn't know much but he did know *something,* even if he didn't realize what it meant. And she wanted to get it out of him before he lost his cool and became entirely recalcitrant. "But Dr. Morgan must've said something that, uh . . . keyed your investigative instincts, right?"

She was still using fancy phrases, but Kowaleski found the current batch far more palatable. "Well, yeah, maybe," he agreed with a condescending nod. "It's a pretty minor thing. But I always like to follow up on details. Small stuff can make a big difference in the long run, you know."

"Oh, absolutely." She nodded her encouragement while Ryson and Frankie exchanged disbelieving looks. Given O'Roarke's paramount contempt for the man, this was like watching Gloria Steinem give Jesse Helms ego strokes.

"I don't even know if Doc Morgan really saw the, uh, possible significance of it." (Big lie.) "But it struck me right off." (Bigger lie.)

"Like a bolt out of the blue, I'm sure," Curtis snarled silkily.

"What the hell's that supposed to mean?!" Calvin jerked his head around and caught the two smirking faces behind him. "Look, Professor, I'm just trying to do my damn job, and I don't need—"

At that inauspicious moment, the beeper clipped to Kowaleski's vinyl belt went off. He jabbed at it ineffectively once or twice, then announced importantly, "I need to use the phone."

As soon as the sheriff was out of hearing, Ryson sighed, "I swear, the man is like something out of an Ionesco play."

"I think you're being a little unkind—to Ionesco," Frankie chuckled. "Eugene wouldn't write a line like 'The deceased's cause of death was—'"

"Can it," O'Roarke snapped at the both of them. "He might hear you."

"So *what?!* Geez, Josh, you know the guy's a total twit," Frankie said, looking to Curtis, her newfound soulmate, for confirmation, which was quickly forthcoming.

" 'Tis pity he's a fool," Ryson quipped.

"No, he's not!" There was a hushed vehemence in Jocelyn's voice that took them aback. "Anyone who knows something you *don't* know is not a fool." Nodding in Calvin's direction, she added by way of explanation, "He's dim, all right, and ignorant, too. But he's got a kind of feral shrewdness—which is probably why he's lasted this long. He knew enough to get his butt up here and make some noise, just *in case!*"

"In case what?" Ryson asked uneasily.

"In case his ass needs covering . . . In case something turns up wrong in the autopsy report. He *knows* he didn't do a proper job following up the break-in report. Whatever the doctor told him was enough to put the wind up his sails."

"You could be right," Curtis murmured anxiously. "The, uh, body was supposed to be released for cremation today. I thought that's what he came to tell me. Still, if he had any solid information, why didn't he say so?"

"Because you stopped him," Josh shot back, "just when I had him loosened up. That wasn't smart, Ryson. Because even if he's on a wild-goose chase, you can't risk the slightest suggestion that Tessa's death wasn't—"

"I know, I know," Curtis whispered hurriedly as Kowaleski approached them.

"Look, I'm outta here, folks. There's been some vandalism up on campus—damn kids! Nothin' serious, but I have to check it out." Calvin was all officiousness again. "Now I hope I don't need to tell ya that everything we've been discussin' is confidential, do I? Goes no farther than these four walls for now, right?"

"Rights" were echoed back all round, and Kowaleski marched toward the front door with the confident appearance of a man who had things under control. Ryson and Frankie collapsed in unison on the sofa, but Jocelyn made tracks to catch up with Calvin just as he was getting into his squad car.

"Look, Cal—uh, Sheriff, I don't want to hold you up. But I *am* going to be staying in this house alone, so I'm a little anxious. You understand?"

"Don't be. I'll keep an eye on you, don't worry."

(Gloria had truly done a magnificent job of snowing Jesse.)

"Oh, I know, I know. But—be a pal—what's the scoop from the doc?"

"I can't get into this now, O'Rourke. And it's probably nothin', anyways. He just said something about her blood alcohol bein' funny is all." For a brief instant, Calvin dropped the Super Cop act and added quietly, "Maybe she got paranoid about those break-ins and drank herself into thrombosis, you know? So relax, we ain't talkin' homicide here. But I'm damn well gonna find out who was spookin' that lady."

On that quasi-tender note, Kowaleski peeled out of the driveway with gravel spewing up from his back tires right into Jocelyn's face. After the dust had settled and O'Roarke's coughing subsided, she wiped her eyes and wondered aloud, "Why the hell didn't she report that first break-in?"

6

"Sir, spare your threats. The bug which you would fright me with
I seek. To me can life be no—"

"Okay, Josh, you rise on this line."

"Uh, I do?" Jocelyn squinted down at the first row, where Ryson
sat with his director's script splayed open on his lap. "Why?"

"Why? Well, uh . . . That's when Tessa rose, darlin'." Curtis was
trying to be the soul of tact, but Josh saw him sneak a peek at his
wristwatch.

After settling the extremely unsettled Angus into the guest house
and wolfing down a damp turkey sandwich Miriam Barnes had left
in the fridge, O'Roarke had collapsed on top of the canopy bed, too
tired to do more than kick off her shoes, and slept until six A.M.,
when the still discombobulated Angus walked daintily across her
face. It was a good thing he had, since she'd promised to meet Ryson
at the theatre at eight so he could give her her blocking.

They were working against the clock now so Jocelyn could be
somewhat prepared for the run-through of Act One with the entire
company, which was scheduled to start at eleven. It was ten-fifteen
already and they had gotten to Hermione's last scene in the first
half—the crucial trial scene where she answers her husband's un-
founded charges of infidelity. Knowing the pressure Curtis was under, O'Roarke had been, in her humble opinion, lamblike in her

acquiescence to his every direction. However, that did not mean she was prepared to be led to the slaughter.

"Well, I—uh, I'm sure Tessa made it play," she said, trying to meet him tit for tact. "But it just doesn't work for me, Ry. See, she's just given birth and this is a long speech—it's my *defense*. And I need to conserve what little strength I've got left till near the end. Where it really counts."

Ryson deftly turned a sigh into a yawn, then gave her a soft smile. He knew the price one had to pay when working with an actor-slash-director. And it was a good sign that Josh had slipped into the first person while discussing her role. It was important that she *owned* Hermione as opposed to just mimicking Tessa's characterization. But he had a run-through in forty-five minutes and it was of the essence that she take possession *fast*.

"Well, you can't stay in the damn chair for the whole speech, Josh. Where do you think you want to get up?"

"On 'Now, my liege, tell me what blessings I have here alive,/ That I should fear to die,' " she said instantly and with great conviction. " 'My *liege*' is what gets her up. Calling him my lord and master at this moment, after all the shit he's pulled—well, it's magnificent irony, isn't it? It triggers her rage and, at the same time, it makes Leontes look real bad. Then, once I'm on my feet, I whack him with the legal stuff—' 'Tis rigor and not law.' "

There was no question now that O'Roarke had moved into the part bag and baggage. This was a radically different interpretation from Tessa's tragically victimized queen and sure to raise eyebrows amongst the cast. Ryson found he rather liked the idea but felt compelled to comment, "Makes her a tad Machiavellian, doesn't it?"

"Sure it does," Josh said with a firm nod. "And why not? She's the daughter of an emperor, remember. She knows how to manipulate—it's right there in the first scene when she talks Polixenes into staying on when Leontes can't. And that's when Leontes starts going off the deep end. Maybe part of his insane jealousy is rooted in the fact that she's maybe more *adept* at the game than he is."

"Hmm, that's mighty fascinatin', Josh. Makes a lot of sense, too." Curtis was of that rare breed of gentleman directors who don't mind where a good idea comes from as long as it comes. His ego didn't require that he be the source of all wisdom and light. However, they both knew that not all men are created equally open-minded. "I—um—wouldn't spring it on your husband . . . I mean Hank, just yet."

"No need." O'Roarke came to the edge of the stage, squatted down on her haunches, and gave him a sly wink. "Leontes doesn't really *know* what's eating him—why should Hank?"

"I see what you mean," Ryson said with a slow smile. "Oh my, oh my, this is going to be a real interestin' run-through."

" 'You had a bastard by Polixenes,/And I but *dreamed* it. As you were past all shame . . .' Wait a sec, wait a sec!" Hank Barnes raised both hands to stop the action and turned in frustration to his director. "Sorry, Ryson, I know this is just a stumble-through for Jocelyn but, uh . . . Tessa used to, you know, do a gesture here, remember? Sort of stretch out her arms. And it really *fed* me." He turned back to O'Roarke with a supplicating smile. "Do you think you could try that?"

Jocelyn returned his smile sweetly but said nothing. She had caught the cut of Barnes' jib within the first twenty minutes of rehearsal; it was clear as crystal that, while Tessa Grant had been on board, Hank had been content to play first mate to her captain, but now, having the largest part in *Winter's Tale,* he obviously felt it was time for him to take the helm.

"You're right, Hank, this *is* just a stumble-through," Ryson interjected, loping down the aisle to the apron of the stage. "And, as such, we're only focusing on basic blocking, not sculpting beats, yes? So let's just get on with it, okay? We don't have much time . . . Take it from your last line—'Your actions are my dreams.' "

With as much grace as he could muster, which was precious little, Barnes resumed his position and picked up his lines as Curtis plopped himself down in the third row with a serious scowl on his face. It was all bluff; he was having a delightful time watching Jocelyn throw a spanner in Hank's works.

The fact of the matter was, despite his grumblings and despite himself, Barnes was doing better with Leontes than he had heretofore. He had been cowed and constantly deferential while playing opposite Tessa. Today, his bubbling resentment of O'Roarke's take on the role, of her very presence, had put some piss and vinegar into his performance. All of which conspired to make Ryson feel both glad and guilty: glad for the sake of the show, guilty for what he knew Hank must be feeling.

Like himself, Barnes had been a student at Corinth with Tessa and he had worshiped her unreservedly, both as an actress and as a woman, from day one. Whereas Ryson, not being of the heterosexual persuasion, had adored her, too, but with a platonic reserve that hadn't blinded him to the harsher facets of her nature. Like many people blessed with great abilities and a great sense of purpose, Tessa, especially as a young woman, had been almost frighteningly single-minded. Seeing herself as being above the usual claims of human affection, she had sometimes used people to her own ends. Back then, the difference between the two men was Curtis had recognized when and how he was being used and Hank hadn't. And, as far as Ryson could tell, Hank had never seen through that potent charm Tessa could exert so easily.

He remembered that first *Winter's Tale* rehearsal when she'd made her oh-so-casual, yet oh-so-grand entrance from the back of the house after the rest of the company had already assembled. Wafting up onto the stage with her script tucked under one arm, she had paused briefly to lay a light hand on Hank's cheek and murmur, "Good to see you again, Barnesy," before passing on to shake hands with the others. Amidst that awestruck gathering, only Ryson had noticed the color rise in Barnes' face as he'd touched the place where Tessa's hand had rested.

Poor Hank, Curtis thought with a fresh pang of guilt. Why did he have to be the one to find her body? That was really too cruel.

"Apollo's angry, and the heavens themselves/ Do strike at my injustice," Barnes wailed convincingly.

They were at the first-act climax now where, having just heard the oracle's confirmation of Hermione's innocence, a servant rushes in to announce the death of the young prince. It was also O'Roarke's cue to swoon. Tessa's faint had been a grand, somewhat elaborate affair; having been a woman of considerable height—five ten in her stocking feet—Grant had collapsed in stages, like a great edifice slowly caving in during a quake. A mere five foot five, Jocelyn was, as Addison DeWitt would say, "too short for that gesture." Instead, she let out a sound that was half moan, half whimper and fell in a heap, like a rag doll. It was a less theatrical, but, Ryson thought, equally effective swoon. However, Barnes looked down at her as if she were a pile of compost and wryly muttered, "How now there?" while rolling his eyes round to the other players as if to say, "You call *that* a faint?"

"This news is mortal to the queen. Look down and see what death is doing!"

Hank's eyebrows shot up as Anita Sanchez, the fourth-year student who played Hermione's maid, Paulina, delivered her line with impressive force, looking daggers at him all the while. Her reading was perfectly in character, as Paulina was deeply attached to her mistress, but there was an extra bite to it that told Barnes, plain and clear, what she thought of his antics.

This surprised Ryson almost as much as it did Hank. Anita, one of the department's most promising students, was known to be a firebrand, but Barnes was her acting teacher this semester and chief mentor. Though you would never know it from the burning look she gave him as she helped hustle Jocelyn offstage. And, when she reentered a few lines later to deliver news of Hermione's demise, she was in full, nostril-flaring steam as she laced into Leontes. Only at the very end of her long speech, her anger exhausted itself and her voice suddenly cracked. She had to fight back tears to get out her last line.

"The queen, the queen,/ The sweet'st dear'st creature's dead, and vengeance for't/ Not dropped down yet."

Her words hung in the air for an eerie moment and Jocelyn, watching from the wings, felt her flesh crawl. Then Anita started crying in earnest.

"Aw, *merde*." Ryson sighed as he hauled himself out of his seat and headed toward the sea of stricken faces onstage. Something like this had been bound to happen after the strain of the last few days, but it was his job to contain the damage as best he could. Luckily for him, Sanchez had the makings of a real trouper. By the time he reached her, she had already dried her eyes and was again in possession of her professional faculties.

"I'm sorry, real sorry, Professor Curtis," she said with one quick sniff. "That was all wrong, I know. 'Cause Paulina knows Hermione's not really dead. She wants to make the king feel bad but she's not—she's just playing a scene. I went way over the top and I . . . I just couldn't pull back, see?"

Bless her little heart, Ryson thought. If this was the way she chose to handle it, it was fine with him. He patted her gently on the back and carefully matched his tone to hers. "Of course, of course. Happens to the best of us, even the great ones. Did you know, when Julie Harris was playing St. Joan in *The Lark,* she got so worked up one night—started crying and just couldn't stop—that they had to pull the curtain *down?*" He raised his gaze to draw in all the other student actors onstage and slipped into professorial gear. "That's a lesson for all of you. The Method folks talk about emotional reality and *really* feelin' the moment and that's fine. But the play comes first—always. Anita just did some great emoting here but she realizes it's wrong for the play. Remember, y'all, emotion is like a racehorse. But *you're* the jockey. You got to ride it and keep the reins or you'll go right off the damn track . . . Now, everybody, let's break and come back to the Antigonus scene in fifteen minutes, okay?"

Smooth, very smooth, Josh thought as she watched the cast scatter to the john, the coffee machine, or out to the lobby for a smoke. Ryson had dismantled the bomb nicely. Had she been in his position, she might have handled it differently, more directly. But Curtis' motto had always been: When in doubt—duck and roll. And he had ducked gracefully, managing to impart a gem of acting wisdom even as he rolled. As he passed by her, delicately dabbing a fluffy white handkerchief at his temples, she beamed at him and said, "Must say, it was a sorry loss to the U.S. Diplomatic Corps when you opted for a life in the theatre."

"You think?" He gave her a watery smile. "But I'd make all those Ross Perot–types *so* uncomfortable. Excuse me while I slip up to my office for a much-needed nip of Southern Comfort . . . Unless you'd care to join me?"

"No, thanks. I want to go over some of my blocking." Actually she had her eye on Anita Sanchez, who was backstage now, gathering up her books and surreptitiously shooting glances her way. Almost as soon as Ryson left, the girl was by her side.

"How you doing, Miss O'Roarke? Rough morning, huh?"

"Well, it was bound to be, wasn't it?" O'Roarke said kindly. "But it'll get easier. It'll get easier faster if you just call me Jocelyn."

"Really? Okay. Look, I just wanted to apologize for making a sce—"

"Nothing to apologize for," Josh said with a firm head shake. "I think you did just fine."

"You do?! But what Professor Curtis said was right. I—I lost the reins but good."

"Professor Curtis was perfectly right. But look at it this way: some actors don't even *have* a horse. You do, and it's a thoroughbred." O'Roarke wasn't just tossing a consoling sop her way. She had watched Sanchez closely during her big speech and been struck by both her command of the language and the variety of colors in her emotional spectrum. "And, as a horse-breeder friend of mine always says—if you ain't been throw'd, you ain't rode."

Anita's mobile features lit up with a huge, grateful grin, then damped down just as quickly. "But Miss O . . . uh, Jocelyn, that wasn't all acting, see . . . I've been feeling so bad about Miss Grant."

"Of course you have. We all do."

"No, no. Not like you think—I mean, yes, that way but—another way, too." Sanchez cast her eyes down and shifted her feet awkwardly. "This is hard to talk about. Do you think . . . Could we go somewhere?"

"Out to the lobby?"

"Uh, outside would be better—if that's okay."

Anita's distress was so palpable Josh could almost smell it. Without saying a word, she jerked her head in the direction of the scene shop. There was a loading dock behind it, which, in Jocelyn's day, had been a favorite place to toke a quick joint. She had no idea if it was used for similar purposes now, but Sanchez obviously knew the spot, as she led the way there without further instruction. Once in the open air, she took a deep breath and turned to Josh purposefully.

"Here's the thing—I'm Mexican and the first woman in my family to go to college, see?"

"Uh-huh. That's a lot of weight to carry."

"Damn straight. Plus I'm here on scholarship and I don't want to do anything to blow it."

"Got it," O'Roarke answered. And she did, since, except for the Mexican part, she had been in exactly the same boat years back. "So—whatever's on your mind, you want it to stay right here."

"Yeah." Anita's face flooded with relief. "That's just it. I couldn't say this to anyone who's, you know, from here. See, there's a lot of old superstition in my family and most of it's hogwash to me. 'Cept this thing about the women in my family having—well, my grandmother calls it the 'Third Eye.' You know what that means?"

"Not exactly. But my guess would be it's something along the lines of precognition—clairvoyance?"

"That's right! You know about that stuff?"

"No, not really," Josh answered cautiously, concerned as to where this was heading, though she felt honor bound to add, "but I had a Grandaunt Maggie from Ireland—she'd see a crow sitting on her bed right before someone in the family died and, they tell me, she was never wrong."

"Uh-huh, uh-huh, that's the kind of thing I mean. And, well— wish to God I didn't—but I think I got that . . . That's really why I lost it in rehearsal."

"Because you, uh, got a sudden premonition?"

"No! Because I *had* one days ago—about Miss Grant. I'm . . . I'm like your Aunt Maggie. I *feel* when somebody's gonna cash in their chips. Only this time it was different."

"Different how?" O'Roarke really didn't want to hear the answer but knew she had to ask.

"See, it never bothered me much before," Anita said quickly, anxious to unburden herself. " 'Cause it only happened with old people—like my grandparents—people who were close to their time, you know? That's why I never thought much about it when I saw the hand."

"The hand?"

"Yeah. Like a wha'd ya call it? A superimposed image. One day when I was seven, I was sitting in the garden with my Grandma Carlita and I see this gray hand pass over her face and I just *knew*. Two days later, she died in her sleep. I thought it was just my

imagination, but it kept happening—but only with my family . . .
That's why I thought I was going crazy when I saw it this time!"

She was breathing hard now, bordering on hyperventilation, so
Josh grabbed both her hands firmly and looked straight in her eyes.
"Just say it, Anita. What did you see?"

"It was at the party at her place the night . . . before, you know?
I was standing by Miss Grant at the buffet table. We were all scarfing
down like crazy. Miss Grant picked up some hors d'oeuvre, then
put it back down on the tray. All I remember her saying was, 'I
can't eat this.' I thought she was just watching her calories 'cause
she wasn't drinking any booze that night. But then I saw the hand
go over her face."

The girl was perilously close to another crying fit and, if what
she was saying was true, O'Roarke was way out of her depth here.

"Anita, that's awful. It must be a terrible thing to live with. But,
hell, death is part of life and it comes to all—"

"No, no, no! I told you, it was *different*." Anita squeezed Josh's
hands urgently. "The hand wasn't gray this time . . . It was red—
blood red. And I've never, *ever* seen that before."

7

"All right, people. I want to jump to the last scene. Then we'll go back and pick up where we left off . . . Jocelyn, could we have you on the pedestal, please."

"Sure, in a sec, Ryson. Let me just finish writing down all this blocking," O'Roarke said, garnering a chuckle from the assembled cast. In the final scene, four-fifths of her "blocking" consisted of standing as still as a statue, since that was exactly what she was playing. This was the moment of "reunion and redemption" as old Professor Hargreaves always called it. The faithful Paulina shows the aged and chastened Leontes a "statue" of his late wife which then comes to life, whether by magic or trickery the Bard never really says; still, it makes for a lovely, hokey ending.

The only problem with it, from the Hermione standpoint, is just that: how to stand stock-still for two pages of speeches all round on how lifelike the "statue" looks. It was tougher than playing a corpse, since stage stiffs are usually lying prone, not standing upright. Having done the role before, O'Roarke was braced for the niggling assortment of itching, twitching sensations that assailed her as soon as she struck her pose and the lines started; still, it was a bitch. She felt like it was an eternity between cue pickups, and everyone sounded as if they were speaking underwater. To keep focused and still, she fixed her upstage eye on Belinda Barnes, who was at the side of her real and fictive father, Hank.

"And give me leave,/ And do not say 'tis superstition, that I kneel and then implore her blessing./ Lady, Dear Queen, that ended when I but began . . ."

Pale-faced, Belinda knelt at the foot of the pedestal, delivering all her lines woodenly to the floorboards. Whether the girl was a woefully deficient actor or still too upset to function normally, Josh couldn't tell. Perhaps there had been a little nepotism behind the scenes when Ryson had cast the part, but at least the girl had the right look for Perdita. That is, she did when Tessa was playing her mother, O'Roarke realized with an inward sigh; she was bang-on *perfect* physically. Whereas Jocelyn's fair skin and dark hair was a total contrast to Belinda's peaches and cream. Damn, I'm going to have to wear a friggin' wig to pull this off, she thought.

Then it was—finally—her cue to get off the pedestal. After embracing her husband, which was no easy matter since Hank was about as yielding as a two-by-four, she let Anita lead her toward Belinda.

"Turn, good lady;/ Our Perdita is found."

Gently cupping Belinda's chin with one hand, she managed to get the girl to meet her eyes if only for a moment.

"You gods, look down,/ And from your sacred vials pour your graces/ Upon my daughter's head! Tell me, my own,/ Where hast thou been preserved? Where liv—"

Before O'Roarke could finish the rest of the line, Belinda jerked her face away, shielding it from Josh and the others with one hand. "I—I'm sorry. I don't . . . feel very well," she managed to get out before flying into the wings.

"Belinda! Come back here," Barnes shouted.

"Shush, Hank. Let her go," Ryson said from the house, more irked with the father than the daughter. "Anita, we'll pick it up from your next speech, please."

They shuffled through to the final exit in a desultory fashion. Once offstage, Barnes, in full parental huff now, forced himself to approach Jocelyn. "Look, I'm sorry about that. She's an emotional kid, but that's no excuse for—"

"It's okay, really. She'll settle down," Josh cut him short, then added pointedly, "if you leave her alone for a bit." While she wasn't the least upset with Belinda, she was furious with her father and wanted out of this little exchange fast before she made some tacky "like father, like daughter" crack. It never ceased to amaze her how some parents had the cheek to get all bent out of shape when they saw their offspring exhibiting behavior that was just a mirroring of their own bad manners. After all, you didn't have to be Dr. Spock to know monkey see, monkey do.

"Well, that's, uh, very . . . generous of you, Jocelyn. I just hope Ryson's as understanding," Barnes mumbled with something akin to real contrition and not just on his daughter's behalf.

She still didn't like the guy much but she was going to have to work with him. Knowing it was better to mend fences than build walls, she looked him square in the eye and said, "Just remember, Hank, I knew Tessa, too. I admired her enormously. So it doesn't take much to imagine how your daughter's feeling now . . . how you're feeling, too. I can't take her place—wouldn't even try to. But I *can* finish this job for her as a way of paying my last respects. Because that's what I think she'd want. Now, if you'll cut me a little slack out there, maybe Belinda will, too, eh?"

"Yes, uh . . . point taken," Barnes said softly, pinching the bridge of his nose in an attempt to check a rising flood of emotion. "Tess would want you here. It's just . . . very hard for me."

With that, he did an abrupt about-face, heading for the sanctuary of his office. That was just dandy by Josh, as she was determined to get to Belinda before he did. As Ryson called places for the top of Act Two, she slipped out into the spacious, red-carpeted lobby, where, just as in her day, students were lolling about in small cliques, smoking, flirting, and gossiping. But there was no Belinda in sight. Not that Josh expected to find her here; the red lobby was the last place one went to lick one's wounds.

Pushing through the mammoth wooden doors that were the portal of the Theatre Arts building, she stepped into sunlight and had to shield her eyes for a moment from the bright rays bouncing off the large reflecting pool, complete with fountain, that was the gem of the campus. The pool was ringed by a raised, cement ledge. Once her pupils contracted, she spied a solitary figure sitting on the far right corner, feet dangling in the water.

Belinda, staring fixedly at her submerged toes, didn't notice Jocelyn's approach.

"I filled this sucker with soapsuds once, you know."

Caught off guard by this surprise opening, Belinda, forgetting herself and her woes for an instant, went bug-eyed. "Really? You serious?"

"Oh, yeah. But it's a secret, see. We never got caught. If you tell, they'll probably rescind my diploma."

"I heard something like that happened *way* back." Belinda spoke as if she were referring to some paleolithic era. "But I always thought it was just, like a campus myth . . . Why'd you do it?"

"I dunno. I guess because, like Mount Everest, it was *there*," Josh answered casually, sliding her posterior onto the cold cement. "Actually, I was just an accomplice. It was my roommate's idea. She bought the soap flakes and I planned the escape route."

"Gawd, that is *way* cool." For the first time in their brief acquaintance, Belinda looked and sounded like a full-blooded college kid. "Who was your roommate?"

This was ticklish, but they were at a delicate point of potential bonding, so O'Roarke felt a slight indiscretion was required to gain the girl's trust. Clearing her throat for full effect, she began with, "If I tell you, you really cannot *breathe* a word of it to anybody, okay? Not even your best pal or your boyfriend. Got it?"

On the word *boyfriend,* Belinda's mouth pursed and she immediately replied, "No chance, no way . . . I won't tell *a soul.*"

"Okay then . . . it was Mrs. Mauro."

"*No!* Professor Mike's wife?! You have *got* to be kidding. I—I didn't even know she went here!"

"Well, I'm not. And she did. And we did the dastardly deed. And they never pinned it on us—so you'll realize how important it is that this stays right here," Josh said, flicking her hand between Belinda's shoulder and hers. Then she started to chuckle as the image of that foam-filled pool came back to her. "Christ, it *was* a sight though. The dean had conniptions."

Then there was the loveliest sound, like wind chimes tinkling, and it was Belinda Barnes laughing out loud as she paddled her toes in the water. "Oh, man, that's *too* good! You and Mrs. Mauro? What a concept. You make these guys look like stooges," she said, jerking her head toward the south end of the building, adding testily, "which they *are*."

"What guys?"

"Didn't you hear? These jerks spray-painted the wall of the building yesterday and got caught red-handed. I'll show you."

Swinging her legs out of the pool in one fluid motion, Belinda pivoted off the cement ledge and headed toward the steps that led down to the parking lot, beckoning Josh to follow. The parking lot, which abutted the south end of the building, was alive with a kind of large-scale, Tom Sawyer–fence-washing scene overseen by the campus security cops. A group of four guys on ladders were scouring the wall, halfway to obliterating a spray-painted image that Jocelyn instantly recognized: a large black circle encompassing a diagonal slash across a wire hanger. She'd seen it everywhere at the Pro-Choice rally in Washington as the companion piece to the "We Won't Go Back" placards. This, she realized, must be the campus vandalism Kowaleski had been called to investigate and, obviously, he had gotten his men.

"Look at those dweebs," Belinda said contemptuously, which took O'Roarke aback. Wasn't this the same girl who'd said she'd wanted to go to the rally?

"Well, hell, Belinda, it makes more sense than filling a pool with soapsuds just for the heck of it, doesn't it?"

"Oh, sure. But they got caught and you didn't. Typical, huh?"

"Typical how? Meaning women are better vandals than men?"

"Yeah, kinda. I mean, we *are* better at subterfuge. We hafta be."

"True enough. But why're you so pissed at these guys? They tried, at least . . . Hey, isn't that our Florizel over there?" Jocelyn pointed to a bare-chested youth laboring at the top of one ladder. "Whoa, what a torso."

"Uh-huh, that's Denny Moskowitz. He's the ringleader. This had to be his idea."

As if he'd heard his name mentioned, Denny turned round and spotted his observers. With a huge grin, he waved his arm in a wide arc over his head, making his ladder sway precariously. Belinda buried her face in her hands and groaned, "He is *such* a jerk."

"Look, even if you hate his guts, wave back or he's gonna tip that ladder."

"Really?"

"Really—wave *back*."

Keeping her face averted, something Belinda was truly good at, she managed to raise one limp-wristed hand in the air long enough to appease Denny and get him back on his scouring track.

"He's such an asshole," Belinda sighed.

"He's your boyfriend, huh," O'Roarke countered.

"Yeah, well, is . . . was. I'm not so sure anymore."

"Either way, don't tell him till he's off that ladder, okay? What —are you pissed that he pulled this prank? Or pissed he got caught?"

Keeping her gaze fixed on the ladder, Belinda didn't reply until it and Denny stopped tottering. When she finally answered, her voice sounded old beyond its years. "I'm pissed because it's too little, too late." Then she shook her head, as if warding off bad memories, and turned to face Josh directly. "But Den's not the only asshole around here . . . I was a real jerk during rehearsal. I'm not trying to make excuses for myself, but—that moment when Hermione lifts up my face? Tessa and me, we had a very heavy connection there, see? I, uh, I'd never felt that way onstage before, Miss O'Roarke."

"Jocelyn's fine. Tell me about it . . . How did you feel?"

"Like— Aw, this is gonna sound artsy-corny, and I hate that crap."

"It's okay—in this case. After all, it's a kinda corny scene, in the best sense of the word."

"Yeah, you're right. But it felt so real with Tessa, like an honest-to-god reunion. Tears would just come to my eyes every time she looked down at me—and that's not like me, 'cause I tend to have a hard time accessing my emotions," Belinda said, slipping into actor-speak. "But I wasn't like me. I'd feel just like Perdita. It was this incredible rush and all I could think was, 'Thank God I've got her *back*.' "

"I understand," Jocelyn said, adding ever so gently, "and today, all you could think was, 'I'll never have her back again.' Right?"

Squeezing her eyes tight to stem a fresh onslaught of tears, Belinda nodded her head rapidly, then, as her face crumbled, turned and headed up the cement stairs, two at a time. O'Roarke followed after and reached the top of the stairs, huffing and puffing, to find the girl back at the reflecting pool and back in throes of despair.

Placing a light hand on her shoulder, Josh asked, "So how do you feel now?"

Flinching from her touch, Belinda gave a harsh, exasperated laugh that sounded nothing like wind chimes and threw her head back. "How do I *feel?* Christ! How do you think I feel? I feel *shitty,* lady."

"Fine. But shitty's a little vague. What else?" O'Roarke stepped toward her, backing Belinda up to the ledge of the pool. "Be more specific."

"I feel—I feel sad, sadder than I've ever felt in my whole life! How's that?"

"It's a start . . . What else?"

"Geez, you're nuts . . . Okay, I feel real . . . gypped. And real angry. And—I cannot stand it that it's you up there and not *her!* Okay?!"

"Atta girl."

Breathing as heavily as Josh had been a moment ago, Belinda plopped down on the ledge and finally let the tears flow. Perching next to her, Jocelyn patted Belinda's knee comfortingly and, this time, she didn't draw away.

"You know, you're perfectly entitled to all those feelings. 'Cause you're right. Death *is* a gyp. It's the Big Gyp. I'm just wondering, love, why you're beating yourself up so bad for feeling the way you feel?"

"I dunno, I dunno . . . My mom says I shouldn't, uh, 'give way' too much or it'll just eat me up, you know? Like in those hokey old novels—'She went mad with grief.' See, I'd been having a sorta tough semester anyway. I guess she's worried this'll put me in the deep end . . . And I'm worried she might be right." Belinda ended in a low whisper, slewing her eyes Josh's way to see if a confirming diagnosis was forthcoming.

After a brief pause, O'Roarke said matter-of-factly, "Ah, I

wouldn't worry about that if I were you—unless you're doing a lot of drugs. LSD, coke, speed—too much of that stuff can push you over the edge if you're shaky to start with."

"Hell, *no!* I never touch—well, I'll take a toke of grass at a party but that's *it* . . . You won't say anything to my folks, will you?" Belinda asked in sudden apprehension.

"Me? When you know all about the soapsuds caper? Forget it." Seeing a wisp of a smile cross Belinda's face, Josh pressed the advantage. "Look, of course your mother's worried—that's her job. But she's a parent and parents naturally hate to see their children in pain. Now I'm not a parent, I'm an actor, so my take is very different."

"What is your . . . take?"

Josh cocked one eyebrow and, much to the girl's surprise, asked, "You know anything about horse racing?"

"Uh, not a damn thing. Is this gonna be, like . . . a metaphor?"

"Yeah, but bear with me. See, sometimes when a horse is hurt —pulled a muscle or something and shouldn't run—a fifth-grade, sleazeball trainer will shoot the horse up so it can race, so it won't feel the injury. And that's when the *ugliest* accidents happen on the track, the really bad spills. The poor animal's leg will go right out from under him. The jockey gets thrown bad and, many times, the horse has to be put down . . . Is this ringing any bells for you, kiddo, or am I being too oblique for life?"

"No, I kinda follow. They do the same thing in pro football sometimes, right? Freeze a guy's knee so he can play, then he shatters it in the next game and his career's over."

"Oh, *good* analogy! You got it . . . Well, I have a parallel theory about emotional pain: Feel it and go through it now, 'cause if you repress it, it'll sneak up later and do you a permanent injury. Of course, there are legions of Anglo-Saxon Americans who'd disagree with me vehemently on this—but they're not actors . . . Trust me, Bel, your feelings won't kill you *or* make you crazy. Ignoring them might."

A beatific smile lit up Barnes' face. "O'm'God! You called me Bel. That's *too* weird."

"Why weird?"

" 'Cause my folks only call me Belinda or Linda and some of my friends—like Denny—call me Bellie, which gags me. Only Tessa ever called me Bel."

"Really?" Josh kept her voice neutral. She was glad that they had reached this rapprochement, but not sure if she was up to a full-blown Freudian transference. Also, she had a hidden agenda that required a deft change of topic. "What did Tessa call Anita? Did she have any pet name for her?"

"Anita? I don't think so. They seemed to work together fine. But they weren't, you know, buddy-buddy . . . Which is kinda funny, come to think of it."

"Funny how?"

"Well, you can see Anita's real gifted," Belinda said with a tinge of envy. "Wish I had half her stage presence. And you know Tess liked talent. You'd think Anita'd be the one she'd, like, take under her wing . . . instead of me."

"Maybe Anita wasn't as taken with Tessa as you were."

"Nah, I don't think it's that. See, Anita's pretty ambitious. Not that she actually sucks up to people, she just charms the pants off 'em. You'd think, with all Tess's big time connections, she'd be someone Anita would be sure to charm—but I never saw her do her number on Tess."

"Could be there was a little competitive feeling there," Josh offered.

"Not onstage. Like I said, they worked well together." Belinda paused, narrowing her eyes thoughtfully. "But *off*stage there might've been. Look, Tessa was no slouch in the charm department either. I mean, she was even older than *you*, but she could still make most of the guys in the show leave tongue marks on the carpet if she just gave 'em a little smile."

"That she could, that she could," O'Roarke affirmed magnanimously while swallowing the bitter "even older than *you*" pill. "Tess was a world-class flirt . . . Did she poach on any of Anita's preserves, maybe?"

"Umm, maybe . . . But I'm not positive. I really don't like talking about stuff like this when I'm not sure." Belinda wiggled uncomfortably on the cement ledge, then gave Jocelyn a severe look. "See, I don't wanna be the source of idle gossip."

"Of course not." O'Roarke nodded her head gravely, biting her lower lip to squelch a smile. "But I'm the new kid in town and I really don't want to make any wrong moves if I can help it, so . . . who's the guy?"

"Professor Mauro. Anita's got a *major* crush on him. Lots of the girls do, actually. But Anita's really gone."

"Does Mik—Professor Mauro know?"

"Oh, puh-leese! What do you think? Good-looking guys always know—they expect it. But he's very cool with it, you know. He flirts some, but that's all."

"Then why would Anita get upset with Tessa?"

" 'Cause—and this is just my opinion, and *please* don't breathe a word to Mrs. Mauro—but I think Professor Mauro had a crush on Tess as big as the one Anita has on him, that's why."

It was Josh's turn to squirm now. "Was, uh, Tessa aware of it?"

"She never said anything to me but, yeah, I think she knew. Their first scene together, where Hermione's playing up to Polixenes to get him to visit longer, you know? She really used to go to town with it—she was great! When they'd finish rehearsing, Professor Mauro looked like he could use a cold shower."

Before Jocelyn could gather her whirling thoughts, something caught Belinda's eye, causing her to gasp softly.

"O'm'God! Who's *that?!*"

Looking like she, too, could use a cold shower, Bel gazed fixedly at a figure that had just emerged from a car parked at the foot of the stairs. But they were very long stairs and Bel had very good, young eyes. Jocelyn squinted down but, in the bright sun, could only make out the silhouette of a male form taking a quick look at the wall-washers before starting to ascend the steps.

"I can hardly see him."

"Well, too bad for you," Belinda joked, suddenly all girlish and fairly flirty herself. "Then I get first dibs. Boy, I've never really gone for older men, but we're talkin' serious cute here."

Ah, the amazing rubber-band resiliency of youth, Josh thought as Bel jumped to her feet like a jack-in-the-box. Whether this was just a distraction or a nifty way to stick it to the laboring Denny or only a sudden schoolgirl fancy, O'Roarke didn't much care; it was a welcome respite from getting the bad news about her good friend's spouse.

So she thought.

"Hi! Welcome to Corinth College. Or maybe I should say welcome back. Are you an alumnus?"

"Sorry, no . . . Just a tourist, I guess."

"Hey, that's cool," Belinda said with all the perky aplomb of a fledgling airline stew. "I'd be glad to give you a tour."

"Well, uh, actually, I'm looking for someone."

The sun was still in her eyes and Belinda was standing between her and "the tourist," but, as soon as she heard the deep voice, Jocelyn knew instantly, knew with a rising/sinking certainty who Bel's new dreamboat was.

Immobilized on the cement ledge, all she could do was clear her throat and offer weakly: "And I guess you found her . . . What the hell are you doing here, Phillip?"

Bel Barnes' pupils went wide as Phillip Gerrard brushed past her and strode toward Jocelyn O'Roarke with an insouciant smile.

"Let's just say—I was in the neighborhood."

8

"What do you mean you're on vacation?! You always take your vacation in August and it's only Apri— *Ow!* Lyle, you stabbed me!"

"That's what you get for jawin' away while I'm tryin' to pin your bodice, girlfriend. Cutting down a costume's tricky business." Lyle Davie, the Corinth costume designer spoke carefully through the row of straight pins he held between his lips as he moved around an anxious Jocelyn, who was standing on a low stool. A slight man with stick-straight, white-blond hair that looked like a last bequest from Andy Warhol, Davie, like Ryson Curtis, was from the South but not a Virginian; he was a good ol' gay boy from Little Rock who had come up the hard way and had the scars to show for it. O'Roarke had met him in her junior year when he'd first come to Corinth and knew him to be a terrific designer, especially when it came to period costumes.

Unfortunately, she also knew him to be a heavy drinker, and his shaky hands, combined with the watching eyes of Phillip Gerrard, were giving her severe *shpilkes.*

"Now hold still, Josh!" He inserted another pin, without inflicting bodily harm this time, and stood back to survey his efforts. "It's coming, it's coming . . . The bitch of it is *La* Grant was taller'n you with broader shoulders. But your tits are bigger'n hers. Plus, you're a few pounds heavier than when you played Jessica, aren't ya?"

"Yes, Lyle, I am. Thank you *so* much for noticing," O'Roarke said with sweet acidity. "It's nice to know you remember my old dress size."

Davie gave a short laugh that sounded like a goose honking once, then abruptly pirouetted round to Phillip with arms stretched wide, flashing him a brilliant smile. "But the color is *fabulous* on her, don't you think?"

Jocelyn was sending him urgent "be nice" signals, so Gerrard, who heartily detested the word "tits," fought to keep his voice level as he nodded at Lyle and said slowly, "Just to die for." Lyle sighed and beamed, and Phillip had the satisfaction of seeing Josh nearly fall off the stool from shock and suppressed mirth.

At least she was smiling now, but this was *not* the reunion Gerrard had had in mind. Not by a long shot.

No sooner had he and Jocelyn said their awkward hellos (he'd expected that part to be tricky), than a pretty Hispanic girl had come running out of the building to tell her that she was due for a fitting. Having been away from the theatre world for some time now, he had naively asked if it could wait while they went to have a cup of coffee. The two pretty girls had exchanged droll glances and giggles while Josh had rolled her eyes and beckoned him to follow her as she'd trotted off.

Hurrying to catch up with her, he had asked, "What do those two think is so funny?"

"Nothing. Just the outlandish idea of keeping a costume designer *waiting*."

"Why's that such a sin?" He had tried to keep the testiness out of his voice and failed. But at least he'd tried; Jocelyn hadn't even made the effort, just growled over her shoulder, "For openers, the play goes up in about a week and *all* my costumes have to be altered. But more importantly—and I'm sure I told you this in the distant past—in this business, you can argue with your director, you can fight with your fellow actors, but you cannot ever, ever piss off the costume designer . . . or you will get screwed to the wall."

It was true; she had told him. Snatches of old O'Roarkian anecdotes had started coming back. "Oh, yeah. I remember you talking about one guy—I think you were doing Jessica in *The Merchant of Venice*—and he hated the girl playing Portia. She was—what? A strawberry blonde. So he put her in pale greens or something for the whole play. And she looked like wallpaper onstage . . . That right?"

"That's right . . . and this is the *same* guy. So let's move it, Lieutenant."

So here he sat on a metal folding chair in the glass-walled fitting room that was perched one flight up from the backstage scene shop, feeling like a fish in a fishbowl. He could hear sounds of hammering and drilling below and there was a flurry of activity everywhere but, still, he could sense the degree of covert attention that was focused on this little room and guessed that it had something to do with his unexpected arrival. And he knew Jocelyn could sense it, too, and she wasn't thrilled by the scrutiny. But Lyle was clearly relishing it. So Gerrard was rather hoping he'd swallow one of his pins.

"You've got a great eye, Phil . . . Can I call you Phil? Swell," he gushed without waiting for an answer. "See, I've got her in emerald greens for the first act—Hermione's preggers then and we want a kind of Vernal Equinox look. Then jet black for the trial scene, natch. And, for the last act, a rose-mauvey number. To fit with the post-Lenten resurrection motif, see?"

"Oh yeah, perfect." Gerrard smiled weakly, nodding his agreement, which was pure bull. He had a good acquaintance with Shakespeare's biggies—*Hamlet, Macbeth, King Lear*—but *The Winter's Tale* was totally out of his frame of reference. Still, vis-à-vis Jocelyn, what the little twerp said made sense. Gerrard was one of those rare men who really noticed what women wore and had a good eye for what they should wear. Emerald green, jet black, and mauve were all great shades for Josh. What surprised him, since these costumes had been built for another woman and, courtesy of Frederick Revere, he'd seen a photo of that woman, was that they weren't particularly good hues for the late Miss Grant. Did that mean Davie had held her in the same disdain as that long-ago, luckless Portia?

Watching Jocelyn pivot toward the full-length mirror hanging on one wall, he guessed, from her half-pleased, half-perplexed expression, that she was entertaining a similar notion. She was in the emerald green gown and, even with the pregnancy padding, she looked smashing. Casting a thoughtful look at Davie, she said casually, "It's lovely, Lyle. Almost the same shade as my Jessica dress . . . Did, uh, Tessa like it?"

"Oh, well, yes and no," Lyle answered with a twitchy shrug. "Loved the cut, hated the colors. But *La* Grant could be very *La* Grand at times. Never let me forget that she'd starred on Broadway and been dressed by Theoni and Santo and Bill Ivey and all that crap. But I stood firm—told her I didn't dress *stars,* I costumed *plays.* That shut her up."

"Did it?" Josh's voice was light and noncommittal, but Phillip was getting his O'Roarke-barometer back in shape; he was starting to pick up on her subtext again. To his ears, it sounded as if she'd just said, "Like fun, fella." And maybe Lyle had caught a whiff of her doubt, as he quickly turned again to Phillip, saying, "Feel this fabric. It's a soft corduroy—dirt cheap—but it hangs just like velvet."

Obligingly, Gerrard got to his feet to finger the fabric. "Very nice," he said, then lifted one hand to lightly pat the pregnancy padding. "Nice tummy, too."

Quick with her reflexes, O'Roarke delivered a short, sharp smack to the back of his hand as she barked, "Can I get out of this damn *schmatte* now? I mean, it's lovely, Lyle, but it weighs a friggin' ton."

Davie did a Jack Benny "Well!" with his eyebrows and drawled under his breath for Phillip's benefit, "Seems like the lady *is* the tiger, huh?" Then he clicked his heels and made a mock bow to Jocelyn. "You may remove the *schmatte,* missy. Just be careful of the pins when you take it off. We don't want your bodice hangin' crooked."

"Oh, I'm sure it'll be fine." Stepping off the stool, Josh gave him an apologetic smile. "You'll do your usual magic and make this old sow's ear look like a silk purse again."

Placated, Lyle gave her rump a pat as she slipped behind a folding screen to change. Then he motioned to Gerrard to follow him out to the hallway. Once there, he lit a Camel, leaned his head against the wall, and blew a thin stream of smoke upward with a world-weary sigh. "Swear to God, I wish I could talk ol' Ry into doing a production of *Caine Mutiny* or *Twelve Angry Men* sometime."

I'll bet you do, Phillip thought but dutifully asked, "Why?"

"All-male casts is why. Heaven! I mean, creatively, it's more fun designing gowns, but the ladies do fray my nerves so . . . Still, Josh is a peach compared to some I could mention."

And will at the drop of a hat, was Gerrard's guess. But he was on vacation and, for a cop, that meant a blessed respite from having to ask questions all the live-long day. So he deliberately misread Davie's prompt to prod. "Well, don't mind the *schmatte* crack. She loves the costume. It's just— I think my turning up without warning threw her a bit."

"Really?! You two old friends?"

"Uh, yeah. But we haven't seen each other in a while. She's been in L.A."

"Oh, I know! Saw that TV movie she did with Austin Frost. Old Corinthians stick together, don't they? You know Austin?"

"Sure. We met when he was still in New York. Great guy," Phillip mumbled. Jocelyn had introduced him to Lyle only as "Phillip," and he had no wish to mention that his acquaintance with both Josh and Austin had begun with a homicide investigation. But the costumer, more interested in fresh dish than ancient history, was already on to a new topic.

"So what've you heard about that guy she was seeing? I heard from a dear friend who cuts rags for 'Another World' that he's— can you feature it?—a hairdresser! But very, very hunky. Trust O'Roarke to find a straight stylist."

Bad new topic.

"Yeah, right . . . So, Lyle, which of the ladies in the company are giving you a hard time?"

"Oh, *all* of them at one time or other. You wouldn't *beleeve!*" Davie French-inhaled and shook his head dramatically. "The Mexican—*la petite* Sanchez—has watched too many Joan Crawford films. I have to keep tellin' her they didn't have shoulder pads in Shakespeare's time! And she wanted to wear heels under her dress, too. What a laugh! Nothin's gonna stop that girl from looking like a chihuahua onstage. The Barnes child isn't too bad—just blond. So she's afraid she'll wash out under the lights and I have to keep reassurin' her. I mean, her body's damn near perfect," he said with grudging admiration. "And I've got her in this simple, clingy number that's so stunning she won't even have to *act*."

"Well, they're young and insecure," Gerrard interjected mildly. "What can you expect?"

"True, true. But Josh was never like that. She had the sense to trust my eye. Which is more than I can say for . . . well, I don't want to speak ill of the dead." Davie paused for effect while Phillip stifled a yawn; if he had a nickel for every time he'd heard that phrase as prelude to a thorough character trouncing he'd have a fine pile of change by now—maybe enough to buy an island. And Lyle was about to make the pile bigger. "*But* Ms Grant—Testy Tessy, I called her—was just impossible! Sweet Jesus save me from Big Fish in Little Ponds is all I can say. Now she was good in her work—can't take that away from her—and good with the other actors. But behind the scenes . . . well, she was the type who knew who had to be charmed and who didn't matter. Obviously, *I* didn't matter a damn." He ended with a sniff as he ground out his cigarette on the linoleum.

It seemed to Phillip that Lyle Davie was patently one of those people prone to see themselves as ill used in any given situation, and there was a tart tang of misogyny beneath his griping. Still, given what little he knew about Tessa Grant and what Jocelyn had said about the perils of offending one's costumer, he was surprised to hear that Grant had flown so strongly in the face of conventional wisdom and couldn't help asking, "What did she do to make you think that?"

"What *didn't* she do is more like it. Everything!" Lyle hadn't just warmed to his topic; he was red hot now. "Look, I stuck her once with a pin—hey, it happens, you know? Usually, like with Josh, you get an 'Ow!' and it's over. With Tessa—oh, my lord!—it was like an assassination attempt. She went screaming to Ryson about how I was trying to sabotage her. How I'm unfit for my job because . . . well, who knows what trash she talked."

Davie suddenly put the brakes on his tirade, either because he felt he had said more than was prudent or, more likely, because Jocelyn was coming out of the wardrobe room.

"Who's talking what trash, Lyle?" she asked, giving him a close look. Phillip, noting that the glass walls weren't all that thick and knowing that O'Roarke's auricular capacities rose sharply whenever gossip was in the air, wondered just how much of their exchange she had caught.

"Oh, now, it's nothin'. I've just been bendin' your friend's ears with the story of my sad and lonely life."

"Not that again," she joked back. "I thought you were over your Tennessee Williams phase."

"Never. I shall always rely on the kindness of strangers," he said overbrightly. "Though I did go overboard a bit, huh, Phil? Didn't ask you anything 'bout yourself—or what you do. 'Cause I can tell, for shuh, you're not in the theatrical trade, are you? I mean, you got the *looks* for it. No question there. But you listen much too well to be an actor."

Phillip smiled and shrugged, then caught O'Roarke's eye with a look that said, "Your call." He was on her turf, uninvited, and if she wanted to pass him off as her agent or accountant or whatever, that was her prerogative.

Instead, she stepped over and tucked her arm through his and said, "You're right there, Lyle. Unlike us, Phillip works for a living. Works for the N.Y.P.D."

"No?! You mean, he's a co—a police officer?"

"A lieutenant, to be exact." Her voice was swift and firm and Phillip fancied he heard an undercurrent of pride in it.

"*Too* fascinatin'!" Lyle's drawl was broadening by the second, but there was a faint alarm behind his eyes. "Now, do tell, what's your, uh . . . special field, Phil?"

Again, he left it to Jocelyn to fill in the blanks as she saw fit. And she did, without missing a beat. "Homicide."

"Well, I *swan!*" Davie sunk back against the wall again as he scrambled to dig another Camel out of his shirt pocket. "Never in a trillion years would I've guessed *that.*"

"But life is full of surprises, Lyle. As Tennessee would tell you . . . Excuse us now, won't you?" She gave Phillip's arm a short tug then started down the corridor.

All Davie could do was light his cigarette and call out after them, "Well—the mind *boggles.*"

"Along with several other parts of the anatomy, I'm sure," Josh rejoined under her breath as she hastened toward the stairs with Gerrard in tow.

He stopped laughing long enough to ask, "He *swanned?* What does that mean?"

"Just a Southernism," she answered, pushing the heavy oak doors open with both hands. "Like 'I swear' or 'I'll be damned.'"

"Then I guess I should be flattered. Means I don't reek cop."

"Of course you don't! You never have," she said brusquely as they stepped out into the sun. "It's your chief asset—makes you lethal."

"If that's meant to be a compliment, I think I like 'I swan' better," Gerrard joked, trying to keep it light.

But O'Roarke wasn't having any. Arms akimbo, she swung round to face him.

"Well, Christ, I hope you didn't traipse all the way up here just to get your ego stroked. 'Cause, boy, are you gonna come up short!"

"No, I did not," Phillip ground out between clenched teeth. "I just thought it might be a . . . nice surprise. That's all."

"That's all? That's bullshit. Face it, Phillip, you are not Mr. Spontaneity. You just don't take holidays on a sudden whim. Hell, you plot out your route before you go to the john! So what's your agenda here?"

"I don't *have* one," he protested hotly. "Look, I just wanted to surprise you, not make you a wreck. If—"

"I'm not a *wreck*," she spat back. "What gall! I just think it would've been nice if you'd *asked* first."

"Fine—point taken. Fine." He lowered his head to catch his breath and gather his wits. The truth was she wasn't far wrong about his having an agenda. On the drive up to Corinth, his mind had been busily concocting a variety of scenarios, all of which had ended roughly the same—with Josh melting gratefully in his embrace. The frosty reality was so far from his steamy fantasies that he was beginning to feel a fool. "You're right. I should've called but I didn't have a number— Aw, shit, forget it, forget it. I don't know what I was thinking. But I didn't come up here to fight with you. If this was a huge mistake, just say so and I'll push off."

"Ah, come on. That's not fair, Phil," Jocelyn objected, but her voice was low and soft now. "You can't put it all on me. You wanted to come and you came. If you want to stick around—fine. But you have to realize that I, uh, I'm in a dicey position right now. Taking over Tessa's part and everything. I'm not going to have much free time and I just don't want to be burdened with any more . . . expectations."

"Hey, I really just wanted to see you again. I've got no expectations."

"You don't, huh?" O'Roarke regarded him closely as a smile tugged at the corner of her mouth. "Well, we'll just have to wait and see about that. You want to get that cup of coffee now?"

"Actually, no—but I'd kill for a cold beer."

"Me, too . . . You're buying."

"You're on."

They walked in silence for a few minutes on the concrete path that ran from the reflecting pool straight to the Student Union. The campus was perched high on a hill overlooking Lake Taconic and a very pretty view it was in Phillip's eyes. He let his gaze drift toward the town of Corinth, nestled at the foot of the hill, and remarked, "You know, I'd better come clean right now. I *do* have a hidden agenda in coming here."

"Uh-huh? Well, 'fess up, fella."

"I'm on a secret mission for Tommy."

"Tommy Zito?!" O'Roarke perked right up at the mention of his right-hand man on the force and her old ally. "How is the old scungilli sucker?" she asked fondly.

"Tom's fine. Sends his love."

"No?! He didn't really say *that*, did he? He probably said, 'Tell her hi,' or 'Give her my best,' right?"

"Wrong. He said, and I quote, 'I really miss 'da dame. Give her my love.' "

"Ahh, what a sweetheart he is." O'Roarke was all aglow and it looked to Gerrard as if he would have done better had he sent his sergeant as emissary; evidently, Zito would have gotten a warmer reception. But then, as Zito would have hastened to point out, *he* wasn't the one who had dumped her. "What's the secret mission?"

"It's a covert shopping assignment. Very hush-hush. You know that gun collection of his?"

"He's still into that?" Jocelyn, no fan of the N.R.A., wrinkled her nose slightly. "When I got him that pasta maker for his birthday, I hoped he'd turn a new leaf."

"Well, that's where false expectations will get you," he quipped brightly. Ignoring her strangled "Me!" he continued, "He's branched out in the last year. Now he's into antique rifles. Orders all these catalogs and scours the 'For Sale' ads religiously. It seems somebody from around here is trying to sell a Remington turkey gun in mint condition. Tom wants me to check it out and see how mint it is before he places a bid."

"I get it. You're supposed to be his—what's the word? His divvy?" Despite her disaffection for firearms, this news cheered Jocelyn considerably. When Gerrard promised a favor, he delivered in spades. For Tommy's sake, he would go all out, applying his meticulous mind and eye to the task at hand. It would keep him busy and give her a breathing space to sort out the confounding array of emotions that had assailed her in the last two hours. So God bless Thomas Zito and all his little instruments of destruction, thought she. Aloud, she asked, "So who's the mark—excuse me, the seller?"

"A guy named Kowaleski. Ever heard of him?"

9

"So then the bartender says, 'Nah, he ain't been doing nuthin' special. Just sitting on that stool all night—lickin' his *eyebrows!*'" Kowaleski slapped his knee and burst into a phlegmy guffaw that ended in a hacking cough.

"Uh, good one, Cal," Phillip Gerrard said tepidly as Kowaleski regained his breath and wiped spittle from his mouth.

"Well, hey, before I bring this baby out, let me get you another brew."

"No, I'm fine. Thanks."

"But I'll have another," Josh said as she pointedly killed the last of her Genesee Cream Ale with a suppressed shudder. She didn't like Genny nor did she want another, only Calvin's brief absence. He got to his feet with a loud belch, then sauntered into the kitchen. As soon as he was out of earshot, she muttered, "Cunnilingus jokes—always a big *fave* of mine!"

"Easy, girl. Remember, we're doing this for Tommy."

"Yeah? Well, I could get my NOW membership revoked for this. *How* did I let you talk me into this?"

"As I recall, I bought you a fabulous dinner and showed you a picture of Zito's new baby and, hey—you fell for it." Phillip gave her a broad grin before walking over to inspect a portrait of Elvis painted on black velvet that hung over the fireplace.

The fact that he was actually enjoying himself, looking more loose and at ease with the world than he ever had in Manhattan, gave her no consolation whatever. It was downright indecent of him and she felt much aggrieved. Yes, the dinner at the Georgian Arms had been exquisite, the baby pictures adorable, and Phillip's conversation light and diverting. Still, he had taken advantage by insisting, "Hey, it doesn't matter what your relationship is. Kowaleski knows you and you know me. And that, automatically, gives me an inside track . . . And Tommy *did* send his love."

He was a swine and she was a sucker, so here she sat.

Never, in her wildest dreams, had she ever imagined herself sitting in Calvin Kowaleski's living room. The sheriff lived in a small ranch house on a dirt road that led down to the lake. The interior looked like it belonged in a *Life* magazine pictorial on Fifties kitsch; all cheap knotty pine walls, linoleum floors, and Formica countertops, and all covered with thin layers of dust or grease. The wholesale absence of warmth, charm, or even eccentricity made it unutterably depressing to her. Worse yet, it made her feel sorry for Cal, and she wished herself a million miles away.

But Phillip didn't. Not burdened with her past history luggage, he approached both the man and his surroundings like an amateur archeologist on a fascinating new excavation. He was having fun and she could have kicked him for it.

"Here you go, O'Roarke." Kowaleski slapped a fresh can into her hand, then trotted over, not to the glass-fronted gun case on the wall above the lime-green sofa where she sat, but to a built-in, paneled cupboard next to the fireplace. Taking a small, metal key from his back pocket, he undid the lock. Like a proud papa holding his firstborn, he slowly turned to present them with the only genuine article in the whole faux household.

It was in a gleaming, cherry wood case, which he delicately unlocked with an even tinier key. Josh didn't know squat about guns but, even to her ignorant, untrained eye, this was a thing of beauty. Phillip let out a long, low whistle as he stepped up to the cradled case.

"May I?"

"Be my guest," Kowaleski said proudly, then, as Gerrard lifted the Remington from the velvet-lined box, added softly, "but be gentle with her."

As Phillip gingerly hefted the butt of the rifle to his shoulder to gaze down the sight, Jocelyn wondered, for the one-hundredth time, why men like Calvin, the ones who showed the greatest disdain for flesh-and-blood women, always endowed their most cherished inanimate possessions with the feminine gender. Maybe it was a subverted yearning for the tender succors they could never achieve in life.

Then Gerrard sighed and said, "God, she's a beauty."

No, it's just *men,* period, O'Roarke concluded sourly.

Gingerly breaking open the chamber, Phillip examined it closely, then looked down the barrel of the rifle. "Never been fired, huh?"

"Nope, she's a virgin all right," Kowaleski answered reverently. "Just like Princess Di on her wedding day—pure as the driven. That's why she's worth so much."

Calvin looked as if he were just warming to his topic. Fearing that he might continue with the *virgo intacta* metaphors, Jocelyn got to her feet abruptly and demanded the whereabouts of the lavatory. Without taking his eyes off the gun, the sheriff pointed toward a dark, narrow hallway.

The bathroom was dark as well, and she had to grope around a bit to find the wall switch. Flipping it on, she caught sight of herself in the medicine cabinet mirror and gasped in horror.

"Egad! 'Midnight is not as kind to me as it once was,' " she intoned mournfully to her reflection. It was a line from Kaufman and Ferber's *The Royal Family.* Said onstage by an eminent but aging actress, it always got a laugh; now the joke was on Jocelyn, who *tsk*'d sadly and plucked out one gray hair, leaving the other four hundred and ninety-nine in place. "But it's only nine-thirty! How truly pathetic."

Of course, the lighting in Kowaleski's john didn't help; white light against white tiles—tiles that had once been white, at any rate—was flattering to few. In O'Roarke's case, it was downright insulting, giving her pale skin a grayish tinge and casting the circles under her eyes into stark relief. She dabbed blush on her cheeks and applied fresh lipstick—which only served to make her look like a decaying clown in some Fellini film.

"*Not* the look I was going for." Squinting at the fixture above the mirror, she groused, "Christ, that's not a lightbulb. It's an interrogation lamp." Deciding that desperate measures were in order, she stuck her head out the door and spotted Kowaleski's bedroom at the far end of the hall. Knowing that her absence wouldn't be noticed for a good hour or so, she tiptoed toward it in search of kinder illumination.

What she found was a lamp with a beer stein base and a burlap shade perched atop an old oak chiffonier with a mirror running its length. It wasn't great, but it was an improvement. Taking out makeup base and a concealer stick, Josh set to work with the care and precision of an artisan restoring a medieval mural, firmly telling herself all the while that this was just professional vanity on her part, having *nothing* whatsoever to do with the reappearance of one P. Gerrard.

Fifteen minutes later, she zipped up her cosmetics bag and assessed her handiwork with a critical eye. While the bloom was not exactly back on the rose, at least she no longer resembled a moldy head of cauliflower. She still looked as tired as she felt, but now it looked like glamorous fatigue—a sort of interesting exhaustion. "Well, you gotta go with what you got," she told the mirror. As soon as the words were out, she remembered who had first said them to her.

It had been Tessa Grant, years ago, up in the ladies' dressing room at the college. Jocelyn, envious of the older woman's tawny complexion, had been experimenting with a new peach foundation base and Tessa had come over and unceremoniously plucked the bottle out of her hand.

"What in God's name do you think you're doing with an Apricot Number Two?!"

"I, uh, just wanted to, kinda lighten my palette. Get a little more color in my face, you know?"

"Oh, sweetie, no! That way disaster lurks. I mean, it's fine for stage. Onstage, you can make yourself look any way you please. You can rub on a ton of Texas Dirt, darken your brows, and look just like a full-blooded Cherokee and it'll play fine under the lights. But this is street makeup and this *won't* play. In life, you can only makeup as who you *are*. You gotta go with what you've got."

"Yeah, but what I got is skin like a ghost's—prison pallor my brother calls it."

"So—who's your brother? Max Factor? What the heck does he know? Squat, that's what. Every woman has her special 'Look.' To find it, you work with your pluses and your minuses—you have to *embrace* yourself in toto. Now take a good look at yourself."

Standing behind her, Tessa had placed a hand on either side of Jocelyn's head and swung her face to the mirror. Bending down so O'Roarke could see her over her shoulder, Grant had narrowed her eyes appraisingly for a minute before delivering her cool and concise verdict.

"You've got a long face and your cheekbones aren't exactly classic, so you need to wear your hair wide at the bottom and never, under any circumstances, let it grow too long or you'll look like Mr. Ed."

Jocelyn had smiled wincingly and asked, "Um, are we getting to the pluses part any time soon?"

"Yes, we are—you're not pretty."

"That's the *plus*?!"

"To my way of thinking, yes. Pretty is for young girls and it doesn't often last. What you've got is a great *acting* face. Big eyes and a mobile mouth. It's expressive as hell and reads to the last row of the house. You're blessed."

"But that's onstage. You were talking about *off*stage."

"Same diff," Tessa had answered with an elegant, economical shrug. "I repeat, your 'Look' is who you are—and you, my dear, are a creature of contrasts. It's in your nature and in your black-Irish coloring. Pastels are your sworn enemy. You can't wear them and you can't play them. That'll be hard on you in your ingenue years, but just tough it out . . . Think of Anna Magnani and those fabulous circles under her eyes! Soul and fire and sheer guts by the truckload."

Despite Tessa's enthusiasm, O'Roarke hadn't known whether to slit her wrists or dance for joy. Having just turned twenty, she hadn't been at all sure if "soul and fire" would be an adequate compensation for the lack of just plain "pretty." But a sharp and sudden wave of nausea had rendered those points moot.

Recalling that she had barely made it to the toilet stall, Jocelyn had a clear image of Tessa's concerned look when she had re-emerged with a sour mouth and moist eyes. Then she shut her eyes tight to erase the image.

She didn't want to remember any more. It was all too much of a muchness.

Sinking down onto Calvin's lumpy mattress, Jocelyn squeezed her eyes shut, as pictures from her distant and recent past crowded in and bumped up against the events of the last few days. This, she thought, was what Lillian Hellman meant when she wrote about pentimento, seeing one's life as a canvas that has been painted and then painted over, but the old colors are never truly obliterated. They still bleed through. If, as Shakespeare said, what's past is prologue—and she had seldom found him wrong—it seemed likely that a tempest was brewing in her very own teacup and she didn't know how she would weather the storm.

Taking a deep breath, O'Roarke blinked and wiped her eyes delicately so as not to undo her handiwork. It was time to see what the boys in the front room were doing. Shakily getting to her feet, she braced herself by putting a hand on a battered nightstand, which tottered under her weight, spilling out the contents of a bottom shelf: some loose change, a key ring, and several loose pages of an official-looking document.

Bending down to replace them, Josh got a jolt when she saw Tessa's name in bold print on the top page of what, she quickly realized, was Kowaleski's typewritten accident report. After struggling with her conscience for all of three seconds, she sat back down on the lumpy mattress for a quick read.

Twenty minutes later, just as Calvin was tenderly putting his baby back in its velvet-lined cradle, she slipped into the living room. The sheriff seemed not to have noticed her prolonged absence, but Phillip had. As Kowaleski put the gun case back in the cupboard, he caught her gaze and raised his eyebrows questioningly.

"Now let me get you another drink, Phil," Calvin said dreamily, still in the afterglow of firearm-fondlings. Standing behind him, Jocelyn shook her head vehemently, then jerked it in the direction of the front door. But Gerrard chose to ignore her for the moment, as he and the sheriff had yet to discuss money. Since Kowaleski was in a mellow mood now, thanks to several beers and Phillip's adroit soft-soaping, it seemed a pity to waste the moment. So he compromised with:

"I gotta pass, Cal. It's been a long day and I don't want to get sleepy behind the wheel. But it's been worth the trip—just to see such a fine piece of workmanship. Have you, uh, decided on an asking price?"

"Well, yeah, I was gonna go for two grand. But—since we're sorta lodge brothers—I'll give you a break. Say sixteen hundred."

O'Roarke, who had sidled over to Phillip, made a small strangling sound in the back of her throat, which he pointedly ignored. Clapping a hand on Kowaleski's shoulder, he replied, "That's mighty good of you, Cal. And don't think I don't appreciate the gesture. But sixteen hundred—well, it's a little steep for me. Can I let you know in a day or two?"

"Sure, sure. You think it over. Take your time," the sheriff said expansively as he saw his guests to the door. "And, say, if you have any time to kill, why don't you stop by the station? I'll give you the grand tour—that'll take all a three minutes."

Both men had a hearty chuckle over Cal's miniwitticism, then shook hands warmly, after which Kowaleski gave Josh a curt nod and grunted a quick, " 'Night, O'Roarke."

Making a beeline for Gerrard's car, she threw over her shoulder, "If that's what they call 'male bonding,' I gotta tell you, Phillip, it's *not* a pretty sight."

"Never mind that," he said, sliding behind the wheel and turning the ignition. "You went snooping, didn't you?"

Stalling, she dug around in her bag for cigarettes, then took her own sweet time lighting one before answering.

"I didn't 'go snooping.' But I did, um, come across something —inadvertently."

"And what would that something be, pray tell?"

Knowing what a stickler Gerrard could be when it came to matters of police protocol, she took a long drag, then took the plunge.

"I, uh, found his report on Tessa—the accident report."

"Jocelyn!" She winced as his voice bounced off the car windows. "And you read it, of course," he said accusingly.

"Jesus! Don't get all Ricky Ricardo on me," she snapped back. To emphasize her point, she smacked her forehead and added in a heavy Cuban accent, "Lucy, I hope you got a good 'splanation for this . . . Of *course* I read it. And it's a damn good thing I did."

"Why's that?" Phillip asked as a ghost of a smile flitted across his face. The problem was he could never stay on his high horse around O'Roarke; she was too good at kidding him off it. "Don't tell me you think Kowaleski's suppressing evidence."

"No, it's not that. Look, I know the guy and he's no Rhodes scholar . . . He's no detective, either."

"Well, I doubt he's had much experience. He's a small-town law enforcer, period. Besides, if the doctor says it was a heart attack, why should he question—"

"Well, if you'd been on the scene, *you* would've had some hard questions, I bet."

"Why would I? I mean, considering that the incidence of cardiac arrest among middle-aged women has nearly doubled in the last twenty years. And we're talking about a woman who, from what I gather, fits the profile pretty well."

"Because it sure sounds like more than your average, garden-variety heart attack to me! Listen, Hank Barnes found her, flat on her back, in the living room, and the place was a shambles! Not just from the party mess, either. There was an overturned easy chair and an end table was knocked over—so hard that a leg broke off."

Downshifting on a tricky turn, Phillip frowned and, trying to keep the incredulity out of his voice, asked, "And they don't think there was some kind of a struggle?"

"No, because the doors were double-locked and there was no sign of forced entry. But—get this—there were pieces of broken glass *embedded* in her hand. It looked like—" Josh paused to take a gulp of air and shake off an all too vivid image. "It looked like she'd been holding a drinking glass, squeezing it so hard that she crushed it. And her face—oh, God—in rigor mortis, her face was set in a— Damn! What's the phrase?"

"Rictus sardonicus," Phillip supplied softly. The death's-head grin. Massaging her shoulder with his free hand, he tried to still the silent alarms going off in his head.

During dinner, he had written off Jocelyn's inchoate concerns over Grant's death as a product of her grief and a form of denial. Now he wasn't so sure. Rictus sardonicus did occur in some heart-attack victims but, given the surrounding circumstances, it was starting to sound as if Grant's cardiac arrest had been triggered by some sort of violent convulsion or sudden seizure. Knowing this was what Josh had been driving at all along, he didn't bother to state the obvious. Instead he asked, "And she had no history of epilepsy? Wasn't taking any special medication?"

"None that I know of. Hell, the woman was like a Valkyrie, Phillip!"

"Okay, take it easy now. Look, there are too many X factors here for you to go jumping to conclusions, Josh. Yes, it sounds like she went into some kind of convulsion. I grant you that. And I can guess what you're thinking."

"I'm thinking she was poisoned, okay? Only—"

"Only the autopsy said nothing about toxic substances. Right?"

"I guess," she admitted grudgingly as Phillip pulled up in front of his hotel, where she had left her car earlier. Hiking her bag onto her shoulder, she reached for the door handle, adding, "But I still think it *smells*. Coupled with those two break-ins, it stinks to high heaven."

Gerrard was getting a few unsavory whiffs himself, but insisted reasonably, "It's quite possible they had nothing to do with Grant. She was just a guest there . . . though I admit it's odd nothing was found missing."

"Odd—just odd? God, you *are* on vacation," Josh said wearily as she opened the car door. "Well, I'll make a point of asking whether it had anything to do with Tess or not when they come back."

"What the devil are you talking about?" Phillip said, grabbing her arm and pulling her back into the car. "Are you staying there?!"

"Sure I am. Her role—her place. Didn't I tell you?"

"No, you did *not!*" Reaching across her, he snapped the door shut. "Are you nuts? You can't stay there by yourself!"

"Yes I can! It's not like I'm going to leave the damn doors open or anything stupid. Anyways, I told you, both break-ins happened when Tess was away. Besides—I can take care of myself." To her discredit, she couldn't resist adding, "So it's no big sweat—since I'm only imagining things, huh?"

"Just can it, Josh! Whatever happened to Grant—and, convulsions or no, I still say it was a heart attack—those break-ins were real enough . . . I'm going back there with you."

"Oooh no, you're not. No way! I'm not playing Irene Dunne to your Cary Grant."

"Huh?! What in the world are you talking about?"

"You know perfectly well what I mean. You're just playing dumb," she insisted.

But his bafflement was genuine and, with a start, Josh realized she had momentarily confused him with Jack Breedlove, old-movie buff extraordinaire and her latest lover. With Jack, it was possible to capsulize any event or situation with a quick film reference. She would come home and tell him that she had had "a de Havilland in *The Snake Pit* day" or given a "*Morning Glory* of an audition," and Jack would do the same—little else need be said. Though, eventually, the constant movie cross-referencing had gotten on her nerves as she found her life in Los Angeles becoming less and less immediate and more and more like some bizarre film retrospective.

But this wasn't sweet, whimsical Jack she was talking to; it was hard-nosed Phillip, the supreme realist. To cover her gaffe, she babbled on, "*The Awful Truth? My Favorite Wife?* In both movies, Irene and Cary play an estranged married couple. And both plots get resolved when the two of them are forced to hole up together in a cozy little mountain hideaway. Get it?"

"Ah, I see. The idea being that proximity breeds, um . . . proximity? A sort of eroticized cabin fever?" he asked in a light, teasing tone.

"Uh, something like that, yeah," she muttered, squirming in her car seat.

Even in the dim light, he could see she was blushing, which pleased him greatly. It had, in his eyes, always been one of O'Roarke's most endearing features; the sudden blush that belied her outward bravado. How was he to know that, in this instance, it stemmed from pure embarrassment rather than impure thoughts?

"Well, I give you my word, Josh—as an officer and a gentleman—*nothing* will happen. Okay?"

There was a shade, just a touch too much *brio con brio* in his voice for her liking. She snapped back with:

"You say that as if it were all up to you. God, what cheek! You're out one fiancée and you come up here without so much as a by-your-leave and plop yourself smack back into my life. Then you *announce* you're coming to my place to play Lord Protector for the night. However, you will *graciously* spare me the full force of your fatal charms! . . . 'I give you my word, as an officer and a gentleman, *nothing* will happen,' " she mimicked mercilessly as she kicked open the car door. "Damn straight nothing will happen, 'cause you're not going to *be* there, sport!"

As she marched purposefully toward her car, Phillip stuck his head out the window and, with indecent gaiety, shouted, "Get some rest—Irene!"

She did not turn or pause, just flipped him the bird over her shoulder. Phillip grinned wryly at his reflection in the rearview mirror and said, "Well, asshole, either the lady's still mad for you—or she's just plain mad."

10

" 'Get some rest, Irene.' What a clown, what a quipster—what a crud! And what the hell is he doing here? Making some Grand Gesture, huh? God, I hate surprises, Angus."

The stoic Angus raised his green-and-yellow eyes above his food dish only long enough to indicate that there was no surprise in life more rude than a delayed dinner. Accepting his censure, Jocelyn roamed about the kitchen aimlessly, stopping to examine the wood slats that had hastily been hammered across the window Hank Barnes had broken to get into the house on that dreadful morning. A sudden chill went up her spine and she rubbed her arms vigorously to ward it—and the thought that it would be rather comforting to have someone else about the house—off.

Tired but still too antsy to sleep, O'Roarke decided to write a quick note to her absent friend Frederick Revere, the only man in her life who didn't give her constant *tsuris*. Having packed so precipitously, she hadn't thought to bring stationery. But there was a small den on the second floor with an antique rolltop desk. Going through the desk drawers, most of which were empty, she finally came to one containing a sheaf of writing paper. As she yanked the drawer wide open, Jocelyn was surprised to feel that its weight was considerably greater than the others, even after she removed the stock of paper. And its depth seemed shallower.

Pulling the now-empty drawer completely out of the desk, she hefted it in her hands. No question—it *was* heavier. Inexplicably she felt her pulse quicken as she flipped the drawer over and, on its bottom, saw small levers around the perimeters, like those on the back of a picture frame.

The drawer had a false bottom.

Holding her breath, she slid each lever open and carefully lifted off the backing. Inside was a loose-leaf notebook. There was no name on it, no obvious title, but she knew instantly, from the distinctive slanting script, that it was Tessa's.

It was also, to Jocelyn's eyes, completely indecipherable.

"What the hell?"

Then she got it. It was written *backward*. In an instant, it all tumbled together in her mind as she recalled, from an old art history course, that Leonardo da Vinci had kept a journal that he'd written backward; a peculiar ability of the left-handed. And Tessa, too, she remembered, had been a lefty. It made perfect sense to Jocelyn that Tess would have protected her privacy by copying a Renaissance genius.

Darting into the bedroom, she wrestled a hand mirror out of her luggage then hustled back to the den. It was slow-going at first and a great strain on the eyes but, thankfully, each entry was dated, and she soon found the one marking Tessa's arrival at Corinth.

> Went to faculty cocktail party. Had some fun playing H. & M. off vs. each other. But am worried about R. Thought I saw signs of his old condition resurfacing. Tried to ask him about it but he cut me off in no uncertain terms. Seems I'm the only one here who knows. Too bad for him, really.

Angus, affectionate again now that his belly was full, rubbed up against Josh's leg and purred inquisitively.

"Well, what do you make of this, Fur Bag?" she said sleepily, hefting him onto her lap. " 'H. and M.' stands for Hank and Michael, right? And 'R.' must be Ryson. But what's his '*condition*'?"

And why had Tessa pussyfooted around it? At first, O'Roarke feared it meant Curtis was HIV-positive, but that seemed unlikely since Ryson, having lived a very chaste life, was homosexual more in the political sense than the physical and, despite all the strain he was under, he seemed hale and hearty.

Angus' opinion, which he expressed by taking an apathetic swipe at the page with one paw, was that it was all Greek to him and not worth a tinker's damn. Rubbing his large head under her chin, he added that it was time for bed. While she disagreed with him on the first point, his latter argument held merit, as her drooping eyelids attested.

But before she went to bed, she took care to replace the notebook exactly as she had found it inside the false bottom. Perhaps Tessa had only been taking pains to protect her privacy by hiding it. But, in light of the break-ins, there was a possibility that the journal contained something potentially damning to someone; so it seemed wise to follow suit.

"Any messages for me?"

"No, nothing, Mr. Gerrard. Have a nice night, sir."

The college kid behind the front desk of the Georgian Arms looked indecently bright-eyed and bushy-tailed and his inflection on *sir* made Phillip feel like a doddering old professor. But then, the boy was used to addressing old professors. He used the same tone as a tall, distinguished man with a halo of fuzzy curls passed through the lobby.

"Good night, Professor Curtis."

"Good night yourself, Denny," he drawled affably. "And do me a favor, son. Though I applaud your commitment to the preservation of *Roe v. Wade,* in future—when you feel the need to make pictorial political statements on campus—use the Phys. Ed. building, okay?"

"Uh, yeah—I mean, yes, sir. I . . . I'll keep that in mind," the boy stammered, staring down at his feet. Then he looked up and saw the sly smile on the older man's face and grinned back. "You gotta admit, it was very flash."

"That it was. Quite theatrical, too."

With his cop's memory for faces, even ones glimpsed briefly atop ladders, Phillip now realized that this was the kid he had seen earlier whitewashing the wall of the Theatre Arts building. But he was more interested in getting his first glimpse of Jocelyn's old friend Ryson

Curtis. Turning round to get a better view, he saw the other man's eyes widen in surprise as he exclaimed, "Bless my soul! You're Phillip Gerrard, aren't you?"

"Uh, yes. How did you know?"

"Easy. I'm Ryson Curtis, by the way." He shook Gerrard's hand warmly and chuckled, "I bet you went to one of those big ol' universities, huh? But you show up on a campus like Corinth—shucks, by the time you reached the Student Union, I'd gotten a detailed physical description and so had the rest of the department."

"Really? New fish in the fishbowl, I guess."

"Exactly! And you're just the man I wanted to see." As an afterthought, he looked round and asked, "Where's Jocelyn?"

"In bed, I imagine. She was pretty beat."

"Oh, splendid! I mean, she deserves a good night's rest. I worked the poor girl like a plow horse today. Besides—I can be so much nosier if she's not around to growl at me, right? Let me buy you a drink."

Gerrard had been more than ready to hit the sheets himself, but he was no match for Curtis' ebullient southern charm and, in no time, he found himself ensconced in a padded leather booth in the hotel's dim but cozy cocktail lounge done in faux coat-of-arms decor. With a Sam Adams draft in front of him, he watched Ryson savor a sip of his Rob Roy.

"Ahh, heaven! I think it's safe to say that ol' Harry, the bartender here, makes the best Rob Roy east of the Mississippi. Care to try it?"

"No, thanks. I'm of the old never-switch, never-worry school."

"Yes, of course. And I'm sure beer is about the only thing Calvin has to offer his guests, rare as they are."

Phillip's eyebrows went up as he let out a low whistle. "Boy! That's quite a network you've got, Ryson. How do you do it—smoke signals?"

"Not quite. You and Josh had dinner here and your busboy was one of my students," Curtis confessed with a guilty grin. "You see, I came down here hoping to find you."

"Impressive. If you ever want to switch careers, I'd be happy to nominate you for the police academy. We could use you," Gerrard bantered and took a long swig, giving himself time to get his bearings. Bright and breezy on the surface, this guy was no lightweight and he clearly had an objective. Whatever it was, Phillip decided to get to it. "What did you want to see me about?"

"I suppose if I said it was just idle curiosity about the famous lieutenant, that wouldn't wash, would it?"

"No chance. I'm not that famous and, according to Josh, you're not an idle man."

"True. But, like our mutual friend, I am curious as the day is long. And I couldn't help wondering—considering your sudden arrival—if Josh had, um, summoned you up here?"

"No, not at all. I just had some free time and decided to surprise her—since I hadn't seen her in a while."

"*Really?*" Ryson put an elbow on the table and leaned forward avidly. Gerrard could see this bit wasn't part of his agenda, just good dish. "That was gutsy of you. Jocelyn *hates* unannounced visitors. As I recall, she won't even buzz you into her building if you stop by without calling first."

"Yeah, I'd forgotten about that," he muttered into his beer. "But why would you think she'd 'summon' me in the first place?"

"Oh, well, I wasn't really sure about that. But I do know something of your, uh—shared history, crime-wise. And I know how upset she is about Tess. When Kowaleski showed up at the guest house asking questions about those break-ins, I thought she might've gotten the wind up and . . . jumped to conclusions."

"Uh-huh. And when you heard we went out to the sheriff's house tonight, you jumped to a few of your own, right?"

"Oh, my, you *are* quick." Ryson gave him an admiring, albeit wincing smile. "Yes, I have to admit I was a bit concerned. Since, as I'm sure you noticed, Jocelyn cares about as much for Kowaleski as she does for Pat Buchanan—who's probably one of Calvin's idols, I'd bet. Anyway, I didn't imagine it was a, uh, *social* call."

"It wasn't. She was helping me do a favor for a mutual friend." Phillip gave Curtis a brief recap of Tommy Zito's long search for the Remington 1187, which had led them to Cal's doorstep. By the time he had finished, Ryson's incredulity had given way to amazement.

"My stars! Josh must be mighty fond of this Zito person."

"Oh, she is, and vice versa. Tom's one of her most loyal fans."

"Ah, well, that accounts for it, then," Ryson said with a firm nod. "O'Roarke values loyalty above riches. But then, she's a very steadfast soul herself—or she wouldn't be here now, would she?"

"Well, you're an old friend in a fix. She's not one to forg—"

"Oh, heavens to Betsy—I didn't mean *me*," Curtis broke in abruptly. "Yes, we're friends and she's done me a great favor by stepping in. But, really, she's doing it for Tessa. You know—you must know—Jocelyn's not a great one for hero worship."

"Uh, no, no she's not." Gerrard answered the twinkle in Ryson's eye with one of his own. "She's usually first on the block to notice the emperor's got no clothes and a pair of clay feet."

"Usually, yes. But not when it came to Tess, you see," Curtis replied carefully. "She out-and-out *adored* her, Phillip. And, whether she shows it or not, she's quite shattered by her death. That's why—well, I've no idea what she's told you about it—but it might be wise to take things with a grain of salt . . . if you see what I mean."

What Phillip saw was Ryson suddenly looking pale and clammy as he raised his glass with a shaking hand. What interested him most, given that it was only after seeing Kowaleski's report that Jocelyn had come right out and voiced her suspicions, was why Curtis had felt compelled to seek him out and make this unsolicited disclaimer. Clearly his own unexpected arrival had disturbed the man. But why would the guy spook so if he didn't have suspicions of his own?

Ryson was waiting anxiously for his response, but Phillip took his time framing it.

"I'm not sure I do. If you mean that Josh's grief might be affecting her judgment, I'd say that's very unlikely. So if you're on a fishing expedition to find out what she thinks about Grant's death —well, you'll just have to ask her yourself."

"Oh, yes, naturally. You mustn't think—I wasn't asking you to betray confidences," Curtis hurried to assure him as he pulled an immaculate white handkerchief from his pocket and dabbed at his temples. "I'm sorry, I'm not putting this very well. It's just this whole thing has been so upsetting and there's so much riding on the success of the show . . . I just don't want the whole mess stirred up again."

"Look, Ryson, if it'll make you feel any better, I'm just here on vacation—period. I'm not looking to start *anything*, okay? But frankly, I think your problem is you're afraid that there *is* something to start."

For a long moment Curtis fixed his gaze on a lion rampant on an argent shield above the bar. Then he let out a low sigh and downed the rest of his Rob Roy.

"Hell, yes, I'm afraid," he said finally. "That night—the party at Tess's place—you could've cut the tension with a dull butter knife. And it all centered around her. I mean, it's not all that surprising. Tessa had a very strong personality. She made a big impact on people one way or the other. You either loved her, as Jocelyn did, or . . . you didn't."

"Uh-huh. And which side of the fence did you fall on?"

"Me? Oh, I loved her, all right," he said simply, as if it were a given fact. "But not as blindly as Josh. She was a fine artist and a great professional, but she could be holy hell offstage. Tessa was a man-eater of the first rank. I don't think she could help herself; it was just her nature. She saw, she conquered—whether she cared a fig about the fella or not."

"And who were her conquests?"

"Oh, Hank, of course, he's always had a soft spot for her. Not that I think he'd actually *do* anything about it. He's really quite a devoted family man. But that didn't stop him from being wildly jealous of Michael Mauro, her latest victim. And Frankie, his wife, noticed, and was none too thrilled. She didn't like Tess to begin with."

"So put her in the Hate Column. Who else?"

"Oh, Lyle, of course," Ryson answered as if he were merely stating the obvious.

"The costume designer? Why 'of course'?"

"Well, the flip side of Tess's courtesan nature was that she had scant use for queers, you see. I believe I was the sole exception to that rule," he said with a modest shrug. "Plus she detested incompetence. Now, I think Davie is a fine costumer, but she had very exacting standards and, apparently, Lyle fell short of them. That night, she made some crack about her pregnancy gown making her look more like a minivan than a mother-to-be."

"What did Davie do?"

"Had a hissy fit—what else? He'd already had a few scotch and waters. So they went toe-to-toe and he told her she didn't really *need* the pregnancy pad. And the hard part for him was—after Hermione gives birth—trying to make her look as if she still weren't carrying a calf."

"Sounds like a swell party. Did anybody throw a drink in anybody's face?"

"No. Mercifully, Miriam Barnes wedged herself between them with a tray of canapés before things got truly ugly. Miriam's daughter, Belinda, was appalled, while her friend Anita was tickled no end. Tess didn't like that."

"Does that mean Belinda was a Lover and Anita a Hater?"

"Oh, no question, Belinda idolized her. And she was very sweet to the girl—which is interesting, come to think of it."

A waitress came by to announce last call and Ryson took her up on it without even asking Gerrard if he wanted another. This minor breach of etiquette in so mannerly a man was, Phillip thought, a testament to how badly Curtis needed to vent his thoughts.

"What's so interesting about it?"

"Tessa was always drawn to fresh talent. That's why she took O'Roarke under her wing way back. She saw Josh had the right stuff and she knew how to encourage it. But Anita is quite gifted—far and away a finer actor than Belinda. So you'd think Tess would've glommed on to her, wouldn't you?"

"But she didn't?"

"No, she went for Linda straight off! The poor girl was terrified of acting opposite her and Tess took great pains to put her at ease. Of course, some of it may've had to do with self-interest. They were playing mother and daughter, and Tessa knew a real emotional bond would read onstage. But I think it was more than that. She was genuinely fond of the child. She even spent one of her days off treating Belinda to a shopping spree in Syracuse. Believe me, that wasn't like her!"

"Did Anita resent Belinda's getting all that special attention?"

"Maybe, maybe not. Anita's pretty secure in her talent, for such a youngster. If she resented anything, it was the attention Tess got from the men. Sanchez is a budding femme fatale herself, but there was no way she could compete with Tess."

"Are you kidding?" A great appreciator of women, Phillip vividly remembered Sanchez's comely form and exotic features. "A nubile twenty-year-old blown out of the water by a woman closing in on fifty?

"Why, Lieutenant, I'm surprised that that surprises you," Ryson joked, back to his wily southern ways. Scouring Phillip's face, he added, "Here I took you for one of those rare fellas who know a thing or two 'bout what makes a woman genuinely fascinatin'."

With a slightly abashed smile, Gerrard shrugged off the personal implications of Curtis' remark and managed to save face with a small assist from Shakespeare. "So age could not wither nor custom stale Grant's infinite appeal—is that it?"

"Exactly. Of course, it didn't hurt that she was a mighty hand-some woman. Have you ever seen her?" Without waiting for Phillip's reply, he whipped out his wallet and riffled through it. "Ah, here it is!" Pulling out a snapshot, he placed it lovingly on the stained oak tabletop. "Now, that was taken some years ago, but it's a good likeness."

In the dim light, Phillip had to lean down to focus on the photo. It was a much better likeness than the one Revere had shown him. Tessa Grant hadn't been a classic beauty, but she had been a stunner—a world-class stunner. In the photo he saw a tall woman with gleaming, tawny hair and a wide forehead. Accentuated by sweeping chestnut brows, her sky blue eyes fairly leapt out of the picture above full, strong lips that were curled into a smile that seemed to welcome and tease at the same time. Dressed in beauti-fully tailored gabardine slacks and a silk shirt, she stood gracefully, with a hand cocked on one hip and an arm casually flung around a young and, by comparison, somewhat disheveled girl.

Hardly realizing it, Phillip let out a low wolf whistle. "I see what you mean. Fair and twenty can't touch *that!*"

"Obviously not." Ryson took a sip of his Rob Roy as he eyed him with great amusement. "Since you didn't even notice who the girl is."

"Huh?" Catching the Cheshire cat grin hovering across the table, Phillip snatched up the snapshot for a closer look. It was true; he had barely given the young girl in the fringed vest and bell-bottom jeans a glance. She was in three-quarter profile, beaming up at

Grant. But now he saw, under a wild mop of dark, shaggy hair, a familiar face. "No! . . . It *can't* be!"

"Oh, but it *is*," Ryson chortled gleefully.

"But she looks like such a baby." He peered even closer at the snapshot, fascinated by this glimpse of a Jocelyn he had never known. A Jocelyn far more open and vulnerable than he had ever seen. Nor had he ever seen such a look of forthright adoration on her face. To his dismay, he felt a twinge of jealousy for the dead woman who had been able to inspire that look.

Reluctantly returning the photo to Ryson, he said softly, "You're right. She must've loved Tessa very much."

"Oh, yes—but it wasn't one of those schoolgirl-crush things, you know." Guessing at how Gerrard's thoughts might be running, Curtis slipped the snapshot back into his wallet and added, "It had more to do with respect and an immense sense of *gratitude*. You see, back then the drama professors were all men. According to what Tess told me later, they simply had *no* idea what to do with O'Roarke. They knew she was damn good, but she just didn't fit their notion of an ingenue or a leading lady. Then Tessa came along and told her to, well, just fuck 'em, if you'll pardon my Olde English."

Phillip nodded his head once, then shook it twice. "Nope, had to be more than that, Ryson. There've been other people since, in her professional life, who've done her a good turn, given her good advice. And, yeah, she's always grateful—but not like *that*."

"Well, first mentors are like first loves. They hold a special place in our affections . . . However, you may be right. There may be more to it. My belief is that Tessa did Josh some great favor—a *personal* favor—at one time."

"Like what?"

"I have my suspicions but I'm not sure." All solemnity now, Curtis raised his eyes to Phillip's. "And even if I were, I wouldn't say. It was their business. And I'm truly sorry if it seems like I've been leading you down a blind alley, Phil. But you'll have to ask Jocelyn. Not me."

11

Blocked first three scenes today. God save me from academics! H. is stiff and too stentorian for words. Really must ask him to remove that very large stick he's got up his bum. (Meanwhile M. watches me like a hawk all the time, but that's to be expected.) The kids are fun thou. Little A. is quite good and B. is a darling, everything I hope—

"Yoo-hoo! Anybody home?"

Perched on the windowsill in front of the boarded-up pane, Angus watched with something approaching interest as his mistress jerked her head up from the pages she had been poring over, mirror in hand. The handle of the back door was rattling, and Jocelyn swiftly shoved the journal into a drawer of spare dishrags, then dropped the hand mirror into her tote bag.

"Just a sec!"

Hustling over to the door, she peeked through the chintz curtain and saw Miriam Barnes tapping a foot on the welcome mat, looking faintly put out. Being a true-blue New Yorker, O'Roarke kept all doors locked at all times. From the expression on the other woman's face, she gathered that such urban paranoia was considered gauche in the homey hills of Corinth.

Unlocking the door, she watched Miriam's frown melt into a

sunny smile as she swept into the kitchen, caroling, "Hi! It's the Welcome Wagon. How'd you like to come up to our place for a nice, big country breakfast? Just the thing to set you up for your first day of rehears—" Her voice faded out as her eyes fell on the kitchen table, which held the remnants of Jocelyn's bagel smothered with cream cheese. Then her face fell. O'Roarke felt an absurd twinge of guilt, as if she'd just plunged a stake through Donna Reed's heart.

Pointing to a bagel-filled paper bag on the table, she mumbled apologetically, "I found those this morning. A housewarming present from Frankie. She knows I've always loved the bagels from Hal's Deli."

"Oh, yes, I've heard they were good," Miriam said doubtfully.

"Heard?! You mean you've never *had* one?" Jocelyn was too surprised to be tactful. During her student days, Hal's bagels were considered the culinary equivalent of the Holy Grail, and O'Roarke had been thrilled to find that they hadn't lost their luster over the years. Happy to share the wealth, she pulled a cinnamon-raisin bagel out of the bag. "You wanna try one? They're great."

"Well, it looks just, uh—delectable," Miriam said without conviction, "but I don't want to spoil my appetite."

They were clearly at a food impasse, as Miriam seemed to be one of those people who wouldn't eat something if she didn't know where it had *been;* so Jocelyn moved on to liquids. "Well, then . . . how about some coffee?"

"Now that would be nice. Thank you." Settling in for a cozy visit, Miriam pulled a chair up to the table while Jocelyn, who, hating all unexpected visitors but most especially unexpected *morning* visitors, slowly poured two cups from the Melitta as she desperately searched for a gracious way to say: "Lovely to see you—here's your hat. And *call* next time."

More liberal in her views on coffee, Miriam took a sip from the steaming mug Josh set in front of her and said, "My, this *is* good! It's not Yuban, is it?"

"Uh, no, Zabar's Vienna Roast. I tossed a bag in my suitcase before I left. It's the only thing that'll unglue my eyelids in the morning."

Miriam nodded and gave an embarrassed, little-girl grin. "I guess

I just assumed all actresses are alike. But I can see you're much more . . . domestic than Tessie. She never had a thing in the house. So she'd often skip breakfast. And I think that's such a mistake because it *is*—"

"The most important meal of the day. You're absolutely right." O'Roarke finished for her, then asked politely, "So did you fix breakfast for Tess every morning?"

"At first I did. But, like I said, Tessie wasn't big on breakfast. Plus she had certain food allergies, I guess. So she told me not to bother."

Josh wondered if the bit about the food allergies was just a bluff on Grant's part to save herself from Miriam's culinary ministrations. Either way, it was definitely time to nip things in the bud.

"Well, I'm in your camp—can't get going without a good breakfast. But, you know, it's such a thrill for me to have a real kitchen for once," she said, sweeping an arm around the room with pointed enthusiasm. "I plan to do lots—just a *ton* of cooking while I'm here. Tell me, do they still have that great farmers' market off Route 13? I could swing by there after rehearsal."

"Um, I think so," Miriam answered uncertainly. "See, I do all my grocery shopping at the A&P in town. It's so clean—and so much quicker."

"Oh, sure." O'Roarke smiled vaguely and nodded. "I'll, uh, have to check it out."

"Yes, do. They have great sales on Wednesdays! We could go together," Miriam said warmly, clearly happy to have found a *McCall's* soulmate instead of the *Vanity Fair* queen she had expected. Then her smile clouded over as she added, "Though I'm afraid the really good values are on large-quantity items. You know . . . *family* size." She spoke the last two words softly and, with great delicacy, averted her eyes from Jocelyn as if to spare her, in her naked, *single* state, further embarrassment. Miriam's presumption was so great and so automatic that it was more comical than insulting, and O'Roarke had all she could do not to laugh out loud.

"Well, I guess it's the farmers' market for me then, huh?" she said with mock regret as she smacked the tabletop and, playing it to the hilt, gave an elaborate life's-so-unfair shrug.

"Oh, now don't be so sure." Miriam patted her hand consolingly.

She gave Josh an impish smile and a wink. "You may be doing a lot of shopping if that policeman friend of yours has a healthy appetite. Right?"

See how quickly the gods smite us when we make mock of Donna Reed, thought Josh as she replied through gritted teeth, "I doubt that. He probably won't be here that long."

"Oh, now that's a pity. Belinda said—oh, she was so cute—she said, 'He's pretty awesome . . . for someone his age.' Isn't that funny?"

"A stitch."

"He'll stay at least till opening night, won't he?"

"Dunno. You'd have to ask him. Like some more coffee?"

"Here, let me," Miriam said, jumping up. Ignoring O'Roarke's mumbled protests, she bustled about the kitchen with proprietary zeal. This was, to some degree, understandable, since the guest house was, in a sense, under her domain. Still it put Jocelyn's teeth on edge as she watched her sweep up some spilled coffee grounds and pinch a few dead leaves off a coleus plant hanging in the window. Lifting the Melitta pot, she saw the wet ring it had left on the counter and stretched a hand toward the drawer containing the dishrags—and the journal.

O'Roarke bolted up, nearly knocking her chair over, and streaked across the room. Just as Miriam was pulling the drawer open, Josh neatly shut it with her hips as she leaned over the counter to pluck a sponge out of the sink.

"Here. Use this." She handed the sponge over and added, as casually as she could, "Cooking I love. Doing laundry I loathe."

"Oh, you and me both," Miriam agreed, mopping away as Jocelyn studied her closely to see if she had caught sight of the diary. Her face was perfectly placid and O'Roarke decided that she was letting paranoia get the better of her. Even if Miriam had seen it, she wouldn't know what it was, since Tessa had obviously kept its existence a secret; if anything, she would assume the notebook belonged to Josh.

Handing O'Roarke a refilled mug, Miriam gave her head a little shake as she tittered and said, "You know, it's funny how wrong first impressions can be."

Sensing this was leading to something but not sure she wanted to go up the path, O'Roarke still obliged with, "First impressions of people you mean?"

"Yes. When I met you, I never would've guessed you were such a homebody."

A *homebody!* Something about the phrase made Jocelyn's flesh crawl as her mordant imagination conjured images of a corpse decomposing in front of a fireplace in a cozy parlor.

"Uh, I don't know about that. But I like my creature comforts as well as the next person," she said dryly. "And, contrary to popular opinion, not all single women eat their meals standing over a sink. Not all single men, either."

"Of course not! I didn't mean that. It's just that, when I saw you and Francine carrying on, I just assumed you were more like her. More, um—bohemian."

Guessing that "bohemian" was Miriam's euphemism for "hippie slattern," O'Roarke sucked in her cheeks and wryly observed, "A professor's wife with three kids? That doesn't sound too counterculture to me."

"Oh, but you haven't seen their home. The way they live. It's like—like something out of . . . of Dickens! The children are adorable, but just totally out of control."

Enough was enough. Josh laid down her mug and looked coolly into Miriam's eyes. "They're young and there's three of 'em. You had one. Think back . . . and do the math."

The other woman flushed to her roots and bit her lip in chagrin. But she apparently had an ax to grind and she wasn't done honing yet. "True. But still, the house is always topsy-turvy, just a mess. Which you could understand if she had a job—but she doesn't! I don't know how Michael gets any work done there. It's no wonder he—"

Miriam stopped herself with a my-lips-are-sealed wave of the hand. Absurdly it reminded Josh of Eleanor Bron's running gag in *Help* where she would firmly tell Paul McCartney, "I can say no more." Paul would nod and reply, "Say no more." Whereupon Eleanor would promptly shoot the works—just as Miriam was itching to do now. If she didn't let her "say more," the woman would likely self-combust.

"No wonder he what?"

"Well, I don't want to make too much of it. And this is strictly confidential, mind. But Michael was very drawn to Tessa. You know, she was so bright and gifted. And so—*serene.* I think he just enjoyed the change. Getting away from the hurly-burly. He was here quite a lot. She didn't like to drive and he'd bring her home after rehearsal. Then he'd come in for a drink and a chat. Now I'm sure it was all quite *innocent* . . . but I don't know if Francine saw it that way."

"Aw, c'mon, Mir. Take a stab. Just how the fuck do you think I saw it, hon?"

The kitchen door swung wide open as Jocelyn and Miriam spun round in their seats to find Frankie leaning against the doorjamb. Miriam gave a strangled "Oh!" and, unlike Eleanor Bron, could truly say no more.

Cursing herself for leaving the door unlocked, O'Roarke decided there was a lot to be said for urban paranoia as she caught the dangerous glint in her friend's eyes and said, "Morning, Frankie . . . How long have you been—?"

"Long enough, toots," she barked in Miriam's general direction before looking down at Josh with an ironic grin. "So—any coffee left?"

12

"Now how do you take yours, son?"

"Just a little cream; no sugar, please." Phillip answered with a nod and a smile; it had been a long time since anyone had called him *son*. Watching the old gentleman pour coffee from an ancient, battered percolator into two chipped mugs, Gerrard, normally a good judge of age, tried to estimate Doc Morgan's, but could only come up with somewhere between seventy and death.

Picking up a creamer shaped like a high-buttoned boot, the good doctor poured the cream as carefully as if he were measuring out a chemical formula, then shuffled across the den, which served as his in-home office, to hand Phillip a mug. The shuffling was not due to arthritic legs but a result of wearing threadbare carpet slippers, which were topped by rather spiffy silk pajama trousers, a Red Sox T-shirt, and an immaculate white lab coat. An eclectic ensemble to be sure, but on him it looked good.

"Smells great," Phillip said, taking an appreciative sniff of the steaming coffee. "Look, I'm sorry about turning up so early in the day. I just thought I'd try to catch you before you started your appointments."

"Think nothing of it. Even if you'd come later, I'd still be dressed like this." Sipping his coffee, Morgan grinned impishly over his mug. "Always told myself that when I retired, I'd stay in my pajamas till noon every day. Then, a few years back, I realized I had no intention of retiring—rather die in harness or wait till they boot me out. But I decided to do the p.j. bit anyways. One of the privileges of eccentric old age. My private patients—the ones I see here in the mornings—are good enough to indulge me. And I don't go to the hospital till one, so it works out fine . . . How's your coffee?"

Gerrard dutifully took a sip and immediately felt his scalp tighten.

"It's—terrific," he managed to gasp from his shell-shocked esophagus.

"Not too strong for you, I hope?" the doctor asked, again with mischief in his eyes.

"No, uh, well, maybe a little more cream."

"Help yourself, son." Morgan genially waved a hand in the direction of the boot creamer, then planted himself in a high-backed leather chair behind his desk as Phillip diluted the liquid TNT. If the old guy drank this stuff every day, no wonder he didn't feel like retiring, Gerrard thought; he's too wired.

"Now—let me get this straight, Lieutenant." Suddenly all business (probably the effects of the mega-caffeine infusion), Morgan fixed Phillip with a gimlet gaze as he nodded for him to pull up a chair. "You're here in no official capacity—that right?"

"Right. What's more, I didn't even know Miss Grant personally. But there's a friend of mine who—"

"That'd be little Joshie O'Roarke, I bet."

"Um, yes. You know Jocelyn?" It was a silly question since, as was becoming increasingly clear to Gerrard, everybody in Corinth knew everybody and, apparently, what they were up to.

"Knew her. When she was in college. Very good in trouser parts. Saw her play Flute in *Midsummer Night's Dream* once. And she was my patient—briefly." Morgan picked up a letter opener and briskly started slitting envelopes, a signal that there would be no more said on *that* particular topic. Despite his cultivated air of eccentricity, there was nothing fuzzy-headed about the man, and Phillip sensed that he would get nowhere fast if he tried to finesse the old fox.

"Well, sir, Jocelyn's concerned about Miss Grant's death. It seems Sheriff Kowaleski made reference to some, uh, discrepancies you found in doing the autopsy and—"

"He did?" After slitting the last envelope, Morgan tossed aside the opener in irritation. "Well, Cal's a fool—a well-intentioned one, but a fool nonetheless. He had no business bandying that information about."

"I'm sure you're right, Doctor. But since he *did* . . . uh, my dad always said a cat that's let only halfway out of the bag does the most damage, if you see what I mean."

Propping his slippered feet on the desk with a disgruntled snort, Morgan squinted up at the ceiling and sighed. "Well, your father knew what he was talking about. Must've grown up in a place like Corinth. Rumors jump around faster'n fleas on a mangy dog in a college town. That's why Cal should've known better. Look, son, I'm no forensic expert, but I've done enough autopsies in my time. If there had been anything seriously amiss, I would've made a full report to the authorities pronto."

"I've no doubt of that. And believe me, I don't want to make trouble here. I'm just trying to, uh—swat a few fleas before they spread."

Doc Morgan regarded Phillip thoughtfully for a long minute and finally decided he liked what he saw. Dropping his feet to the floor, he sat upright with hands clasped on the desk blotter.

"All right, I'll tell you what bothered me. But let me preface it by saying that, despite all our knowledge, the human body remains a very mysterious thing, even in death. And no two are exactly alike. Physicians hate to admit it, but there are things—the way one person's body synthesizes certain substances in a unique manner, for instance—that we have no way of accounting for."

Phillip nodded his agreement. "I know what you mean. I've seen it more than once."

"Good. Now, in doing the autopsy, I found a small trace of alcohol in the deceased's blood."

"And that worried you because the witnesses said Grant hadn't been drinking that night," Gerrard put in too quickly.

"Oh, crapola on that," Morgan shot back in disgust. "You know—we both know better'n that. You don't have to be drinking booze to show blood alcohol. Lots of things, once the body breaks them down, will leave a trace of alcohol." He leaned forward and added pointedly, "But it'll be *methyl* alcohol every time."

"Of course." Suddenly Phillip felt his scalp tightening again, but it wasn't from the doctor's coffee. "But wasn't that what you found?"

"Nope." Gerrard was a much better, more perceptive listener than Kowaleski had been and the doc couldn't help but pause for effect before adding, "It was *ethyl* alcohol. Again, it was a very low amount. Not enough to do her damage or cause the heart attack. But you tell me—what the hell did the woman eat or drink that would turn into wood alcohol?"

"Now tell me, just tell me—'cause I really want to get this straight—why the hell were you trashing me with goddamn Miriam?"

Frankie hung a sharp right on Sequoia Street, throwing Josh against the car door.

"Ow! I wasn't trashing you. She was just blathering."

"Yeah, right! Just blathering about me and Mike and Tess. And you just *sat* there and let her—"

"Hey—what was I supposed to do? Pour my coffee down the back of her blouse . . . like you did to Sue Kratz at that Ten Wheel Drive concert?"

"Why not? It shut her up." Frankie's cheeks were still flushed, but her temper was cooling down; O'Roarke could tell by the way she was driving, only a scant ten miles per hour above the speed limit now, and by the way her eyes lit up at the mention of the besmirched Sue.

"Like fun it did! She screamed bloody murder and we got tossed out of the concert, remember?"

"Yeah, but it was worth it," Frankie said with a nostalgic sigh, her spirits restored by the happy memory of past mayhem.

In retrospect, Jocelyn found it somewhat amazing that she and Frankie had never really locked horns in their school days, considering that they both possessed classic Irish tempers, the straw-fire kind that flares suddenly but burns out just as fast. The difference between them lay in how that anger manifested itself. Of the two, O'Roarke had the shorter fuse, but when she lashed out, she lashed out verbally—the Tongue Slayer, as a short-lived boyfriend had once dubbed her—whereas it had been Frankie's wont to stew silently for a bit, then out of the blue, she'd put her cigarette out in the middle of your egg yolk or swipe your favorite sunglasses and lob them into the center of the reflecting pool or execute some other unexpected act of retribution. Back then, since it was never directed at her, Josh had found her antics funny and outrageous. But how would it play now? And how far would Frankie go, these days, to get back at someone?

Finding a lollipop glued to the side of her bucket seat, Jocelyn dislodged it and, as she leaned forward to stick it in the ashtray, snuck a sidelong glance at her friend before asking, "So why's ol' Miriam on your case? Is it just because you won't do the faculty wife bit?"

"Who knows! She's always been a pain in the butt. Only lately it's gotten worse. I figure it's either the onset of menopause or she's pissed 'cause I wouldn't suck up to Grant like she did. Miriam, shit—she thought we should all fall to our knees and salaam every time that broad walked into a room!" Her tone was calm and matter-of-fact, but Josh saw her hands tighten on the wheel.

"You, uh, didn't care for Tessa much?"

"No, not much . . . But not for the reasons Miriam was hinting at, if that's what you're thinking." They were on the steep hill that led up to the campus and Frankie shifted into third as she locked eyes with Josh in the rearview mirror. "Just for the record —that stuff about Tess and Mike? Maybe yes, maybe no. I know his eye wanders a lot, but I don't think the rest of him does—I just don't know, see? But that's not why I didn't like Grant. Hell, if Mike were cheating on me—and I'm only saying *if* now—I wouldn't blame the other woman. I'm not *that* stupid . . . I'd just cut his balls off."

"Of course you would, you sweet, old-fashioned thing, you," Jocelyn joked with more levity than she actually felt since she didn't believe her friend was being the least bit facetious about the in-home castration bit. "So what didn't you like about Tess?"

"Oh, God, you're being *so* cas about it! You bullshitter. I know you think Grant walked on water, okay? And that's fine. That's as it should be. She was good to you. But Tess had blinders on. She only saw two types of people—*men,* natch, and the talented elite. You had to be in one of those two categories or you were just plain invisible to the lady. You had no worth at all . . . I didn't like that."

"But you're talented! Hell, you played first cello when you were just a sophomore and—"

"Past tense, past history. You just don't get it, do ya, Joey?" Pulling into the parking lot, Frankie killed the ignition and turned to her with a sad, rueful smile. "When Tessa looked at me, all she saw was a messy married lady with a cute husband and a passel of noisy brats. That's all most people see, really. And they either feel sorry for you or they feel contempt. She was just more open about her contempt, that's all. She made me feel . . . small, you know?"

"Aw, Jesus, Frankie, that's crappy. I'm so sor—"

"You say 'sorry' and those nifty Cool Rays you're wearing are going straight into that pool, missy," Frankie warned, waggling her brows ominously, then breaking into a broad grin. "Hey, I'm used to it. It's the price you pay during the child-rearing years. And I happen to like my noisy brats—they're a rush. So it's worth it."

"And Mike? Is he worth it?"

"Hey, he's a *great* dad. Changes diapers without a groan, picks 'em up from Little League practice and reads 'em bedtime stories without me holding a gun to his head. And he doesn't give a damn that I'm not on the Ladies' Auxiliary, so . . . it evens out."

O'Roarke wasn't sure if she bought the last bit, but she let it drop. She was a slave to the idea of parity in relationships between the sexes. But experience had taught her that such parity, a genuine give-and-take between equal partners, was as rare as the dodo. So she marveled at her friend, at all the women she knew who had that capacity for self-sacrifice she lacked.

It seemed grossly unfair to her, remembering the hours upon hours Frankie had spent practicing, remembering the sweet ache she would get in her throat listening to Frankie's lyrical cello glide through Barber's *Adagio for Strings,* that anyone would dismiss this woman out of hand as a household drudge. And she was furious with her late mentor for being one of them.

Guessing some of what was going through Josh's mind, Frankie gave her a little nudge. "Hey, you know what Will said. The world must be peopled! And it's a dirty job, but—"

"Somebody's gotta do it. Yeah, yeah." Wanting to leave on a brighter note, Josh added, "Speaking of which—when do I get to see your progeny?"

"Anytime. Wanna come for dinner tonight?"

"Sure! That'd be great. What should I bring?"

"Food would be good—unless you like Fluffernutters. Just kidding! I'll make lasagna in your honor. And you can help me force-feed Shane. He thinks ricotta looks like decomposing cow's brains."

"What an imaginative child! And thank you *so* much for sharing that appetizing image with me, Frank."

"Ah, you ain't heard nothin' yet, whoosie."

Gathering up her bag and script, she jerked the car door open just as Hank Barnes' Ford Escort pulled into a parking space across the lot. Watching him extract his lanky frame from the compact, Frankie reached out to put her hand on O'Roarke's arm.

"By the way, Josh—I'm not trying to play get-back here, but I don't think Miriam had any idea how far gone yon Hank there was on Tessa. If you ask me, it's even money between him and Mike as to who got tapped to play prince consort to the queen."

13

"O my most sacred lady,/ Temptations have since then been born to's, for/ In those unfledged days was my wife a girl;/ Your precious self had then not crossed the eyes of my young, uh . . . *friend? lord?* What the hell's the word?"

Michael Mauro broke character and squinted down at the boy holding book in the first row who cleared his throat self-consciously and called out, "My young playfellow."

"Oh, right. Shit, I *always* forget that," Michael muttered as he resumed his position opposite Jocelyn with an apologetic shrug. "Guess I've got a mental block. *Playfellow* just sounds so faggy, though."

Ignoring the remark, a remark she felt sure Mauro wouldn't have made if Ryson had been present, O'Roarke picked up her cue and plowed through her next speech. Then Hank as Leontes crossed over to take her arm, interrupting their tête-à-tête.

"Is he won yet?"

"He'll stay, my lord."

Only the king swung his queen round a bit too quickly and bumped smack into her pregnancy pad.

"Oops! Sorry, Josh."

"Way to go, Hank! Break her water in the first scene—that'll shorten up Act One just fine," Mike quipped, breaking up the other actors onstage and effectively destroying what little concentration they had.

Ryson would have cut him off and gotten things back on track, but he had left word that he was going to be late and they should start without him, which they had. But, despite Jocelyn's best efforts, the rehearsal had taken on a let's-play-hooky air from the start, thanks largely to Mauro's clowning. She knew full well that, had it still been Tessa onstage, they wouldn't dare pull this crap and it irked her. Still, there was something to be said for the salubrious effects of goofing off, especially for a cast that had been under so much tension of late. So O'Roarke contented herself by making a silent vow never, ever to work with amateurs again as she waited for the laughter to die down.

Then she turned to Hank and sweetly asked, "Lee, honey, could you give me my next cue? So your little snookums can make her exit—and get this goddamn cement sack off her gut!" More laughter, but Hank settled down enough to get through the rest of the scene.

As soon as she hit the wings, Josh wiggled out of the pregnancy harness. It had been her decision to start working with it right away, because she wanted to get the walk down; this was vital to her. Whereas Laurence Olivier, very fond of elaborate makeup in his Shakespearean heyday, always built his characters on the fake noses he created for them, O'Roarke built hers from the ground up. The first question she asked herself about any role was: What has she got on her feet? Frederick Revere teasingly called it Josh's Moccasin Method, referring to the old Indian saw about not judging a man until you've walked one day in his moccasins. But it had never let her down.

In the case of Hermione, in the early scenes, that walk was largely determined by the fact of her pregnancy. And it was no mean feat to walk not just like a pregnant woman, but like a pregnant *queen*. So she considered the pregnancy pad a must. But she detested it heartily.

Free of the loathed encumbrance, she darted up the stairs to Ryson's office. She knocked once and heard a raspy voice croak, "Yeah? What?"

Behind a battered desk in the outer office sat the chairman's secretary, Trudy Feeney, just as she had sat for the last twenty years, and maybe longer for all Josh knew, through a whole string of department heads; typing away on an old Underwood with cigarette ash sprinkled on the keys while smoke from an unfiltered Camel, always dangling from the corner of her mouth, spiraled up to mingle with the hair spray in her teased bouffant. Wearing a frilly blouse with shoulder pads any linebacker would envy, she was, as she had always been, an imposing Cerberus to the inner sanctum.

Upon seeing O'Roarke, she said with the warmth of a bug exterminator toward an encroaching roach, "Wha'd ya want?"

"Hi, Miss Feeney." Jocelyn couldn't help herself; no matter how she tried, the word *Trudy* would not form on her lips. "I was just, um, wondering—do you know when Ry . . . Professor Curtis is due back?"

"He'll be here when he gets here."

"Uh-huh. Makes sense."

Trudy Feeney had lived in Corinth all her life. She was, in the deepest sense of the word, a "townie" and, as such, regarded all transients on campus as interlopers and therefore highly suspect. Too late Josh wondered what benighted impulse had brought her up here. Pure hubris, she decided, since stones bled more readily than Feeney. Still she had to give it one more shot or Trudy would mark her down as a total feeb.

"It's just that I was a little worried. Professor Curtis is always so punctual." Nothing from the Stone. Making a desperate last stab, she added, "I hope he's feeling all right."

The heavily penciled arcs that had long since taken the place of eyebrows jerked infinitesimally upward as Trudy ground out her cigarette in an overflowing ashtray and growled, "He's fine . . . Why'd ya ask that?"

A nerve had been struck. Feeney never asked questions, only refused to answer them. Since Jocelyn couldn't say, "A little journal told me," she vaguely replied, "Oh, I just think he's been looking a bit tired. He's had a hard week after all. It'd take a toll on any—"

"Well, don't worry your little head, missy. He's doin' just fine." That was to be the end of it. But Josh stood there with a calculated look of concern and skepticism on her puss and it worked. Trudy lit another Camel, then blew smoke and brimstone in O'Roarke's face. "Looky here, it's only natural for a body to get a little wore-out when he's pulling more than his fair load! My lord, what that man has had to put up with—slackers and such. It's no wonder."

"And such what?"

"Huh?"

Having gotten this far, Jocelyn decided to shoot the works.

"Look, Miss Feeney, I'm not trying to be a nosy parker. Ryson is an old friend of mine and if there are any problems—if anyone's giving him a hard time—I'd like to help, okay?"

Trudy took a long draw on her Camel and gave Josh a hard look. Then, as sphinxlike as possible for a woman with a henna bouffant, she said, "Well, I'm not gonna go into partiklers, missy. But this place ain't nothin' but a nest a' vipers if you ask me. Everybody always jockeying for position with an eye on the prize." By way of explanation, she jerked a thumb in the direction of Ryson's office. "Now Professor Curtis, he's as fine a chairman as I've seen in all my years. But there's some folks—past and present—who think they'd make a better job of it. They're *wrong!* But they're always lookin' for a chink in the armor, see? And the professor's no fool —he knows he's gotta watch his back . . . That can get pretty tirin' is all I'm sayin'."

And it was. After this uncharacteristic burst of loquacity, the por-tals slammed shut as Trudy pointedly resumed her mile-a-minute typing. Jocelyn eased herself out the door and, back in the hallway, took a deep breath. She had forgotten about the intricate politics of academia, but Trudy had given her a succinct refresher course. Chairman of the Corinth Theatre Department had long been a revolving-door position; she'd seen two come and go in her college years. But exactly *who* had his or her eyes on Ryson's job now?

It was a warm day for spring and, since it was school policy not to turn on the air-conditioning till June, the backstage area felt stale and stuffy. Stepping into the wings, Jocelyn saw that they were still some ways away from her next scene and that rehearsal decorum had sunk even lower as Hank, delivering one of Leontes' jealous tirades, had adopted Richard III's limp and Peter Lorre's accent to the vast amusement of all. So she stepped out to the scene dock for a breath of fresh air.

Directly behind the scene shop, the scene dock was a cement

platform used for painting the larger flats and set pieces. At the moment the dock was deserted save for a series of flats depicting the woods of Bohemia, drying in the sun. O'Roarke walked over to the east end of the platform, which looked out over the parking lot and the soccer field, hoping to catch a glimpse of Curtis' car pulling into the lot. But there was no car in sight. So she began a series of stretching exercises to get limbered-up for the next scene, only to be stopped mid–neck roll by the sound of a tenor voice.

"These your unusual weeds to each part of you/ Do give a life— no shepherdess, but Flora/ Peering in April's front—and, speaking of fronts, yours is looking extremely fine these days, babe."

"Just bag it, will ya? You said you wanted to run lines—so cue me . . . And I told you not to call me babe."

Peering over the edge of the dock, Josh spotted Belinda and Denny Moskowitz three feet below her, sitting on the ground with their backs against the base of the platform. Denny reached out to lay a hand on her shoulder, but the girl flinched away.

"Geez, what is with you?! You been treating me like a fuckin' leper ever since—"

"I don't want to talk about it, Den! Okay?"

"Fine, fine. It's just— Gimme me a *little* break here, huh? I know you don't want to go out with me right now, but—"

"I don't want to go out with *anybody*. I'm . . . not ready yet."

"I know, Bellie. And that's cool. But look, I'm really trying to be sensitive as shit about this thing, really. I know you had a hard time and I just want to be your *friend*—that's all, honest."

"Then why won't you do like I ask and just leave . . . it . . . *alone?*"

Damn me and my fetish for footwear, thought Josh. If she hadn't been wearing Hermione's soft-soled slippers, Belinda and Denny might have heard her approach and she wouldn't be in this position—eavesdropping unintentionally, but eavesdropping all the same. It was a low and loathsome thing to do and she was ashamed of herself, though not enough to tiptoe away and maybe miss something really good.

" 'Cause I don't understand why you're so supremely pissed at me! Belinda, you know I didn't do it on purpose. It was an *accident!*"

Twitching with curiosity now, O'Roarke forced herself to stay perfectly still. From a far corner of her brain, the actor's corner, a small voice said that this was great practice for the last scene, where she had to be a statue. She told that small voice to take a hike. Though the argument had been maddeningly vague thus far, she had her suspicions about its cause. Having already debased herself, she wasn't about to miss the payoff.

Belinda gave a small, mirthless laugh and in a voice that sounded old beyond her years said, "Yeah . . . isn't it always."

That pretty much cinched it for O'Roarke. Peering down at the top of Belinda's blond head, she felt a keen and aching empathy for the girl. There was only one "accident" that could cause a young woman—any woman—such distress, she knew.

She knew because she'd been there once herself.

"Hey, dude, gimme dat, please."

Assuming he was the dude in question, Phillip looked around, but saw no one else in Aisle 5 of the Super Shopper. Then he felt a sharp tug on the strings of his windbreaker. "Dat bag by your head—the bwown 'n' gween one."

Dropping his gaze, he was confronted by a pair of big brown eyes set in a small, rather grimy face. The little boy in jeans and a Corinth College sweatshirt couldn't be more than four or five but he had the forthright air of a Wall Street power broker, and a will to match. Pointing insistently at a large bag of Snickers on the top shelf, he said helpfully "See, it has a big S on it. I can't weach it."

There was no adult in sight and the little man was getting impatient. Afraid the child would either burst into tears or, more likely, give him a swift kick in the shins, Phillip took the Snickers bag down and was just about to hand it over when a tall, buxom woman wheeled a crammed shopping cart around the corner and came barreling down on them. Just as the boy was reaching for the bag, she deftly made a one-hand grab for it, tossing it neatly back from whence it came.

"Aw, nuts, Ma!"

"And nuts to you, too, mister. I told you no more candy today."

Mother and son locked eyes in a silent battle of wills. Gerrard watched the boy's face redden as he filled his lungs with air. Just as he seemed about to let loose with a shriek, his mother squatted down to his eye level and said, "One squawk, Shane, and I hide your T-Rex for a *week*."

Quickly reversing tactics, he clamped his lips together in an attempt to turn from red to blue. But his mom, a clever adversary, darted out a hand to tickle his belly, chanting, "Shane, Shane, gives me a pain in the brain."

He pushed her hand away but started to giggle despite himself. Knowing the battle was lost, he came back fast, trying to win a concession. "Can I wide down there?" he asked, pointing to the metal rack beneath the cart.

"Yeah, okay. But only as far as the check-out line . . . and don't run your hands over the floor this time."

The child threw himself belly down on the rack and proceeded to make racing car sounds. Laughing, Phillip turned to the woman.

"Sorry about that. I should've known better. But he was just so —sure of himself."

"Oh, yeah, he's got his act down pat," she replied with a disarming smile. "Ditches me when I'm not looking and goes in search of some lone sucker— Whoops, sorry."

"No, no, you're right. I was an easy mark."

"Well, don't feel bad. He's very shrewd. Always picks guys. You're single, right?"

"Uh, yes. Does it show?"

"Oh, not to me. To him—he's got a sixth sense about it. Preys on unsuspecting bachelors. Kid's got no scruples, none." With a twinkle in her eye, she added, "Takes after me."

"Ah! I see, a second-generation felon."

"Yep. My husband's already started a trust fund to cover his bail when he's old enough to be tried as an adult."

"Really? Sound planning."

Shane had had enough of the grown-ups' banter and started to rock the cart back and forth.

"Com'on, Ma! Let's *woll.*"

As this was the pleasantest exchange he'd had since coming to town, Gerrard fell in to step with them. The woman was also wearing a Corinth College sweatshirt, so he asked, "Do you work at the college?"

"No, my husband does." Shooting him a quizzical look, she quipped, "You're not from around these parts, are ya, pardner?"

"Heck no, ma'am," he twanged back. "I'm from New York—the city, I mean."

"I *knew* it!" Her face lit up as she stopped in her tracks. "You're Joey's friend, huh?"

"Joey?"

"Jocelyn. You're Phil the fuzz! Damn, I never would've taken you for a cop."

"Well, I'm not at the moment—I'm on vacation."

"What a relief! So I don't have to worry about my shady son?"

"I wouldn't go *that* far. But since I don't even know his last name—"

"Oh, geez, I'm bein' even ruder than usual. Sorry. I'm Frankie Mauro, O'Roarke's old roomie."

"You're kidding? You two *roomed* together?!" Gerrard's jaw nearly hit his chest.

"Yeah, for three years. Why the big shock?"

"I—I dunno. It's just, um . . ." Phillip was too taken aback to be his normal, tactful self. "And you never came to *blows?*"

Wheeling her cart into the shortest check-out line, Frankie threw her head back and hooted with laughter. "No. But there were probably a lot of side bets that we would. We did raise some hell together, though."

"I can imagine."

"No, Phil, I don't think you can even begin to," she said with an enigmatic grin. Then she abruptly transferred her attention to the meager contents of his shopping basket. "Why're you getting that crap?"

"There's a little fridge in my room, so I—"

"Oh no, no way, man. Eating alone in a hotel room is too lame. Come to my place for dinner."

"I couldn't do that," Phillip protested, but Frankie had already taken the basket out of his hand.

"Sure you can. Just dump this stuff and spend the money on a primo bottle of wine," she answered breezily. "Something red, I guess. We're having lasagna."

From under the cart Shane started making retching sounds. "Uck! Not with dat white goop dat looks like—"

"Can it, Shane." Frankie gave the cart wheels a firm kick. "Look, you *have* to come, Phil. I've already invited Josh. We'll just spring it on her."

"Uh, I don't know if that's a good idea. Jocelyn sort of hates being—"

"Surprised—I know," she said with breathless glee.

Gerrard looked into Frankie's dancing eyes and found himself laughing again.

"What time do you want me there?"

14

"My God, she's making *lasagna?* Frankie only makes it 'bout twice a year, when my folks visit and on my birthday—if I beg and grovel enough." Checking himself out in the rearview mirror, Michael Mauro smoothed a curly black lock into place—most men just have hair but Mauro really did have locks—and winked at O'Roarke. "I guess you really do rate!"

"I guess," Jocelyn said listlessly; she wasn't feeling up to Mike's level of jocularity. "Should we pick up some wine on the way?"

"I guess." He mimicked her Sad Sack tone, but Josh hardly noticed; she was too busy internally fretting. To keep him occupied, she asked questions about his children, then only half listened to his detailed answers while rerunning the day's events in her mind's eye.

Her inadvertent eavesdropping on Belinda and Denny had been interrupted by the sight of Curtis' car pulling into the lot, which had sent the pair scuttling back into the theatre. Still undiscovered, O'Roarke had stayed on the scene dock and watched Ryson getting out of the car. Closely observing him mount the long flight of steps up to the Performing Arts building, she had thought she detected something odd about the way he was walking, an unevenness in his gait. And he had held on to the stair rail with concentrated effort.

Hiking her rehearsal skirt over one arm, she had dropped down from the cement platform and scurried around the side of the building to intercept him on his way in. Upon spotting her, he had swiftly shifted a startled look into a polite smile.

"Well, I guess it's not just the fog that comes on little cat feet."

"You know what they say, Ry—forewarned is forearmed," Jocelyn had said in a spritely, mock-conspiratorial tone as she drew close to him, close enough to make sure there was no trace of booze on his breath or flush on his cheeks. She had rattled on, "Just thought you should know that—despite the valiant efforts of your poor stage manager—the run-through has rather . . . degenerated."

"Hmm, I was afraid of that. How bad is it?"

"Uh, right now it kind of looks like the Shakespearean version of *Animal House*."

"Ah, well, only to be expected. I suppose a little cutting loose will do them good. My apologies to you, though, darling."

"Oh, it's okay. We got through my first scenes in fair order. I was just worried that you wouldn't get here in time to settle 'em down for the trial scene."

"Couldn't be helped, I'm afraid. I was summoned by our illustrious president this morning for some emergency hand-holdin'. He needed reassuring that we'd be ready for the big night."

"What did you tell him?"

"Said, 'Harmon, rest easy. O'Roarke's back and Corinth's got her. And she's gonna do us all proud—real proud,' " he had said, tucking her arm in his and giving it an affectionate squeeze.

It had been very flattering, very plausible, but not all-together reassuring. Curtis had always had a silver tongue and, though she hadn't doubted his sincerity, she had still felt she was being stonewalled in some way. But the reticence of a true son of the South is like the Great Wall of China; there's just no getting around it.

Then Ryson had taken her completely by surprise when he ever so casually remarked, "I met your friend Gerrard last night."

"You did?! Where?"

"At the hotel. We had a nightcap and a nice long jaw. He's quite a fellow. Smarter'en a swamp fox."

"And what did you two *jaw* about, pray tell?"

"Aw, well—you'll just haf'ta ask him 'bout that," he had drawled, getting folksier by the minute. "But I'll say this much—you could do worse, girl."

"Michael, just wait here. I'll get the wine—my treat, okay?"

O'Roarke jumped out of the car as soon as they pulled up to Watson's Liquors without waiting for a reply. Mauro was, as his wife had said, a doting dad. But she had had as much as she could take of cute tales about the birth of each child. And the sound of his voice, mellifluous but one step away from D.J. oily, had given her a pounding headache.

The problem was, she told herself as she scoured the aisles for a decent bottle of cabernet, she worried too much about other people. And worried to no avail. Where her own affairs were concerned, she was far more blithe, having always had a strong sense of self-sufficiency coupled with a healthy *que será, será* fatalism; i.e., shit happens and then you deal with it. It was only with other folks that she went into overprotective overdrive, which was—she knew—largely futile, since there is usually precious little one can do. And worrying accomplishes nothing. She had told herself this countless times over the years, especially when she had been seeing Phillip and getting the shakes every time she knew he was going out to make an arrest. When their relationship had ended, her one consolation had been that at least *that* fear was behind her—or so she thought.

She marveled at people who had the nerve to bring children into the world. Once you had kids, it was your duty—your full-time *job*—to worry. And it was one of the reasons parenthood had never attracted her. But what was the point of blessed bachelorhood if she was going to fret herself into a frenzy anyway? she wondered. How was it going to help Ryson or Belinda . . . or Tessa?

Josh knew what Freddie Revere would say; what he always said: "We're like radios. Worry just creates static. Whereas, *action* clears the airwaves and improves the reception."

"Yeah, but *what* action, Freddie?" she mumbled, causing one of the other customers to give her a wide berth. Now she knew how Hamlet got so twisted. Spotting a good Napa Valley label, she grabbed two bottles and marched over to the counter, making a firm resolution to check her brain at Frankie's door and just enjoy the evening.

"Hi, guys!" Frankie smiled at her spouse and friend through a crack in the front door.

"Hi, yourself. You gonna let us in or what?" Mike asked.

"Sure." Frankie yanked the door open and threw one arm out wide. "Look what I picked up at the supermarket today!"

In the living room, ensconced in an overstuffed armchair that had three children hanging over the back, Phillip looked up from the *Where's Waldo?* book in his lap and offered cheerfully, "They were having a special on me."

"Honey, this is Phillip Gerrard, Joey's friend from New—"

"No kidding? I heard you were in town. Pleased to meet you," Mauro said, striding across the room with hand extended.

"Same here, Mike. You've got quite a brood." Phillip stood up to shake hands as Shane ran up to his father.

"Dad, Dad! He's a *police*. And he's got his own gun!"

Jocelyn turned slowly to her old friend. Ignoring Frankie's 'Ain't I the dickens?' look, she held out a paper sack to her and said stonily, "There are two bottles of Napa Valley red in there. Go uncork them right *now*."

Steve Martin once said, "If you ever think you want to have kids, just go out to a restaurant and sit next to one." Frankie recalled the quip as she watched Josh and Phillip contend with her high-octane crew over dinner, keenly observing their different techniques. Gerrard was patient, kind, and diffident; a little overwhelmed by the onslaught. Whereas Jocelyn, still disgruntled over the curve she'd been thrown, was far more comfortable with the kids and much less indulgent. When Shane started playing "Look" with the ricotta in his mouth, she leveled him with: "That's dumb. Only babies do it." To a five-year-old, it was the ultimate insult and Shane swallowed the lump in one mortified gulp.

The girls, Jennie and Terry, were smitten silly with Phillip, but a little in awe. Jocelyn they found less impressive but more approachable. Frankie was amazed at how quickly they took her for granted in the physical sense; plopping themselves in her lap to try on her bracelet or, as seven-year-old Terry was prone to do, peeking down her shirt to see her breasts. Unfazed, Josh let her get a good gander before easing her to the floor, saying, "Someday this, too, will all be yours," sending both Jennie and her father into smothered giggles.

And Frankie watched Gerrard watch Josh as if she were a wholly new and strange person. And he had plenty of opportunity to watch, since she had scarcely spoken to him or Frankie, dividing her attention between children and father. Not that she was flirting, Frankie knew. Just as she knew O'Roarke was about the only girl in her class to graduate from Corinth without having had an affair or serious flirtation with a married professor. Back then she had had a rock-solid rule about avoiding married men, and it was pretty clear she'd kept to it. Frankie guessed it was a holdover from her Catholic upbringing; apparently she respected the married state as much as she feared it.

As soon as the table was cleared, Mike clapped his hands, saying, "Here's the drill. Terry, take your bath. Shane, get into your jammies and brush your teeth. Jennie, you can stay down here till—"

The younger siblings cried in ritual unison, "Aw, how come she gets to?!"

" 'Cause she's got—*seniority*." Josh pronounced the last word so ominously it sent the little ones skittering up the stairs.

Following her into the kitchen with a pile of dirty dishes, Frankie said, "God, I gotta remember that one. Works like a charm."

"Not for long. Terry'll come downstairs tomorrow and ask what it means," Josh said, scraping lasagna noodles into the garbage. "You'll have to tell her, 'cause you're a good mom—then the jig'll be up."

"You really think I'm a good mom?"

"You must be. They're all bright as pennies and secure as hell."

"And holy terrors. That's what Miriam thinks, anyway."

"Then screw her. I'll wash, you dry." O'Roarke handed her a dish towel, adding, "If Miz Barnes thinks she's the distaff version of Dr. Spock, how come she only had one kid?"

"Well, in all fairness to Miriam—and you know I hate being

fair—she had a hell of a time having just one, I hear. For awhile there it looked like they weren't going to, you know, be able to. Then Hank took a sabbatical and they went to Italy for a year. Came back with baby Belinda, much to everyone's surprise."

"Hmm, must've been all that olive oil," Josh said brusquely, thrusting a dripping plate at Frankie. "Now—speaking of surprises—"

"I know, I know. You're pissed at me." Frankie sidled away to uncork another wine bottle. For all her bravado, she had never been able to bear Jocelyn's censure. "I, uh, overstepped the bounds here, huh? Inviting Phillip?"

"You could've *told* me!"

"Okay, I'm sorry. It's just, when I met him, I thought he was so *cool*."

"Yeah, so I noticed." And she had. All through dinner, it was apparent that Frankie was as fascinated by Gerrard as her offspring. Not that she blamed her; out of the city and out of his work mode, Phillip made quite an appealing impression. In his faded, fit-like-a-glove jeans and slate-gray corduroy shirt, which picked up the gray of his eyes, he looked downright hunky. But Josh could see that Frankie, always a big fan of comely males, was taken by more than his looks; behind his easy laugh and attentive conversation, there was that innate complexity of mind that gave him a subtle air of mystery. And Frankie was a sucker for a man of mystery.

"Oooh, methinks the lady is just a tiny bit jealous, methinks."

"Then thinks again, you libidinous harlot. Those goo-goo eyes you were making at him might work on Mike, but I am made of stronger stuff. Besides, Phillip and I are just—"

"Don't tell me. Just good friends." Frankie groaned out the old cliché. "If that's so, you have ree-ally lost your touch, Jo. 'Cause he is *fine*."

Wiping a fresh plate, she broke into a rowdy rendition of "He's So Fine" until Jocelyn flicked soapsuds in her face.

"Cut it out! They'll hear you," O'Roarke said, jerking her head toward the living room.

"So what? Maybe it'll get Mikey's motor running." Frankie picked up her dish towel with a snap of the wrist. "Heck, I haven't flirted with anybody in *ages*. 'Course, I haven't had much material to work with . . . No panting coeds hanging round my door like Mike's got."

There was no self-pity in her voice, just the faintest tinge of wistfulness, but it was enough to tug at Josh's heartstrings. Whipping the dish towel away from Frankie, she jostled her toward the doorway.

"Then go make the most of it. I'll finish up here. And take this with you." O'Roarke handed her the uncorked bottle. "You can get 'em both revved up and then—"

"Leave 'em both hanging!" Frankie cried, clasping the Napa Valley to her bosom and batting her eyelashes in mock ecstasy. "Just like the good old days."

"You two really *did* that? Filled the whole pool with soapsuds?" Phillip laughed aloud as Frankie, who had been regaling him with tales of her college exploits with O'Roarke, replenished his wineglass. She was a natural raconteur, with an earthy humor and a lively turn of phrase. Even better, she was direct and wholly devoid of pretense; just a damned comfortable woman to be around.

"Yup, to the brim. Took 'em *days* to drain the sucker. And we never got nailed for it. 'Cause Josh fixed up an ironclad alibi. She had us volunteer to serve at a banquet at the president's house that night—the kind of suck-up job the sorority girls usually did. We just snuck out after serving the entrée—did the deed—and got back in time to serve dessert!"

"Yeah—but it almost backfired on us." O'Roarke finally emerged from the kitchen to pick up the story. "Remember?"

"Oh, yuck—yes!" Frankie shuddered at the memory. "The fish."

"What fish? In the pool?"

"No, for dinner." Josh plopped down on the sofa next to a dozing Mike as Frankie handed her a glass of wine. "We had a freak heatwave and the president's wife had ordered fish for dinner. And I guess the cook got a little careless, 'cause the fish went off."

"Like a *bomb*," Frankie interjected. "Everybody got sick. The whole campus reverberated with the flushing of toilets."

"Right. Now we—the servers—were given the same meal as the

guests. Only Frankie and I didn't eat any 'cause we were out, uh—"

"Wreaking havoc," Phillip supplied helpfully.

"Yeah. But Josh just saw right away that we had to get sick, too, or our cover would be blown. So the next day she made this foul goop with coffee and cream of tartar and made me *drink* it!"

"Hey, I had to drink it, too."

"The wages of sin," Phillip said solemnly. Frankie threw a pillow at his head but he caught it one-handed and fired it back at her. "This why they call them throw pillows?"

"Stop! You two start a pillow fight and I'm leaving," Jocelyn warned and then yawned, "I've regressed enough for one evening."

Gerrard heard Frankie murmur, "The hell you have," under her breath as she slipped over to the stereo. He didn't know what she had up her sleeve, but he didn't think it would work; O'Roarke looked like she was about ready to join Mike in Slumberland. Then the room filled with the heavy twang of a bass guitar chord followed by a cascading drum beat and the velvet growl of a woman's voice wailing, "I've been lost before!" The voice, if not the song, was dimly familiar to him. But before he could venture a guess, Jocelyn leapt to her feet, quivering like a bloodhound that had just been given the scent. Pumping her fist in the air once, she cried, "Oh, Tracey—*yes!*"

Then Frankie shimmied over to bump hips with her and the two women launched into what was obviously an old and well-rehearsed dance routine, an eclectic, hopped-up version of the Green Onion, while Tracey Nelson backed by Mother Earth sang "Temptation Took Control of Me and I Fell." Watching the pair, who were now completely lost to the music, gyrate like twin cobras in heat, Phillip felt as if he were privy to an arcane female ritual, a dancing celebration of—not eroticism—but sensuality for its own sake. Mike, jarred by the music, was awake now, and Phillip saw he felt it, too. And it was enough to make a guy need a shower.

Then Jocelyn bumped against the coffee table and a piece of paper fell off it and fluttered to her feet. When she caught sight of it, she stopped cold. Both men said "Awww," at the same time but she didn't hear them. As the song came to a close, she bent down to pick up the paper and asked, "Who wrote this?"

"Phil did," Mike answered. "Just a little parlor trick to bribe Jennie into going to bed."

A flicker of surprise crossed her face as she walked over to a wall mirror and held the paper in front of it. Slowly she read aloud, "Jennie Mauro is one smart cookie if she can read this."

Puzzled by her reaction, Phillip said, "Jennie's a southpaw like me. I told her if she practiced, she could do it, too."

"What? Write backward, you mean?" Frankie asked. "I didn't know that! Mike and I are both right-handed; so're Shane and Terry."

"Yeah, well, it's a minor compensation for having your brain in backward. A lot of lefties can do it," Gerrard explained; then asked, "What's the big deal, Josh?"

"Uh, nothing, nothing really," she answered vaguely. "I knew you were left-handed. I just didn't know you could do this . . . Tell me something, can you *read* backward, too? Or do you need a mirror?"

"I don't think I do . . . if the writing's legible enough."

"Really? That's good, Phillip . . . That's *very* good."

Frankie and Mike probably thought she had had a little too much wine. But Gerrard knew her drinking capacity as well as he knew the little click that had just gone off behind her eyes.

15

Should go to bed but I'm a little edgy. Came home tonight and got the feeling somebody had been in here while I was away. Nothing's missing that I can see. But a few things—like my papers—seem not quite the way I left them. Maybe it's paranoia born of fatigue—or dieting! Or maybe Pinkie's up to his old tricks. If so, I'll know for certain by Opening and this time I'll fix the little bugger but good. (Or maybe everyone living in a woods gets a Goldilocks sooner or later, eh?) Must get to bed, thou. Tomorrow's our "shopping expedition."

"Who the hell is Pinkie?" Gerrard wondered aloud. Removing his reading glasses, he pinched the bridge of his nose and blinked his tired eyes. Though he didn't need to use a mirror, it was still quite an effort deciphering Grant's backward scrawl.

After having orchestrated a hasty exit from the Mauros', Josh had told him all about her find on the way back to her place. Practically begging him to take charge of the notebook, she had pointed out, quite rightly that: "It'd take me forever to get through it and I might miss something crucial. 'Cause I wouldn't be as objective as you. Besides, if—and I don't think it's at all likely—but *if* someone broke in again, well, better it's just not around, right?" Then, without even inviting him in for a nightcap, she had given him the diary, along with a chaste peck on the cheek, and sent him off to do his homework.

It was nearly two A.M. and he had been lying in bed with the journal for over an hour and had only gotten through five entries, most of them chiefly concerned with the progress of *Winter's Tale*. Reading between the lines, Phillip got the distinct impression that Tessa had seen herself as more than a guest star; it seemed she had considered herself the co-director as well. How Ryson Curtis had felt about that, he could only guess. Affable as he was, Curtis didn't strike him as the sort of man who would welcome another hand on the helm.

This last entry was the most intriguing. It was not only the first mention of a possible intruder, but the first time Grant had used a full name. Usually she wrote initials—H. for Hank Barnes, R. for Ryson, and so on. M. was a bit confusing as it sometimes referred to Mike Mauro, sometimes to Miriam Barnes, though Miriam was once or twice called the G.W. The Good Wife was Phillip's guess. Pinkie had to be a code word or nickname. But whose? He would have to ask Jocelyn if she knew, though he wasn't looking forward to their next conversation.

For one thing, he would have to tell her about his interview with Doc Morgan since he was becoming more and more convinced that her instincts were right. But it wasn't merely the traces of wood alcohol in Grant's bloodstream that troubled him now. It was Tessa herself. Terse and cryptic as her journal entries were, they still offered a rare glimpse into the writer's psyche. And the picture they painted was of an intelligent, determined woman of great vitality, passionately dedicated to her craft . . . with an ego as big as the Great Outdoors.

And it wasn't just what she wrote, but how she wrote it. During his police academy days, Gerrard had once taken a course in graphology, much of it forgotten now. But it didn't take an expert to see that Grant had perceived herself as the center of the universe or, at the very least, as the sun in the solar system. Other people were merely satellites rotating round her in order to reflect the light she gave off. There were intimations of invincibility as well in the way she crossed her *t*'s and finished off the lower loops of her *g*'s and *j*'s. All this, coupled with her comparatively blithe response to the initial break-in, told him that, if real danger had been lurking, Tessa Grant would have been the last to know.

"Hey, soldier, mind if I join you?"

"Oh, Ms O'Roarke, hi! What're you doing here?" Denny Moskowitz asked, sliding his tray over to make room for hers.

"It's Jocelyn. And would you believe me if I said I had a nostalgic yearning for Corinth cafeteria food?"

"Get out! Nobody'd eat this crap if they didn't have to," he said, shoveling in a forkful of watery scrambled eggs despite his epicurean sensibilities. "You must really *hate* cooking."

"Actually, I love to cook and I love a good breakfast." Pointedly poking the sodden lump that was supposed to be hash browns, she added, "So what's your next guess?"

"I dunno." Looking a little hot under the collar, Denny shifted his eyes around the room for possible clues. "Uh, you like the view?" They were in the Tower cafeteria, one of the highest vantage points on campus, and its floor-to-ceiling windows did offer a splendid panorama of the college, but it wasn't worth risking major acid indigestion as O'Roarke indicated by flicking her gaze from the window back to her plate and arching one eyebrow. Denny got the message. A hopeful, nervous smile lit his face. "You got a thing for young guys, maybe?"

"Forget it, Den. You're adorable but I've got nephews older than you."

"No *way!*" His incredulity was flattering, but it soon gave way to frank discomfort. "Then I guess you maybe, uh—want to talk to me about something?"

"Now you got it. There's something I—"

"Hi, Jocelyn. Hi, Denny." Anita Sanchez sauntered over to lean across the table, giving Moskowitz a melting look and a nice glimpse down her V-neck, tie-dyed T-shirt. It was amazing to O'Roarke that the tie-dyes of her youth had come back in style, but not as amazing as the gravity-defying tilt of the girl's breasts. She could remember once having a shirt very like Anita's but, for the life of her, she couldn't recall ever having *those.*

Denny, however, seemed far less impressed by the sight. "Hey, Nita," he mumbled. "What's up?"

"This, that, and the other," she answered coyly. "Got room for one more?"

Josh was halfway to formulating a polite rebuff, but the boy beat her to it. "Sorry, babe. I got here first. Jocelyn's helping me flesh out my character. You mind?"

"Oh, no! You know me. I'm all for . . . fleshing out," she cooed, leaning heavily on the double entendre. But the little darts she shot O'Roarke's way said she minded very much indeed. "Maybe you'll do the same for me. It'd be a big help. 'Specially since my character's almost your age."

"I'd be glad to," Jocelyn said warmly and meant it. It was worth a small slur on her age to have inspired the jealousy of a girl with Anita's anatomy. But then, paraphrasing Shaw, she reflected that anatomy was wasted on the young.

As soon as Sanchez was out of earshot, Denny shook his head sagely, saying, "I don't get her. She is so hot onstage. But off, man, there is just no—no subtlety. Know what I mean?"

"Yes, I do. I'm just surprised that you know what you mean."

"Hey, gimme a little credit, okay?" His smile was utterly disarming as he added, "We're not all dickheads."

"Far from it, I'd say." To make her point, she extended a forefinger toward the Performing Arts building. "A dickhead would've spray-painted a pair of tits on that wall. Not a Pro-Choice slogan. I was just wondering if that was a political act on your part or a . . . romantic gesture of sorts? A kind of apology?"

Some scrambled eggs seemed to have gotten caught in his esophagus. Denny swallowed hard twice before asking, "Wha'd ya mean?"

It wasn't fair to toy with him so she came right out with it.

"Look, Denny, I was out on the scene dock yesterday. When you and Belinda were . . . running lines?"

"Oh, shit, no! You didn't—?"

"Yeah, I did. It was an accident, but it would've been so awful to bust in—so I didn't. And I'm sorry, truly sorry."

"How much did you hear?"

"Pretty much all of it. And it wasn't hard to guess the rest." Leaning toward him, she dropped her voice as low as possible. "You got her pregnant and she had an abortion, right?"

Denny gave his confirmation with one short nod, then stared

down at his cold eggs for a long minute before asking, "Are you gonna tell anyone?"

"Of course not. The only reason I brought it up is . . . well, Belinda sounded pretty upset. Does she have anyone she can talk to about it?"

"I don't know. She sure doesn't want to discuss it with me," he said sadly. "And she's scared shitless her parents will find out."

"How could they? You wouldn't tell them."

"Hell, no! That's the *last* thing I'd do, 'specially since Mrs. Barnes is a Pro-Lifer. Though I think her dad would be pretty cool about it . . . after he beat the crap outta me, I mean." Something nearly resembling a smile crossed his face as he added, "Belinda may hate my guts right now but she knows I'd never spill. Anyhow, I'm not the one she's worried about."

"Who might that be?"

"Lyle Davie. At least, Bellie thinks he guessed. She had her first costume-fitting when she was about four weeks gone. Then she had the, um—operation over two weeks ago. Right after that she had another fitting and she swears he noticed something. But she never showed, you know? So I don't see how—"

"Mmm, it's possible. He's got that kind of eye. From fifty paces, Lyle can look at a fully clothed woman and tell if she's gained two pounds—and where she's gained it. Still, even if he jumped to the right conclusion in Belinda's case, why would he tell anyone?"

"That's what I said! But Belinda thinks he might want to make trouble for her just 'cause she was Tessa's pet. He hated her something wicked, you know. But he was scared of her, too, least I always thought so. Now that she's not around to, like, shield her . . . well, Bellie's afraid he'll say something out of spite."

"I doubt it. If he pulled a trick like that, I'd say he could kiss any hope of gaining tenure good-bye. Lyle may be vindictive, but he's not stupid." Though she spoke with assurance, hoping Denny would pass it along to Belinda, O'Roarke refrained from adding "unless he were planning a little blackmail." Not that Belinda would've been his target, but she could imagine who might have been—which prompted her to ask, "Do you think she told Tessa about it?"

"Oh, yeah! She *must've*. I mean, she didn't tell me so—she

wouldn't discuss the, uh, arrangements, though I made her take money for it. But Tessa took her up to Syracuse."

"So that's what their little shopping spree was about." Jocelyn sipped her tepid coffee and looked out the window. "I should've guessed."

Struck by something in her tone, Denny glanced up and saw that his breakfast companion was a million miles away. She sat with her chin propped in her hand, staring down at the theatre building, lost in reverie.

"So, how far gone are you, cookie?"

Josh could hear Tessa's crisp, cool voice echoing through the years and could see the clinical but not unkindly look Grant had given her when she had emerged, sweaty and shaking, from the toilet stall in the dressing room, the acrid taste of vomit still in her mouth.

"Just three weeks. I . . . I found out right away 'cause I'm always so regular."

"That's lucky . . . What're you going to do about it?"

"I don't—well, it's tough. My boyfriend says we can get married . . . if that's what I want."

"How magnanimous . . . Is it what you want?"

"Well, I love him, but I never thought much—I just can't *see* us married."

"And you have a vivid imagination. So that should tell you something, Jocelyn."

"Like what? I don't want to be married?"

"Maybe not forever—but not at the moment, perhaps?" Grant had kept her tone carefully neutral and kept her gaze intently fixed on Josh. "And how do you feel about the prospect of motherhood?"

"Lousy!" She remembered the small, keening sound that had swelled up from her chest as her knees went watery. Tessa had helped her over to the makeup table as the sobbing erupted. With her face buried in her arms, she had wailed, "I'm not *fit* for it. I can't be 'cause I've hated every damn second of this. It just—sucks!"

"Well, contrary to all the romanticized claptrap about it, few women enjoy pregnancy."

"But I really, really *hate* it . . . and I want it over! Now."

As soon as the words were out, Jocelyn had felt light-headed with relief. Having finally admitted the worst to herself about herself, she had suddenly found her course.

"Fine. That can be arranged fairly easily—since you're in a state with decent laws," Grant had said in a calm, businesslike way that soothed O'Roarke far more than any maternal coddling would have. Then something had compelled her to ask, "I suppose you've considered the idea of adoption?"

"No! Not for a second. I could never do that."

"Why not?"

Even now Jocelyn could see Tessa vividly in her mind's eye, perched on the edge of the makeup table, looking down at her with keen interest. In that moment, all her inchoate and divisive feelings had crystallized. Glancing down at her belly, she had spoken urgently.

"Now this, right now, this isn't a life. I mean, hell, I've got twelve years of Catholic schooling telling me it *is* . . . but I can't believe it. Not because I don't want to—because I don't feel it in my bones. But—once it *was*—I couldn't drop it on someone else's doorstep. So I can't let it go that far—that's all."

Grant's mouth had twisted for just a second, as if suppressing a twinge of pain. Then she had leaned forward and, with a sudden and surprising tenderness, wiped a lingering tear from Josh's cheek, saying, "You're gonna be all right, cookie."

"Uh, Ms O'Roarke—Jocelyn, you okay?"

"Huh? . . . Oh, yes. Sorry. I spaced out for a bit, didn't I?"

"Yeah, kinda. I hope I didn't upset you."

"No, no. Hey, you're the one who's entitled to be upset. I've been mucking in your affairs, haven't I?"

"Aw, that's cool—it's kinda a relief really. See, I haven't talked to anyone about it either. And it's hard with Belinda being so pissed at me."

"Sure it is. It's hard on both of you," she said, giving his arm a friendly pat.

This small gesture of comfort seemed to undo the boy in a big way. Shaking his head vehemently, he blurted out, "Damn right! I mean, we weren't careless, you know? It was just—the stupid rubber broke—just once. And bingo! And I really love Bellie. Last thing in the world I wanna do is hurt her. But I did. I put her in that position. Made her go through that."

"You mean you told her to have the abortion?"

"No! I would've done whatever she wanted. We'd already talked about getting married . . . later. But she knew she wasn't ready, so—"

"So she made her choice and did what was right for her . . . So you're not the heavy here, Denny. It's a mutual responsibility and you didn't leave her in the lurch. Deep down she knows that. Just give her some time and some room, okay?"

"Yeah, I'm tryin'. I'm just afraid she'll never feel the same about me." Ducking his head, he looked at her sideways. "Was it like that for you?"

"Was what like what for me?"

"When you had yours—did you hate the guy after?" Seeing the stark surprise on her face, he added, "Sorry. But when you went into deep rev there—I thought maybe you were déjà-vu-ing. Uh, feel free to tell me to fuck off."

"You're quite a perspicacious fella, Denny." When thrown for a loop, O'Roarke always resorted to four-syllable words, but her big vocabulary didn't throw young Moskowitz. He just shrugged nonchalantly and gave her a rueful smile.

"Like I said—we're not all dickheads."

She bought a crooked cat, which caught a crooked mouse.
And they all lived together in a little crooked house.

Phillip paraphrased the old nursery rhyme as he approached the guest house. He had phoned Jocelyn first thing in the morning only to be greeted by endless ringing. So on the spur of the moment he had set out to do a little reconnoitering. Since O'Roarke persisted in keeping him at arm's length, it was quite possible he would never be invited inside her current bivouac. But he had only seen the house twice, late at night, and he was itching to get a better sense of its physical layout, especially after reading the journal entries.

Drawing closer he could see that the house wasn't really crooked; it was just the cobblestone chimney, which was in need of some repair. The house itself, a small two-story structure—two and a half if you counted the dormer attic—was set on a gentle swell of land, which showed foresight on the builders' part, Gerrard thought as he eyed the flat, soggy ground around the edge of the large pond. As it was, he guessed that the fruit cellar would flood a bit in a heavy rain.

But with its ivy-covered walls and leaded-glass windows everywhere, the place had a certain ramshackle elegance, like a grand duchess in rustic retirement. He went along the north wall first, but the shrubbery along the side was so thick and dew-soaked that he couldn't get a good look in the windows. But he saw enough to make out the basic structure; there was a small study that led into a modest dining room. The largest room, as in many country homes, was the kitchen, which took up the whole west end of the building. About ten yards from the northwest corner of the house was a large compost pile. Coming around the south corner, he finally found a good vantage point; there was a stone patio just outside the kitchen door with a low wooden bench positioned directly under a wide window with one boarded-up pane.

The bench was a bit worm-eaten, but sturdy enough to hold his weight. Still, he nearly lost his balance when he pressed his face against the glass and immediately found himself staring into two yellow eyes.

"Whoa, Angus! Long time no see, pal."

The cat blinked once but quickly regained his composure. To make his indifference manifest, he casually stretched out a paw to bat a tiny spider off the window and proceeded to chew it matter-of-factly in Phillip's face.

"Well, don't get all soppy on my account, sport," Gerrard muttered, wondering if all those silly tales of pets adopting their owners' antipathies had any basis in fact.

But he didn't wonder for long.

A hand yanked the back of his shirt collar roughly. As he and the bench went toppling over, he heard a voice grunt, "Gotcha!"

16

"What the—? Get off me, asshole!"

"Not till you settle down, mate."

The redheaded guy straddling his upper chest wasn't all that big, but then neither was Phillip. And he was well knit, with good upper body strength. Gerrard could tell by the pressure he was now applying to his windpipe.

Unlike many of his peers on the N.Y.P.D., Phillip had never developed much interest in any of the martial arts. However, in his youthful days as a Boy Scout, he had once earned a merit badge in Indian wrestling, a form of self-defense that emphasized lower-body agility—which was Gerrard's strong suit.

Grinding his elbows into the stone patio, he managed to raise his chest just enough to throw his assailant off-balance for an instant. Then Gerrard let his chest fall back as he swung both legs up high and scissor-locked the guy around the neck as he twisted over onto his side. The redhead gasped and struggled but couldn't break the hold. Keeping the pressure on, Phillip watched him losing wind and strength, then asked, "Had enough?"

"Bloody . . . bastard! I'll—"

"Will? Is that you, Will?"

Both men looked up to find a little mouse of a woman in a cardigan over a frilly blouse and skirt with a bulging net shopping bag over one arm peering down at them. The men froze, looking like a bad still-shot from the wrestling scene in *Women in Love*, as she blinked in horror.

"Will, dear, I, uh—I think you've just assaulted a police officer." Then Miriam Barnes turned to Phillip. "You *are* that nice lieutenant I've been hearing about, aren't you?"

Nodding weakly, Gerrard released a chagrined Will from the scissor lock. The younger man rubbed his neck for a moment, then gave the other two a watery smile.

"Think we'll all laugh about this someday . . . perhaps?"

"Now you two get acquainted while I rustle us up some lunch," Miriam said as she bustled about her chintz-covered living room, plumping pillows and pouring sherry for her two unexpected guests. Phillip was just about to try the sherry as she whisked out of the room, but Coltrane raised a warning hand.

"At your peril, Lieutenant—unless you have a wicked sweet tooth."

"I don't. Thanks," he said cordially, putting down the glass. "And it's Phil."

"Um, yes. I suppose we should be on a first-name basis after such an . . . informal meeting, eh? Awfully sorry about that."

"Hey, it was my fault. Really. Call it cop hubris. I just never expected to be taken for a skulker."

"Well, yes, you did look rather suspicious. But I should've known—since it was broad daylight and blatant as hell . . . not like the other time."

"What other time?"

Coltrane glanced toward the swinging door and lowered his voice. "Let's keep it down a bit. I wouldn't want Miriam to get wind. But, you see, the reason I was rather, um, overzealous today . . . well, I think I saw the interloper once. But I didn't say anything at the time because—well, because Tess hadn't said anything yet."

"What was it you saw?"

"Very little, I'm afraid. It was, oh, maybe two weeks ago. I was at the far side of the pond—across from the guest house—gathering specimens. About four in the afternoon, but it was starting to rain, so it was rather dark. For some reason, I glanced up and saw someone coming out the kitchen door. At the time, I thought it was Tessa, but I found out later that she'd stayed on campus for a faculty dinner that day."

"Why did you assume it was Ms Grant?"

"Well, it is her place, after all," Coltrane said defensively. "And it was someone in a slicker with the hood up. So I supposed it was a woman. A man usually just lets his head get wet, doesn't he?"

"Unless he's a man trying to cloak himself."

"Precisely. Which is why I feel rather filthy about the whole business." Will ran a hand through his hair, then dropped it heavily on the arm of the sofa. "It's the curse of the bloody British race! Polite passivity—then doing the right thing when it's too damn late. I might've saved her!"

"From a heart attack? I don't see how—"

"No! From what *caused* her heart attack. Like a face in the window," Coltrane hissed vehemently. "Listen, Gerrard, I was there that day—Hank called me right after he called the police—and I saw her! Her face—Christ! It was terrible. She looked like someone who'd been frightened to death."

Displaying remarkable charity toward a man who had just recently tried to throttle him, Phillip poured Will's sherry into a nearby ficus plant and slipped over to the liquor cabinet to replace it with whiskey. Then, stifling his own misgivings, he calmly started to tell Coltrane about the fairly common occurrence of rictus sardonicus. But his explanation was cut short by Miriam's triumphant reentrance with a tray stacked with watercress sandwiches and bowls of tomato soup adorned with Ritz crackers.

Playing Lady Bountiful to the hilt, she waved them over to a table by a large bay window, saying, "The watercress sandwiches are compliments of Will, Lieutenant. He picked some for me just yesterday. Do you know, before he came, I didn't even *know* watercress grew here? I thought it was the sole property of merry ol' England!"

In fact, the watercress looked as if it had been shipped from merry ol' England, but the two wrestling buddies were too polite to say so. They made their way through the salty soup and limp sandwiches in manly silence as Miriam rattled on.

"It's been *such* an eye-opener having Will here. All this flora and fauna on our doorstep and we had no idea! And his greenhouse is just a jewel. You should see it, Phillip."

"I'd like to."

"Great idea," Will concurred, taking a sip of his faux sherry. "I'll take you over after lunch."

Miriam was scheduled to work at the Corinth soup kitchen in the afternoon so Coltrane and Gerrard were, mercifully, left on their own. But she was right about the greenhouse: it was a jewel. And, once inside it, Will dropped all his English upper-crustiness and became a boy in his favorite sandbox.

"What's been really fascinating for me working over here is to see how many similarities there are between the herbs and plants in England and North America. Especially in the Finger Lakes region. Which is why I wanted to come here, of course. It's been a big undertaking but, thank God, I've had help."

"You mean Miriam?"

"Christ, no! Try as I might, she still can't tell the difference between a mushroom and a toadstool. But one of the other professors' wives has been very helpful. Mrs. Mauro has been quite—"

"Frankie? I'm not surprised. She's a very bright lady."

"Uh, yes, she is. And she's got a fine eye for plants as well."

Standing behind him, Phillip noticed the tips of Coltrane's ears turning pink at the mention of Frankie's name. One of the things he liked about redheads, from a professional standpoint, was that their coloring always gave them away. Judging from Will's, he surmised that the limnologist had quite a crush on the lady. Sensing the scrutiny, Will cleared his throat and added lightly, "Of course, Belinda lends the odd hand when she has the time. Which hasn't been often lately. Small wonder."

By way of explanation, he nodded toward a snapshot thumbtacked to a wall. It showed Will and a very pretty blond girl, both of them mud-smeared and grinning, triumphantly holding up identical leafy stalks of something. Leaning in for a closer look, Gerrard said, "I think I met her the other day. Up at the college." Jerking a thumb toward the Barnes house, he asked, "You mean, *she's* their daughter?"

"Yes. Hard to fathom, isn't it? Nice girl. My theory is fairies left her at the bottom of the garden. Said as much to Hank once when I'd had a few. He nearly bit my head off."

"Gosh, I can't imagine why . . . What's that stuff you're holding?"

"That stuff is *Cicuta virosa*," Will sniffed. "The photo was taken the day we first spotted it. Would you like to see it in the flesh?"

Without waiting for an answer, he sidled down the narrow aisle between the two long wooden tables that held his vast array of foliage and Phillip sidled behind as it seemed the only safe way to travel. Pulling up alongside three parallel plant boxes, Coltrane waved a hand, magicianlike, above the three separate rows of stalks. "Can you pick out the *Cicuta virosa*?"

"Uh, no, Will, afraid I can't. See, to me they all look like, um—celery."

"Exactly! But they're three very different specimens." Rubbing his hands together, he expounded with great zest, "One of them is celery, actually. And one is garden angelica—beloved by homeopaths for its supposed health-enhancing properties. And the other is *Cicuta virosa*. Now you're a detective; you should be able to figure it out."

Throwing down the green gauntlet as it were, he stepped aside so Gerrard could make a closer inspection. In his element now, Coltrane was enjoying himself. Though Phillip suspected his pleasure was tinged with a desire for revenge after his overthrow on the patio, he felt the only gentlemanly thing to do was to take this little challenge seriously.

He started by feeling the stalks and leaves of each plant. Then he leaned over to smell the leaves. Straightening up, he pointed to the box on the far right, saying, "That's not celery. The stalks are too thin and the smell's wrong."

Then he quickly reached out and snapped off a small stalk from the middle box. Just as he was about to bite into it, Coltrane lunged toward him and yanked it out of his hand.

"Sweet Jesus! Have you gone *balmy?*"

"Sorry . . . I didn't think these were your only specimens." Judging from Will's wild-eyed gaze, Phillip assumed he had just broken some cardinal rule of herbology. And he had.

"Oh, specimens be damned! Don't you know that you never, bloody *ever* ingest a plant that you haven't damn well identified?!"

"I, uh . . . I know you have to be careful with mushrooms," Gerrard stammered. "I guess that isn't celery, huh? So how do you tell?"

"Here's how." Coltrane agitatedly plucked a stalk from each box and waved the roots in Phillip's face. "By the roots, mate, the roots! And you make sure you've got a damn good reference text . . . if you care to live long enough to publish your findings, that is."

Pointing to the offending stalk, Phillip asked, "How sick would that've made me?"

"*Sick!* Are you daft?" Coltrane said in a strangled voice. "Sicker than you've ever been in your life. A piece the size of a fingernail can kill a child. One centimeter is lethal to a full-grown adult—unless you receive immediate medical attention. And even then it's dicey since a doctor could easily make a wrong diagnosis."

Winded after his outburst, Will did the sensible British thing and dug a pack of Winstons out of his shirt pocket. After a few soothing puffs, he said in somewhat milder tones, "Sorry, I didn't mean to take your head off. But in my line of work, you hear so many horror stories. So many needless deaths. All because people don't take the time to educate themselves about their natural surroundings. Up here, everywhere you look—*if* you look—there are hundreds of different herbs and plants growing wild. Many of them are medicinal. But some of them, like *Cicuta virosa,* are toxic as hell. So you have to know what you're about."

"Can I bum one of those?" Gerrard asked, pointing to the cigarette pack. Will forked one over, assuming his companion's nerves also needed calming. But he certainly didn't look rattled. In fact, he looked cool as a *Cucumis sativus* as he lit up, blew a tiny smoke ring in the air, and watched it diffuse. But had O'Roarke been present, knowing as she did that Phillip had quit smoking years ago, she would have recognized the signs of intense cogitation.

"So, Will, what's *Cicuta virosa* called when it's at home?"

By way of reply, Coltrane turned the plant box around so Gerrard could read the label on its side. After the Latin name there was a slash, then neatly printed: "water hemlock."

"Hemlock." Phillip's pupils snapped to attention as he stubbed out the half-smoked cigarette. "Like they made Socrates drink?"

"No, that was probably *Conium maculatum.* A fine-leaved plant with small white flowers. Greece doesn't have the right climate for water hemlock. It's usually found in England and North America." Having regained his clinical detachment, Coltrane went on. "As you might guess, it grows near bodies of water, seas and riverbanks mostly. Belinda and I found these by the stream that feeds into the pond. Looks and smells like celery. Tastes—so I'm *told*—rather like parsnip."

"And if somebody eats it, what are the initial symptoms?"

"Whew—that's difficult to say. There are a whole slew of possible reactions. Depending on the individual. You know, size, weight, what they've had to eat or drink that day. As I said, that's what makes it so tricky to identify. But . . . let me see." Coltrane squatted down and dragged a beat-up file box out from beneath the table. "The good old *F & F* should have a full listing."

"What's the *F & F*?"

"*Friends & Foes: A Dictionary of Beneficial and Toxic Plants.* Written by the illustrious Sir Edmund Henshaw. In my field, it's the equivalent of the Saint James Bible, really. Now . . . where the hell—?" Will started tossing papers and files onto the dirt-strewn floor. "It *must* be here somewhere. I never leave it out. Damn! Did that fool girl borrow it?"

At that moment, Belinda Barnes burst through the door. Wearing a Pink Floyd T-shirt and overalls, with trowel in hand, she called out, "Hey, Willie! I got out of rehearsal early. Wanna go digging? . . . Oh, sorry. I didn't know you had company. Hi, Mister Gerrard."

Before Phillip could return the greeting, Coltrane leapt to his feet and bore down on the girl full steam.

"Belinda, did you take my Henshaw without asking?"

"Heck, no. I'd never do—"

"Oh, come off it! You're always popping in here when I'm away. Filching fags and borrowing things left and right."

"That's not fair, Will! Yeah, I sneak a smoke in here sometimes 'cause I don't want Mom and Dad to know," she pleaded.

"What about the other week when you took my binoculars, eh?"

"That was just *one* time. When you weren't around to ask. And you *said* I could use the *F & F* for my botany class. But I always make my notes right here and put it back!"

Belinda's eyes were welling up, but Will didn't notice or didn't care.

"Yeah? Well, maybe *one* time you thought it would be easier to make notes in your room. Just *tell* me, for chrissake! You know that book costs a bloody fortune."

"I know, I know. But I *didn't!*"

Then the girl started weeping and headed for the door. But her exit was impeded by her father's entrance. Hank Barnes threw a protective arm around his daughter's shoulder and stroked her head, murmuring, "Don't cry, honey, don't cry. I heard what this jerk-off said and he's full of crap." Then he gently nudged her out the door and made his way purposefully toward the retreating Coltrane.

Phillip thought it quite likely that the unlucky limnologist was headed for another wrestling match.

17

"Five, right? That one skipped five times!"

"Nope. Four. I counted."

"Damn! I used to be much better at this. Here, your turn."

Jocelyn bent down and selected a nice piece of shale for Gerrard. He hooked his lower arm in and then snapped his wrist out, sending the rock skimming across the broad, shallow stream near the foot of Tomahawk Falls.

"Now *that* was a five-er," he said with some satisfaction.

It was late afternoon and, despite the bright sunshine, there was a spring chill in the air, but he didn't mind. Returning to his hotel after the fracas at Coltrane's, he had been pleasantly surprised to find O'Roarke waiting for him with a six-pack of Rolling Rock and two meatball heros she had picked up at a place called Johnny's Big Red, a local legend, he gathered. Then she had suggested an impromptu picnic at Tomahawk Falls, a small state park about forty minutes from Corinth filled with hiking trails, deep, narrow ravines, a very pretty waterfall, and, as Josh had pointed out upon arrival, "the best skipping stones in a hundred-mile radius."

On the drive up she had been fairly quiet, only asking the occasional question as he had recounted the showdown between Will and Barnes, then observing, "Coltrane must've been awful glad to have you there."

"I guess. People do tend to think twice about assault and battery when there's a cop standing by. At least, Hank did—once he found out. Otherwise, I think he would've ripped the guy's head off."

"Really?" Her amused expression had suggested that such an outcome wouldn't have been entirely tragic. Then, concentrating on a tricky piece of road, she had fallen silent for the rest of the trip. But once they had arrived and immediately devoured the huge, sauce-soaked, and deservedly legendary heros at a weathered park table, her mood had shifted to hoydenish high spirits.

"Lucky throw," she said, handing him another piece of shale. "Bet you can't do it twice."

This time his stone made six hops, finally bouncing out of the water and landing on the other side of the stream. Whistling casually, Phillip bent over and tossed her a small rock. "Your move, Slick."

"Hey, don't get cocky, mister. I told you these were great skippers." Using a backhand motion, she flicked the shale out low to the water and nailed a decent five-er.

"Well, you're . . . improving."

"Cheeky bastard," Josh said, giving him a playful poke in the ribs. "I'll get Frankie to take you on. She'll dust you."

Then she lost her footing on the slick shale and fell against him. Phillip steadied her by putting both arms around her waist. It was the first time he had held her in many, many months, and the soft, familiar swell of her hips brought on a flood of sweet memories that made him shut his eyes for a moment. Jocelyn stayed very still, hardly breathing, in his embrace, but when he opened his eyes to meet hers, he found them filled with a pained wariness. Brushing his knuckles against her cheek, he whispered, "Ah, love, I never meant to hur—"

"No! Uh uh—Sollocks, Sollocks!" Next thing he knew, she was ten paces away from him with her hands clamped over her ears.

"Sollocks? Wha'? What the hell is Sollocks?!" He overenunciated so she could read his lips.

"A contraction for Solomon Isaacs," she said brusquely and started to trudge up toward the falls. "You *know*—it's from *Private Lives*. It's Amanda and Elyot's code for *this topic is off-limits*. Geez, you've got a crappy memory for a cop."

Stung, he followed after her shouting, "What're you talking about? I didn't even see it on Broadway. I mean, Joan Collins isn't exactly my idea of a Coward—"

"Forget Broadway! Forget Joan Wigs-R-Us fucking Collins. See, see? You forget everything." She stopped and spun round to shake her finger in his face. "You forget that I dragged you up to Long Wharf to see that goddamn lovely production with my friends Sharon and Chip in the leads. Remember? Then, when we got back to your place after, we decided to try . . . Aw, screw it." Her spleen all vented, O'Roarke abruptly plopped down on a nearby boulder and sighed wearily. "I'm just being idiotic. There's no point."

The utter hopelessness in her voice cut him far more than her sudden anger had. Squatting down in front of her, he grabbed both her hands, forcing her to look at him. "Yes, there's a point! There's got to be . . . Why do you think I came up here, Josh? It wasn't some silly whim. I *had* to. I've tried, but I can't get on with my life until—until we resolve some things."

"Old history, you mean? I know how you feel," she said softly, looking over his shoulder to the flowing water. " 'So we beat on, boats against the current, borne back ceaselessly into the past.' But, you see, right here, right now, I'm caught up in a past that predates you, predates us . . . Look, I know I've been ducking the issue. But I can't help it. Being back here and dealing with Tessa's death, it's pulled me so far back that it's like—like the old movie houses!"

Inexplicably she started laughing and he had to grit his teeth to ask, "Care to explain that segue?"

"Oh, sorry. See, there used to be four movie houses around the college—maybe they're still here. I don't know. Anyway, we never called them by name—just by their, uh, proximity to campus. There was the Near Near, the Near Far, the Far Near, and the Far Far." Lest he doubt her sanity, she hastened on, "So, in a, um, metaphorical sense, I'm at the Near Near while you're watching flicks at the Far Near . . . That sounds fey as fuck-all, huh?"

He would have liked to, loved to, say yes. But he couldn't. Even at her tempestuous, illogical best, Jocelyn always managed to make emotional sense. It was what made her not only an exceptional actor but, as he knew from past experience, an insightful second-guesser. Like all good detectives, Phillip knew where his strengths lay; he had an immediate and excellent grasp of physical evidence. He could see the possible permutations of a crime the way Einstein saw $E = MC^2$. As, in fact, he was beginning to see all sorts of permutations around Grant's supposed heart attack. But, for him, it was a kind of mental chess. For Jocelyn, it was and had always been a matter of instinct.

So he took a long breath, kissing whatever hopes he had had for this vacation adieu, and said, "No, it doesn't. And, for what it's worth, I think you've got cause to be uneasy."

"You do? What changed your mind?"

"A couple of things."

"Like what? Tessa's diary?"

"Yuh, that and some things Will told me . . . And the feeling I get that Doc Morgan isn't entirely satisfied with the autopsy findings."

"You talked to Doctor Morgan?!"

"Yeah, I saw him yesterday morning—right before Ryson's appointment."

O'Roarke shot out a hand to grab his sleeve. "Ryson was at the doctor's? He told me he'd been with the—never mind. You're sure it was a professional visit? What did he say to you?"

"Nothing. Morgan had me leave through a back door. I saw Curtis pull in as I was getting into my car. I don't think he saw me, though."

"Just as well. If he had, he never would've lied to me. He'd have just said it was a checkup or something equally plausible. Ry's a good fibber."

"But why's he covering up? You don't think it's—"

He didn't bother finishing the sentence. The look on Jocelyn's face said that she had already considered the worst possible diagnosis.

"No, I don't think it's AIDS. For one thing, Ryson's always led a pretty celibate life. Of course, according to Tessa, he's had this condition for a while, too. But his weight's good and I can usually see the signs. No, whatever it is, I think it's been in remission—until recently."

"Is that why rehearsal ended early today? He wasn't feeling well?"

"Hard to know. We're doing our first full-dress tech tonight. So he made a witty little speech about dress techs being like true love—'A course that never does run smooth. And this one promises to be long and truly gruesome, my dears. So why don't you all run along and get some rest—blah, blah.' Like I said, Ry's always plausible."

"Unless, of course, he's just being kind to his cast. Whatever he's got—well, it could just be something minor." Phillip stood and pulled Josh up from the boulder. "Come on, let's get a beer."

O'Roarke had left the six-pack in the stream, wedged between two rocks. He yanked two cans out of their plastic loops and handed her one. Jocelyn took a sip that made her teeth chatter—the stream was icy cold and so was the Rolling Rock—then shook her head.

"No, it might not have anything to do with Tess, but it's not minor or he wouldn't be hiding it."

"Well, then why don't you try the direct approach? Just *ask* him."

"The direct approach?" She screwed up her face in distaste. "I hate the direct approach. It's too—"

"Direct?"

"Yeah. Besides, how could I broach it? I don't want to mention the journal and I can't say I know he lied about yesterday."

"Then say you've noticed something—you have, haven't you?"

"Sure, but it's pretty piddling. He's . . . walking funny. Not limping exactly, but sort of listing to the side once in a while."

"Hell, that could be anything. An inner-ear infection can mess up your balance. There must be something else."

"Well, sorry! It's tough to scrutinize someone sitting in a dark house when you're up on a lit stage, you know."

"Okay, okay. Tell you what, you act—I'll scrutinize."

"Huh? Wha—when?"

"Tonight. I'll sit in on the dress rehearsal. How's that?"

"Uhhh, I dunno, Phillip." She was as filled with misgiving as he was with relish. "That might not be such a hot idea."

"Why not?"

"For one thing, you march into that theatre and a lot of already jumpy folks might get downright rattled."

"I'll slip in in the dark."

"But the lights go up at intermission."

"So what? If someone gets rattled—we might learn something."

"True, true," she said, still ambivalent. "Only . . . I don't want to catch flak for it later."

"From Curtis, you mean?"

"No. From *you*. Look, I know, in most circumstances, you are the soul of patience. But Ry wasn't whistlin' Dixie. Dress techs *are* long and truly gruesome affairs. You stop. You start. You have to go back 'cause a cross-fade cue was late or the sound came in too soon . . . I mean, it might not be so bad if this were a professional company. But it's not. And it's gonna be ugly. Really ugly. I'm just not sure if you can—"

"If I can *hack* it? Are you serious?!" Gerrard laughed derisively. "Don't you know that ninety percent of police work is pure tedium, woman? You actually believe a little aggravated boredom is gonna put me off stride?"

Sensing the professional outrage beneath his ridicule, she backed off.

"All right, okay! Suit yourself. Maybe I'm wrong. Maybe you'll find it friggin' fascinating." Under her breath, she added, "And maybe there'll be pork in the treetops by morning."

Not catching the last bit, Phillip threw an arm around her shoulder and joked, "Or maybe someone's just a wee bit nervous about having me sitting out front again, huh?"

Which only proved O'Roarke's earlier assertion re how quickly men forget. Josh never rattled in front of civilians and, only rarely, in front of critics. Had memory served him well, Gerrard would have been uneasy now to see Jocelyn merely shake her head as she bent down to pluck the remaining beer cans from the creek. He didn't know that simple pity for the ignorant was all that stood between him and a nasty knee-decapping.

Around eleven P.M. that night, when they finally reached the intermission break, his powers of recollection, along with a renewed sense of humility, came back in full force.

The dress rehearsal had started promptly at seven-thirty. Had ground to a halt at seven forty-five, when Josh had started to visibly miscarry onstage and been whisked into the wings for some emergency costume surgery. Had resumed at eight-ten for a full twenty minutes—until Hank Barnes found that a key prop, a wine goblet, hadn't been preset because it had been repainted that afternoon and was still tacky. And on and on—or, rather, back and back.

By nine-thirty, when his butt had long since turned to cold, hard cement, Gerrard had a painful epiphany; he recalled all the times past when Josh had said, "Don't come opening night, love. We'll still be rickety. Come a week or so into the run, when the kinks are worked out." (What a kind and merciful woman she was, really, under all that crust.) And he recalled Christopher Walken's Oscar-winning performance in *The Deer Hunter* as well. Back then he'd thought Walken's depiction of a soldier ravaged by prison-camp torture an amazing feat of acting. Now, not to take anything away from his performance, he realized that ol' Chris was stage-trained, and probably all he had had to do was cast his mind back to *this* —and bingo! You had agony by the bucket.

Not to say that there weren't some saving moments, mostly supplied by Jocelyn. Even to his biased eye, it was clear that she was the pro among the acting proles up there; always quick to foresee disaster, quicker with a joke when the disaster finally struck. While the company was waiting for her pregnancy pad to be resewn, she had hollered out from the wings, "I'm ready for my Ob-Gyn now, Mr. deMille!" Sitting in the row behind Ryson, Phillip had seen the harried director watch his cast roar with laughter, then throw his head back and hoot, "Thank you, Miss Desmond."

A miniature Tensor lamp clamped to the arm of the director's chair gave him light enough to take notes; it had also given Phillip a better chance to study him. But the only thing that had struck him as out of the ordinary, since Curtis had been jotting down notes galore from the start, was his eschewing cursive script in favor of block printing. It wasn't the form of writing normally employed by people in a hurry, but then, Gerrard thought, Ryson might have particularly illegible handwriting.

As soon as the houselights came up, Ryson rose—a little stiffly, but who could blame him? Phillip felt soldered to his seat. Stretching his arms above his head, Curtis yawned while the cast scurried in various directions, either to change costumes, repair makeup, or grab a smoke. Spotting Gerrard, he blinked, owllike.

"Why, Phillip, what're you doing here? Penance for past sins?"

"No, not at all." Though, come to think of it, there was a grain of truth in Ryson's flip remark, and he seemed to know it, too. "I just wanted to see Josh back in action again. It's—it's been a while."

"Yes, I imagine it has," he replied cryptically, then grinned. "And it's a far cry from her most recent work, eh? What did you think of her trial scene?"

"Uh—very moving."

In truth, he had found it not only moving but, as he had had no prior acquaintance with the play or its plot line, unsettling as well. Watching Barnes as this insanely jealous king who lashes out at his wife for something she didn't do—infidelities he's imagined—and seeing Jocelyn's Hermione answering his absurd charges with stoic dignity had given him a nasty jolt of déjà vu. Having once made some similarly harsh and unfair accusations himself (though not in iambic pentameter) in the aftermath of the Burbage Theatre affair, it had given him a chill when Jocelyn had looked at Hank with stricken eyes and said, "The crown and comfort of my life, your favor, I do give lost, for I do feel it gone,/ But know not how it went." Of course, it was just a play and she had just been doing her job. But Christ, she'd been convincing. And he couldn't help but wonder, seeing that portrait of a woman profoundly betrayed, how much he may have contributed to the performance.

"Damn right," Ryson exclaimed, surprised by Gerrard's apparent lack of enthusiasm. "It's a hell of a piece of physical acting."

"Physical? What's so physical about it? She sits for most of the scene. Then rises once toward the end."

"But *what* a rise! It conveys everything she's just been through —child labor and the loss of the child. You can see the woman's bone-weary and near collapse. But it's very economical, no frills. Seein' as how O'Roarke's never had children, her sense of physical condition is uncanny. That's not sense memory—*that's* acting, my boy."

"I see what you mean." Something he couldn't put a name to prompted him to ask, "How did Ms Grant play that scene?"

"Oh, brilliantly, of course." Ryson narrowed his eyes and looked up at the stage as if he were watching her phantom rehearse. "But Tessa leaned more on the language to make her effect."

"Why? Because she didn't have the what's-it? Sense memory?"

Shaking his head thoughtfully, Curtis spoke softly, as if some

long-buried notion had just broken through to light. "No, I think—
I think maybe it was just the opposite."

"*Madre de Dios,* did I stink up the joint or what?!" Anita Sanchez
added a few obscure Spanish curses as she repenciled the age lines
on her smooth olive skin.

Standing in back of her, adjusting her gray-haired Act Two wig,
O'Roarke said, "Relax. You did fine."

"Are you kidding? I completely lost my character tonight."

"But you remembered your lines. In a dress tech, that's enough.
And better than your elders did."

"No way. You didn't go up or lose character." Then the girl
wailed, "And you haven't even had a week's rehearsal!"

"But I've done the role before, Anita. And I'm not the one who's
in almost every other scene. So don't beat up on yourself, okay?"

To Jocelyn's surprise, hot tears sprung to Anita's eyes as she im-
pulsively grabbed her hand. "God, you're so nice. I can't tell you
what it means to—to finally get some encouragement."

"What're you talking about?!" Even though she knew exactly
what Sanchez was talking about, O'Roarke gave her a little "don't-
be-silly" pat, adding, "Professor Curtis thinks you're aces."

"I didn't mean him. I meant—"

She stopped short as Belinda came into the dressing room looking
like a sylvan vision in Perdita's peasant costume. She also looked
like she was ready to commit hari-kari.

"Oh, m'gosh, it's not going too good, is it?"

"Gee willikers, no, Orphan Annie," Anita spat back. "But I'm
sure, once you're out there, it'll be smooth as silk."

"Nita! I didn't mean you," Bel protested. "Don't get on my case,
huh? I'm nervous enough as it is. I feel sick to my stomach."

"Well, at least you don't have to worry about blowing chow—
now."

The pure spite in Sanchez's voice, as much as her implication,
froze Josh. The bobby pin she had been holding fell to the floor
with a small ting that echoed Belinda's sharp gasp. The three of
them held tableau for an eternal minute—until Lyle Davie whisked
through the door with Anita's costume and body padding in hand.

"Come on, my little Mexican jumpin' bean. Time to gain twenty pounds in twenty seconds."

She climbed into the garment quietly with carefully downcast eyes. Oblivious to the high voltage in the room, Lyle prattled on as he adjusted the dress, "I swan, on this show I've spent most all my time trying to make fat women look thin and thin women look fat. And let me tell y'all, that is no small job."

O'Roarke was about to tell him exactly which part of his anatomy was in immediate danger of getting fat when he looked down and *tch*'d, "Damn threads." Kneeling on the floor, he whisked out his ever-ready pinking shears and cut the offending fibers from the hem of the dress.

"Oh, thanks, Mr. Davie," Sanchez mumbled, acutely aware of Belinda's stricken gaze and anxious to get away from it. "It'll be fine."

"No, hold still, Anita," Josh said firmly. "Let the man do his job. One lose thread can trip you up onstage." Prodding Lyle's foot with her canvas slipper, she added, "Isn't that so . . . Pinkie?"

The scissors almost slipped from his grasp as he looked up at her in alarm. Making one final snip, he jumped to his feet saying, "You're fine now, Nita."

The girl bolted from the room and Davie paused just long enough to give Jocelyn a searing look before he backed out the door holding the pinking shears behind his back.

Distraught as she was, Belinda still knew some sort of confrontation had just taken place. Turning to Josh, she said, "How'd you know about that?"

"About what?"

"Tessa's nickname for him. Nobody else calls him Pinkie—and she only did behind his back mostly . . . He hates it!"

"Yeah, I gathered as much. Why is that?"

"I dunno. But I think it has something to do with when they worked together before."

"When was that?"

"In Minneapolis. Maybe five years ago, I'm not sure. They did a production of Ibsen's *Ghosts*. I don't know what happened—Tessa never said—but they sure didn't come out of it best buddies."

"Well, it happens. Nothing like doing the classics to put people on edge," O'Roarke said casually, though it was her guess that Grant and Davie's feud had gone far deeper. So she gave the girl a little push toward the makeup mirrors. "You better get ready. Here, let me give you a little help."

And Belinda needed it. She was still pale from the salvo Anita had shot her way. Pulling up a chair beside her, Josh took one glance at her makeup case and sighed. "Uh, sweetie, this stuff ain't gonna cut it."

"It's not?" Sensing fresh disaster, Bel gulped and quavered, "But it's what I wear all the time!"

"Sure, it's fine for the street, but it'll never read onstage," Jocelyn said kindly, realizing that she had played this scene once before; only last time she was the insecure ingenue.

"Oh, shit. Can I—can I borrow some of yours?"

O'Roarke shook her head. "No good. Our coloring's too different."

"What am I gonna *do?!*"

The girl was about a heartbeat away from hysteria. Jocelyn cast her eyes around the room and spotted a battered tackle box on the floor beside the costume rack. She knew instantly whose it was— or had been. Hauling it over to the dressing table, she said, "This should do the trick."

"But that's Tessa's. I couldn't!"

"Sure you could. She'd want you to," Josh said swiftly. Eyeing the small tin lock on the case, she yanked a bobby pin from her wig and went to work. A minute later she was laying out powder, rouge, shading sticks, and eye shadows. Her panic momentarily deflected by O'Roarke's lock-picking prowess, Belinda gushed, "Boy, that was fast. How'd you learn that?"

"I have a friend named Tommy Zito . . . who's enriched my life in many ways. Oh, this'll do fine!" Josh examined a really good mink makeup brush with professional admiration, then dabbed it in Amber #2 blush. "See, your coloring is very similar to hers. And Tessa knew what it takes to make a blonde stand out under the lights. She was a master. Now hold still."

What Jocelyn lacked in the way of Grant's cosmetic artistry, she made up for in speed. Five minutes later, when Denny came to get

Belinda for their first scene, his eyes bugged out when she opened the door.

"Man, you look bitchin'!"

"Get a grip. It's just makeup, Den," she said briskly. But she seemed pleased and actually deigned to smile up at him. "Jocelyn did me."

Moskowitz gave Josh a look of gratitude as he put one hand over his heart and lowered his voice solemnly. "Awesome. On behalf of horny guys everywhere—I thank you."

"Denny!" Belinda gave him a quick chop in the ribs then giggled, "You're such a *jerk*," before taking off down the stairs with her swain in hot pursuit. Wanting to see her little Pygmalion under the lights—and see if the couple's reignited chemistry carried over into their love scene—O'Roarke headed for the house.

But Anita was waiting for her in the hallway.

"*Psst!* Jocelyn, can I talk to you?"

"Bet your ass you can." Grabbing the girl's elbow, she hauled her back into the dressing room. "And I've got a few choice words for you, too."

"Look, before you get started, I just want to explain something."

"Like why you took that cheap shot, maybe?"

"I know, I know. But I was upset, see?" She paused for dramatic effect. "I mean, do you know Belinda had an abortion?"

"That's none of my business. And it's none of yours, either."

Ignoring the icicles that Josh had left hanging in the air, she pressed on. "But I just found out, you know. And it *really* upset me . . . 'cause I'm Catholic."

"So's the pope. Big fucking deal."

This time she made her effect; Anita's eyes flew wide in shock. "But, I mean—aren't you?"

"No, I left the fold a long time ago. But my mom goes to church every Sunday. She's devout as they come. And do you know what she'd say?" O'Roarke put her face very close to Anita's and spoke with steel-blade precision. "If you don't believe in abortion, don't *have* one. Period . . . And F.Y.I., in case you haven't kept up, there's a group called Catholics for Choice. I know quite a few nuns who've joined it."

"But that's not— How *could* they?!" The girl's enormous eyes grew larger as her old universe took a new tilt.

"Because they believe in a little thing called primacy of conscience. Look it up sometime. They also feel that private religious beliefs shouldn't be *mandated* to the public. Now, that has to do with a little thing called separation of church and state—which is getting swept under the rug some these days. But let me tell you what *I* believe in." She was on a white-hot roll and seeing red, and poor Sanchez, backed into a corner now, had nowhere to run and nowhere to hide as O'Roarke bore down on her. "I believe in the individual's right to *privacy*. And the U.S. Constitution backs me on this one—or it's supposed to. But, bringing it all back to basics, what this means vis-à-vis Belinda's medical history is—you keep a lid on it or I will go out of my way to make you the sorriest little thespian who *almost* had a brilliant career . . . Need I go on?"

Throwing both hands in front of her face as if in fear of being vaporized, Anita shook her head repeatedly, swallowed hard, and then burst out sobbing.

"But it's not *fair*. It's not fucking fair! I've had to bust my butt all my life. Get jobs, get scholarships so I could break out. And she—she gets everything handed to her! Tessa's little pet. Denny's girl . . . Do you know how few *straight* guys there are in the drama department?"

Struck with instant contrition for spewing old venoms on such a young head, Jocelyn reached out to gently draw Anita's hand from her face and looked into her watery eyes. "Hey, I'm an alumnus. I know exactly how many there are. Three—and one has bad zits."

Hiccuping and laughing at the same time, Anita nodded. "Yeah, and the other one's *short!*"

"Well, try dating the music department," Josh said consolingly as she wiped running mascara from the girl's cheek. "They're weird, but randy. And, given your religious background, I'd suggest drummers. I hear they've got the best . . . rhythm."

Anita's strangled laugh ended in a moan when she caught sight of herself in the mirror. "Jesus—look at my face! I've gotta be back onstage in a few minutes."

"Never fear. Mighty Ms Make-Over is here," Josh said, reaching for a Pan-Cake stick.

18

"Oh my, doesn't she look lovely!"

Slipping into the seat next to Gerrard's, Miriam Barnes sighed blissfully as Belinda made her entrance with a boy who looked familiar to Phillip. It only took him a second to realize Prince Florizel was also the night clerk at his hotel. That connection made, his eyes shot back to the girl. Miriam had good cause to *kvell* over her daughter; a pretty girl offstage, under the lights Bel was the quintessence of loveliness and youthful grace. So it was no strain at all to concur with Mom.

"Yes, she's a vision all right."

"I'm not supposed to be here. Bellie'd have a fit if she knew," Miriam whispered with guilty excitement. "She didn't want me to come till opening. But I've sneaked into rehearsals once or twice . . . I just *had* to see how she was doing."

Obviously she was doing just fine in her mother's eyes, but Phillip wasn't so sure. After watching countless films and plays in O'Roarke's company, he was without doubt the N.Y.P.D.'s foremost authority on actors and acting. While Belinda, despite a few flubbed lines here and there, seemed well cast as the demure and dutiful Perdita, for him she lacked that indefinable something Josh called "presence." As she had once told him, "It's that thing—and I think you have to be born with it—that draws the audience's eye before you even open your mouth and keeps it on you. In film, a good director can create some of that focus for an actor. But onstage, it can't be manufactured. You've just got to *have* it."

The little spitfire Sanchez had it in spades, as did Jocelyn. But Belinda was so achingly beautiful that whatever presence she lacked was hardly missed.

"Oh, rats! I can't see her," Miriam hissed and leaned forward to tap Curtis on the shoulder. "Ryson, they're blocking Bellie."

"That's because they're dancing *around* her, Miriam," the long-suffering director hissed back. "It's a May dance. She is, symbolically speakin', the maypole. Get it? Now hush up. She'll be down front as soon as we get to Autolycus' song."

Only they didn't get to the song because Autolycus strummed his lute once and broke a string. The choreographed merrymaking came to a dirgelike close.

"Props!" Ryson rose to his feet as the Prop Master came onstage, and pleaded, "Please, please, tell me we have a back-up lute."

"Uh, yuh, yuh, we do." The Prop Master, a black girl in horn-rimmed glasses and a T-shirt with the logo ANITA TOLD THE TRUTH, stood far right wringing her hands. "It's in one of the trunks. I'm just not sure . . . which trunk."

"Well, *find* it," Curtis boomed, and the girl shot like a cannonball into the wings. "All right, people, let's take it back to—"

"Uh, Ry, 'scuse me. But long as we've stopped, can I make a little adjustment?" Lyle Davie sauntered down the aisle plucking a threaded needle from a pincushion fixed on his wrist with an elastic band. He skipped up the escape steps without waiting for permission, adding, "Prince Denny's about to lose his cloak, see."

"Sure . . . go ahead " Ryson threw up his hands as he sunk back in his seat with a sigh. Miriam Barnes made a clucking noise as she watched Davie restitch the cloak to Moskowitz's shoulder, then she turned a sour face to Phillip.

"This could take forever . . . Let's go stretch our legs a bit." His legs were all for it and quickly vetoed his mind's protest that he should stick close to Curtis. As soon as they reached the red-carpeted lobby, Miriam heaved an exaggerated sigh.

"Well, there you have it. The Old Bubba Boys Network in action."

"Bubbas? You mean Curtis and—?"

"Lyle, of course. Ry goes and bites that poor black girl's head off and then lets Lyle prance up on stage—disrupt everything—just so he can look important and . . . and, well, there's no nice way to say it. So he can fiddle around with the poor boy."

Phillip stared at the little woman in frank amazement. Homophobia was something he was used to on the job; every precinct house in New York had its fair share of obnoxious gay-bashers. But it was something you seldom ever encountered in or around the theatre. He felt compelled to remark, "Didn't look that way from where I was sitting. I mean, the cloak *was* coming loose. It's not like he went up there to reposition the kid's codpiece."

"Well, I'm sorry to tell you," she began primly; Miriam was one of those people who always claim that they're "sorry to say" when they're actually quite thrilled to deliver the bad news, "but that sort of *thing* does go on in a drama department. Now Ryson's an excellent chairman and a real gent—but he is a homosexual from the South like Lyle. And, believe me, they stick together! Mercy, who else would've given Lyle a job with his—"

She cut herself off with a nice imitation of someone biting their tongue. Phillip would have liked very much to drop the matter just for spite. However, he had a hunch about what she was hinting at and wanted to confirm it. But, to spoil her fun, he went with his hunch and said nonchalantly, "If you're talking about a police record, that's no big deal."

"How did you kno—I mean, how can you say that?!"

" 'Cause it happens a lot. Gay men are very vulnerable in certain states. Especially where there's crummy cops. Look, you get a speeding ticket—it stays a speeding ticket. In the wrong town, somebody like Lyle gets a speeding ticket . . . and maybe gets a little roughed-up in the bargain. Next thing you know, he's up for resisting arrest. So, like I said, no big deal."

It gladdened his heart to bust her little bubble of righteous indignation. But he had to hand it to her, the woman regrouped fast. Placing a hand to her cheek, she assumed a philosophical air. "Well, you'd know better than me, I'm sure. And I gather it all happened a few years back. In Minneapolis, I think." Apropos of nothing, she added, as if it made everything all right, "And he's built perfectly divine costumes for Belinda, hasn't he?"

Feeling a little like Alice at the Mad Hatter's tea party, he nodded and muttered, "Yeah . . . nice threads."

"Well, shiver me timbers! Is that ol' Phil? The S.O.B. who's stolen my demento son's affections?" As Miriam winced, Gerrard looked up to see Frankie, in a khaki jacket, black tights, and lumberjack boots, whisk into the lobby. "How the hell did Joey get you to come to a goddamn dress tech? Lemme guess—promised to show you her appendectomy scar later, huh?" Then she paused, as if she'd just that second caught sight of the other woman and purred wickedly, "Why, hello, Miriam . . . Love that skirt and sweater set. Is it new?"

"No, I'm sure you've seen it a hundred times, Francine."

"Have I? Well, you know me. Ms Fashion Amnesiac of Corinth College."

"Yes," was all Miriam said as she eyed Frankie's getup sorrowfully.

Phillip was having some fun now, watching Frankie beam down at Miriam as she casually flapped her jacket open to reveal the Grateful Dead T-shirt underneath. "Well, you know, some of us can pull a look together, and the rest of us just have to wing it."

"Yes," again from the skirt-and-sweater contingent as she started to wave one hand in front of her face. "It's getting a bit hot in here. I think I'll get some air." Heading for the oak doors, she gave Gerrard a come-along look, but he was quite happy where he was. After the doors swung shut behind her, he turned to Frankie.

"Was that just for my benefit—or do you always yank her chain that way?"

"Ahhh, a little bit of both," Frankie confessed sheepishly. "Mir just presses my Bad Girl button somethin' fierce. Mike reads me the riot act about it weekly, but I can't help it. First she calls me Francine, then I start obnoxing. It's kinda like a sick vaudeville act we've worked up over the years . . . Hey, at least it keeps the faculty cocktail parties interesting."

"Let me ask you something—and try to keep your bias out of it—that lady likes to gossip. How much of it is hot air?"

"Oooo, tough one, Phil. She'll trash me six ways from Sunday behind my back, I know that. But, in general terms, Madame Barnes is the one person round here who knows where *all* the bodies are buried. Walk softly and carry a big set of ears is her motto. If there's dirt, she'll find it."

"So she likes to stir up trouble, then?"

Sucking in her cheeks, Frankie shook her head. "No, can't say that. *Love* to, but can't. No, with Miriam I think it's more like— like buying insurance. She's super-protective of her family, see? She wants to know stuff for *ammunition* . . . just in case. She may go overboard but, much as it barfs me, I gotta say she's a hell of a wife and mother."

Coming from her Number Zilch fan, this was quite a testimonial. Phillip nodded, then put his hand on Frankie's arm. "Look, I've got to go back to my hotel. When Josh comes offstage, will you tell her I'll meet her back at the guest house?"

Holding up one hand in an Indian salutation, she nodded and intoned, "Can do, Kemosabe."

"I knew it. I knew he'd never make it through a dress tech," O'Roarke groused with some satisfaction from the backseat of the Mauros' station wagon. It was nearly one A.M. and she was tired, hungry, and cranky after the long rehearsal.

"Aw, give the guy a break," Frankie said, turning round in the passenger seat. "He's on vacation for chrissake."

Josh couldn't tell her friend that she was irked because she had run all over the building trying to find Gerrard so she could tell him about Pinkie's real identity, so she sniffed peevishly, "Oh, you. You always take his side."

"Somebody's got to. You sure don't cut him any slack . . . What'd he do to get you so permanently pissed, anyway?"

"Honey, honey, lay off," Mike chimed in, taking one hand from the steering wheel to pat his wife's thigh. "It's been a long night. So why don't you cut *us* some slack. Just drop it, 'kay?"

Ordinarily O'Roarke would have been grateful for his intervention, but she guessed it had less to do with chivalry and more to do with Mike's reluctance to let another man be the focus of female attention for too long. Nettled, Frankie bumped his hand off her leg and replied, "Hey, I'm only trying to help. What can I say—I *like* the guy."

"Gee, color me stupid. I *never* would've guessed," was her spouse's sarcastic comeback.

"Look, it's kinda refreshing to have one man around who doesn't treat me like—like furniture!"

"One man? Pfft! What a crock, Frankie. You've got little Willie Appleseed dropping by all the time." Mike pursed his mouth and adopted a phony British accent. "With his little cuttings and wild herbs and snotty wisecracks."

They were warming up to it now, getting ready to put on the marital boxing gloves. Jocelyn, who preferred watching old Ronald Reagan movies to seeing couples squabble, squirmed in her seat, though it was difficult because something kept poking her behind.

"Oh, excuse me. *Two* men—and one of 'em's English," Frankie snorted disdainfully. "That still doesn't put me in your league, does it, lover boy?"

"What the hell's *that* supposed to mean?!"

"You know damn well what it means. Just remember, fella— what's good for the goose is good for the gander." To emphasize her point, Frankie leaned over and honked loudly in his right ear. Mike jumped in his seat and nearly drove into a ditch.

"Jesus! Are you trying to kill us? You are wacko, just plain—"

"Kids, kids, I don't want to spoil your fun," O'Roarke interjected, "but you just missed the turnoff to my place."

Cursing in Italian, Mike swung a big U-ie while his wife smiled triumphantly. The smile seemed to indicate that, according to the Mauros' own Marquis of Queensberry rules, swearing in a foreign tongue was the equivalent of going into the ropes. So Frankie must have won the first round.

While the partners retreated to their separate corners, Josh seized the opportunity to search for whatever was perforating her backside. Under the jumble of lunch boxes, baseball mitts, and kids' jackets, she finally felt a hard object wedged between the seat cushion and backrest. Tugging it out, O'Roarke found herself staring at a large, flat book. But it wasn't a *Where's Waldo.* Judging from its worn condition, it was—it had to be—Will Coltrane's copy of *Friends & Foes.*

Tapping her friend on the shoulder, Josh asked, "Uh, Frankie, did you know Will's been looking for this?"

"He has? What is it?" Frankie squinted in the dark to read the title.

"Probably another small token of his esteem," Mike barked, but he was too busy trying to negotiate the twists and turns on the unlit lane to put much spin on it.

"A plant dictionary?" Her face a perfect blank, Frankie shook her head, saying, "For the life of me, I can't remember—"

"Holy shit!"

Mauro slammed on the brakes, pitching both women out of their seats. O'Roarke's nose banged into the headrest, making her eyes water, and she heard Frankie's head clunk against the glove compartment. Sitting back up, Josh could see they were just yards from her front door.

"*Ow!* Geez, Mike, what happened?"

"I almost hit something. Saw the eyes in my headlights," he said, gulping for air. "Must've been a raccoon . . . Look—there it goes!"

Swiveling her head to the right, Josh saw a furry rump diving into the shrubs. It was just a glimpse, but it was all she needed. Kicking open the car door, she ran pell-mell toward the bushes.

"Joey, wait! What're you doing?"

She spun round just long enough to shout, "Don't go into the guest house. Go to the Barneses' and call Phillip."

Afraid the jolt had shaken her friend's senses, Frankie wailed, "Where are you going?"

"To find my cat," she hollered as she plunged into the woods.

19

"Do me a favor. Just keep him the fuck away from me 'cause I am really, *really* pissed. And I just might blow, see?"

"Yes, sweetheart, I'll do that. Now just take a sip of this, okay?"

Gerrard gently drew one of Josh's hands away from the bedraggled Angus and placed a brandy snifter in it while positioning himself so as to block her view of Sheriff Kowaleski striding importantly around the den of the guest house. For once in her life, O'Roarke did as she was told and took a swig of Martell's. Huddled on the staircase with her cat on her lap, her face crosshatched with nicks and scratches and a red welt on her nose, she glared into space, paying no heed while Phillip dabbed at her wounds with a damp washcloth.

Wincing as he touched a tender spot, she looked up at him and asked, "Do you think that asshole will *finally* take the hint and open an investigation?"

"Uhh . . . that depends, love," he offered warily. "So far there's no sign of forced entry, and nothing's—"

"Look, I *told* you! I shut this place up tighter than a drum this morning." Phillip nodded and refrained from pointing out that one escaped feline hardly constituted proof of illegal entry. But she seemed to read his thoughts anyway. Brushing away angry tears, she whispered, "Damn, Phil—we nearly ran him over!"

"I know, Josh, I know." He sat beside her, putting an arm around her rigid shoulders. "But he's all right now."

He had arrived just moments after Angus' near-fatal accident. After getting the news from Frankie, he had grabbed Mike's flashlight and called out to Jocelyn that he was coming to help her search.

"No, don't!" Her disembodied voice had floated eerily out of the woods. "He must be scared shitless. He won't come out if someone else is around."

So the three of them had waited in silence for nearly an hour, listening to Jocelyn move through the brush, cooing soft and low to her pet. When she finally emerged with Angus, wet and whimpering in her arms, Phillip had felt a wave of relief, knowing as he did that sticks and stones wouldn't break her bones and names would never hurt her—but if anything had happened to that cat, she would have folded like a pup tent in a sandstorm.

He also knew that, even though Angus was safe and sound, her resolve about getting to the bottom of things would now be trebled. Someone would be made to pay for this, and woe to Calvin if he tried to get in her way.

Massaging his gut with one hand, Kowaleski walked out of the den saying, "Tell me again what you did before you left here this morning."

Despite her ill humor, O'Roarke knew better than to wise-off to an investigating officer, especially one she had summoned. Stroking Angus' neck, she dutifully repeated, "I got up around seven-thirty and showered. After I got dressed, I came down and fed Angus. Then I went around the house and checked all the doors and windows to make sure they were closed."

"Closed? Not locked?"

"Both. I fastened all the windows and shot the bolt on the kitchen door."

"But not the bolt on the front door, eh?"

"No. How could I? I went *out* the front door," she said through gritted teeth. "But I turned both the locks on it when I left."

"And both locks were still turned when you got back tonight. Right?"

Avoiding Calvin's gaze, she stared at his belt buckle and nodded her assent.

"And all the windows were still closed. Right?"

"Yes, but—"

He held up a beefy hand to silence her. "Now wait a sec. Hear me out. This is an old house and it's kinda rickety. I 'spect there's a few gaps in the baseboards here and there. Don't you think it's more likely your old puss cat squeezed through one of them and got out through the basement?"

At the words "puss cat," both Angus' and Jocelyn's eyes narrowed dangerously. "About as likely as Ali making a big comeback." Josh caught herself and continued mildly, "Listen, Sheriff, I *know* this animal. He makes Garfield look like an overachiever. There's not a feral bone in his body. His chief aim in life is to always stay within a five-yard radius of his food dish." As if to illustrate her point, Angus belched softly, then gave an elaborate yawn. "You could leave the door wide open and he wouldn't go near it—unless somebody spooked him."

Hooking his thumbs in his belt, Cal rocked on his heels, a superior smile on his face. Assuming that he was gearing up to say something really obnoxious, Gerrard decided to leave him to his fate and take a look around the den. Sure enough, as he slipped unnoticed into the next room, he heard Kowaleski heave a deep sigh and say, "Well, you know, I been around animals all my life, O'Roarke. So take it from me, even a city-bred kitty like yours—you get it out here in the woods, it's gonna hear the call of the wild, see? Makes 'em act funny. Do strange things."

"Oh, please! Spare me the Marlin Perkins routine, okay?" Jocelyn was now well and truly past her meager limits of patience. "Somebody came in here tonight—like they did twice before! Just what does it take to light a fire under your butt?"

"Hey, now! There's no call for you to—"

"Calvin, wake up! This is not Mayberry RFD. You've got a felon in them thar woods and you're not doing squat about—"

"Sheriff, you want to come in here?" Phillip called from the den. Glad for the reprieve, Kowaleski trotted in with Josh on his heels. Standing by the window to the left of the writing desk, Gerrard pointed to the other two windows in the room and said, "Those two are shut and fastened. This one's just shut."

"So? She must'a missed one of 'em."

Jocelyn opened her mouth to protest but Phillip caught her eye and shook his head. To Kowaleski, he said, "I don't think so. Hand me your flashlight, will you?"

Throwing the window open, he leaned over the sill and shone the beam down into the shrubs. Leaning over his shoulder, Calvin muttered, "I don't see anything."

"Look at the bushes here—right below the window. They look a little . . . dented-in, don't they?" Then he swung the light to the left and right. "Those others are smack up against the house."

Standing on tiptoe, trying to get a glimpse, Josh asked, "So what do you think?"

"I think you should go make a pot of coffee," he said as diplomatically as possible, "while the sheriff and I take a little stroll outside."

Near four A.M., O'Roarke yawned as she poured the last of the coffee into Phillip's mug and growled, "I can't believe that man hasn't ever taken a plaster cast."

"Wouldn't've done much good anyway. One stepladder's pretty much like another," he said, rubbing his stubble as he added a drop of Martell's to his mug. "Just be glad that you've got proof of your intruder now."

"I am. And grateful, too." Sitting opposite him at the kitchen table, she added softly, "You were pretty swift tonight. Helping ol' Cal play connect-the-dots."

"Ah, give him a break, Josh. He's used to college pranks and drunk drivers. This is somebody very subtle."

"I'll say. Leaving a stepladder outside the window and coming in through the front door. If it hadn't been for Angus, I'd never have noticed a thing."

"You better ask Ryson who has access to the spare keys to this place."

"That's the funny thing, Phillip. Tessa changed the locks after the second break-in. I thought I had the only set."

Frowning, Gerrard stretched out an arm to steal one of her cigarettes. "Where do you keep them?"

"In my purse . . . or here." She tapped the window ledge next to the table.

His frown deepened as he remarked, "Either way, they're obvious places. Lots of people had a chance to take an impression."

"But who'd have the equipment to do— Oops, sorry, I'm tired. Don't tell Tommy, okay?"

Phillip grinned, remembering, as Josh just had, the day Zito had shown her what nefarious miracles could be worked with a little bar of soap. "I won't. He'd be *so* disappointed with his star pupil." He gave her arm a little nudge and she smiled back. Then her eyes lit up.

"Still, still—anybody can use a bar of soap, but they can't cast the duplicate keys, right? They'd have to take it to a locksmith or somebody like that. And it'd be a pretty queer request."

"True. In any of New York's five boroughs, they'd laugh you out the door. And even up here—even if the person had a perfectly plausible story—they'd remember."

The light went out of Jocelyn's eyes as she nodded. "Yeah, they would. But this is someone crafty. They wouldn't have the duplicates made in Corinth. And there are tons of little towns round here and they've all got locksmiths and gunsmiths in 'em . . . Even if we could talk him into it, I don't think Cal's up to doing that kind of legwork."

"He may not have to." Phillip arched a brow meaningfully in her direction.

"Really? Why's that?"

"Because we've got someone with a B & E record in our midst. I called Tommy and he did some checking."

Sensing that she was just about to get scooped, Josh blurted out, "It's Lyle, isn't it?!"

"How the hell did you know that?"

" 'Cause I called him Pinkie tonight and he went a whiter shade of pale. And it fits with Tessa's diary."

"Gee, do you know how to spoil a guy's fun. But you're right. It was back in Minneapolis. Four years ago. The charges were dropped, though. Want to know who dropped them?"

"Tessa, right?"

"Yeah, right—killjoy," He sighed. "You were a lot more fun back when you were a neophyte, you know."

He expected a cocky smile and a snappy comeback, but Jocelyn seemed to have suddenly lost her zip. For a while there, they had been really cooking, just like the old days, but now he saw a hesitation in her eyes. She seemed to be wrestling with some inner scruple. There was a time when he would have leaned on her to come out with it. But he had learned the hard way that it was disaster to get between O'Roarke and her conscience. Besides, this was more her case than his; her friends, her past. And her call. He sat back and waited for her to make it. Finally she looked up at him, her face a study in conflict, and spoke haltingly.

"Listen, you've been knocking yourself out trying to help me. And I—I haven't been, uh, completely forthcoming in return. There are a few things I haven't told you because—well, I didn't know if they really applied to the case. And I didn't think they were any of your business, frankly . . . And maybe I wanted to handle things on my own—not need you. But now, now I'm getting the feeling there's a lot of back story here that—"

"Uh, back story? What's that?"

"Oh, sorry, that's film-speak for the story that happens before the opening credits. Things that set the plot in motion. Like, in *Streetcar;* Blanche DuBois' husband commits suicide after she taunts him about his homosexuality. That happens way before the start of the play, but it's a crucial part of Blanche's back story because it sets her on the road to ruin."

"And you think there's something is Grant's back story that—what? Preordained her death?"

"That's my gut feeling, yes." O'Roarke nodded once, then shook her head twice. "But I can't be sure. I may not be a neophyte, but I think I'm too close to this to see all the possible angles. So I'm gonna come clean. But you've got to understand something first."

"What's that?"

"This isn't one of your investigations, Phillip—hell, there's no official case at all yet. So what I tell you stays between us. I don't want you to use it to lean on anybody . . . unless I say so. Got it?"

It was a lot to ask of a man with his sense of duty to the letter of the law. She knew it and he knew she knew it. But he also knew he owed her one Free Ride and he trusted, not her regard for legalities, but rather her innate ethics.

"Got it. When the time comes—you drop the dime, not me . . . So, what gives?"

"Well, it has to do with Belinda . . ."

By the time Jocelyn finished telling him about Bel's abortion and the part Tessa played in it, the sun was starting to rise, filling the kitchen with a gray and rose light. Gerrard stood at the west window, which offered a nice view of the pond to the left and the compost heap over on the right.

Going over to the sink, Josh splashed her face with cold water, then turned to him. "So what do you think?"

"Two things: If you're right in your back story theory, I think it goes back farther than Belinda's pregnancy—though, for the life of me, I can't say why. But right now it doesn't much matter because, until we come up with the *how*, the why isn't . . . What the devil is he doing up?"

"Who?" O'Roarke crossed to the window and saw Will Coltrane trundling up the hill from the far end of the pond with a canvas hip-sack over one shoulder. "I haven't the faintest . . . We could go ask him."

"No, no. Let's wait a bit."

In silence, they watched Coltrane wander in the general direction of the house, stopping here and there to examine the ground and uproot a plant or two. Josh wondered aloud, "Is it just me—I mean, I know I'm not a plant person—or is that guy a little squirrelly?"

Phillip waved a hand to shush her as Coltrane, just yards away now, stopped suddenly beside the compost pile. Picking up a long twig, he poked around the pile for a minute, then squatted down to take a look at something. When he stood up he was red-faced and scowling. Breaking the twig over one knee, he flung it angrily at the compost heap.

"*Now* we go ask him," Phillip said, grabbing his jacket and heading for the kitchen door. It took O'Roarke a minute or two to find her sweater. When she came round the corner of the house, Will was in full splenetic flight.

"I ask you, how's a body to get a job done with these—these ignoramuses about?!" He jabbed an accusing finger in the direction of the Barnes home. "Bloody Hank had to go mow down the south side of the pond and I *knew* there'd be specimens there. And I was right!" He bent down and pushed aside some grass cuttings, grabbed a limp stalk of something, and shook it in Gerrard's face. "See, see!"

Stepping in for a closer look, O'Roarke, who felt it was too early in the day for major outrage and too late for Will to still be grousing about the mowing, said, "Looks like a piece of celery to me."

"Well, it's *not*," Coltrane spat back contemptuously. "It's *Cicuta virosa.*"

"You don't say." Grown comfortable with her horticultural illiteracy, she shrugged casually. "So what's that when it's at home?"

"It's water hemlock," Phillip put in.

"Really? Like the stuff Socrates had—"

"No!" Both men answered as one, then Gerrard added, "Though it's just as poisonous . . . But Will, that stalk wasn't mowed. Look at the grass cuttings. Barnes must have a pretty powerful mower. They look like they've been through a Cuisinart, don't they? That stalk is almost three inches. It was hand-cut."

Getting a twig of his own, Phillip started poking around the pile while Coltrane's face assumed its normal color, but he still wasn't ready to let go of his grudge against the Barnes clan. "Well, that's just as bad, really. They've no right to be cutting my specimens. I mean, honestly—first they do this. Then Belinda swipes my best reference book and her father nearly bashes me when she refuses to admit—"

"But she didn't, Will."

"Of course she did," he insisted. "Who else would've waltzed in and—"

"I think maybe your memory's playing you false." Despite the early morning chill, O'Roarke suddenly felt warm under the collar as Phillip froze midpoke and looked up at her in surprise. "I, uh, saw the book in Frankie's car last night . . . You must've lent it to her."

Coltrane's jaw went slack and he shook his head muzzily. "No, I didn't. It's not a book I lend out *ever*—to anyone. Not even Frankie." His cheeks flushed again. "And I can't imagine her wanting to borrow it. She's not—well, she's been very supportive about my work, but she's not that keen herself . . . Why would she want *Friends & Foes?*"

"Maybe she picked it up accidentally with . . . other stuff," Jocelyn offered with faint hope, which grew even fainter as the look Will gave her said: *Fat chance.*

And the look Phillip gave her, as he plucked out another piece of the poisonous plant, said something far worse.

20

"Water hemlock, you say? Well, that's a new one on me. Hold on a minute."

Gerrard jumped as Doctor Morgan's phone receiver clunked against a hard surface. Over the line, he could hear the distant sound of pages turning punctuated by an occasional slurping noise, which, he assumed, was the good doctor enjoying his morning java. This went on for quite some time until Phillip began to worry that the old man had become so engrossed in his research that he had forgotten about his caller. Then he heard the approach of padding feet and, a moment later, a cheery voice.

"My, my, I can see why you've reached your station in life, young man. Though, I must say, it's a pity you didn't go into forensics."

"Does that mean what I think it means, Doc?"

"Yes. Lord knows how you tumbled to it, but, yes. *Cicuta virosa*, after digestion, will leave traces of methanol in the bloodstream . . . And you're right about the other bit as well."

"The onset symptoms?"

"Umm-hmm. Severe convulsions—much like a grand mal seizure—followed by rictus sardonicus in some cases. Though, in an autopsy, it'll just look like heart failure, you understand."

"Of course. Believe me, Doctor, there are M.E.s who wouldn't even have picked up on the wood alcohol."

"Kind of you to say so, Lieutenant . . . But I'm still not happy about releasing the body for cremation."

"Don't be. Exhumation orders are hell to obtain. And, in this case, I don't think it would help all that much," Gerrard said softly, not just to soothe the old gentleman; Jocelyn had company in the kitchen and he didn't want any of this exchange overheard.

"Yes, you're right about that," Morgan agreed. "There was almost no food left in the stomach when I did the autopsy. So there'd be little chance of finding any water hemlock . . . Do you think I should call the sheriff?"

"Not for the moment, if it's all right with you. We're still dealing in suppositions." To put the doctor's mind at ease, he added, "And you did mention the methanol in your initial report, so it's not as if we're holding out on Kowaleski."

"That's true." Phillip could hear the relief in the other man's voice. "I leave it in your hands then. Frankly, I don't think poor Calvin's up to this sort of thing . . . My God, he *knows* these people—so do I, for that matter—it's hard to believe one of them's capable of something so foul."

"Yes, well, that remains to be seen. But I'll let you know what develops."

"Please do . . . And good luck, son."

Putting the receiver back in its cradle, Gerrard cocked an ear toward the kitchen, trying to gauge if it was safe to make an entrance.

After their discovery at the compost pile, O'Roarke had sent Will on his way, promising him that she would get his book back posthaste if he'd keep mum about it. Then she had trudged back into the house and, avoiding Phillip's gaze, muttered, "I know what you're thinking, but I can't talk about it right now, okay? I'm too beat. Let's both grab a few hours' sleep. Then we can start fresh." Seeing the sense of this, he had retired, without protest, to the spare bedroom and, despite the little hamster running round the wheel inside his brain, had fallen promptly asleep, only to be roused around two P.M. by the seductive smell of bacon frying, telling him that Josh was up and feeling feisty enough to defy the American Heart Association's dietary credo.

And he had been more than ready to join her in sin, but Belinda

Barnes had beat him to it. Sitting with her back to him at the kitchen table, she had been nibbling on a strip of bacon and sniveling, "I know I was lousy last night. I just got to thinking how *shallow* Perdita is and I got pissed at her."

Spotting Phillip in the archway in nothing but his boxer shorts, Jocelyn had waved him away, deftly miming a suggestion that he shower and shave over the girl's head, as she asked without missing a beat, "Why do you think she's shallow?"

" 'Cause here's this sweet old shepherd who took her in and raised her as his own after her own father left her on a hill to die like some damn Spartan! And she forgives him in a heartbeat so she can go off and marry a prince. I mean, what an ingrate!"

Deep in her misery and a plate of scrambled eggs, Belinda had missed their little semaphore routine as Gerrard signaled: "You're doing this *now?*" And Josh had signaled back something along the lines of: "Can't be helped. Show must go on." Then she had plopped herself down opposite the troubled ingenue and said firmly, "First off, you're giving yourself needless grief here. This play's a pastoral—it ain't *Hamlet*. The supporting characters aren't too fleshed-out. So, if you need to build a through-line for Perdita, here's what you do . . ."

Now, some forty-five minutes later, it seemed the discussion had progressed from the professional to the personal. Peeking in, Gerrard could see that Belinda had stopped sniveling. She was crying outright as Josh, oblivious to his reappearance, stroked her shoulder gently.

"It's stupid to say I know how you feel. I'm sure it's different for every woman. For me, it's like that Sondheim song—'Always Sorry, Always Grateful.' At the time, I was very sad and very guilt-ridden because I was *so* relieved."

"Yeah, me, too," Bel sniffed. "Does it ever go away?"

"Maybe, for some. Not for me, not entirely. Because I think we define ourselves by our choices in life, so I don't really want to forget. But listen to me, sweets." Josh leaned over and took hold of the girl's hands. "Don't confuse pain with shame. You took responsibility for yourself and made a decision. That takes guts. And you don't have to apologize to anybody about that *ever*. Because it's none of their damn business."

"No, it's really not, is it?" Wiping her eyes, Belinda sat up straight and spoke in a steady voice. "You know, Tess said some of this stuff, you know . . . before. That it was my own affair, nobody else's. But she was real careful not to sway me either way."

"Yes, I'm sure," said O'Roarke, and she was.

"It's just—I dunno, you're, like, cooler with it, somehow. I always got the feeling with Tessa that . . . that she was almost as upset as I was. And she never even had one." Belinda got up from the table to put her arms around Jocelyn's neck. "Anyways, you're the best! I know I still have stuff to work out, like with Denny—I've been a real shit to him. But I won't forget this, Josh. I mean, you didn't have to tell me about yours but you did. And I promise, someday I'll pass it on—if I meet a girl who's in trouble." With that, she planted a kiss on O'Roarke's cheek and plucked her sweater from the chair. Heading for the back door, she caught sight of Phillip, who did a masterly job of appearing as if he were still drugged with sleep, and called out, "Hi, Mr. Gerrard. Boy, you sure sleep late. Don't worry. We saved you some bacon." Then she breezed out the door.

Entering the room like a man about to cross a mine field, Phillip found Josh looking neither alarmed nor outraged, but vaguely puzzled as she followed Belinda with her eyes. Then she turned to Phillip with a rueful smile, saying, "Oh, Grandma, what big ears you have."

"Sorry about that. I didn't mean to—"

"Hey, one good eavesdrop deserves another," she said, going to the stove to fix him a plate. "That's how I heard about hers, so it's only fair, I suppose." Shrugging philosophically, she deposited the food in front of him.

"What I meant to say is," he began quietly, trying to quell his inner turmoil, "I'm sorry I had to hear it this way . . . Why didn't you ever tell me, Josh?"

Pouring herself a fresh cup of coffee, she gave him a sharp look. "I guess you weren't listening all that closely, huh? Let me reiterate—it's nobody's damn business."

"Not even mine? Not after—what? Two years together?" He gave up on the quelling bit and dropped his knife and fork as a safety precaution. "After you turned me down flat with some bullshit about not being fit for marriage?"

"That wasn't bullshi—"

"Maybe so, maybe not. But don't tell me that your having had an abortion wasn't goddam *germane* to the issue!"

"Shut up, Phillip, just shut up *now.*" Her voice was low and level but there was an edge to it that made him pay heed. "I'm only going to say this once, so pay attention. The world is filled with women who had abortions in their youth and went on to marry and raise a family, believe me. So, no, I didn't think it was necessary to tell you about mine. What I will tell you now is: Terminating a pregnancy can be a kind of litmus test for some women. It changes you and makes you come to terms with what you really want in your life. I found out I wanted my work, my friends, and my freedom. You wanted a wife and family. I bet you still do."

"Don't try to tell me what I wan—"

"Whatever, whatever." O'Roarke waved a hand in front of his face as if to clear away a low-hanging mist. "The point is—whether you know what you want or not—I *do.* So just don't glom on to my abortion as some hidden motive for my aversion to matrimony, okay? Because, even if it were true, it's all water under the bridge. I just don't want you to go on kidding yourself that someday I'll turn into the kind of woman you'd like me to be." Placing the tip of her finger tenderly to the cleft of his chin, she whispered, "It ain't gonna happen, love."

Had anyone, he wondered looking at her sad, smiling face, ever planted a stake in the heart of one's illusions so sweetly? She was right, of course. His secret hope in coming to Corinth was to find her changed, bored with the hollowness of Hollywood perhaps, and ready to turn a new corner in life arm in arm with him. What a chump! If he weren't so disappointed, he could almost laugh at himself. Because his fancy was all of his own manufacturing. Because O'Roarke, as long as he'd known her, had always been as she was now: a solo player.

Shoving his half-eaten meal aside, he grabbed his coffee mug and went for a refill. Keeping his back to her, he said dryly, "So I guess I should take a hint and take a hike then."

"Are you kidding?!" It gratified him to hear the sudden rise in her voice; she was sounding far less philosophical now. "You cut out on me and I'll—I'll never speak to you again . . . And I'll tell Tommy you left me in the lurch, too!"

"Calm down." He turned round to find her right under his nose. "You know I always finish what I start—well, in this case, what you started. I'm not about to turn my back on a probable homicide."

"Well, thank the lord." She gave a sigh of relief that was immediately followed by a snort of indignation. "So what was that 'take a hike' crap, then? Or were you just trying to scare me?"

"No, I wasn't," he lied just a tad, then continued formally, "I was speaking figuratively. As in, I dunno, as in we'll just stick to business from here on in, okay? And I won't, uh, trouble you with my unwanted attentions. How's that?"

"Uh, excuse me. Did I miss something here?" Josh blinked owlishly and looked about the room in mock confusion. "Did we just get zapped into a Jane Austen novel? If so, shouldn't we be in the drawing room? Shouldn't you be in tails? And where the hell are my crinolines?"

"Oh boy, you are really pressing your luck this time, sweetheart," he said tightly, ready to wipe that smartass smile off her face with a Brillo pad. "You've given me nothing but a hard time since I got here. And I've let it ride because—because I felt, in some ways, I deserved it. But I *don't* deserve this kind of bullshit when I'm just trying to play by your goddamn rules. What's more—I'm in no mood for one of your brilliant displays of slice-and-dice sarcasm. So stuff it."

"Phillip, take it easy! I was only joking."

"Yeah, right. You always make jokes—at other people's expense."

"Well, I'm sorry. I couldn't help it. I mean, geez—'your unwanted attentions?' I thought you were gonna whip out a snuff box or something."

"There you *go!*" Gerrard grabbed his head with both hands in lieu of grabbing her throat. "You can't stop yourself, can you? You're an impossible woman, O'Roarke, you know that? And, where men are concerned, you've got about as much tenderness as a boa constrictor."

"You're right." Any sane woman would have stepped back for

safety's sake. Jocelyn took a step in, raised her chin, and darted her tongue in and out rapidly in snakelike fashion. "But, you know, boa constrictors are very misunderstood animals, really . . . And they've got a hell of a sex drive." To illustrate her point, she wound her arms around his waist and let her hands slide up his back.

"Cut it out," he snapped, trying to disentangle himself. "I know what you're up to."

"What am I up to?" She drew her fingernails lightly across the nape of his neck.

"Your old tricks, that's what. You always get horny when you make me lose my temper. Stop it!" He gave her hand a smack. "You're just being perverse."

"Sorry." She let her arms drop to her sides and assumed a hang-dog expression. "I'm a disgrace to my gender. I was being brazen and shameless, wasn't I?" Putting the back of her hand to her temple, she sighed dramatically and added, à la Elizabeth Bennet, "And, I must confess, my intentions toward you were *not* honorable, sir. Nay, I blush to say, they were downright—"

"Oh, shut *up*," Phillip groaned, shot out one hand to grab her neck, and pulled her mouth to his, hard. Before he released her, he made damn sure she had little breath left to babble. For added insurance, he cupped her jaw in his hand. "Say 'Uncle.'"

"Uncle . . . Oh, lord, Phil—"

"Shush. That's enough." He lowered his face to hers and gathered her in his arms.

He didn't care if this was the right, the smart thing to do; caressing Jocelyn, suddenly soft and yielding and in thrall to him, had effectively short-circuited all his brain cells. He leaned back against the counter, pulling her with him. She inched one leg up his until her foot landed in the sink, rattling the dirty dishes. Neither of them heard the noise, only the sound of their own gasps and the blood pounding in their ears. Which is why neither one heard the soft pad of espadrilles on the patio or the faint tap on the kitchen door or the knob turning.

But they heard the high-pitched squeal well enough.

Jocelyn hopped back on one leg to get her foot out of the sink while Phillip sprang sideways like a startled crab and shot out an arm to keep her from falling backward.

"Oopsie! I've come at a bad time, haven't I?"

Miriam Barnes stood in the doorway, her face as pink as the cherry gingham dress she was wearing, with her eyes carefully focused on the oak floor; for which Gerrard, whose soldier still saluted, was deeply grateful. With both feet now on the ground, O'Roarke, who felt Miriam's remark won hands-down for Understatement of the Nineties, was undone by her sense of the ridiculous. Patting her rumpled curls down as best she could, she smiled warmly at Miriam and said daffily, "No, no, not at all. We were just about to do . . . the dishes."

Hearing this, Phillip felt a rumble of insane laughter building in his chest. The only way he could stop it was to blurt out, "Yeah, we were arguing about who'd wash and who'd dry."

To their mutual delight, Miriam nodded as if it all made perfect sense, smiled at Phillip sweetly, and said, "It's nice to know there are some men around who don't mind helping in the kitchen."

It was more than he could take. To save himself and justify Miriam's good opinion, Phillip spun round and started filling the sink with Ivory Liquid, not daring to meet Josh's eye.

"So, Mir, what's up?"

"Well, I feel awful asking. I mean, I saw Sheriff Kowaleski downtown and he told me about the trouble here last night and I know how concerned you must be."

"About the break-in? Well, nothing was taken so it's not so bad . . . You didn't see anyone around the place, did you?"

"Oh, no! Of course, I left here in the afternoon—for my bridge club. Then I grabbed a bite in town and went up to catch the rehearsal. Whoever it was must've come after dark."

"You're probably right. Anyway, what did you want to ask?"

"A *big* favor, Josh." Miriam looked at her imploringly. "I was going to have the cast party at our place, you know? Lord, I was shopping all morning! Then I come home to find our gas stove's sprung a *leak*. It's shot and we can't replace it until—well, until Hank gets paid at the end of the month, I'm afraid . . . So do you think we could have the party here? I'll still do all the cooking, of course."

"Sure, that's no problem. I haven't been here long enough to mess the place up much. So it won't take me any time to straighten up."

"And I'll have the dishes done by then," Phillip muttered for her ears only and got a sharp jab in the ribs.

"Oh, you don't need to bother about a *thing*," Miriam gushed gratefully. "I've got everything planned out. And Cal said he'd come up and help with—"

"Uh, Cal as in Kowaleski?" Not trusting her hearing, Josh thumped an ear with the heel of her hand. "Calvin's moonlighting as a caterer these days?"

"Don't be silly!" Miriam giggled like a schoolgirl. "No, whatever people say about him, Calvin's just a teddy bear, really. He's helped me with lots of parties before. He likes to do his bit for the college, you know."

"No, I didn't know." Jocelyn glanced sideways at Phillip, who immediately shut off both faucets. "I gotta say, I think I've misjudged the guy . . . Did he help you with the last party? The one Tessa had here?"

"You bet he did!" Miriam's face suffused with pride in her friend. "He knew I'd been down with the flu that week so he picked up my groceries for me. And he even cut up all the crudités. Like I said, there are still a few men who don't mind helping out in the kitchen."

Struck by a novel thought, Miriam gave Josh a nudge and a daring wink. "I guess the secret is to find yourself a good policeman, huh?"

21

"Wait a minute, just let me get this straight! You think somebody killed Grant with a friggin' *canapé?*"

Sheriff Kowaleski leaned back in his creaky swivel chair and gave Gerrard a skeptical smile as if he were half sure that his leg was being pulled. When the punch line didn't come, he folded his arms across his beer belly, shaking his head with regret. "You're serious, huh? You really think she got whacked by a piece a' celery."

"Uh, no—water hemlock. Like I said, it—"

"Looks the same, smells the same. Yeah, yeah." But Calvin's disgruntled countenance spoke eloquently of his distress that a fellow officer would entertain such feeble fancies. This had to be the result, his sad eyes seemed to say, of overexposure to the lunatic O'Roarke. What he didn't know was that, if the lunatic had had her way, Phillip wouldn't be in the sheriff's office now.

After Miriam's surprise visit had effectively broken up their steamy tête-à-tête, he had announced his intention of calling on Calvin, eliciting a deep groan from Josh.

"Now why do you want to go do *that?*" she had groused. "He's not going to believe you. And even if he did, all this is way over Cal's head."

"Maybe. But even a blind hog can find an acorn."

"Really? And what does that mean, Tennessee Ernie?"

"It means that somebody like Kowaleski, who's wrong most of the time, can't be wrong *all* the time," Gerrard had explained patiently. "Now, we're fairly sure we know what killed Tessa, but not the how, who, or why. Calvin lives here and knows these people. He probably knows things he doesn't *know* he knows. Get it?"

"Yes. But you heard Miriam. He sliced the crudités! I know it's farfetched, but that makes him a possible suspect."

"All the more reason to pay a call. To see if he squirms."

And, in fact, Kowaleski was squirming a bit, but it seemed he was more troubled by his undershorts bunching up than by a bad conscience. Once he had readjusted himself, he gave a satisfied grunt and gazed wistfully out the window as if to say: It'd be a hell of a lot more fun to be out setting up speed traps than doing this bullshit. But Gerrard ignored this little pantomime and bided his time. Finally, Cal leaned forward, propping his elbows on the desk, and said, "Look, Lieutenant, I know you got a lot more experience with this stuff than me. So let me ask you—outta all the cases you work on in a year, say—how many of 'em involve poisoning?"

"Statistically, less than three percent," Phillip answered quickly, then paused for effect before adding, "of apparent homicides, that is."

"Wha'? You saying there are some that get by you?" Cal looked surprised and just a little pleased by the thought that Gerrard was not omnipotent.

"Oh, yeah. Lots, I'm afraid. Sometimes you know it but can't prove it—that's always a bitch. But I'm sure there are others where we're not even called in—or we are and we miss something—so it's chalked up as natural causes. In those cases, there are no statistics, of course. But my guess is most of them involve some kind of drug overdose . . . or a poison that's hard to trace."

The certainty and matter-of-factness of Phillip's delivery made its impression. Slack-jawed, Kowaleski gazed at him in sudden alarm.

"And you *really* think this is one a' those cases?"

"Given that the medical evidence jibes with the effects of water hemlock poisoning—yes, I think it's a very real possibility. But look, it's your show and I'm not going to tell you how you should run it," Gerrard said deferentially, though just then Calvin looked as if he desperately wanted some stage directions.

"But who'd do it? I mean, what *for?!*"

"I don't know. You just start with the Three P's—Passion, Profit, or Past Injury," Phillip offered, trying not to sound as if he were giving a seminar. "Of course, Passion—or jealousy—is way out in front most times."

"Right, right, that makes sense. Grant was quite a looker, wasn't she," Kowaleski said as if that fact had just occurred to him. "And I hear she was real cozy with Mike Mauro. If the wife found out . . . Hey! Poison's supposed to be a woman's thing, huh?"

"Well, let's not forget Doctor Crippen." As it became clear that Cal had never heard of that gentleman, Phillip added, "Anyway, crimes of passion are usually impulsive and sudden. Poisonings are methodical and calculating. So I can see Fran—Mrs. Mauro finding her spouse in the sack with another woman and maybe picking up a gun or a carving knife . . . But I don't see her as the type to plot and plan a killing, do you?"

"Uh, no, guess not," Kowaleski agreed grudgingly. Then his eyes lit with something akin to cunning. "But hold on a sec! How do we know it was planned? I mean, here's Coltrane always running off at the mouth about this herb shit and he's buddies with her, right? So she's at the party and she knows the woods are loaded with the stuff. And maybe she spots Mike and Grant canoodling in a corner. Pops out the back door and cuts herself some hemlock, then slips it to her victim. That'd be pretty darn impulsive, huh?"

If Jocelyn had been present, Calvin would be short one larynx by now. As it was, Phillip was none too thrilled with his theory, though he admitted to himself it had some merits. It also had some flaws.

"Well, I guess it's possible. But it's one thing to know there's water hemlock on the property. It's another thing to find it quickly . . . in the dark."

Loathe to relinquish his pet theory, the sheriff pressed on. "Coltrane could, I bet. What if they were in cahoots?"

"Then you're back to a planned killing. People don't whip up murder schemes over cocktails."

"Well, what if—what if it were just Coltrane? We don't know squat about the guy. Could be a whacko. Maybe he had the hots for Grant, too. Or maybe he did it for Francine's sake."

Knowing how Doctor Frankenstein felt when the monster started getting too frisky, Phillip said, "Even the British don't carry chivalry that far, Cal. Though you've got a point about Coltrane's past. It might not be a bad idea to check it out." Seeing Kowaleski make a mad grab for the phone, Gerrard coughed pointedly and cut him off middial. "Thing is—you don't want to narrow your field too soon. You've got a lot of possible players here. You need to know *all* their scorecards."

"Yeah, but you said yourself passion always tops the chart."

"On average, yes. But not always. People will kill for money, too."

"Shit! Did she *have* any?"

"I don't know," Phillip muttered, growing tired of spoon-feeding. "But her lawyers do. And they can also tell you who inherits it."

"Aw, why bother? It's probably just her family."

"Well, Jocelyn says she was an only child and her parents are dead. So—bother."

"Okay, okay, I'll look into it. But I don't know about this Past Injury thing. I mean, who'd she have a past *with*?"

"Lyle Davie, Hank Barnes, and Ryson Curtis." Phillip raised three fingers in the air. "How's that for starters?"

Taken aback, Calvin grumbled, "Shoot, I didn't know about Davie. But Hank and Curtis—they're good people. I don't think they'd—"

"No! You mean you don't *like* to think they're possible suspects." Gerrard rose to his feet in frustration. "But—if you accept that a murder was committed—you can't *assume* anyone's innocence. If you do, you'll be totally ineffectual. You'll also be doing them a disservice—strange as that sounds—because the guiltless deserve to be cleared, see? And you can't do that by shielding them."

"Yeah, I see." Kowaleski shifted his gaze to a distant corner of the room. Something Phillip had said dropped like a stone in the murky pond of his mind, sending out disturbing ripples. Leaning against a damp and sweaty wall, Gerrard watched and waited for the ripples to reach the shore. Finally the sheriff jerked his head from side to side and blurted out, "I know Ryson's been worried about his job, but I don't see where Grant was a threat. I mean, she didn't know."

"Know what?"

"About his health . . . Hell, I wouldn'a known if I hadn't been in Doc Morgan's waiting room during his exam."

"Know *what*, Cal?"

"Ah, fuck. I hate talkin' 'bout people's private stuff. But I guess it can't be helped . . . Ry's got multiple-what's-it. You know, MS. Seems it hasn't bothered him for a while but now it's flarin' up again. That's why he's worried about his job. There's always people gunnin' for chairman. I don't think Grant was one of 'em, but maybe he thought different. Still, how would she know?"

"Past history, that's how," Phillip said softly as he gazed upon the blind hog who had just found his acorn.

"Damn, I'm blind as a bat in these things!" Jocelyn cursed and yanked off a pair of steamed-up goggles after slamming her hand against the wall of the Corinth College indoor pool for the second time in ten minutes.

After Phillip had left for the sheriff's office, despite a first-rate display of carping on her part, she had decided to while away the time until the final dress rehearsal by swimming laps, a pasttime she usually found both soothing and conducive to clear thinking. But it's difficult to clear one's mind when one's vision is blurred. Having left her trusty Technisubs in New York, she had cadged a pair of goggles from a hunky young lifeguard who must have possessed dolphinlike radar and so had no need of his optic nerves in the water. No matter how often she adjusted the rubber straps and rubbed spit on the lenses, she couldn't keep the goggles from leaking or misting up or both. And in the water, as on land, O'Roarke liked to see where she was going.

Rubbing her bruised knuckles, she exchanged the goggles for a kickboard and set out to do another ten laps. Halfway through her routine, she started to feel somewhat better. After all, the presence of Coltrane's book in Frankie's station wagon wasn't, in and of itself, damning. When Josh had drawn her attention to it, Frankie had seemed genuinely surprised. But the question remained: How had it gotten there, and when? If Will was to be believed, he never took it out of the greenhouse; so the possibility of his accidentally leaving it in the car was paper thin. But was he to be believed? Could he have engineered the whole thing as a blind of some sort?

She rather liked the idea but, as the chlorinated water restored her better judgment, she was forced to admit that she liked it because she didn't much like Will. And since, of everyone involved, he had the least connection with Tessa, he may have had the means, but not the motive.

But then who did? That was the infernal question. Phillip, she knew, would be focusing on the Three P's by now, and there was no denying the sense in that. But Jocelyn was plagued by the feeling that, in this case, the usual standards didn't apply, that some more arcane purpose had prompted the killing. Firmly convinced that the break-ins were tied to it, she wondered how so efficient a murderer could be so hopeless a burglar. Three shots at the place and nothing to show for it!

Then, as she was completing her last lap, the obvious finally occured to her: "You can't find what's not *there!* It has to be something in the diary and the killer doesn't know Phillip's got it." However, by the time she hauled herself out of the pool, another obvious fact reared its nasty head: Who even knew about the existence of the diary? Tess had taken pains to keep it hidden, and she herself had only discovered it by pure fluke. So scratch that, she thought, unless it's something *in* the diary. A piece of paper—or a will.

The thing to do was to get ahold of Gerrard as soon as possible and get back to his hotel room. Jocelyn looked up at the wall clock to see if she had enough time, but her view was suddenly obscured by the wet head of Lyle Davie, looking angry as a wet hen.

"I'd like a word with you, missy," he hissed through chattering teeth.

"Really? Can it wait, Lyle? I'd like to—"

"No, it can*not.* I want to know what you were gettin' at, calling me 'Pinkie' last night."

"Well, gee, I didn't mean to be insulting . . . Isn't that your nickname?"

"It was—back in Minneapolis. But nobody up here knows that."

"Tessa did. She worked with you then, didn't she?"

"Uh, yes—and she was the one who came up with it, too. But she never called me 'Pinkie' up here. So how'd you—"

"Why not? I think it's kind of cute."

"Well, I don't! And I asked her not to use it anymore."

"And she obliged you because you two were such old friends, that it?"

"Hardly," he sniffed, drawing a towel around his thin shoulders. "We were—just tryin' to, uh, turn a new leaf, you might say."

"What was wrong with the old leaf? Come on, Lyle, you can tell me . . . Did Tess get you canned or something?"

It is difficult to feign wounded dignity when one is turning blue and wearing a striped bikini brief, but Davie took a stab at it, saying, "I will be butt-fucked by a Ubangi before I discuss my personal affairs with you. So just mind your goddamn business, O'Roarke."

"Face it, Lyle, he who dishes gets dished. It's a natural law. And speaking of the law—my friend the lieutenant tells me you had a run-in with it . . . back in ol' Minnie, right?"

Like a true Confederate, Davie went from blue to gray as his mouth worked soundlessly for a moment.

"You had him check me out? *Why?!*"

Glancing down at the water as if it were the Rubicon, O'Roarke decided it was time to make a crossing.

"Because I found a journal Tess was keeping in the guest house —that's how I got your nickname . . . I also got the feeling she thought you might've had something to do with the break-ins."

"But that was a whole different thing! Just a gag that got outta hand," Lyle sputtered, agitated and anxious to tell all now. "Look, we were doing Ibsen's *Ghosts* and Tessie was directing and playing Mrs. Alving. So, okay, she had a heavy load to carry. But, I swan, she was just a bitch on wheels through rehearsals. Now opening night's coming up and the tech guys got together and decided—for a lark, Josh, that's all!—that we'd get into her apartment and rig up a li'l faux ghost, see? So I built the ghost and swiped her keys after the curtain went up that night . . . And I slipped into her place to rig it 'cause I was the only one who didn't have to be backstage. Anyway, she gets home after the party and the thing's hanging in her bedroom—and she pitched a fit and called the cops."

"How did she know you'd done it?"

Professional pride overrode self-preservation for an instant as Lyle smiled modestly. "Well, it *was* a pretty piece of work. I'd drawn a caricature of Tessa's face on it and sprayed it with iridescent paint. Made a very startling effect."

"And she brought charges."

"Well, yes. But she dropped them after she cooled down."

"But you lost your job anyway."

"Uh . . . true. Minneapolis is not known for its sense of whimsy. But hey, once burnt, twice shy. I am the *last* fucker on earth who'd go into Grant's place without a formal invitation, girl."

"Okay, but weren't you worried that Tess might tell Ryson about it?"

"No, 'cause *I* did. Right from the get-go. Ry, bless him, *has* got a sense of whimsy . . . And he didn't mind a joke at Grant's expense from time to time. Just to take her down a peg or two." There was a trace of smugness in Davie's voice but Josh caught it, dropped her grand inquisitor tone, and adopted the pose of a fellow hell raiser.

"So what was the new gag?"

"Well, see, Tess loved Ry, but she treated him like a baby brother sometimes. Not in rehearsal—I must admit she took his direction well. But she always had ideas 'bout how he should run his department. He was very funny and charming takin' it from her, but, you know, there are limits to even Ryson's good breeding. So we got together for drinks and commiseration one night—and that's when I came up with the second costume thing . . . Frankly, I'm surprised you didn't notice, Josh."

Feeling like a cow struck between the eyes with a two-by-four, O'Roarke shook her head and said slowly, "You made two sets of costumes for her, didn't you? A right size and a too-small size—so she'd think she was gaining weight. That's why you didn't need to alter them much for me. You just put me in the smaller set."

Lyle laid a finger along the side of his nose and winked. "Bingo! So it was real convenient—as things worked out."

"Wasn't it just," Jocelyn said blithely as she swiftly clamped a hand on his wrist and deliberately gouged her nails into cold flesh. "You little scum-sucking rat turd."

"Aiyee! Leggo—it was just a joke!"

"No, it wasn't. It was mean and malicious. And let me tell you something else, asshole." Lyle's writhings were attracting attention now but she didn't care. "You deserved to lose your old job and you deserve to lose this one, too. I don't care how talented you are—you're no damn professional. Your job is to make the actors look right and feel good onstage—period. Not fuck with their psyches. Past history be damned."

"Josh—it's not like I'd have let her go on in the wrong cost—"

"No, you'd just let her feel like a fat slug while she was in rehearsal, you slimy pissant. And you'd *never* pull that crap on a guy—not even the pretty boys who turn you down flat, huh? Because they're not as vulnerable. Their livelihoods aren't as dependent on physical appearance." Davie tried to shake his arm free, but her nails were as embedded as tenterhooks. "Hey, I know Tessa was no day at the beach. But I bet you've worked with a dozen men who've given you as hard a time or worse. And you didn't sabotage them, did you? Face it, Lyle, you're a hard-core misogynist. You love a guy who's got bigger balls than you, but you hate a woman who does."

"You *bitch!*" O'Roarke had released his arm and he stared in horror at the four deep crescent-shaped marks that swelled up, quickly turning from white to crimson. "You're crazy, O'Roarke, just plain— Christ! Look at that. I'm bleeding!"

Looking down, Josh saw a single drop of blood oozing up from one welt, which, in her book, did not constitute bleeding, but it succeeded in calming her down, though not to the point of genuine contrition. Draping her towel over his arm, she grumbled, "Well, you're not a Romanoff, so don't get hysterical."

"Me?! You're the one who's outta control. And don't think I won't tell Ry 'bout this. It's—it's gay-bashing, is what it is."

"Oh, Lyle, grow up. This has nothing to do with sexual orientation. I just don't like *you*." She poked his chest with one finger to emphasize her point and he jumped back as if he'd been branded with a hot iron.

"Just keep away from me, hear? You're a fucking menace!" With that Lyle scuttled off to the showers, leaving Jocelyn, a wet pariah, on the pool deck. But before she could beat a retreat, a small, dripping boy came up and tugged at her arm.

"Hey, Josh, what's a missoganis?"

"Huh? Shane—what're you doing here?"

By way of explanation, Shane jerked a thumb over one shoulder and Jocelyn looked up to see Frankie, clad in a green Speedo, sauntering over, shaking her damp head ruefully.

"You know, I like to get the kid out of the house, away from all the violence on TV. So what happens? We get here just in time for the gunfight at the OK Corral. *Tch*—the times we live in."

"Oh, stop," O'Roarke protested, genuinely embarrassed now. "I hardly laid a—"

"A *nail* on him, I know. Gee, and you didn't even break one!" Frankie gazed with elaborate admiration at Josh's lethal talons. "You should call Sally Hansen or somebody. I bet it'd make a great product endorsement spot." She grabbed one of Jocelyn's hands and held it up while solemnly intoning, "Yes, it's true, ladies. With new Nuke 'Em Nail, you, too, can claw your way through a whole football squad without a chip or a snag!"

"Frank, I know you're really enjoying this," O'Roarke whispered hotly, "and I hate to spoil your fun—but are you almost done?"

"Ma, what's that thing she called him?" Shane persisted. "A missoganis?"

"That's misogynist, hon," she corrected her boy tenderly. "A guy who hates all girls."

"Like me!"

"No, you just hate your sisters—that's normal. Now be a sport and go get your water wings, huh?" For once, Shane did as he was told, leaving his mother behind to savor her friend's discomfort a little longer.

"Boy, what a show. I don't know what Lyle said but I've never seen you go off like that! It was great—no premeditation, no—"

"Circumspection? Yeah, well, I'm glad you had a good time but I'm not too proud of myself. It'll be all over campus by the time I get to the theatre."

"Yeah, and they'll probably give you a plaque!" Her smile faded as she added, only half joking, "But I'd check my costumes to make sure he hasn't sewn razors into the seams if I were you."

Shane reappeared, looking a little blue and prune-y, with his water wings under one arm. "Ma, I'm cold! Let's go." He turned to

Josh and offered gallantly, "You can come, too. Will's taking us to Burger King."

"Ah, thanks, but I can't." At the mention of Coltrane, Frankie started busying herself with towels and robes, carefully avoiding Jocelyn's eye. "Hey, Frankie, I saw Will this morning and told him you had that book of his."

"Oh, right! Good thing you reminded me. I completely forgot after the, uh, ruckus at your place last night." Waiting till Shane was out of earshot, she asked, "What happened after we left? Did you find anything missing?"

"Not that I could see . . . But I think I know what they were after."

"Really! What?"

"Something of Tessa's. A diary she kept."

"You're kidding? A diary?" She almost slipped on the wet tiles and grabbed Jocelyn's arm to keep her balance. "Hell, I didn't think Tess was the introspective type. Have you read it?"

"No, I couldn't. It's written backward. Phillip has it."

"So *that's* why you dragged him out of our place the other night." Frankie was no slouch at putting two and two together and she was already on to higher math. "But what's the big deal about a diary?"

"Nothing—unless there's something in it that somebody needs to find out . . . or wants kept private."

"You're not talking about just kiss-and-tell stuff, are you?" It wasn't really a question. Sensing the gravity of her friend's concern, Frankie was rapidly formulating her own equation. Her body stiffened as she swung Josh round by the arm. "You don't—? You think it has something to do with her death?"

"I told you, I haven't read it so I can't—"

"Jo, come *on!* Don't blow smoke at me. Christ, I can feel it." She shook O'Roarke's arm. "You're tense as piano wire! You really believe somebody was out to get her?"

"Yeah, I do . . . and I think they succeeded."

22

"No! You didn't? Tell me you didn't, Josh."

"I just told you I *did*. Now calm down." Wedging the receiver between her right ear and shoulder, O'Roarke wiped salad dressing from the corner of her mouth. It was no mean feat to eat a chef salad while sitting in a phone booth with an irate cop on the other end of the line. "Just get out that journal and start—"

"Kowaleski hasn't decided to open an official investigation yet and you go and tell two people about the diary—both of them possible suspects!"

"Come on. Frankie would never—"

"Can it. You know damn well if a case *were* opened she'd have to come under consideration. Look, I like her, too. Okay? But even if she's innocent as a newborn babe, you still shouldn't have told her you think it's a homicide."

"She guessed, Phillip. Even if I lied, she'd have known. Frankie's got a built-in shit detector."

"Oh, hell . . . Look, I'm coming up there."

"No! You can't—I told you, you've got to finish that journal *tonight*."

Luckily, Gerrard, who was also dining, though in the comparative comfort of his hotel room, had thought to order a scotch on the rocks with his meal. He took a sip to quiet his nerves, then spoke with a semblance of calm.

"Thing is, Josh, if you told two people two hours ago, that means eight people know by now, right?"

"Right. That's why I did it," she answered with equal equanimity.

"But don't you see? That makes you a *target!*" So much for the scotch.

"Wrong. It gives me insurance," she insisted, glancing down at her watch. It was nearly seven and she had less than an hour to get into costume and makeup, and less time than that to make Phillip, who liked to play things close to the vest, see why she had chosen to lay out her cards. "Look, we can't wait on Calvin if he ever *starts* an investigation. Meanwhile, the killer's been thinking he's safe to do as he pleases. But *now* he'll know he isn't."

"You call that insurance?!"

"Yes, because I've let it be known that *you* have the diary, not me . . . By the way, did you bring your gun with you?"

"Of course not. You know I never carry off-duty. Anyway, this perp's not going to come after me."

"Exactly—and that's my insurance," she said, trying not to sound too smug.

"Oh, you little devil, you." Despite his misgivings, he had to chuckle; somehow Jocelyn always managed to convert her Gaelic rashness into Gaulish cunning. "So you're setting me up as the patsy, huh?"

"Well, isn't that what you overprotective, manly types are for?"

"Hey, don't get cute with me. I know what you're up to, Josh," he said, back to all-business again. "You're trying to flush the perp out and that's not smart. Or prudent."

"Phillip—we'll be *old* before Cal ever mounts a case And, honestly, I don't blame him. I know we're light on hard evidence. But everything we've got is going staler by the moment. It could all slip away if we don't stir something up soon."

"Point taken. But listen to me, Josh. It's better—*safer*—to watch and wait for a bit." Gerrard paused to kill the rest of the scotch before making a mighty reversal of a long-standing position. "And, frankly, I'd rather let the trail go cold than have you in jeopardy."

Many women, most women, would have been touched by such

solicitude. But most women hadn't been on the hard receiving end of Phillip Gerrard's sense of justice as Jocelyn had during the Burbage Theatre case, when she had been the one who had, despite his rancor, let the trail go cold for very good reason. Now he was trying to do the right thing at the wrong time.

And it didn't play.

"So you're saying, because I might get hurt, it's okay to let Tessa's killer walk?" As far as loaded questions went, this was a fully packed Magnum, so Gerrard chose his words carefully.

"That's not what I meant, no. But yes, I don't want you sticking your neck out *now*. And not just because of the overprotective manly shit, either," he said, backpedaling adroitly. "You press things too soon and you risk blowing the whole case."

"What do you mean?"

"I mean, you can't solve a case before you've built one. Only rookies try for shortcuts, and they screw themselves in the end 'cause they ignore due process in some way. Then the whole thing gets thrown out of court."

"But I'm not a cop," she protested. "So how could I—?"

"You'd be a key witness for the D.A., most likely. A half-decent defense attorney would bring up your relationship to Grant, implying that you were hot for revenge. So if any of your actions were seen as deliberately incendiary, your testimony would be tainted in the jury's eyes. Get it?"

"Damn, I never thought about that," she said. Then there was a long pause while Phillip pictured the clockwork mechanism ticking over in her mind. Impervious to soft soap, O'Roarke was a sucker for hard logic and she realized Phillip's knowledge of the inner workings of the legal system far outstripped hers. "All right, I'll make you a deal," she said finally. "I'll lay low tonight if you promise to stay put and finish that journal."

"Deal. But that means you just look and listen. No poking and prodding, right?"

"Right . . . you just do your homework like a good fella. I'll stop by after rehearsal—if it's not too late."

"Don't worry. I'll be up. Just take care, Josh."

"Sure. I'll be good." Then she rang off and Phillip rang room service for another scotch. Somehow, despite her assurances, he wasn't at all sure that he and Josh shared the same definition of being "good."

For her part, she had made the promise in good faith and had every intention of keeping it. How was she to know that the first person she'd run into, coming into the theatre lobby, would be Ryson Curtis, pacing the red carpet and wringing his hands like an overwrought hall monitor.

"Jocelyn! Where've you been? It's nearly half hour."

"Well, it's been a busy day, Ry," she said brusquely, heading for the stairs to the dressing room, trying to ignore the swell of anger rising in her breast. "Don't worry, I'll be ready on time."

"It's not that. I wanted to have a word with you," he said, dogging her steps. "Lyle came by my office earlier. He's very—upset."

"Yeah? Well, tell him to file charges if it'll make him feel better."

"Oh, don't be facetious! I've had my hands full calming him down. And, frankly, I'm upset with you, too."

"Well, golly, that makes three of us." She swung round on him at the head of the stairs. " 'Cause I'm not exactly pleased as punch myself. In fact, I'm disappointed as hell that you'd go along with him on that nasty number he pulled on Tess. That was just plain *low*, Ry."

His hands fluttered up in the air, then dropped to his sides. "If it's any consolation, I'm none too proud of it myself, darlin'. I'm afraid he caught me at a weak moment. I'd had a hard day with Tessa in rehearsal and one drink too many that night. Tell you the truth, I hardly remember that conversation with Lyle. But, yeah, I guess I must've given him the nod to pull that li'l prank."

She was almost disarmed by such a forthright confession, but the "li'l prank" bit set her off again. "That was no *prank*. It was goddam sabotage. And you should've stopped it. Hell, she was doing you a favor, Ry."

"Yes, yes, she was," he admitted, dropping his head and shaking it from side to side. "Always Lady Bountiful, our Tess. I think that was part of my problem."

"What problem?"

"Oh, it's hard to describe. Let's just say that I now have a greater understanding of why, after the United States has showered so much foreign aid over the globe through the years, we, as a nation, are *so* despised by so many."

Some people would have found this an elliptical remark, but Jocelyn instantly saw the sense of it.

"So she made you feel like a poor relation, huh?"

"Um, yes. Quite impoverished, actually."

"Well, I don't know what to say, hon. Other than—that's bullshit."

"Beg pardon?" One hand flew to his chest and he honestly looked as if he couldn't believe his ears.

"You heard me. That's crap. Look, I'm not denying your feelings. But I think you were a jerk for giving in to them. Tessa didn't come here out of pity! She came because she believed in you—in your ability. She'd never put her ass on the line for an incompetent, just out of friendship. She wasn't *that* bountiful, for chrissake."

"How can you know that?" There was something half fearful, half hopeful in his face as he drew a breath and asked, "Did she say so in her . . . diary?"

"No—she said she was worried about your health. Did you ever discuss it with her?"

"What? Discuss what?"

It was the wrong moment for this conversation and O'Roarke cursed herself for raising the topic. But it was too late to retract, so to hell with going up on time, she thought, and plunged ahead. "Ryson, I know about the M.S., okay? I'm sorry, it's your business, no one else's. And, just like Tess, I'm not going to tell a soul. But I wish to God you'd felt you could've confided in one of us—that's all."

"Half hour, people! Valuables, please." The stage manager's voice echoed down the corridor but Curtis hardly seemed to hear. He wet his lips several times before he could find his voice.

"I—I had no idea she knew. I mean, not this time. We were both starting out in New York when I had my first onset . . . she picked me up from the doctor's office after I got the news so, of course, I told her. But we almost never talked about it after that. See, I've been very lucky. Long periods of remission. Then, just recently, there was a flare-up and I've had to go back on steroids . . . But I didn't think she noticed."

"Sure she noticed, Ry. She had a good eye . . . and she cared about you."

"Oh, sweet Jesus! What a fool I was." Curtis folded up and sat down on the top step with his head in his hands. "I thought she was trying to one-up me . . . and she was just trying to shoulder some of the weight."

The stage manager was bearing down on them now, intent on getting Jocelyn into the dressing room. She squatted down and put a hand on Ryson's heaving shoulders. "Look, I'm sorry I sprung this on you. For what it's worth, I think Tess understood what you were going through . . . You gonna be all right?"

"Not immediately, no. But by curtain, yes," he said, reaching up to pat her hand. "And I thank you for telling me, Josh. Now—go be brilliant."

"Sure, no sweat," she said softly, then sprang to her feet before the S.M. could catch sight of his director in tears. By way of diversion, she threw her fists up with a mock snarl and did a Cagney.

"Aw, you dirty rat! You'll never take me alive, I tell ya." The blank look on his face told her he'd never seen Cagney alive, but, determined to keep up the act, she held out her wrists for handcuffing and quipped, "Do your worst, copper."

Thinking he got the joke, the boy grinned and said, "Don't tell me. That's Angie Dickinson in *Big Bad Mama,* right?"

"No . . . just some other blond."

Forty minutes later, just as the S.M. called places, she was flying down the back staircase toward the wings as quickly as her pregnancy pad permitted. She hadn't had time to heed Frankie's warning and check her costume for possible booby traps. But after their poolside peccadillo, she didn't really believe Lyle would be booby enough to try anything cute. It was probably just paranoia, enhanced by Gerrard's safety-first lecture, that made her fancy the pad was a pound or two heavier than usual. Placing a hand on either side of the fake belly, she was somewhat consoled to find there was no internal ticking.

In the wings, Hank and Mike were warming up each in his own way. Mike was flopped over, bouncing gently as his knuckles brushed the floor, then he took a deep breath and exhaled slowly as he rolled back up to his full height, while Barnes, who carried a heavier load of lines, was limbering up his lips with an old bit of actor's doggerel: "I had a hippopotamus. I kept him in a shed. And fed him upon vit-a-mins and veg-e-table bread."

"Lovely, Hank," Jocelyn whispered as she came up behind, engaging in her own form of warm-up. "Now do 'Sally sells seashells.' That one always gets me all choked-up."

Hank spun round and hissed in her face. "Where the hell've you been?"

"I, uh, had a call to make," she said, taken aback. "What's the matter? I still made it in plenty of time." By way of justification, she pointed at the two boys in heavy age makeup who shared the first scene. "Camillo and Archidamus haven't even gone on."

"I know. But you're always early!" This was the price one paid, she thought, for being compulsively overpunctual; people get pissed when you're merely on time. "I wanted to talk to you."

"Well, the way today's gone, you'd have had to take a number and get in line. Sorry," she said brusquely just as the curtain rose with the slow, elegant sweep that always worked on O'Roarke the way a red cape worked on *toro;* she was instantly in character and in Sicilia. And the real world was, mercifully, light-years away.

Alas, Hank was not so easily transported. Tugging at her sleeve, he persisted. "Belinda was at your place today, huh? Did she mention anything about that so-called shopping trip she took with Tessa?" Mike tried to shush him while Josh just shook her head. " 'Cause I think they did more than shop! What do *you* think?"

"I think you should talk to your daughter, not me." A faint alarm went off on one side of her brain, but it didn't stand a chance now against the acting side of her cerebellum. "I'm here to do a part, not family intervention. So drop it."

He did, but only because he had no choice. Archidamus was winding up the first scene.

"If the king had no son, they would desire to live on crutches till he had one."

With a pleading smile, Mauro urged, "Come on, kids. It's *show* time!"

23

"Christ on a crutch! Do you know what time it is?"

"Yeah, I do," Phillip lied; he was on his second pot of coffee and Time as an actual dimension no longer had meaning. "And I'm sorry, but I have to know—did you get in touch with the lawyers?"

"Well, kinda. Not really though," Kowaleski cranked at the other end of the line. "I called after you left. But geez, those guys keep pussy hours! There was nobody round to talk to."

"That's okay—just tell me the name of the firm."

"You kiddin'? They all got names long as my arm!"

"I know, I know they do," Gerrard said, trying to control his voice. If it were any of the guys on his squad making this sort of stink, he would have busted an eardrum by now. Instead he asked gently, "But you made a note of it, right?"

"Sure, I did . . . but it's on my desk at work."

"All rightie." He sighed so deeply it made him light-headed. "Let's just try for the initials then. Think you can remember them, Cal?"

"Shit, lemme see now. I know it was a bunch a' Jew names." In the background, Phillip could hear the creak of mattress springs accompanied by the tinkle of beer cans falling to the floor, then— "Wait a sec. I gotta whiz."

"Oh, swell. Oh, peachy-fucking-keen," Phillip addressed the ceiling, trying to ignore the scatological sounds echoing over the line. "I'm here, out of my jurisdiction, trying to build a case with Bubba the Clown. *Great* vacation! Wish I'd brought a camera."

But it seemed that there was some odd connection between Kowaleski's bladder and his brain; perhaps, as one emptied, the other filled, for, when he picked up the receiver, his voice was loud and clear as he said, "Myers, Abrahms, Moses and Allen—that's it."

"Ah, that's beautiful. Thanks, Cal. I'll talk to you tomorrow." Happy to resume his REM cycle, the sheriff grunted his assent as Gerrard hung up the phone and gazed happily at the open page on his lap.

"Myers, Abrahms, Moses and Allen spells *MAMA*. Just like I thought."

Then there was a sharp knock. The door flew open and he was confronted with a heavily made-up Valkyrie.

"Ho, boy, I hope you kept your end up. 'Cause I *was* good and it was *hell*," Jocelyn gasped as she yanked a pack of cigarettes from her purse before heading for the bottle on his dresser. "Where are the glasses?"

"Bathroom," he said with a jerk of the thumb. "Ice is in the bucket."

She came out of the john, puffing up a storm with ice tinkling edgily in her glass as she crossed to the armchair farthest from the bed and threw herself into it in a sprawl. "So—ask me how it went tonight."

"Can I first ask if you're upset about the case or about the run-through?" It was a sincere question since he knew she was as apt to be disturbed by a bad scene as by a bad alibi.

"Oh, hell, I wish I knew! The final dress was far from brilliant, but it wasn't god-awful. If it were a professional gig I'd be worried, but amateurs never really come alive till there's an audience out front. Of course, once they do come alive, they start doing cute bits they never did in rehearsal. So you have to be on your toes. I'll be grateful if Hank just remembers all his lines for once."

"How many times did he dry up tonight?"

"Three. But then he was somewhat distracted." Jocelyn told him about Barnes' suspicions regarding Belinda.

"How did he get wind of that?"

"Well, it can't be Denny. He and Bel seem to have patched things up, so he wouldn't want to rock the boat."

"What about Lyle? Or Anita?"

Opening the palms of both hands, O'Roarke offered, "Take your pick. It's a fifty-fifty chance either way. They both avoided me like the plague tonight. But at this point, I don't exactly trust my judgment. How can you tell—when you're about to open a centennial production that a lot of people's reputations are hanging on—what's guilt and what's plain nerves?"

"Tough call," he said softly. "Toss me a cigarette, will you?"

She shook her head until she noticed the pinwheels spinning round his pupils. "O'm'gosh! You've been hard at it, haven't you? Did you find something?"

"I think I might've. So fork over a coffin nail . . . and finish telling me about the final dress."

He lit up and took a hungry drag as she recounted her run-in with Ryson. Then she snapped her fingers. "I almost forgot! That idiot Lyle *did* pull a number. He rigged a hot water bottle inside the pregnancy pad. So I started leaking before my first exit."

"What'd you do about it?"

"Nothing. Didn't say a word to anyone. That'll make him real nervous. Now, what've you come up with?"

"This." He flipped a page of the journal toward her and Jocelyn craned her neck to the left, then to the right trying to decipher the backward writing, pulled out a compact mirror, then gave up in frustration.

"I can't make squat out of it."

"Don't feel bad. Neither could I. It's in Italian."

"Well, geesh, you could've told me!" She massaged the back of her cricked neck with one hand and walked over to hold the diary up to the dressing table mirror. " '*Nel mezzo del cammin di nostra vita/ Mi ritrovai per una selva oscura,/ Che la diritta via era smarrita.*' Well, all I can make out is *nostra vita*—our life. But it sounds like poetry. Of course, most Italian sounds like poetry to me."

"No, you're right. It is—Dante, in fact."

"How do you know? You don't speak Italian."

"No, but Zito does. I read it to him over the phone and he translated it for me. It's from *The Divine Comedy*."

"Tommy—our Tommy—knows *The Divine Comedy*? In Italian?!"

"This bit he does. It's from the first canto of *Inferno*. His grandmother used to read it to him when he was little—just to keep him in line, I guess."

"Well, I'll be. He never fails to amaze, does he?" Jocelyn chuckled with delight. "So what's the translation?"

Picking up a scrap of hotel stationery from the nightstand, he cleared his throat and read: "In the middle of the journey of our life I came to myself within a dark wood where the straight way was lost."

"Really?" There was no mirth in her voice now. "What did she write after that?"

"Nothing, it's the last line of her last entry."

"Oh lord, no. That's too sad. Too eerie." She sighed, rubbing down the gooseflesh on her arms. "Tess wasn't melancholic by nature . . . What brought that on?"

"Can't say for certain." Phillip reached over to take the diary from her and leaf through the pages. "For a private journal, it's surprisingly impersonal for the most part. When it's not, she gets very vague, downright obscure sometimes. She must've been an innately secretive woman, Josh."

"It's funny, I never thought of her that way, but you may be right." Sinking down on the foot of the bed, she leaned over to run her index finger along the spine of the book, like a medium trying to contact the Other Side. "In one way, she was very direct. Tess always told you what she thought—if a scene was going badly or she felt your work was shoddy, or solid. But it was always about the work, not about her. I—I know almost nothing about her personal history, just her career record."

Hearing the timbre of regret in her voice, Phillip countered, "You knew some stuff. About her being an only child and her parents' being dead."

"Yes, but even that came up in a work context. She was lecturing me about fleshing out a character's back story." Jocelyn shook her head and smiled wryly. "I was doing a scene from *Private Lives* in class. Playing Amanda and making a hash of it. So she stopped me and asked." O'Roarke paused to straighten her shoulders and raise her chin; when she spoke, it wasn't her voice that came out. " 'Tell me, lovey, how many siblings does Amanda have? And are they older or younger?' When I said I didn't know because there was no mention of her family in the script, Tess laid into me . . . 'It's your *job* to know! Coward's done *his* work—written a wonderful role with some of the most delicious comic lines in the English language—but you can't expect him to drop the whole ball of wax right in your lap. The poor man can't write your subtext for you!' "

Enjoying the performance, Gerrard still felt compelled to interject, "But what does subtext have to do with brothers and sisters?"

"Everything! It affects how we deal with people for the rest of our lives—a youngest child tries to resolve conflicts in a very different way from the eldest, say." Rising to her knees as she warmed to her topic, she poked his chest for emphasis. "A guy who grew up without sisters is at a big disadvantage in the dating game compared to one who had a slew of 'em. Now Amanda and Elyot—Tess felt that they were both only children. That's why they fight all the time. They're each used to having their own way, so they're rotten at making compromises, see? God, she was a great teacher . . . Anyway, that's how I found out *she* was an only child."

"Hmm, interesting. I always thought it would be tough to grow up alone. Maybe that's why she was so fond of Belinda. They had that in common . . . since, as you say, she's very honest about talent and she had no illusions about Bel's."

"What did she write?"

He leafed through the pages to find the entry. "This is after the first week's rehearsal: 'A.S.'—that's Anita—'has ambition to equal her talent, which is raw but raging. My sweet B., I fear, lacks that essential fire in the belly. Still she'll be lovely in the role, despite herself. Was ever a child so perfectly cast? The truth always reads onstage.' "

Plopping down beside him, Jocelyn frowned as she stared at the page. "So how did she get from here to losing her way in a dark wood?"

"It's hard to trace, Josh. She didn't make an entry every day and some days it's dry notations, like this one." Phillip pointed to a date with two lines scrawled beneath it. " 'H. still struggling with lines. Would like to help him but don't dare.' She didn't think Hank was any great shakes as an actor but I get the impression she felt sort of sorry for him."

"What does she say about Mike?" Jocelyn braced herself for the worst.

"Says he can act. That he's funny and charming. They obviously spent time together but, if it was in the sack, it's not mentioned here."

"Then it was just flirting! *Had* to be." Attempting to leaven her relief with logic, she said, "I mean, there's not a woman in the world who'd keep a diary and *not* write about a new love affair, right?"

"I . . . don't know. To every rule, there's the exception. And she was an exceptional woman." She knew he was working up to something and she had an uneasy hunch it had to do with the final entry.

"You think she was unhappy about having an affair with a married man?"

"I don't know if it was unhappiness. More like regret." As she feared, he turned to the last pages. "Two days before she died, Mauro came by her place with his kids—'the terrible trio' she calls them. But she got a big kick out of 'em. Said they were all 'natural hams in the best sense of the word.' And she was surprised Mike was such a good dad."

"So she got the guilts?"

"Maybe. Who knows? Christ, she's so—slippery!" Frustrated by wrestling with a phantom, he flipped to the final page. "Anyway, Mike and the kids leave. Then she says: 'They made me think of Italy again. But the Past is immutable and there's precious little I can do about the Present at present. So I'll tend to the Future. Have decided to call MAMA and make new arrangements. Something has to be salvaged from this mess I've made.' Then she ends with the Dante quote."

"Who's MAMA?"

"Myers, Abrahms, Moses and Allen. That's my guess."

"Lawyers?" Phillip nodded slowly and Josh nodded back with, "She was going to change her will."

"That's my other guess." He smiled and gave her thigh a pat. "But we won't know for sure till tomorrow."

"Tomorrow. Terrific. We open tomorrow and it'll probably take all day to pry the dirt out of her lawyers, huh?"

"Most likely. Especially with Cal doing the prying."

Groaning, Jocelyn flipped over on her stomach and buried her face in a pillow, muttering, "So if I'm lucky, we'll hear right around curtain time. Great!"

"Well, how about I take your mind off it with a little back rub," he offered, kneading her shoulders with his hands. Two pots of coffee had stimulated more than just his mind.

"No, Phillip, I don't think that's a good ide— Ooh, God, that feels great!"

"It's a nice view from up here, too," he said as he slipped a leg across the small of her back and went to work on the knots in her neck. After a few minutes, he could feel her muscles relaxing as he let his hands trail down to the bottom of her sweatshirt. But when his hands made contact with skin, she stiffened suddenly.

"What's the matter?"

"Get off, get off," she hissed, then, without waiting for him to comply, she dislodged him by flipping over onto her back.

"Josh—it's just a massage for Pete's sake—"

"Shh! What's that noise?" She sat up as her eyes flew around the room.

"I don't hear any—" Then he heard it. "Christ, has it started to hail?"

"Yeah, but just around your window." O'Roarke pointed across the room as a handful of gravel plinked weakly against the glass. "I think you're being summoned."

The window was two stories above the hotel parking lot. Leaning over the sill, Gerrard looked down on the moonlit, smiling faces of Denny and Belinda.

"What's going on down there?"

"Oh, Mr. Gerrard, we're *soo* sorry," Bel called up in a loud whisper. "But I'm looking for Jocelyn. Do you know where she is?"

"I'm sure this strikes you both as a very, um, Shakespearean gesture—but you could've used a damn phone!"

"Oh, gee, I never thought of that," the girl yelped, then collapsed

in giggles and buried her face in Denny's bomber jacket while her
swain flapped his free arm helplessly.

"Sorry 'bout this, sir. Belinda's, uh—she's kinda tanked."

This announcement brought a scream of laughter from his lady
love as Josh came to Phillip's side and he informed her, "Youth is
wasted—period."

"Bel, it's me. Now keep it down," O'Roarke warned as she
watched the young couple swaying in each other's arms. The girl
did look crocked, but Denny just seemed off balance. "Den, how
many has she had?"

"Just a couple beers—well, five. She's just not used to it, see?"

"No—but I'm gettin' there!" Bel gave a whoop that turned into
a hiccup as she broke away from Moskowitz, yanked something
from her jacket, and waved it high above her head. "An' after I get
there—I'm goin' to *Italy!*"

"If you don't go to jail first," Denny scolded. "Now cool it or
we'll have the cops up here." He plucked the long white envelope
she was waving from her grasp and held it up toward the window.
"She got this tonight. It was sent care of the college. She didn't even
open it till after rehearsal."

He looked over at Belinda expecting her to pick up the story, but
the girl was lost in her own private bacchanalia now, spinning round
and round with arms stretched wide, golden tresses bouncing off
her shoulders. It was a sight to behold, and O'Roarke couldn't help
observing, "Wish she'd move like that in the pastoral dance."

Phillip gave her a severe look, then turned his attention back to
Denny.

"So what's it say?"

"It's from Tessa—from her lawyers, I mean." Moskowitz looked
at the envelope and shook his head in wonder. "Says Belinda's the
what's-it, the chief beneficiary of her estate."

"Well, I'll be—ow!" Jerking back in surprise, Josh banged her
head against the raised sill as Gerrard sucked in his breath and
finished for her. "A son of a bitch. That was fast . . . Does it ment on
the size of the inheritance, Den?"

"Sort of. I'm not good with legal lingo. But it looks like she'll get
about—"

"Fifty thousand cool ones!" Belinda halted her ode to joy long enough to raise both fists above her head and shout, "Thank you, Tess!"

Then the gods of malt and hops pulled the plug and she went down with alarming speed, her head making a nasty crunching noise as it struck the gravel.

24

"Excuse me. Are you the parents?" a voice as starchy as the white uniformed figure it came from asked the two people slouched against each other on an orange vinyl couch in the hospital waiting room.

Rubbing sleep and clotted mascara from her eyes, Jocelyn jerked up and said, "Uh, no, just friends. But we called her folks. They should be here any second . . . How is she?"

After taking in their disheveled appearance with distaste, the Nurse Ratchet–clone finally allowed, "Oh, she'll be all right. She got a cut on the back of her head but it only took four stitches. There doesn't appear to be any sign of concussion so far."

"No, it's not likely she'd have concussion," Phillip put in, squinting his sore eyes against the harsh fluorescent lights. "She wasn't knocked-out. She, uh, passed out."

"So I gather," the nurse sniffed from atop her high horse. "I hope you weren't the ones who supplied the inebriates. She *is* underage."

"Ever hear of false I.D., lady?" Josh asked with heavy sarcasm, but Gerrard stopped her with a sharp look.

"No, we didn't. I think she'd been partying with friends before she came by the hotel." Thinking it best to keep Denny out of the picture, Phillip and Jocelyn had persuaded him, despite his vehement protests, to make himself scarce. Nursie, however, was still looking skeptical, so he turned up the professional charm. "But I certainly understand your asking. In a college town, you must get a dozen accidents like this a week. Some much more serious than this. I see a lot of it in my line of work, too. And it's a damn *shame*, isn't it?"

A hot gleam came into those cold R.N. eyes as she asked, "By any chance, are you a policeman?"

"Yes'm. Phillip Gerrard, N.Y.P.D.," he said as he drew his badge out of his jeans pocket and flipped it open in one smooth move that he had perfected years ago.

"Oh, my. And a lieutenant, too!" Two faint dots of color rose on her starchy cheeks. O'Roarke nodded and told herself, A cop groupie. Born and bred. She had met dozens over the years and could spot one at thirty paces. All Phillip had to do now was show her his gun—had he been carrying it—and this Ice Queen would melt all over him like a popsicle in August. As it was, she was thawing fast. "Do you know, my father was a policeman."

Bingo! Thank you, Dr. Freud. Josh didn't say it, but Gerrard knew she was thinking it and pointedly ignored her smirking look. "Really? Where did he work?"

"Gee, I think I'll get some fresh air," O'Roarke announced as she dragged her numbed behind off the couch, leaving the acolyte to worship at the Temple of Phil. But instead of heading for the exit, she veered toward the swinging doors that led to the Emergency Room. She had been here years before when she had caught a baseball with her lower lip instead of her catcher's mitt, and nothing much had changed. It was a long room packed with beds cordoned off by immaculate white curtains. Apparently it was a slow night so all she had to do was follow the sound of sniffling. Pulling aside a curtain she found Belinda, looking weepy but impossibly pretty for someone who had just taken four stitches, sitting up in bed with a silver-haired old gent holding her hand and clucking soothingly.

"Don't fret, my dear, don't fret. You'll have one hell of a headache tomorrow, yes. But the show *will* go on and you'll go on with it."

"You really think—? Oh, Jocelyn!" Her appearance brought a

fresh onslaught of tears from Belinda. "I'm so embarrassed. You must hate me."

"No, sweetie, not at all." Smiling at the old man, she added, "Doctor Morgan can tell you I pulled bigger boners than this in my time. Right, Doc?"

"Is that Joshie O'Roarke? My, my, despite Calvin's dire predictions, you're alive and well and not behind bars! Good to see you, dear." He came over to give her a peck on the cheek, then beamed back at Belinda. "And she's absolutely right, Bellie—she *did* pull bigger boners. Much bigger."

He knew whereof he spoke since it was Morgan who had stitched up her inner lip after the ill-fated ball game; it was he who had given her a medicated hand cream to clear up the rash she had gotten from dumping all that detergent in the reflecting pool. And it was he who had given her the news about the rabbit dying. All this he had done with solicitude and without censure.

"Ah, Doc, in thy orisons be all my sins remembered—but let's not go into details, okay?"

"Never. All your secrets are safe with me."

"What are you doing here at this ungodly hour anyway?" Josh asked, seeing the dark circles under his eyes.

"Well, babies get born at ungodly hours. Almost invariably." He stuck out a liver-spotted but rock-steady hand. "Congratulate me, Joey. I've just delivered my one-hundreth set of twins."

"Are you kidding? That's wonderful, Doc! If it weren't such an ungodly hour, I'd buy you a drink." Wanting to include Belinda if only to distract her from her guilt-ridden funk, she asked, "Did you deliver Bel, too?"

"No, Josh, I wasn't born here," Bel said when Morgan failed to answer. "But he's taken care of me ever since. And I was real lucky he was here tonight." She gave him a watery smile. "He gives great hypo."

Patting the girl's shoulder, Morgan murmured modestly, "Well, I try. And you were never a baby about getting injections." Pointedly addressing the ceiling, he added, "Unlike some patients I can recall." Belinda had no trouble following his drift, having seen Jocelyn suppress a shudder at the mere word *hypo*.

Catching their pitying glances, O'Roarke snapped, "I can't help it! I *hate* needles, okay? It's very wussy, I know, but I must've been a pincushion in a previous existence."

"God, that's so—lame." Belinda shook her head sadly and raised the bed sheet to hide a grin. In O'Roarke's experience, there was nothing like the abject humiliation of an adult to raise the dampened spirits of Youth, and Bel, all guilt and gloom a minute ago, was no exception to the rule.

But her fun was short-lived.

They heard a commotion in the waiting room, then the swinging door made a whooshing noise accompanied by the patter of many feet. A second later the curtains were yanked wide and Belinda was confronted by two distraught faces; one, Barnes *père*, a bright red, and one, Barnes *mère*, a sickly gray.

Having obviously steamrolled his way past Nurse Ratchet, who hung on Phillip's arm making shushing sounds in the background, the incarnadine Hank demanded of everyone and no one, "Just what the hell happened?!"

"Now, honey, don't yell," Miriam said. "She's upset enough."

"Mom, Dad, really, I'm fin—"

"She's upset? *She's* upset! What about us? Getting a call like that in the middle of the night. Jesus Christ!"

Seeing that Belinda was none the worse for wear, Gerrard considered saying as much, but knew it would be folly. Hank Barnes was one of those fathers who, when given a bad fright, alchemized that awful fear into a more comfortable emotion—anger. Having grown up with a dad who had the same M.O., Phillip knew that Hank's fury wouldn't abate until his panic did.

From her end of the tiny cubicle, Jocelyn watched Miriam wedge herself between Hank and Belinda as she simultaneously ascertained her daughter's condition while attempting to soothe her husband's wrath. It was a classic demonstration of one of the cardinal rules of matrimony: Only one partner can go crazy at a time. And though Miriam was as shaken as her husband, it was clearly *his* turn.

"Hank, Hank, she's all *right*," Miriam insisted. "Now let's just get her things and get her *home*. Okay?"

"It's *not* okay, Mir. Somebody's been damned irresponsible! She's a minor for chrissake." Phillip prayed that Josh wouldn't make another crack about fake I.D. in a college town and, for once, his prayers were heard. "What was she doing in a hotel parking lot at that hour?" Barnes glared accusingly at one and all while Belinda begged O'Roarke and Gerrard to keep mum with big eyes.

Swinging her legs off the bed, she tugged her father's arm. "Daddy, please. Don't make a case, huh? A bunch of us got together after rehearsal and had a few beers—which, I admit, was dumb of me 'cause I hadn't had much to eat. Then somebody said 'Let's have a scavenger hunt.'" Belinda paused for breath and a fresh load of horse manure. "Only it wasn't a regular scavenger hunt—it was a, uh, Shakespearean one, see? Instead of finding silly stuff, we had to find a . . . a scene from one of the plays. And I got the balcony scene from *Romeo and Juliet.* Only I had to be Romeo, a' course." Here she paused again, this time to bat her lashes at Phillip with maidenly modesty. "So I picked poor Mr. Gerrard and got him up. But he was real sweet about playing along. Then I guess I got carried away and just—passed out."

Thunderstruck, Phillip gaped at the girl, then looked over at Josh, who was no help at all; she was gaping, too, but with deep admiration, he could see, for Belinda's amazing improv skills. Having no idea why she was so keen to keep the news of her windfall from Hank and Miriam, he had no choice but to join the Liars' Club.

"Well, sure I played along. It seemed harmless enough. Lord knows I pulled worse pranks in my college days." He tagged on a hearty chuckle at the end for good measure, figuring O'Roarke would probably critique his performance later.

"So what were *you* doing there?" Barnes, still huffy, swung round on Jocelyn. "Playing the *Nurse?*"

"No, Hank, I was holding book," she said mildly but, having had her fill of the outraged papa act, added, "not that it's any of your damn business."

"Oh, cute, very cute," Hank bellowed as he went from pink to purple. "What do you career bitches know about having kids? Fuck all, that's what! So don't you tell me what's my business and what isn't or I'll—"

"Henry, you're being an ass now," Morgan said as he blocked

Barnes' threatening advance toward Jocelyn. "I know you're upset, but just take your girl and get out of here. Or you'll do her more injury than that little cut on her head will. *Comprendez?*"

The stern voice of the Family Physician prevailed where all else had failed. Hank stepped back like a dog whose nose had just been rapped with a rolled newspaper and Miriam seized the moment to gather up Belinda's things. Herding her daughter and husband toward the swinging doors, she paused long enough to look over at the old man and whisper, "Thank you, Gideon." Then she made little apologetic head bobs all round and was gone.

The R.N.-cum-Cop-Groupie tore herself reluctantly from Phillip's side and followed them, saying, "You'll have to sign a release form, folks," leaving Phillip, Josh, and the good doctor to bask in the afterglow of domestic angst. Doc Morgan pinched the bridge of his nose and asked, "Coffee, anyone?"

"No thanks, I've had plenty." Gerrard sighed.

"A little brandy, then? I keep a flask in my office for . . . just such occasions."

"Now *that's* what I call a doctor," Josh said to Phillip, nodding at Morgan as he led them down a long corridor to an office nearly as small as the cubicle they had just vacated.

Unscrewing the flask, Gideon looked round and said, "I'm afraid I don't have glasses—but these should do." He picked up three specimen cups and smiled gleefully. "Don't worry. They've never been used."

They all clicked plastic and took a slug. Morgan smacked his lips appreciatively as he cocked an eye at Jocelyn. "Don't think too badly of Hank. He's a hyperprotective parent. Miriam, too. It's common with an only child."

"Oh, I don't," she reassured him. "But I thought his choice of words was interesting. 'You career bitches'—plural. I got the feeling he wasn't just mad at me. So who's the other 'career bitch' he had in mind?"

"If you mean Tessa, I don't see why he'd be mad at her," Gideon said carefully, topping off his specimen cup. "Henry always seemed very fond of her—almost adoring. You think it might have some bearing on her death?"

Phillip and Jocelyn held an eye conference over the doctor's head;

by various lifts of the brow, nods of the head, and esoteric hand gestures, they jointly determined that the issue of Belinda's abortion should not be raised as it might compromise Gideon's professional code but that her recent inheritance was fair game.

So they told him.

"Chief beneficiary? Bless me! That's a ripper."

"You know the family. Why do you think Bel wants it kept secret?" Phillip asked.

"Oh, it could be for a dozen different reasons and not one of them would have any bearing on Ms Grant's demise," he said, waving a hand airily. "Belinda's always been a rather secretive child. My guess is she has some sort of hidden agenda."

"So what's on that agenda?" Josh asked.

"I'm not sure. But I know what it'd be if I were in her shoes." O'Roarke and Gerrard pressed him with questioning eyes and he added without prompting, "Just to get away. To get out. My God, tonight was just a sample. Just think of it—that constant battering ram of love, concern, and worry. And nothing like other siblings to deflect it . . . Wouldn't it make you want to head for the hills?"

Jocelyn nodded her agreement but confessed, "I can't imagine it, really. There's four of us in my family and we were always vying like performing seals for the best sardine. So it's beyond my ken."

"Not mine," Phillip interjected. "I have sisters but I was the only son."

"Spelled *s-u-n*, right?" O'Roarke asked flippantly, having witnessed the endless parade of hand-knit sweaters, homemade bundt cakes, and sheepskin slippers that appeared, without fail, at his door on Christmases and birthdays.

But Gerrard was too preoccupied to rise to the bait; instead he asked, "What did you think of Belinda's ad-libbing in there?"

"The Shakespearean scavenger hunt bit? I thought it was a stroke of genius." Jocelyn spoke with the appreciative air of an experienced bullshitter. "It was just silly enough to be perfectly plausible—the kind of nonsense drama-ramas get up to after a few drinks."

"Like putting detergent in the reflecting pool," the doctor offered with a sly smile.

"Exactly." Josh grinned back. "Or spray painting the side of the theatre building. Now Bel's pseudo-prank was much milder, but she hit just the right note. That's the hallmark of good fibbing. Gotta admit, I didn't think she had it in her."

"Still, I don't quite see the point of it," Gideon said, dropping his specimen cup into a wastebasket. "She'll have to tell her parents about the inheritance sooner or later."

. "Maybe she just felt the timing was wrong. That it'd be too much of a double whammy for them right now," Jocelyn suggested.

"Or maybe there's a reason why she wants it to be later, not sooner," Gerrard said. "Though she was certainly keen enough to tell us."

"She wasn't keen—she was in her cups," O'Roarke replied, sensing that something was nagging at Phillip. But Doc Morgan was fading fast and she didn't want to prolong the discussion. "Can we give you a lift home, Doc?"

"Oh, there's no sense in that. I've got a patient coming in at eight for tests. So I'll just camp out here. I've got a cot in the back room." As he straightened up the office, the old gentleman clucked his tongue and spoke more to himself than his guests. "Poor woman's been trying to conceive for two years with no luck. We've already tested the husband and there's nothing wrong with his sperm count. So now it's her turn. And I expect she'll require some major hand-holding."

"Well, she couldn't wish for a better hand to hold," Josh said with a yawn as she patted Gideon's back, adding sleepily, "and if the tests don't show anything wrong, tell her to go on vacation—to Italy, maybe. That seemed to do the trick for Miriam."

"Hmm—what?" Morgan blinked uncomprehendingly for a moment, then nodded. "Oh, yes, yes, I see what you mean. Well, it couldn't hurt, could it?"

After bidding the doctor good night, even though it was nearly morning, Josh stuck her head into the waiting room, then whispered to Phillip, "Coast's clear. Your groupie's gone—probably giving some poor sod an early-morning enema."

"Oh, she isn't *that* bad," he insisted, but O'Roarke had to run to keep up with him as he scooted for the exit and freedom.

"Neither is the common cold. Just tough to get rid of. Tell me, did she ask for an autograph—or a lock of your hair?"

"Stuff it—damn, it's chilly!" Phillip rubbed his hands together, surprised to see his breath misting in the parking lot air. "Isn't it supposed to be *spring?*"

"Yes, but this is upstate New York, where spring is more often a concept than a reality. I can't tell you how many Easter Sundays—when I was a kid—I had to put on snow boots over my new Mary Janes to go to Mass. Then I'd bitch and snivel all the way to church."

"Ah, well, that explains it," Gerrard said darkly as he got into Josh's rental.

After turning the ignition and turning on the heat she demanded, "Explains what?"

"Many, many things." Giddy with fatigue, he waved an all-encompassing hand. "Your profound agnosticism, for one. A just and merciful God surely would not snow on a little girl's fashion parade, right? I'd say it'd also account for your—how should I put it?—your ingrained contrariness and distrust. See, I read a book once where the author maintained that our personalities are really shaped by the climate we grew up in . . . And you, my pet, grew up in a *miserable* climate."

"So now is the winter of my discontent made glorious summer by this son of a bitch," Jocelyn said as she swung out of the parking lot at a fast clip. "I'd make you hitch back to the hotel if I didn't know you were just trying to get my goat to distract me . . . You're bothered about Belinda, aren't you?"

"Yeah, a bit," he admitted, too pooped to prevaricate. "Look, here's a girl who's supposedly only a so-so actor, right? But she put on one hell of a show in the E.R. tonight, didn't she? I saw how surprised you were."

"Sure I was. She lied like a bandit. But, Phillip, good acting isn't the same thing as good lying. Some fine actors are rotten liars." She made a slicing motion with one hand to cut off his coming objection. "Okay, okay, so I happen to be the exception that proves the rule. Still, acting is all about revealing. Lying is about concealing. And Belinda is obviously much better at the latter, that's all."

"Fine, I get the distinction. But I can't help wondering if, maybe, she was having a two-show night."

Meeting his eyes in the rearview mirror, Jocelyn bit her lip and said, "You think the first performance was in the hotel parking lot?"

"Could be. Why was she so hot to give you the news?"

"Offhand I'd say she's transferred her feelings for Tessa to me."

"Yeah, that was my first assumption, too. But now I'm not so sure."

"Hell, she was crocked, Phil. That could be reason enough."

"But Denny said they'd only had a few beers. And he was sober enough. Maybe she knew exactly what she was doing."

"All right, maybe she did! But what's so sinister about that?"

"Nothing—unless she wanted to make a big show of her surprise about the inheritance."

"Why would she want to—?" O'Roarke stopped herself as her brain leapt onto Phillip's track. "Unless she already knew about it and didn't want anyone to guess she did. Is that what you're thinking?"

"Yup. How do you feel about that?"

"Not so hot." Jocelyn pulled up to the curb in front of the hotel. "But I think I'm going to feel even worse in a minute."

"Why's that?" Following her gaze, Phillip looked up at the hotel veranda just as an unshaven, grim-faced Calvin Kowaleski came down the steps.

"That's why."

25

"Okay, lemme get this straight. The Barnes kid shows up outside around two A.M., right? She passes out in the parking lot and you drive her to the hospital, arriving there by two-thirty-five." Calvin stopped scribbling long enough to wet his pencil on the tip of his tongue just as Jocelyn was about to bite into an English muffin.

Suddenly devoid of appetite, she dropped the muffin and nodded. "That's right. And we were there just over two hours."

Standing at the foot of his unmade bed, Phillip gazed at the spray-painted logo above the headboard, which read: POWER TO THE PEOPLE—DOWN WITH PIGS, and asked, "When did you get the call from the front desk, Cal?"

Flipping back a page, Kowaleski scowled at the notepad, trying to decipher his own writing. "Um, they got a complaint from the room next door a little before four-forty. But the night clerk knew you weren't here. So he came up with the passkey and found . . . this." Cal waved a beefy hand at the chaotic jumble all around them: overturned chairs, clothes ripped from drawers strewn everywhere, spilled ashtrays, and all of it topped with a light snow of shredded paper. It looked like the aftermath of a demented ticker-tape parade. "Called me at four-fifty. I got here just ahead of you two. Had a little trouble getting the car started," he added somewhat sheepishly, then shifted to a bearish growl. "Goddamn kids! Their folks slave to send 'em to a good college. Then they spend their time pulling crap like this. Fucking ingrates, they oughta be shot!"

O'Roarke's second attempt to make lip contact with the muffin failed as she gaped at the sheriff, then swallowed hard and tried to speak in a level voice. "You mean you think this is just a—a prank?!"

"Damn straight. And I know just the punk who'd pull it, too." Sensing which way Kowaleski's wind was blowing, Josh and Phillip locked eyes and winced as one. "Belinda's little lover boy didn't go to the hospital with her, did he?"

"No, but that was our idea, not his," Gerrard interjected. "And he got in his car and left before we did."

"Phil, come on! Wake up and smell the java. He coulda just taken a spin around the block and come right back. The kid works here, you know. Probably knows a dozen ways to get in without being seen." Calvin favored them with a pitying smile as he pointed to the spray-painted wall. "This's got Moskowitz written all over it."

Too exhausted to come up with something suitably scathing, Jocelyn took an angry bite of her muffin and mumbled, "Aw . . . your mother wears army boots."

"Wha'did you say?" Calvin glowered at her. "Hey, O'Roarke, you don't have to be friggin' Kojak to see—"

"See *what*? Look, spray-painting a Pro-Choice logo on the drama building may be an act of vandalism, but it's also a political statement. You may not like it but it comes under the time-honored tradition of student protest."

"Yeah, well, you'd know *all* about that, huh?" he said dismissively.

"I know it's not the same as *this*," she shot back, nodding at the surrounding wreckage. "It's just not Denny's style. And he's not the only person around who knows how to point a nozzle, for chrissake!"

"Aw right, aw right! So maybe, just maybe, he ain't the perp. Could be one of his buddies."

"You know, Cal, I'm not so sure about that." Gerrard clapped a chummy hand on his fellow officer's shoulder, then asked diffidently, "Do you think we could be looking at a copycat crime here?"

"Huh? Like somebody trying to make it look like a college prank?"

"Exactly! If this was the work of some punk kid, just done for spite—don't you think it'd be worse than it is?"

"Worse? How? It looks pretty bad to me."

"Nah, not really. This is just—messy. A hard-core vandal would've really ripped up the place. Broken some mirrors, pissed on the bed sheets. That kind of shit."

"Uh, Phil, no offense, but I'm just talking about college kids and you're thinking of city punks. And we both know they're *real* animals."

"Good point, good point, Cal," Gerrard said admiringly as Josh tossed aside her muffin for the last time. She knew Phillip was only playing up the cops-in-arms bit to soothe Cal's ego, but the performance was sufficiently convincing to turn her stomach. He walked over to the dresser and shook his head bemusedly as he picked up the bottle of scotch. "Only thing is, this bottle hasn't been touched since we left, see? Now we both *know* if some young turk had tossed this room, it'd be empty—or gone."

For a two-fisted drinker like Kowaleski, this was one-hundred-proof positive. Looking up at Phillip with puppy dog awe, he sighed, "I tip my hat, Lieutenant. No question, that'd be one dead soldier. So wha'd ya think? Maybe I should go question the people next door and the staff, huh?"

"Yeah, I think so. That'd be good, Cal."

Heaving himself off the bed, the sheriff grabbed Gerrard's hand and pumped it. "It's an honor working with you, fella. What's say we meet for lunch and I'll give you the lowdown. Okay?"

"Sure thing. And, hey—I appreciate you taking me into your confidence."

"Pleasure's mine."

For a second there O'Roarke thought Calvin might buss Phillip on both cheeks in the French military fashion, but he contented himself with the old one-two boxing feint instead. As his footsteps faded down the corridor, she hauled herself up to give Phillip a lethargic standing ovation.

"John Simon called it gut-wrenchingly real. Frank Rich writes

'Phillip Gerrard is the new George C. Scott.' Clive Barnes says 'Is it over yet?' . . . Geez, I think you just lost your amateur standing, fella."

"Jocelyn, you can't expect a man like that to function at top capacity—whatever that may be—without encouragement. Just remember what the good sisters used to tell you—'You can catch more flies with a teaspoon of honey than with a barrel of vinegar.' "

"Remember what I used to tell them? 'Who wants to catch *flies?* "

"Right—then they put you in detention. Point is, like it or not, we need Cal's help. I can't do the legwork and neither can you. So let him. Who knows? He might turn up something."

"Your faith is touching. Color me touched."

"God, if cynicism were an Olympic event, you could win the gold, Josh."

"Oh-ho, *me?!* I think you just earned a silver, friend. There was your thickheaded buddy sitting knee-deep in the *Obvious* and you never said *boo.*" Before Gerrard could answer, Jocelyn opened her left palm, which held a scrap of paper, one piece of the rough-hewn confetti scattered across the floor. Phillip didn't even need to look at the few Italian phrases scrawled in reverse on it. They had both realized, as soon as they had stepped into the room, where those shredded scraps had come from: Tessa's diary. "Calvin's probably the *only* person in Corinth who didn't know the journal was here."

"Yes—thanks to you. Your little scheme kind of backfired there, Josh."

"Oh, great! Blame it all on me . . . Where did you leave the diary?"

Grimacing, Gerrard scratched the back of his head then mumbled, "On the, uh . . . nightstand."

"Ah, I see. Using the ol' hide-in-plain-sight ploy, were you?" she sniped smugly.

"Hey, gimme a break! I was trying to patch Bel up. You could've tucked it away when you came back up here to call the hospital."

Realizing that they were both loopy with fatigue and one step away from a Kramdenian free-for-all, O'Roarke did a rare thing: she apologized. "You're right. We both screwed up, okay? . . . Even if we had thought to hide it, I'm sure the perp would've dug it up any—"

"That's right! But they didn't have to because it was right out in the open." Phillip flopped down on the bed and smacked himself between the eyes. "Man, either I'm losing it or I've been hanging around Kowaleski too long. Talk about missing the obvious."

For a moment, Jocelyn followed his gaze as it drifted around the room, then snapped her fingers. "Of course! Whoever it was could've just waltzed in, picked up the journal, and waltzed out without disturbing a thing. Heck, you might not have noticed it was gone for hours. So why'd they bother to do all this?"

"Judging from that"—Phillip pointed to the spray-painted scrawl over the headboard—"I'd say it was a deliberate attempt to implicate Denny. A pretty lame attempt at that. I mean, 'Power to the People'? It's so Sixties."

"I dunno. Somehow I don't think it was done just for show." Staring at the floor, Josh trudged around the room like a zombie. "Somebody's trying to mislead us, all right. But I get the feeling it's somebody who's genuinely angry—or very frightened. Look at this." She bent down to scoop up more of the shredded paper. "Why not just grab the diary and *go*? Why take the time to do this? That was risky."

"Because the perp didn't want it to look like he was after the diary. That's why," Phillip supplied as he flipped wearily onto his stomach. "Now I don't mean to be rude but could you maybe, um—go home? I'm fading fast here."

"Yeah, me too. I'll call you before I leave for the theatre."

Eyes already shut, Gerrard nodded gratefully. He could hear Josh rustling through the paper scraps on her way to the door, then the sound of the doorknob turning. Then something in his mind turned with it and he bolted up in bed.

"Wait!"

"What?"

"You're right, Josh. It makes no sense! Why would somebody break into the guest house three times to get their hands on the damn book and then tear it up without even reading it?!"

In a flash she was beside him, bobbing her head up and down excitedly as a new notion took shape.

"Because—because maybe they already *had* read it, or—"

"Or they knew it existed and just wanted to make sure no one else read it. Or . . ."

The same thought struck them at the same time but, Jocelyn formed the words first. "Or maybe they were after something besides the diary all along. Something like . . . the will?"

Phillip nodded and amended, "The *old* will."

"Goddamn cobwebs," she cursed, then sneezed.

Like all actors, O'Roarke had a personal ritual she followed religiously on the day of an opening. Hers involved sleeping late, making a mammoth breakfast, then working it off with a long swim followed by a light snack and maybe a catnap in her dressing room before getting into costume and makeup. Though she may have varied it slightly once or twice in the past, she had never before strayed so far from her routine as to incorporate spring cleaning, something she detested with all her being.

"Oh, Jocelyn, don't bother with that," Miriam Barnes said as she whisked by the den with yet another tray of hors d'oeuvres. "I'll dust in there later."

"No, no, Miriam, it's okay. You've got enough on your plate," she joked feebly, eyeing the tray of cheese puffs. "I'd feel like a louse if I didn't do my bit."

"I must say, you really are something. So down to earth." Miriam beamed adoringly at her. "Most actresses I've known would've spent the day in bed—especially after the night you had. I can't thank you enough for this . . . and for helping Bellie."

"Well, you had quite a night, too, so it's only fair." Though the perennially perky Mrs. Barnes looked better-rested than Jocelyn felt after a scant five hours' sack time. Roused from sleep by the first wave of Miriam's food parade, O'Roarke had been forced to play charwoman to mask her real purpose: searching for the old will. The fact that Phillip was to spend his day lunching with Calvin, then, as they had agreed, putting some long-distance pressure on Tessa's lawyers, did little to cheer her. In this man's world, the housework end of detecting always fell to the woman. Now if she could just get Miriam safely into the kitchen so she could get on with it. "Say, I think your puffs are, uh, curdling."

"Oh, gosh, you're right! I better get them in the fridge—but don't you work too hard now, hon."

"Don't worry about that."

Once Miriam was out of the way, Josh pulled the old rolltop away from the wall, examined its dusty back, and found nothing. Then, after pulling out all the drawers, again turning up squat, she tried to tilt it up in order to look at the bottom. But, being an antique made back when they really knew how to build 'em, it weighed about as much as a baby elephant.

"Want a hand with that?"

Nearly dropping the desk on her toe, Josh spun round to find Frankie standing in the doorway.

"Oh, hi! Yeah, sure. Just grab a couple of thick books and prop them under when I lift, okay?"

Without comment, Frankie did as she was bid, then watched Jocelyn get down on her knees and wipe the bottom with a dust rag with one hand (as the other surreptitiously felt along the surface to no avail).

"Mind if I ask just what the hell you're doing?"

"Can't you see? I'm dusting," O'Roarke grunted, then signaled for her friend to remove the props as she got to her feet.

"Like fun you are. I lived with you and people don't change *that* much."

"Okay. I was searching for buried treasure." Given Frankie's first-class shit detector, she figured a half-truth would serve better than a full fib. But to be on the safe side, she segued swiftly with: "What're you doing here? Don't tell me you've come to give Miriam a helping hand with the party?"

"Aw, shit! *She's* here?" Frankie's shoulders sagged as she dropped into a wingback chair. "That's the last thing I need."

Smelling trouble, O'Roarke asked, "What's the matter . . . Is it the kids?"

"No, they're fine—for now. Jennie's on a Girl Scout camp-out and Terry and Shane are visiting . . . my mom."

This meant something was really wrong since Frankie's relationship with her mother had always been about as cordial as Nancy Reagan's with Kitty Kelley. Then Jocelyn spotted the overnight bag lying in the doorway.

"And where's, uh, Mike?"

"If there's a god—in a three car pileup on Route Thirteen."

Then Frankie did something Jocelyn had only seen her do once before, when her father had died: she cried like a baby.

Positioning herself on the arm of the wingback, Josh rubbed her friend's back and, being a firm believer in the cleansing effects of a good weep, said nothing. She merely nudged the den door shut with one foot, since this was turning into a torrential weep and she didn't want Miriam to get wind of it, and carefully examined Frankie for signs of welts or bruises. There were none, and that was a small relief as it obviated the need to find an ax and hack off Michael's nether regions. Clearly Frankie's wounds were psychic, not physical, and she confirmed the fact when she finally caught breath enough to say, "The shit heel never came home last night! Never even called."

"Aw, honey, I'm sorry," Josh soothed. "Is this the first time he's done it?"

"Hell, no! He pulls this once or twice a year. Usually when he's in a show. But he's always called before with some lame-o excuse." Yanking a used Handi Wipe out of her bomber jacket, Frankie blew her nose soundly then wailed, "This time he didn't even bother to *lie!*"

"*Tch,* bad form that, very bad form . . . What did he say when he got back?"

"Nothing. Not a damn thing. Walked right by me and the kids having breakfast and went upstairs and conked out. He's still asleep."

"You mean he doesn't know you've left yet?!"

"Nope. And I didn't leave a note either," she said defiantly, but her bravado was brief. "I bet the dickhead won't even notice until my lawyer calls his."

"Frankie, don't you think you should talk to him before you do anyth—"

"No! No way. I'm not putting up with this crap anymore." Frankie jumped to her feet, nearly knocking Josh off the chair arm, and started pacing up and down the den. "Tessa was the last straw. It wasn't so much Mike having the hots for her—it was that he *admired* her so damn much. 'Tess is so accomplished, so talented, so . . . everything!' Then—did you know?—he brought the kids here once? *My* kids! So they could see for themselves what a friggin' paragon she was and what a slob their mother is. Christ, I coulda kill—" She caught herself, but not soon enough. White-faced, she whispered, "I—I didn't mean that, Joey."

"Really? Sounds like you did. Also sounds like you're angrier at her—even now—than you are at Mike. But he's still alive, so you can take it out on him."

"Jesus, that's a rotten thing to say!" Frankie looked at her as if she were a stranger. "I thought you'd be on my side."

"Damn it! Don't give me that crap, Frankie." Five hours' sleep had left O'Roarke even shorter than usual on patience and understanding. "This isn't about taking sides."

"The hell it isn't!" Frankie went off like a powder keg. "You've been in her corner all along. Rolled into town like some goddamn avenging angel. And I know why. It's 'cause you've changed, Jo. You've gotten just like her—talent is all, the work is everything— and screw other people's lives and other people's families . . . And you're afraid you're gonna end up like her, too."

Stung and stunned by the venom in Frankie's voice, Jocelyn backed off.

"Look, can we drop this? You had a bad night and so did I and—"

"Don't tell me! And you've got a show to do, right? Right, and that's what really matters to you. Not me and my crummy problems. And not that poor schnook Phil—who's fool enough to care about your selfish ass—he's only here to do your dirty work. We're all just jokes to you, huh?"

"No, I don't find you the least bit funny." Afraid of her own temper now, Jocelyn forced herself to speak softly. "Hysterical, yes —funny, no. And if I believed you really meant it, I'd snatch you bald-headed, sister . . . But I think you've got me confused with someone else. Someone you're so jealous, so envious of, that you don't even give a damn that she was murdered. Murdered, Frank! That outweighs marital discord by a *lot*. And it's made you so nuts, you don't have the sense to see that you could be—in a bad spot."

"Ha! You're not serious." What began as a sarcastic chuckle turned into a choking noise as O'Roarke's face told her friend just how serious she was. "That's crazy! Okay, okay, I was jealous, I was p.o.'d. I didn't *like* her. But, shit, I'm all mouth. You know that."

"Yes, I do. But Phillip's room was broken into last night and Tessa's diary was destroyed. You knew about the diary and where it was."

"Only because *you* told me. I didn't ask!"

"True. But you knew, see, so—"

"So don't tell anybody I knew."

"Uh, even if I was willing to do that— Wait! Don't blow a gasket. Did you tell anyone else about that conversation?"

"No, nobod— Oh crap, yes, I did. I told Will . . . But he wouldn't say anything."

"Frankie, Frankie, you can't count on that! And that's not the *point*." Nearly at the hair-tearing stage, Jocelyn grabbed the other woman's shoulders and shook them hard. "During a police inquiry, it's very stupid and dangerous to tell lies, even lies of omission. And it's lunacy to think anyone with an ounce of self-preservation will lie to cover your ass while theirs is hanging out there."

"Well, Will would." Frank spoke with supreme confidence, then eyed Josh warily. "What about you?"

"I wouldn't—I couldn't."

"Oh, man! It's nice to have *friends*," she spat back, trying to wrest herself from Josh's grip. But Josh wasn't giving.

"Because I think you're innocent, you asshole! Lying would only make things look worse."

"But I was home last night!"

"But Mike wasn't. And the kids go to bed early."

"You think I'd leave my kids alone?!"

"No! I'm just trying to show you what a D.A. could make of it . . . That and the fact that Coltrane's missing book turned up in your station wagon."

"What's the big deal about the dumb book?"

"Frankie, in all your woodland rambles with Will, didn't he ever talk about water hemlock?"

"Maybe. I'm not sure. But what's that got to do with—?"

Before O'Roarke could expand on the finer toxic points of water hemlock and Coltrane's book, there was a rap on the door, then the door swung open. Both women held their breath, expecting to see Miriam all agog.

"Hallo, ladies. Thought I might find you here, Frankie." Will Coltrane strolled into the room with an expansive smile. "Saw your car in the drive. I'm not interrupting any serious girl talk, am I?"

As Jocelyn nodded "yes," Frankie shook her head "no" and said, "Hi, Willie. What's doin'?"

"I've had a rather good morning, actually. Found one or two new specimens." Adroitly placing himself between the two women, he turned to Frankie. "Care to come take a look?"

Using their old roommates' code, Jocelyn pinched her nose to signal: "Lose this guy." Laying her middle finger against one nostril, Frankie signaled back: "Fuck off." Then she tucked her arm in his and brazened, "I'd love to see your specimens, Will. Tell you what. You show me yours—then I'll show you mine."

26

"So, Phil, how about another Slamburger?"

"No thanks, Cal. One's my limit."

Pushing aside the last of his Slamburger, a charred chiliburger topped with processed cheese and fried onions, Gerrard belched discreetly and made a mental note to pick up some Maalox. It would have consoled O'Roarke somewhat, had she but known, to learn that Phillip's day was going no better than hers. Kowaleski had elected to treat him to lunch at his favorite hangout, a dingy little dive called the Chanticleer. Eyeing the denizens seated at the long, smoky bar, Phillip wondered if the sheriff came here because he actually liked the noxiously greasy food or because it was an easy way to keep tabs on Corinth's undesirable element, as the Chanticleer appeared to be the watering hole for all "the usual suspects."

Or maybe he liked the service. One snap of his fingers brought the blowsy, redheaded waitress to his side.

"What can I get ya, Sheriff? We got that apple pie you like."

"Yeah, that sounds good, Dorrie. With a slab a' cheese on it and a cup a' coffee. Same for you, Phil?"

"No. Just some more iced tea, please." *And a stomach pump*, he would have added, but tact forbade it.

"Suit yourself." Dorrie gave Gerrard a pitying look, then winked at Cal as she sashayed off to the kitchen.

"So, anything interesting turn up at the hotel, Cal?"

"Not much. But I told George—he's the owner—that his security sucks. There's a back entrance that's supposed to be locked at night but it wasn't." Kowaleski shook his head in disgust, then brightened. "But we found a used cleaning smock in one of the linen closets."

"Okay, so the perp had easy access to the hotel itself. But how did he get in my room? They can only have so many passkeys around the place. Right?"

"Uh, George says twenty, but he's not exactly sure."

"Twenty?! Christ, why bother having doors at all! Who has them?"

"George, a' course, and the night manager. And all the cleaning staff—that's the trouble, see. They're supposed to turn 'em in when they go off duty. But they forget sometimes and just leave 'em in—"

"Let me guess. They leave them in the pocket of their smock."

" 'Fraid so. And all the smocks hang in the maintenance closet on the first floor."

"So someone just slipped into the closet and rifled the pockets till they found a key."

"Yeah, kinda looks that way," Calvin admitted. "I questioned the night staff. Turns out there was a hot poker game going on in the kitchen. I figure you coulda marched a twelve-piece band by 'em without anybody noticing. But we got one break! The perp left the passkey in the used smock. I'm having it dusted for prints right now." Kowaleski smiled proudly until Phillip burst his balloon.

"I don't think that'll be much help. A metal key won't hold prints."

"But—but what about the tag on it? That's plastic!"

"You might get a partial print from it. But right now that won't tell us anything. Unless it's somebody with priors, like Lyle Davie."

"Or Will Coltrane."

"Coltrane's got a record?!"

"Not really. But I've got his prints on file. Pulled him over for drunk driving once, about a month after he got here. Judge let him off with a slap on the wrist— Oh, geez, I forgot to tell you! I heard from England."

"Heard what?"

Phillip had to wait for an answer while Dorrie deposited the dessert and drinks on the table. Then Cal took a big bite of pie and savored it along with his recent discovery. "I faxed the college where he used to work. They said—lemme think how they put it—oh yeah. He wasn't fired, but he left 'under a cloud.' That's it." Taking a slurp of coffee, Kowaleski chuckled. "Those limeys talk so fuckin' quaint, huh?"

"Yeah, cute as the dickens. But did they say what *kind* of cloud? Are we talking about boffing an undergrad or misusing grant money or what?"

"Uh, now wait a sec . . . I think I got their fax on me, maybe."

Kowaleski made an elaborate show of patting his pockets while Phillip wondered if the guy was even dumber than he seemed or if he was just playing at it, having himself some fun at the city boy's expense. When Cal finally flipped out his notebook with the fax right on the front page, Gerrard suspected the latter and seethed inwardly as he snatched it away. After a quick read, he gave his companion a hard look.

"You should've shown me this sooner, Cal."

"Well, you know, it didn't come in till late yesterday. After the mess at the hotel, I kinda forgot about it." He shifted uneasily under Gerrard's gaze, then added defensively, "Besides, they're pretty damn vague there."

"Maybe you should keep a dictionary in your office, then. This part seems clear enough." He jabbed a finger at the last paragraph, which read: "Mr. Coltrane proffered his resignation after an unfortunate classroom incident; a student under his supervision inadvertently ingested a highly toxic plant substance and required hospitalization. Had he remained on the faculty, an investigation into Mr. Coltrane's possible negligence would have been mandatory."

Shoving the fax across the table, Phillip said acidly, "That's one damn big cloud, Calvin."

"Oh, sir, I shall be hated to report it./ The prince your son, with mere—um." The page, a freshman girl playing her first britches part, bit her lip as she groped for the rest of her line. Waiting for her cue to "swoon," O'Roarke held her breath until the page broke into a relieved smile and continued proudly, "With mere conceit and fear/ Of the queen's speed, is gone."

"How? gone?" Barnes' voice quavered as he drew back from the girl in dread. It was an effective move, though one he had never made in rehearsal, and Jocelyn suspected it had more to do with fear of going blank, since some actors regarded drying up as a contagious disease, than with inspired improvisation. Still, it worked for the scene—except that it left Hank positioned directly downstage of her, blocking her from the audience's view.

"Is dead."

Now her swoon cue was coming up and Barnes still hadn't budged. In rehearsal, she had always done an accordion faint, a straight crumple to the floor like a puppet with its strings suddenly cut. But now that wouldn't play.

"Apollo's angry, and the heavens themselves/ Do strike at my injustice."

Wishing she still had the pregnancy pad to cushion her, Josh did a little improvising of her own: clutching her breast, she let out a low moan, took a short step away from the throne she had been leaning on, and let herself fall, fully extended, stage right of Barnes.

It was a cheap save, but it worked. The audience gasped in surprise, as did Hank when he looked down and saw her sprawled at his feet, but he got out his next line. "How now there?"

"This news is mortal to the queen," Anita said, doing some fancy footwork of her own to get to O'Roarke's side. "Look down/ And see what death is doing."

Then the ladies-in-waiting gathered round, upstaging Barnes now, and helped Anita hustle their fallen queen off right. Once in the wings, Josh rubbed her bruised hip as she turned to Sanchez and the others. "Sorry about that, ladies. I had to cheat right of him."

"Shit, yes," Anita whispered angrily. "We couldn't play the swoon *behind* him! What was he thinking of?"

"His next line probably. Anyways, you adjusted well and the house bought it. Nice work, Nita."

"Aw, it was nothing. You're the one who saved it." Having studiously avoided Jocelyn since their last encounter, Sanchez gave her a bashful look. "Listen, I know I was a jerk the other day. I—I hope you're not still mad at me?"

" 'Course not—not after that save, sweets." Josh gave her elbow a squeeze and the girl's face flooded with relief.

"That's great! 'Cause something happened and it made me think about what you said and— Whoa! That's my cue!" Spinning away from O'Roarke, Anita staggered out of the wings, tearing at her bodice and wailing like a banshee.

"Woe the while!/ O, cut my lace, lest my heart, cracking it,/ Break too!"

Smiling with satisfaction as she watched Sanchez's Paulina rip into Hank's Leontes, Josh remarked to no one in particular, "No question—the kid's a trouper."

"Hey, Jocelyn, nice recovery," Mike Mauro offered as she came into the hallway. "You really aced that scene. Wanna go out back for a smoke?"

"No thanks," she said, brushing by him. "I have to help Belinda with her makeup."

"Sure, sure. But I just wanted to ask you." He placed himself between her and the stairs. "Do you know where Frankie is?"

"Nope. And even if I did, I don't know that I'd tell you."

"Oh. So you know—? Uh, you spoke to her today?"

"Yes, I did—you should try it sometime." She elbowed past him, but he bounded up the stairs to block her.

"Wait, wait! I can explain, Josh."

"Well, that's just peachy-fuckin'-keen, Mike. But tell it to your wife, not me. I'm working, damn it!"

"But she'll listen to you. I—I don't think she'd believe me."

"So who's fault is that?"

"Mine, all mine. I haven't always leveled with her and I should've." Mauro slumped down on the top step dejectedly. "And now I'm going to lose her."

If this was an act it was better than any performance she'd seen him give onstage. Haunted by Frankie's earlier remarks about her callousness, O'Roarke decided, performance or no, to lend an ear. Hiking up her train, she plopped down next to him and said, "Okay, level with me then . . . Were you having an affair with Tess?"

"No, I swear! I was bowled over by her at first. She—hell, she was one sexy lady. But we just flirted, you know. Then I got to know her better and I saw she was real . . . sad. And I felt kind of protective toward her. So when Frankie got jealous and started making cracks, I—I let her think the worst."

"That wasn't real smart." While restraining herself from further comment on the shortcomings of so-called male logic, she couldn't keep from asking, "What was Tess sad about?"

"I'm not sure. I just sensed she'd had some big regret in her life. For a while there, I thought it might have to do with Hank."

"Hank?! You think she was in love with *him?*"

"No, no. But I heard he'd been in love with her—and I'm pretty sure they had a little fling once. You know how you pick up signals between two people." He arced his fingers, making quotation signs in the air. "People with 'A Past.' Maybe seeing him with Miriam and Belinda made her feel she'd missed out on something. Who knows."

"So why didn't you tell Frankie any of this?"

" 'Cause I'm an asshole! And I'd been getting sort of jealous myself ever since Coltrane showed up and started drooling all over her." Mike rubbed his jaw and gave a mirthless chuckle. "Funny thing is—Tess really admired Frankie. Talked about a recital once where she heard her play a Mahler piece and she told me—what? Oh yeah, she said, 'Your wife's an artist. The real goods. When she's ready to get back to her music, don't stand in her way.' "

Smacking him smartly on the arm, Josh said, "And you never told her *that,* either? Why not? It would've made all the difference!"

"Because *that* made me jealous, too! I couldn't help it, Jocelyn. I know what I am. I'm a good teacher and a fair actor. But no artist. Tess made me think about that and what Frankie's given up and it made me feel . . . small."

"So you made her feel small to keep you company. Figures." She wasn't even angry now, just depressed as hell over the damage men and women did to one another in the close quarters called love. "Is that what last night was about, too?"

"No, it wasn't! I was, uh, with someone—but it was completely innocent."

"Fine. Run it by me," O'Roarke said with dry skepticism, "and we'll see if it flies."

From the house there was a burst of hearty applause signaling the end of Act One. Hank came into the hallway wiping sweat from his brow and Anita, pumped up with actor adrenaline, was right behind him. But when she spied Jocelyn and Michael on the stairs, she pumped down. Nodding in her direction, Mauro sighed, "I was with Anita."

"Uh-huh, I see . . . That flies about as well as the Hindenburg."

"But nothing happened—I swear! Anita will tell you so herself."

"Come on, Mike. She's your student. She'll say anything you want her to."

"But it's the *truth!* Damn, I can't believe this." In frustration, he pounded his knee with his fist. "The one time I do somebody a favor and it's going to cost me my marriage."

"If it was so damn innocent, why didn't you tell Frankie about it this morning, huh?"

"I was bushed and I didn't want to get into it in front of the kids. Then when I woke up, she was gone . . . Please, Jocelyn, just tell me where she is."

Before she could answer, her attention was drawn away by the sight of an unexpected visitor. Coming down the upstairs hallway, dressed in his best bib and tucker, was Gerrard, looking around anxiously.

"Phillip! What're you doing back here?" Leaving Mauro on the top step, she rose to intercept him.

"Looking for you, of course." Suddenly recalling all the theatrical taboos he had learned from O'Roarke, he stopped short. "God, I hope I haven't broken some cardinal rule. Is this bad luck—like seeing the bride before the ceremony or something?"

"No, no. It's just, um"—she drew close to him and lowered her voice—"if any of the cast ask you how it's going out front, for chrissake, lie your ass off if you have to and tell 'em it's bloody marvelous . . . How was I, by the way?"

"Bloody marvelous," he said with a wicked grin.

"'Atta boy. Keep up the good work," she chuckled, patting his shoulder. "Now, what's up?"

"I've been looking for Coltrane all afternoon and he's nowhere to be found. Miriam said she saw him leave the guest house with Frankie. I thought you might know where—"

"Frankie's with Will?" Mauro broke in, jumping to his feet. "And you can't find them?!"

"Well, they're not out front. And they're not at at his place or your place. I checked."

"Oh, great! That's just terrific."

"Psst! Jocelyn, I can't get my makeup right," Belinda called out desperately from the dressing room door. "You have to come do me!"

"Be right there." Turning back to Gerrard, she whispered, "Say anything. Just get him calmed down."

Nodding, Phillip whispered back, "See, it is bad luck to go backstage at intermission." Then he raised his voice cheerfully. "Hey, Mike, you were bloody marvelous out there."

Fleeing to the comparative calm of the dressing room, Jocelyn found Belinda sitting in front of the mirror staring helplessly at Tessa's makeup case opened in front of her. Seeing O'Roarke's reflection, she moaned, "I'm a wreck. I can't remember which blush to use or anything!"

"Amber Number Two." The girl's hands were shaking so badly, Josh took the mink brush from her. "Here. Let me . . . How's your head?"

"Head's not too bad. Stomach's rotten. Feels like midgets are playing kickball in there." Raising her face so Jocelyn could highlight her fine cheekbones, she asked, "How's Dad doing?"

"Bloody marvelous. He hasn't dried up once . . . Now lift your chin."

"That's good. I was worried about him . . . He was acting funny today."

"Well, he's probably just as nervous as you are."

"Nah, it's more than that. See, while Mom was busy getting stuff ready for the party, I told him the truth about last night. 'Cause I couldn't handle the guilt, you know? Then I showed him the letter from Tessa's lawyers. I thought it'd make him happy but he just got real quiet for a long time. Then he said not to tell Mom or anyone for a while."

"Did he say why?"

"Nope. Just got up and went for a drive. He didn't even come back for dinner . . . I hope he's not mad at me."

"Because of the inheritance? Why should he be?"

"No, not that—that just shocked him, I guess. But I get the feeling he knows about my, um—you know." Keeping one eye on the door, she added, "Maybe I should level with him. Dad's a pretty understanding guy deep down. But Mom would just freak."

"Like I said, sweets, it's your business. Now pooch your lips so I can do your mouth." Deftly applying burnt-umber lip liner, she cautioned, "Just give it some thought first."

"Tessa said I shouldn't tell them ever. She felt it'd be unfair to them, sort of. After you make a choice like that, she said, it's yours to live with. You shouldn't try to dump it on other people."

"Here, blot your lips," Jocelyn ordered, handing her a Kleenex. "Tess was made of stouter stuff than most of us, Belinda. And she could be a bit rigid in her standards . . . You do what's right for you."

"Belinda, you almost ready?" Anita stuck her head in the door. "They just called five minutes to places."

"Cripes, I'm not even dressed," she shrieked in fresh panic. "I'll never make it!"

"Yes you will," O'Roarke asserted, forcing her back in her seat. "There's a whole scene before your entrance and Autolycus is such a ham, he'll milk it for days. Now hold still while I powder you down. Where's Lyle? Oh, forget it. Nita, can you get her costume ready?"

"Sure thing. I think Lyle's in the shop getting wasted. He's always a wreck at openings. We'll do better without him." Sanchez sped to the clothes rack and started unhooking the back of Perdita's shepherdess dress with flying fingers.

Finished with her handiwork, Josh released Belinda to Anita's ministrations and went in search of the garlands and wreath that went with the costume.

"Why the hell he can't just use Velcro beats me," Anita grumbled as she struggled to do up the back row of tiny hooks while Jocelyn laced up the bodice. Their task was made no easier by Bel's sudden attack of Saint Vitus' Dance.

"Honey, you gotta hold *still* if you don't want your tits to fall out on your first entrance," O'Roarke threatened.

Sanchez gave a bawdy whoop. "Yeah, then Denny'll go up higher than a kite and you'll have to do the scene as a monologue!"

"Ow! You hooked my skin," Belinda squealed, jumping away from Anita and knocking Jocelyn back against the dressing table. Her hip, the one already bruised from the big swoon, made sharp contact with the makeup case, which went crashing to the floor.

"Oh, shit! Now look what I've done," Bel wailed.

"Don't worry, don't worry. I'll clean it up." O'Roarke positioned the wreath on Belinda's head and draped the garlands around her shoulders before giving her a gentle shove toward Anita. "You're all set."

"And you look totally awesome, babe," Sanchez said as she ushered her toward the door. "Man, there'll be some hard-ons in the ol' house tonight!"

The maidenly Perdita let out something between a gasp and a guffaw. "Nita, quit it! You are *too* rude and *too* raw, girl."

They giggled their way into the hall, leaving Jocelyn alone at last with a hell of a cosmetic mess at her feet. Bending down, she gingerly uprighted Tessa's tackle box to assess the damage. Luckily, she had replaced the lid on the box of face powder so that hadn't spilled. But brushes, blushes, shade sticks, and eyeshadow compacts were strewn everywhere. And the magnifying mirror adhesived to the inside roof of the case had cracked. Placing the case back on the table, she pried the broken glass away from the metal. Behind it was a square, yellowed envelope. When she saw it, something grabbed at her entrails.

Kicking aside the debris on the floor, she pulled up a chair and sat down to peel out the envelope. Then she leaned down to retrieve a nail file, which she slid carefully under the sealed flap. Now her hands were shaking as badly as Belinda's had earlier as she drew out one thick piece of vellum.

She saw at once that it was some sort of official document. But it was in Italian. Nevertheless, it contained several names that would be the same in any language.

"Jesus, Mary, and Joseph—*this* is what they were after," O'Roarke said aloud.

Then she ran to find Phillip.

27

"Gawd! Will somebody *puh-leese* light me!"

Standing in the foyer of the guest house in his opening night getup, black leather pants and an olive silk calypso shirt, Lyle Davie brandished a carved ivory cigarette holder in one hand and a bottle of Cutty Sark in the other. "Let's all get lit!"

Used to Davie's flashy party entrances, most of the cast and crew merely looked up for an instant, then carried on with their assorted merrymaking. Only Denny Moskowitz paid heed, flicking a lighter in front of the costumer's flushed face.

"Just don't breathe on it, Lyle, or you'll set the house on fire."

After sucking hard on the ivory holder to get the cigarette going, Davie coughed, blowing smoke in the boy's face. "What *are* you insinuating, Dennis, old dear?"

"You've had a few already, huh, Lyle?" Moskowitz sniffed the air pointedly.

"Just a stray nip here and there to calm my nerves," Davie said loftily, shoving the bottle at him. "Now why don't you take that over to yon drinks table and make me a stiff one."

"Sure, in a sec." A good head taller than the older man, Denny shoved the bottle back forcefully, propelling Davie into the den. "After we talk."

Rubbing his arm, Lyle laughed nervously, "Ooh—rough trade! I didn't know you went in for that sort of—"

"Cut the crap," he ordered, swinging the door shut. "I'm not in the mood for your dumb fag jokes, okay?"

"Okay, fine," Davie said, edging away from the boy. "What is this? Manhandle Lyle Week or somethin'? Have you been talkin' to Jocelyn?"

"No, I've been talking to Anita. She says you told her Belinda had an abortion. That so?"

"Aw, shucks, you can't count on women to get these things right. They always exaggerate." Then Moskowitz grabbed at the sleeve of Lyle's shirt, making him cry, "Please—watch the fabric! You'll rip it."

Having had a few snorts himself, Denny growled, "I'll rip you a new asshole if you don't tell me what you said!"

"Nothing—well, not much. Just that I thought, only *thought*, that maybe B'linda had gotten herself in a speck of trouble. But that was in strictest confidence. Anita should know better than—"

"No, *you're* the one who should know better . . . You got a big fuckin' mouth, Lyle. You know that?"

"Yes, yes, I do. It's a big problem." Unswiveling the top of the Cutty Sark, Davie took a swig, then gulped. "I swan, I think it's a gene I got handed down from my Grandma Culverton. That woman never could keep a—"

"Screw your grandma and screw you, too." Yanking the bottle away, Denny lowered his face to Lyle's. "What I want to know is —did you say anything to Professor Barnes?"

"No, no! I wouldn't ever do somethi—"

He was interrupted by a soft rap on the door. Then Miriam popped her head in the room. "Oh, it's you two. I didn't know you were here, Lyle . . . Lovely blouse—uh, shirt."

"Thanks, darlin'. Made it myself." Grateful for the reprieve, he scuttled toward Miriam and gave her a peck on the cheek before adding wryly, "Run one up for you if you like."

"Um, that's a sweet offer. But I really don't think it's *me* . . . Den, have you seen Professor Curtis anywhere?"

"Not yet, Mrs. Barnes. He's probably still at the alumni reception."

"No, he's not. I stopped by on my way out. And, lawdy Miz Mawdy, what a bore it was," Davie drawled, having recovered his usual aplomb now that he was out of harm's way. "Poor ol' Ry was doin' his chairman thang. Getting his hand pumped like he was the backyard well. But, when I was leaving, I saw him and Jocelyn heading for the cloakroom . . . They oughta be here by now."

"Tsk. I wonder what's keeping them." She frowned in consternation. "I don't want to put out the hot food till Ryson arrives. He just loves my chipped beef."

"Don't we all, darlin'. Don't we all," Lyle said with patent insincerity as he retrieved his bottle from Denny's hold and swept out the door.

Leaning against the doorjamb, Miriam watched him make a bee-line for the ice bucket, calling out extravagant kudos to various cast members on his way. Then she gave a little sigh and said, "He really is a nasty man, isn't he?"

Surprised, Denny gave a short snort, then cleared his throat. "Yeah, sometimes. When he's had too much to drink."

Rolling her eyes in Davie's direction, she observed dryly, "When *hasn't* he?"

"Mir, I can't believe my ears! You just gave somebody a *shot*." Frankie's voice boomed from the opened front door, causing Miriam to nearly jump out of her skin. Then Frankie, with Will Coltrane close behind, flew to Miriam's side and gave her a big, wet smack on the forehead. "Good for you, girl. Never thought I'd see the day. Next time, say it louder so the little pisser hears ya."

"Francine, please, keep it down," Miriam hissed. "Where have you been all night? Michael's been asking for you."

"Yeah? Well, he's a little pisser, too, so who cares," she said defiantly, rocking back on her heels. Only Coltrane's outstretched hand kept her from capsizing as he murmured, "Frankie, love, what say we go to the kitchen and get some coffee?"

"What say you get your sweaty mitts off my wife, you creep," Mauro hollered, bursting out of the crowded living room into the foyer. "Then you can go stick a sapling up your as—"

"Michael, please, there are ladies present," Will huffed.

"Really? Where?" was Frankie's looped contribution.

"Denny, take Francine into the kitchen," Miriam commanded as she pushed her in Moskowitz's direction. Then, staunchly placing herself between the two glowering men, she said, "I don't know what's going on here and I don't think I want to. But you will not, *not* spoil this evening for the others. I won't have it! I'm very good friends with Dottie," she added, heavily dropping the name of the college president's spouse, "and she hates scenes as much as I do."

"You're right, Mir," Mauro agreed grudgingly as the threat of lost tenure sunk in. "This isn't the time or the place . . . But I'll talk to you later, Coltrane."

"When you're in a saner frame of mind, I hope," Will answered with face-saving bravado.

Michael took a step toward him, then backed off with, "Hope all you want. I'm going to see to my wife."

He started down the hall to the kitchen but Anita Sanchez blocked his entry at the door. "Don't come in here now, Professor Mauro. I'm talking to your missus."

"For God's sake, Nita, don't! She'll tear your head off."

"Just chill . . . and let me handle this, okay?"

"Okay," he replied doubtfully, trying to peek around her into the kitchen. "But try to get some coffee into her first."

"Nah, I don't think so," the girl said sagely. "This ain't one a' those Café Vienna moments, trust me." Then she shut the door in his face.

Sitting at the kitchen table, slicing lemon wedges, Frankie looked up and asked, "Is zat my worser half out there? Tell 'im to take a hike. He doesn't do tequila, anyway." Then she poured two shots of Jose Cuervo and held out a salt shaker to Anita. "You know the drill? You must—you're Mexican."

Sanchez nodded her assent, then licked the salt from the side of her fist, downed the shot, and bit into the lemon wedge as Frankie followed suit. Both women gasped in unison. Blinking rapidly to clear her vision, Frankie squinted at the girl and asked, "So, tell me, were you Mike's little, uh . . . extracurricular activity last night?"

"Yes—and no. I mean, it's not what you're thinking. Not at all."

"Oh, hell, you don't have to bullshit me. I don't blame *you.*"

"But you shouldn't blame him, either!" Anita tugged Frankie's hand urgently. "Look, I know you're pissed off and a little plastered, but you gotta listen. He—he did a real *nice* thing last night."

Shutting one jaundiced eye, Frankie peered out through the other. "Really? Do tell."

Meanwhile a car pulled into the driveway. Shutting off the ignition, Ryson Curtis turned to Jocelyn and asked, "Are you really sure about this?"

"No, not one hundred percent. I told you, it's all circumstantial at best. But it's also the only scenario that makes any sense . . . especially after what you've told me."

"Hell, I almost wish I hadn't," he sighed. "Tessa had *lots* of affairs, Josh."

"I know. But if you're right, it's the only one that fits the time frame. Hopefully, Phillip can verify the rest."

"Is that why he left after intermission?" O'Roarke nodded and Curtis sighed again. "So what's going to happen next?"

"I'm not sure, Ry. Wish I were. But I think we'll have to wait till Phillip shows."

"And then what?"

"Then . . . we'll wing it."

"Oh, gawd," he groaned, "How I hate improv."

Not wanting to make a big entrance, Josh and Ryson slipped around to the back door. Stepping into the kitchen, they were surprised to find Frankie and Anita half laughing, half crying over a tray of sodden stuffed celery.

"Joey! Where the hell you been? Here—have a wet hoor-durvey. They're a little salty, but that's not Mir's fault."

"At least she didn't put all that awful crab crap in 'em this time," Anita giggled, then hiccuped.

Eyeing her half-smashed friend warily, Josh asked, "So, does this mean I'm no longer the scum of the earth?"

"Gee, I dunno. You'll hafta ask Will. He's the expert on pond scum," Frankie quipped, sending her and Sanchez into a fresh burst of hilarity. Then some shards of remorse penetrated her inebriate armor as she leaned over the sink to splash cold water on her face before enveloping O'Roarke in a bear hug. "Joey, I'm sorry, I'm sorry. I didn't mean to go off half-crocked— Hah! I mean, half-cocked like I did. You were only trying to help. And you were right."

"Well, that's great," Jocelyn said, trying to disentangle herself from Frankie's suffocating embrace. "What was I right about?"

"About Professor Mauro," Anita interjected. "And about a lot of stuff you told me. See, I wanted to tell you backstage—I *get* it now! I—I had a bad scare yesterday. My period was late and I threw up in the morning. So I got one a' those home pregnancy things. But I was too freaked out to even try it. All I could think of was my scholarship and everything I worked for going down the tubes . . . Mr. Mauro found me crying in the parking lot last night and got me to tell him what was wrong. Then he took me back to my dorm and waited downstairs while I did the test. It was negative—thank you, Jesus! But I was so damned relieved, I just conked out. And poor Professor Mauro fell asleep in the lobby."

"No kidding?" O'Roarke gave Sanchez a noncomittal smile before turning to Frankie and whispering sotto voce, "Are we buying this or what?"

"Oh, sure. It's too cornball for words." Frankie sighed. "That's just like Mike. He's got a thing about protecting his students' privacy. Big jerk just picked the wrong time to be noble."

"So all is forgiven?"

"Yeah—but I'm gonna let him sweat a little longer," Frankie chuckled. "Just for the hell of it."

"What a swell idea," Josh said mordantly. "I can tell it's going to be a hell of a party."

Looking down, Anita saw what Jocelyn was carrying in her left hand and said in surprise, "What're you doing with *that?*"

"Excuse me, ladies. I think I'm about to be summoned." By prearrangement, Ryson had already gone into the living room to congratulate his cast and set up O'Roarke's entrance. Now he was clinking a spoon against his glass and calling for everyone's attention.

"Quiet everybody. Hold it down for just a sec." There was still a low buzz of conversation but Curtis had no trouble projecting above it. "Y'all did a super job tonight. You've made me and the department and the whole college damn proud." He was interrupted by a burst of applause and several rebel yells. Clearing his throat he continued, "But there's someone I'd like to single out. Someone who came here at a moment's notice to help us in our hour of need. A great lady and a fine actor, Jocelyn O'Roarke . . . Where the hell are ya, Josh?"

On cue, O'Roarke stepped into the archway between kitchen and living room. There was another round of applause and the de rigueur call for a speech. She waited for the noise to die down, then walked over to Curtis, deliberately letting the tackle box she was carrying thump against her left leg so that it made a metallic chinking sound somewhat reminiscent of Old Marley's rattling chains. Handing the case to Hank Barnes, she accepted a glass of wine from Ryson, which she held high.

"Um—unaccustomèd as I am to public speaking," she began lightly, "I'd just like to thank all of you for making me look good tonight."

"By comparison, you mean," one young wag called out to general guffaws.

"Well, in your case, yes," she riposted, topping his laugh. "But I really want to thank you, not just on my behalf, but on Tessa's as well." Immediately the laughter died, along with all undercurrents of conversation; she had every eye in the house. "I know that sounds odd, but I think she'd want me to. I met Tessa at Corinth when I was the same age as most of you. Back then I thought I knew a thing or two about acting, but Tess taught me what it meant to be a professional. To have standards and to care about the work for the work's sake. As heartsick as I was—as we all were—to lose her, it's been a rare privilege for me to be able to come back here and show some of what I learned from her. She was a great teacher. A good teacher's like a good parent: the example they set gets handed down, not just to their children, but to their children's children. By your hard work and the generous support you've given me through a difficult time, you've proven that . . . If Tessa were here now, I think she'd say to you what Hermione says to Perdita: 'Mine own, mine own.' " Raising her glass higher, she said, "Here's to Tess!"

A hushed silence followed as glasses raised all round. Then Denny echoed, "To Tess—and Josh!" And the room went wild with whistles and foot stamping. Trying to fish a hankie out of her pocket, a teary Miriam nearly dropped a tray of crudités. In the archway, Anita sniffled and said to Frankie, "God, that was something."

"Yup. It was something all right," she replied, watching Jocelyn closely as people gathered round her. "Something out of *Julius Caesar*, maybe."

"Huh? What do you mean?"

Drifting back toward the kitchen, Frankie said vaguely, "Oh, you know the bit. Marc Antony's speech."

"What? You mean—I come to bury Caesar, not to praise him." A scholarship student who bothered to read plays, not just Cliff Notes, Sanchez frowned suddenly. "I don't get it. That speech isn't just a eulogy. It's political, too. Antony's trying to manipulate the crowd and make Brutus look like a piece of shit."

"Umm-hmmm," was all Frankie offered. Poking her head into the fridge, she said, "I wonder if there's one damn piece of celery around that hasn't been *stuffed*? Aha!" Triumphantly she raised a Baggie filled with virgin stalks and spun round to find Anita staring at her with a strange expression.

In the living room, having been hugged and bussed by many as well as groped a bit by a stewed sophomore, Jocelyn turned to Hank, saying, "Sorry to leave you holding the baggage. I'll take that upstairs now."

Surrendering the makeup case, Barnes asked, "Isn't this Tessa's? Where did you—?"

"Oh, Josh, that was *so* awesome, what you said," Belinda interrupted. Her misty eyes widened when she spotted the case. "Uh-oh, I broke something, didn't I?"

"No, just loosened the hinges," Josh said quickly. "It'll be easy to fix. I've got a mini-screwdriver in my suitcase."

"Whew! That's a relief." Smiling up at her father, Bel said, "Did you know Josh has been doing my makeup with Tessa's stuff?"

"No, I didn't. But don't you think we should return it to—someone?"

"Why? The colors are perfect for her, Hank." Giving him a cajoling wink, Josh added, "Besides, don't you think Tess would want her to have it?"

"Yes, I suppose so . . . But let's not make a big deal of it just now, okay?"

"Oh, Daddy, you're so cute," Bel giggled, giving him a peck on the cheek. "Like I'm gonna post a notice on the call-board or something." Then she sailed off to her friends as her father looked on wistfully.

"Well, let me put this in my room." Jocelyn started for the stairs but Hank grabbed her hand.

"Uh, Jocelyn, I—I just wanted to thank you for taking care of her last night. And I'm sorry about the things I said."

"That's okay. You'd had a bad scare."

"Yeah, but that's no excuse. It's only—Christ! I don't know what I'd do if I lost her." Shaking off some dire imagining, he regained his composure and offered, "Look, you want me to take that? I've got some tools in the garage and—"

"No, don't bother. I can fix this in no time." Then she slipped up the stairs before he could stop her. Miriam, still moist around the eyes, was just coming down them.

"Oh, Jocelyn, what a lovely tribute that was! Especially the part about teachers and parents."

"Well, you know, you're both unsung heroes. Heck, you're the one who deserves to take a bow. Up all last night and then slaving all day to get this party together. I don't know how you do it."

Flushing with pleasure, Miriam demurred, "What can I say? It's my job."

Then the doorbell rang and she flew down the stairs to answer it.

"Phillip, there you are! We were getting worried about you."

"Sorry, Miriam. I had some business to take care of," Gerrard said as he entered the foyer. "Then I ran into a friend and convinced him to come along."

Peering behind him, she gasped, "Why, Gideon—is that you?!"

" 'Fraid so, Miriam." Doc Morgan stepped forward to take her hands in his. "Hope you don't mind a gate crasher."

"Don't be silly. It's just such a surprise." Drawing him toward the living room, she asked, "Didn't you two just meet last night?"

"Oh, no, no. The lieutenant has been consulting me on a, uh, professional matter recently." Switching subjects abruptly, he said, "Now where's Belinda? I want to take a peek at that lump on her noggin."

From the staircase O'Roarke caught Phillip's eye and motioned for him to follow her. On the landing, she whispered, "Was I right? What did he say?"

"He couldn't *say* anything, Josh. That would be a breach of ethics," he whispered back. "I had to do all the talking. I laid out everything we've pieced together and said, 'Stop me if I've got any of this wrong.' "

"And did he?"

"No, not once. When I suggested he come with me, he just grabbed his coat and said, 'Let's go.' " Catching sight of the makeup case, he cocked an eyebrow and asked, "What're you going to do with *that?*"

Raising her lips to his ear, she said, "Okay, here's the plan . . ."

Several minutes later, Gerrard came downstairs and peered purposefully around the living room. Spotting his quarry, he elbowed his way through the crush of revelers. Coming up behind Will Coltrane, who was in earnest conversation with a pretty young coed, he clapped a hand on his back, nearly sending Coltrane out of his shoes.

"Will! Just the man I was looking for."

"Really? How flattering," the other man answered dryly, clearly displeased by the interruption. "Might it wait a mo? Stephanie and I were just discussi—"

"No, it might not." Flashing the girl a dazzling smile, he hooked Coltrane's arm and said, "Sorry, Stephanie. I'll return him to you good as new. Promise."

"Oh, no prob." The girl looked more relieved than disappointed. "Take your time."

As Phillip steered him toward the den, Will shook off his hand, grousing, "God! Where are your manners? It must be true—what one hears about pushy New Yorkers."

"Now take it easy, Will. I probably did you a favor." Dropping his voice, Gerrard added, "Besides . . . you don't need more trouble with undergrads of the fairer sex, do you, sport?"

Sucking in his breath, Coltrane looked at Phillip, opened his mouth, then clamped it shut again. Making his way through the throng, Gerrard didn't even bother looking over his shoulder; he knew Will would be right behind him.

28

"Eeek! Who put that ice cube down my back?" Belinda spun round and spotted Denny Moskowitz's smirking face. "Den—you creep! I'll get you." Picking up a bottle of seltzer water, she shook it vigorously and took off in pursuit of her beloved. Ryson Curtis flattened himself against the kitchen wall as the two sped past him and out to the back patio.

A good time was being had by almost one and all.

Under normal circumstances, Ryson would have been among the good timers. A veteran of countless cast parties, first during his years in Manhattan and then throughout his academic career, Curtis had found he preferred the latter to the former. They both start out the same, with much hugging, kissing, and cries of "You were so good I *hate* you!" (in New York) or "Blow me away. It was totally bitchin'" (in Corinth). But in Manhattan a certain strain creeps in as the time for the morning editions draws near; a kind of French Revolution paranoia comes over those vulnerable souls who have poured their guts or pocketbooks into a production as they wait to learn upon whose neck the guillotine's blade will fall. Even with a hit, one or two poor suckers usually come out headless.

But in academia there are no Frank Riches or John Simons, wielding their pens like Madame Defarge's knitting needles, to skewer you. If you got through the performance without tripping over the furniture or your tongue, you were a success. For this reason, Ryson always watched his students partying with a tender regard for their high spirits and blissful ignorance; as yet none knew about the critics' abattoir that awaited them.

This particular party was a shade rowdier than most, which he attributed to relief and release after a trying rehearsal period and the fact that rather more liquor than food had been consumed despite Miriam's dutiful efforts to entice one and all with bean dip, cocktail wienies, and what not. Determined to keep his wits about him while others, notably Lyle, were losing theirs, Curtis had been nursing a Jack Daniel's for over an hour while looking in vain for O'Roarke. Then he had gone in search of Gerrard only to find him sequestered in a corner with Mike Mauro, oblivious to all Curtis' gesticulations. Even Doc Morgan, who rarely missed an opportunity to take him aside and quiz him on his health, seemed to be avoiding him.

Like Tony in *West Side Story,* he felt something coming, but, in this instance, he didn't think it was going to be great. Oddly enough, only Anita seemed to share his unease. Bumping into him, after having firmly sealed her friendship with Francine Mauro for all time in a bottle of Jose Cuervo, she patted her damp brow with a napkin, then confided, "Ya know, Professor Ry, I'm pretty wasted 'bout now. So I *should* be havin' a good time. Right? But I'm feeling kinda weird."

"Could be the tequila, dear," he suggested kindly. "Want me to lead you to the, uh, facilities?"

"Nah, nah, I'm not gonna hurl. Iz not that." She blinked her eyes rapidly. "I just keep gettin' these strange flashes . . . everytime I look at the stupid 'frigerator. Like a warning sign."

"Well, best not look at it, then."

"Can't help it. It sorta *draws* me, you know?"

Still suspecting the effects of too much tequila, he said, "Maybe it means you want to *eat* something?"

"Oh, get real!" She rolled her eyes and snickered. "After one a' Mizz Barnes' spreads, the cafeteria crud doesn't look so bad."

"Shh! Don't let Miriam hear . . . she works so hard at it."

"Yeah, you're right. I shouldn't— Jesu! What the hell was that?"

A loud crash drew their attention to the living room. Darting to the archway with Anita, Ryson saw Michael and Coltrane standing on opposite sides of an overturned coffee table, heaving like bulls.

"Now look what you've done, you clod," Will shouted, pointing to a broken table leg. "That's an antique, you know . . . No, you probably don't. You wouldn't know something of value if it bit your behind!"

"What does that mean? Tell you what I *do* know," Mauro said ominously, coming round one side of the table, "I know I'm god-damn sick of your pissant limey cracks. I'm sick of your stupid, smug face, too!"

"How sad. Lucky for me your wife doesn't feel that way," he shot back with a thin smile. "Quite the contrary, I'd say."

"Oh shit, I'd better find Ms Mauro," Anita said, suddenly sober as a judge, as she shot out of the room.

"Okay, okay, let's hear it, asshole! I want to know just where you two went today." Like a fighting cock, Michael butted his chest against Coltrane, who pushed him away forcefully. They were the only two figures in the center of the room now but the perimeter was packed with aghast and titillated onlookers. A fight over a pretty girl was not an uncommon occurrence at college parties; but when it involved a professor and his wife—*that* was something new and not to be missed. In the past, Curtis had broken up a few student fracases with little trouble and no harm to his person. But this, he feared, was going to be a nastier kettle of fish. Feeling like the Reluctant Dragon, he stepped forward and raised his voice full volume.

"Gentlemen! Have you lost your ever-lovin' minds? This is not the time or place for such discussion."

"Aw, hell, Ry, this ain't a discussion!" In his cups, Lyle Davie brayed from across the room, then hiccuped and added with Southern solemnity, "A lady's honor's at stake . . . They gotta duke it out."

"Just shut *up*, Lyle," Curtis barked. "You're only—"

"Hey! I got no trouble with *that*," Mauro broke in belligerently, then stabbed Will with his finger. "How 'bout you, pantywaist? Wanna take it outside?"

"It would give me great pleasure to knock your tiny block off," Coltrane answered.

Hoping to avert disaster, Ryson scanned the room for assistance until his eyes came to rest on Gerrard, who stood near the foyer, looking on dispassionately. "Phillip, can't you do something?"

With a resigned shrug, as if to say "This'll do no good," he came forward and broke the two men apart. "Look, fellas, it's late and you've both had a lot to drink. Why don't you just take a breath, count to ten, and—"

"Ten!" Coltrane caught the other two off guard and shot out a fist, which missed Michael but came round to thwack Gerrard soundly on the shoulder, knocking him to the floor. Never in his life had Curtis seen a man go down, then come up so quickly, like a human jack-in-the-box, which he could only suppose was a testament to Phillip's years on the force. In a twinkling he had the two larger men by the back of the neck as he railroaded them toward the front door with the crowd following in his wake.

"All right, you clowns—you want to mix it up? Fine!" Shoving them both out onto the front lawn, he hollered, "Go ahead—knock yourselves out."

Bathed in the light of a full moon, Mike and Will squared off while the others silently formed a circle around them. Mauro made the first move with a lunging jab that caught Will's shoulder and sent him staggering backward. Ryson prayed for some sort of deus ex machina to appear and thought his prayers had been answered when Anita propelled Frankie through the front door, saying, "See, I *told* you they were gettin' crazy!"

"Oh, Frankie, thank God you're here," Curtis cried. "Make Mike stop."

Cigarette in one hand and a Miller Lite in the other, Frankie squinted at the two combatants, who were slithering around on the wet grass, and asked, "Lemme get this straight—they're fighting over *me?*

"Yes, yes, you've got to do something fast!"

Just then Will tackled Mike around the middle and the two men hit the ground rolling. Frankie gave a small sympathetic grunt, then turned to Ryson with a beatific smile. "What're you, nuts? You think I'm gonna break *this* up? No way!" She patted his sagging shoulders affectionately then pointed at her spouse. "Look, there's a guy who's forgotten anniversaries, forgotten Valentine's Day. Even forgot my birthday once. To my way of thinking, Ry—this is the *least* he could do."

"Oh, good God almighty," Curtis sighed, dropping his face in his hands.

As Will and Mike broke apart and struggled back to their feet, Frankie looked over the crowd and asked, "Where's Josh? Damn! I'd hate for her to miss this." Spotting Gerrard, she called out, "Hey, Phil! Have you seen Jocelyn?"

Keeping one eye on Mike and Will as they danced around each other, he shrugged and shook his head, but Frankie was keen to have her old roommate in on the action. "Well, go look for her! She's gotta see this."

From behind Phillip, Hank Barnes called back, "For pity's sake, Francine, get a grip. This isn't funny!" Just then Mauro, the home town favorite, landed a blow on Coltrane's jaw and a cheer went up from the younger spectators. But Will countered with an underhook to Michael's rib cage that made even Frankie wince as she watched her husband grunt and sink to his knees. Rubbing his jaw in surprise, Will started to turn away from his opponent but Mauro threw his arms around Will's knees and both men went once more to the ground.

"Oh, this is too much. I can't watch this," Ryson said to thin air since no one was paying him the slightest attention. Deciding to go look for O'Roarke himself in hopes that she might talk some sense into Frankie, he headed for the front door. He walked through the living room, which was entirely deserted, as was the kitchen.

Then, just as he entered the small dining room, the house was plunged into total darkness.

Curtis gasped and put out a hand, feeling for the wall. "If this don't take all! What a time for a fuse to blow." From the crowd noises outside, he gathered that the others hadn't noticed the blackout as yet, thanks to the full moon. Locating the wall, he got his bearings as his eyes adjusted to the dark. There was a small mahogany dining table in the center of the room with two pewter candlesticks at either end. Grabbing the nearest one, he fished a book of matches out of his pocket and fumbled to light the wick.

"So shines a good deed in a naughty world," he quoted the Bard as the candlelight threw the room into eerie relief. Then he heard someone moving up the staircase. From the lightness of the step he assumed it was a woman, hopefully O'Roarke, but, for some reason, he didn't call out to her. Instead he went through the dining room into the den.

The door to the foyer was shut. When Ryson opened it, the candle went out as a hand clamped down on his shoulder.

Upstairs a slash of yellow light fell on the carpet and moved down the long hallway, stopping at the door to the master bedroom. A hand turned the knob gently, opening the door. Once inside, the hand holding the flashlight jerked back and forth across the room until it caught a gleam of metal. Then there was a sharp intake of breath as the torch drew close to the makeup case, illuminating the small padlock on the front.

The hand yanked furiously at the lock to no avail. In a frenzy, the interloper raised the butt of the flashlight and brought it down, again and again, until the tin loop broke away from the body of the lock. Voices wafted up from the lawn below as the scuffle seemed to reach its climax. A girl's voice called out, "Look! The lights have gone out." And the general hubbub grew louder as people drifted back toward the house.

Inside the darkened room, urgent hands opened the case and overturned its contents on the bed. Then the beam of the torch went flying across the bedspread, searching for something that wasn't there. There was a sound like the moan of a wounded animal, then the hands, shaking now, uprighted the case and felt round the insides, coming to rest finally on the small mirror attached to the roof. Nails scraped against metal as the mirror was pried away; then there was a faint rustle as an envelope slid to the bottom of the case.

The dry sound of paper tearing was followed by a gasp of profound relief.

"Sweet Jesus! I *got* it."

In that instant the lights came back on and another voice spoke from the far corner of the room.

"Yes, you've got it . . . but you didn't have to kill for it."

As Jocelyn stepped out of the shadows, Miriam Barnes gave a

small cry and crumpled the paper in her hands. "What—? What're you doing here?"

"I was waiting for you. I knew you'd come looking for that," she said, pointing to the document in Miriam's hands as she cautiously approached.

"Don't! Don't come near me . . . Please, Jocelyn, just go away, please?" Even in her terror, she managed a polite smile. "This really doesn't concern you. Doesn't concern anyone, really." She started to tear the paper in two but O'Roarke stopped her with:

"There's no point, Miriam. I've seen it and so has Phillip . . . Besides, it's on record in Salerno. We can always get a copy."

"No, *no*, you can't! You mustn't." Her smile grew tighter as she clutched the certificate to her breast. "She can't ever know."

"Is that why you killed Tessa? You thought she'd tell?"

"I *knew* she would. As soon as I saw them together in rehearsal. Saw the way Tess looked at her when she said, 'Mine own, mine own.' I—I couldn't let that happen." Shaking the mangled paper in her fist, she cried, "I don't care what this says—*I'm* her mother."

"Yes, you are," O'Roarke said soothingly as she looked into the other woman's desperate eyes. But she took care to keep her distance. At that moment Miriam reminded her of a cocker spaniel she had had as a child; normally the most affable of animals, the bitch had once bitten clean through Josh's hand when she had tried, too soon, to touch one of the pups in her litter. She sensed the lurking volatility that Grant had missed or ignored and proceeded gently. "Belinda knows that. Do you really think—even if Tess had said something—it would make a difference to her? Hell, Miriam, you didn't have to—"

"Yes, I *did!* Oh, what do you know—about children! About how they take you for granted," Miriam snapped, finally showing her teeth. "You raise them and protect them . . . but they grow *away* from you. They want something different, something more exciting. So how in *hell* could I compete with someone like Tessa?! Even if that selfish bitch had kept her mouth shut, she was still going to take my girl from me somehow. And she would've *ruined* her! Once I found out about the—the baby and what Tess made Belinda do . . . I knew I had to stop her!" Then she paused and gave Josh a cunning little smirk that froze her blood. "But, technically, I really didn't *do* anything, you know."

"No. You just made food for the party—things Tess didn't like or couldn't eat, like the crabmeat. And you put a Baggie filled with water hemlock in the fridge."

"Yes, because I knew she was dieting. But I was *very* careful. I hid it way in the back so no one else would find it. Why should they? There was tons to eat. But I knew she'd get hungry and go looking. And she did—I watched her. Then, when she left the kitchen, I grabbed the rest and dumped it out back on the compost."

"That was very clever, Mir. And you're right, technically it's not murder," Josh said, still maintaining a neutral tone. "But it *is* manslaughter."

"Well . . . *maybe*," Miriam allowed with a little sniff. "Though I don't see that it makes much difference. See, I'm not the little ninny you all take me for . . . You have no *proof*, do you? A birth certificate doesn't prove anything." So saying, she ripped the paper apart defiantly. "And this conversation doesn't mean a thing, either. It'd only be—what do they call it?—hearsay. And, since you're the only one who heard and everybody knows how you crazy you were about Tess, it'd just be your word against mine. In this town—no jury would believe you."

"No, they wouldn't," O'Roarke agreed softly.

Then the door swung open, revealing Phillip standing alongside Ryson Curtis, who looked over at a stunned Miriam and spoke with deep regret.

"But they'd believe me, dear . . . And I'm afraid I heard every word."

Miriam's mouth worked soundlessly as she backed away from the two men. Gerrard could see from the frantic look in her eyes that she was in a precarious state. Not wanting to frighten her further, he held his position in the doorway and spoke soothingly.

"Miriam, you know I'm not here in any official capacity, but I'd like to help you, okay? Why don't you let me take you down to Kowaleski's office right now. No one needs to know—we'll just slip out the back door."

"Why . . . why do you want to take me there?" she asked, still fighting the fact that her worst nightmare had just come true.

"So you can make a full statement to the police. If you come forward on your own, it'll be much better in the long run, honestly. You were under extreme emotional duress at the time and the court will take that into consid—"

"I can't do *that!*" Miriam flushed to her roots as if he had just made an indecent suggestion. "It's not—I don't care about me. But my family, how could I shame them like that?"

Phillip looked to Jocelyn for assistance, but she stood frozen a few feet from Miriam with her eyes downcast, mired in some shame of her own. Finally, Ryson came to the rescue with: "Darlin', nobody's gonna turn their backs on Belinda and Hank, I promise you. Phillip's right—this is the best way for you and them."

Miriam's eyes flew back and forth from one's man face to the other, searching for some sign of reprieve. Finding none, she finally gave a small shrug of resignation and sighed, "Yes, yes, you're both right. I see that."

Thinking that the worst was over, both men gave sighs of their own and started to cross the room to Miriam. Only then did O'Roarke raise her gaze from the carpet, but what she saw made her suck in her breath in alarm. One moment Miriam seemed rooted to the floor but, as soon as Phillip and Ryson came within arm's reach, she made a sound that was half sob, half shriek and catapulted her body away from them, directly toward the bedroom window.

Gerrard made a grab for her, only to catch an armful of air. Ryson, too, reached and missed. But Jocelyn, a few crucial inches closer, threw herself between Miriam and the windowpane. At first, she heard but didn't feel the impact. Then she felt a warm, trickling sensation down her back and knew she was about to pass out.

___

29

"A woman without a child is like a man without an arm . . . a right arm."

"Sorry, Grant—Bette. We are *not* amused!"

From her hospital bed, Jocelyn raised the TV remote and banished Grant Mitchell and Bette Davis from the small screen. Normally she got a big charge out of rewatching *The Great Lie*, a chestnut from 1941 that featured Bette and Mary Astor at their bitchy best, vying for the affections of the ever-stolid George Brent. But she was in no mood for Mitchell, as the sage physician, holding forth on the old biology-is-destiny theme, managing to insult lefties as well as women in the bargain.

Anyway her back, stitched and bandaged, was starting to itch like mad. Just as she was trying to slip a hand behind her, Doc Morgan strolled in and promptly commanded, "Cut that out, miss. You're not to touch those stitches."

"But they itch," she mewled. "What'd you do—dip the catgut in ground chili peppers or something?"

"Oh, don't be such a wimp," he scoffed, then winked. "You don't know what real torture is till you've been in a body cast."

"Gosh, look at that little twinkle in your eye . . . You're all ghouls. You realize that, don't you?" Then she saw the X rays in his hand and raised herself up stiffly. "So, what's the damage?"

"Medically speaking, I'd say we'd have to chalk this one up to the luck of the Irish," he quipped, dropping the X rays on her lap. "No broken ribs and no damage to the vertebrae. Just a few nasty cuts and a lot of contusions."

"No kidding," she grumbled. "I never would've known."

"Getting snippy, aren't we? Well, in your case, that's probably a good sign. If you promise to stay *still*, I might let you out tomorrow."

Stir crazy after a day and a half in bed, she was pleased by the prospect of release but suddenly fearful of what awaited her on the outside. Dropping her eyes, she said, "That's great . . . but what about Miriam? How's she?"

"Her injuries were minor, though she's in the hospital, too," he answered quietly as he drew up a chair. "But not here. They've got her up at Saint Loyola."

"Loyola? That's—that's a psychiatric hospital, isn't it?"

"Yes. She's had what we used to call a nervous breakdown. They have fancier terms for it nowadays. But what it boils down to is— well, the strain was just too much for her. Even if you hadn't, uh, forced the issue, I think she would've broken down in a matter of days. Miriam's essentially a gentle woman, you know. What she did was as much a violation of herself, her own psyche if you like, as it was a crime."

"I know." Despite the sunlight streaming through the window, she felt a numbing chill; a side effect of painkillers mixed with remorse. "I hope she gets a decent lawyer. She's got a good shot at a temporary insanity defense." Then she locked eyes with Gideon. "Can I ask you something?"

Morgan nodded; he had been expecting this. For almost two days, even when she wasn't groggy with drugs, O'Roarke had lain in bed, fixated on the television set, purposely oblivious to her surroundings. She hadn't even given him a fight when he had outlawed all visitors. But he knew, once the pain subsided, she would have questions. And he felt he owed her some answers.

"You must've known that Belinda wasn't Miriam's child. But . . . did you know whose child she was?"

"No, not really, though I had my suspicions. Hank and Miriam tried for years to conceive and I was their physician. I ran all the tests. That poor woman was distraught when she found out she was infertile. Then Hank took that long sabbatical—soon after he got back from a teachers' conference in Manhattan—and they returned from Italy with the baby. Miriam claimed she'd gone to a special clinic in Switzerland, but I was dubious to say the least. Then she switched to another doctor, never came to see me again, and I was sure they'd arranged an adoption."

"But you said you suspected."

"Yes, that was later. You see, Hank and Belinda were *still* my patients. And, over the years, I started to see real similarities. Same blood type, same allergies, same carriage. Lots of little things that, taken together, couldn't be just coincidental . . . But I never knew about Tessa. If I had, Jocelyn, believe me, I would've said something."

"I feel like such an idiot. It seems so obvious *now*. Bel looks just like her. Miriam must've been in a cold sweat from the day Tess arrived." Falling back against the pillows, she gazed up at the ceiling, trying to imagine how it must feel to want a child so badly that you'd forgive a husband's infidelity and beg the other woman to have his baby. But it bespoke a desperate determination that was beyond her ken. Suddenly angry, she banged her hand against her knee. "Hank had to know that! He should've helped her—reassured her somehow."

"He didn't know how, Josh."

"Huh? Did he say that?" O'Roarke jerked up in bed, then winced from pulling her stitches. "That is *so* lame!"

"My dear, judge not, lest ye be judged," Gideon said in soft rebuke. "I went up to Loyola last night and had a talk with him. According to Hank—after they brought that baby back to Corinth—they never spoke of her real antecedents, not *once* in all those years. Miriam even started telling their friends long, detailed stories about her pregnancy and labor. Hank thinks, after a while, she came to believe them . . . and he found himself joining in, adding little touches about holding her hand in the delivery room and watching Belinda's head come out—things like that."

"Jesus Christ! No wonder he kept still, no wonder. They fine-tuned that fantasy together for nearly twenty years," Josh gasped in awe and pity.

"Yes, exactly," Gideon agreed somberly. "How did Coleridge put it? 'Fancy is a mode of memory emancipated from the order of time and space.' Something like that." Then his mouth turned down as he added tersely, "All the same, he was a damned fool not to have warned Grant to keep her distance!"

"True—but I'm not sure it would've done any good," Josh said sadly. "God, it's like Greek tragedy. Hubris cometh before the fall. And Tess had plenty of hubris. My guess is, much as she was taken with Belinda, she never intended to tell her the truth. She wasn't one to break a pact. So it wouldn't have occurred to her that Miriam would feel seriously threatened—and do something desperate. She dismissed women like Miriam—'the domestic types' she called them. Tess thought violent passions were only for the stage, not for people like Miriam." Jocelyn's throat constricted as she felt a fresh pang of grief for the folly of this brilliant, flawed woman she had so admired. Rubbing her eyes, she quoted softly, " 'Being transported by my jealousies/ To bloody thoughts and to revenge'—that line comes right after her swoon . . . I guess she wasn't paying attention, huh?"

Gideon saw her jaw clinch in pain as she stiffened against the pillows and said, "I think it's time for another shot, Josh."

Before she could answer, a candy striper breezed into the room with a small but exquisite arrangement of sweetheart roses and baby's breath in a china teacup and saucer. "These just arrived for you, Miss O'Roarke. Aren't they precious?" the girl gushed as she handed Josh a tiny envelope.

Having already received a joke horseshoe of carnations with a "Rest in Peace" ribbon from Frankie and a sheaf of her favorite rubrum lilies from Phillip and Ryson, she slid a fingernail under the seal with quizzical anticipation. Gideon watched her read the enclosed card, gulp, and blink back hot tears. Stretching out a hand, he asked, "May I?"

O'Roarke nodded weakly, handing him the card. It read: "Best wishes for a speedy recovery. Our thoughts are with you. Sincerely, Hank & Belinda."

All Morgan could do was shake his head in wonder and murmur, "My, my, despite all, that's quite a family, isn't it?"

"Yes, it is, Doc," she said, barely able to speak. "Do me a favor, please? Help me get dressed."

"So, how about another drink, Phil?"

"What a good idea," Gerrard said. He was about to hand his wineglass to Frankie but Mike swooped down and took it.

"I'll get it, babe." He paused to give her shoulder a squeeze. "You deserve a rest after making that fabulous meal."

She watched him go into the kitchen, then turned to Phillip with a sheepish grin. "Ahh, marital bliss . . . Kind of sick-making, ain't it?"

"No, no it's not. In fact, it's great to see."

"Yeah, I guess—not that it'll last. Two months tops and we'll be sparring and spatting and taking each other for granted again." But her shining eyes belied her cynicism.

"But you'll be together and that's something."

The newly uxorious Michael returned with an uncorked bottle of Frog's Leap cabernet sauvignon and handed out refills all around, saying, "If you don't mind talking about it, Phil, there's one thing I wanted to ask—"

"Wait, wait, sweetie," Frankie whispered urgently, jerking her thumb toward the ceiling. "Better check the stairs first."

"Oh, right!"

Mauro tiptoed halfway up the stairs while his wife explained, "Thanks to you, Shane's decided he wants to be a detective now. Past two days, he's been skulking around the house, hiding in nooks and crannies. It's like living with the C.I.A."

Giving the "coast clear" sign, Michael came back to the living room chuckling. "Yeah, his teacher called today to say she found him behind a sofa in the faculty lounge . . . One of us had better talk to him, hon."

"Fine. Scissors, paper, stone?" Mauro nodded his agreement and shot out a closed fist as Frankie shot out a flat palm and snickered, "Paper beats stone. You get to be the heavy this time."

Accepting defeat good-naturedly, he sat down, putting an arm around his wife's shoulder, and addressed his guest. "What I can't figure is, *when* did Miriam go to your room to destroy the journal?"

"It's all in her statement. Miriam made a full confession this afternoon."

"She *did?!* Everything?" Frankie jerked her head up from Mike's shoulder. "Boy, that'll make for a short trial, huh?"

"Not necessarily. A smart lawyer could get it thrown out—say it was made while she was under duress." Phillip paused to sip the superb wine, then added, "Or use it to bolster an insanity plea."

"Well, what do you say? You think she was *really* out of her gourd?"

"Hey, I'm no shrink. And I've seen sociopaths who've faked it convincingly enough to fool even them. But I do believe Miriam was genuinely and deeply distraught over a period of weeks. Whatever the reality of the situation was, she really *believed* she was in danger of losing her child. That's enough to send certain people over the edge."

"God, yes! I've got three kids, but if I thought somebody was gonna take any one of them, I'd—" Placing her fingertips to her temples, Frankie gave a little moan of empathy. "And Miriam only had Belinda . . . Damn! I wish I hadn't been so bitchy to her all the time. Maybe if she'd had somebody to talk to, she wouldn't hav—"

"Uh, sweetheart, before you don your sackcloth and ashes, remember the woman *did* plant Will's book in *your* car," Mike reminded her gently, then looked over at Gerrard. "The lady really got around. That was the same night she staged the third break-in, huh?"

Phillip nodded. "Right. She said that all Tessa had asked for—after having the baby—was the original birth certificate. And she was convinced Grant had brought it with her."

"And she was right," Frankie added as a new thought struck her. "So Miriam wasn't after the diary at all. She didn't even know about it till later."

"Yes, but when she did find out, it made her even more frantic. That's when she broke into my room."

"But, Phil, how the hell did she get in there without being spotted?" Mike asked. "That took a lot of nerve."

"Well, thanks to Denny, she knew the general layout—where they kept the smocks and cleaning stuff. It was a gutsy move, all right.

But Miriam had the advantage of being one of those women that people look at but don't really see."

"That's true. She practiced self-effacement like it was a religion." Then Frankie sniffed, "But where was ol' Hank during all this?"

"On a cot in Bel's room," Phillip supplied. "It seems Miriam insisted that one of them stay with her in case she woke in the night, and he volunteered. Once they were both asleep, she drove by the hospital first, saw Josh's car was still parked there. Then she went to the hotel and slipped in the back way."

"Still, you could've come back any moment." Frankie sipped her wine, then pursed her lips. "So why didn't she just grab the journal and scram? Why'd she take the time to trash the room?"

"That was to implicate Denny. The lady may've been desperate, but she was canny, too," Gerrard replied with a touch of admiration in his voice. "Every time she made a move, she covered it with a false clue. Like leaving that ladder by the den window when she already had a set of keys to the guest house."

"Talk about still waters," Mauro said, shaking his head in wonder. "Here I thought she was just this nice, dull hausfrau."

"Me, too," Frankie admitted. "Well, actually, I just thought she was dull. It's spooky to be at close quarters with someone for so long, then realize you never had a clue what they were really about. Christ, I feel like such a dunce!"

"Well, don't. I've met some very kindly killers along the way. Folks who take in strays and visit shut-ins on Sundays. People who normally wouldn't hurt a fly, then a button gets pushed, a button they didn't even know was there . . . and they react violently, lethally. Then they often go right back to being their old, sweet selves."

Frankie and Mike's eyes met and rolled in unison, then she turned to Phillip with a sarcastic smile. "Gee, thanks for sharing that. We'll both rest easy *now*."

The doorbell rang and she turned to Mike with a frown. "Are we expecting anyone?"

"Not that I know of," he answered, heading for the door. Looking out the front window, he gave a surprised whistle. "Good grief— it's the sheriff."

"Evening, Mike. Sorry to butt in like this," Calvin said with an apologetic bob of the head. "But I was wondering if Gerrard was here."

"Hi, Cal. What can I do for you?" Phillip asked, joining the other two at the door.

"I, uh, just wanted a word with you . . . in private, if that's okay."

Leading Kowaleski out onto the front porch, Phillip said, "Excuse us, will you?" as he shut the door behind him. "Anything the matter, Cal?"

"Uh, no. I mean, it's nothin' about the case. I was just wondering—that rifle of mine? You still interested in buying it? 'Cause I'm ready to take your original bid."

"You are?" Having not given a second's thought to the matter in days, he was taken aback both by Kowaleski's offer and his peculiar sense of timing. "Well, that's great. But it's a fine piece, Cal. You could probably get more for it."

"Sure I could, but I don't got the time. I need the money fast."

"Okay—mind if I ask what for?"

"No, you got a right. It's just—I never been in a situation like this before. With the Grant case." Struggling to find a way to frame his feelings, Kowaleski kicked a booted foot against the porch glider, making it shudder and swing. "I may not be much of a cop, but I want you to know I'll do everything I can to help the D.A. in my, um, professional capacity. But personally—shit, this'll sound weird—I'd like to give the family a hand."

"You mean you want the money for the Barnes'?" If Cal had nudged Phillip with his other foot, he would have sent him, in his stunned state, toppling over like a granite statue.

"Yeah. I know she did it, Phil, and she's gotta pay. But Mizz Barnes's always been real decent to me, see? Not a snob like some of 'em. And I feel like I owe her."

"Owe her?" All Gerrard could do was echo back.

"Maybe if I'd a took those first break-ins more serious—done a better job—I mighta' been able to stop her in time." Looking up at the clear night sky, he cleared his throat, then continued, "So, if Hank'll let me, I'd like to give him something so's he can get a first-rate lawyer for her. That's all."

In all his years with the N.Y.P.D., Phillip had never heard anything like this. Only in Corinth, he thought, but said, "That's extremely generous of you, Calvin. But you know, Belinda will be coming into some money, and—"

"Not soon enough. You know how long that legal crap takes. 'Sides, that's Grant's money. Bellie might feel funny about using it for her—her mother." Squaring his shoulders, he looked down at Gerrard with something very like nobility in his face. "And like I said—I owe the lady."

"Yes, well, if that's the way you feel, I, uh—I'd like to pay you your asking price. Okay?" Putting out his hand, he added, "Let's shake on it."

As Kowaleski's squad car drove off, Phillip reentered the house to find Mike on the sofa and Frankie on the phone saying, "That's great, Doc. Yes, sure, I'll tell him." Hanging up, she turned to Phillip with a radiant smile. "That was Doc Morgan. He said you can go pick up Josh!"

30

"Easy now, easy," Gerrard said as he helped Jocelyn from the wheel-chair into his car. "We don't want to pull any of those stitches out."

"Uh, Phillip, for two days now people have been addressing me in the plural," Josh said through gritted teeth. "And let me tell ya, *we* are pretty fuckin' sick of it. Okay?"

"Point taken," he said humbly, grabbing a car blanket he'd borrowed from the Mauros and spreading it across her lap. "There. Think you'll be warm enough?"

"As a bug in a rug," she drolled, adding, "especially since it's sixty out, at least."

He cocked an eyebrow but said nothing as he trotted around the car and slid behind the wheel. Keeping his eyes on the rearview mirror, he backed out of the parking space and ventured mildly, "Feeling lousy?"

"No, not really. Gideon gave me a little Percodan for the road."

"That's not the kind of lousy I meant, Josh."

"Oh," was all she said, then, after a long silence, "yeah, pretty filthy, actually . . . Aren't these lovely?" She held up the rose-filled china teacup that had been cradled in her lap. "They're from Hank and Belinda."

Phillip winced inwardly; that was a killer. But he kept his tone noncommittal. "Really? What did the card say?"

"Just the usual." O'Roarke's voice was high and brittle now. " 'Get well soon—and thanks for destroying our family.' "

Yanking the steering wheel hard to the right, Gerrard pulled over to the side of the road and turned to face her. "Stop it! Stop it right now, Josh. Don't torture yourself for doing what had to be done."

"Ah, Christ, Phillip—what's the point of it, though?" She leaned back and shut her eyes, but that didn't stop the flow of tears. "That woman's no menace to society. She did a horrible thing, yes, but she's no criminal. She'd never do it again."

"Really? You're absolutely positive of that?" Gerrard had seen Jocelyn like this before; crippled by remorse in the aftermath. She had as strong a desire to get to the bottom of things as any of the best pros he'd known. But she took it hard when it came time to pay the piper. He didn't want to see her wallowing in senseless guilt. "You know, earlier I was telling Frankie and Mike about one-shot killers. Essentially harmless folks who get backed into a bad corner and resort to murder as a way out. But I'm not so sure Miriam really fits that mold."

"What're you saying? You seriously think that poor woman has the makings of a repeat offender? Come *on!*"

"I'm saying that 'that poor woman' killed rashly, *needlessly!* She was paranoic and delusional. Adopted kids grow up and seek out their birth parent all the time. But they don't turn their backs on their adoptive parents. A rational person knows that. It may make them uneasy at first, but they don't go shopping for a meat cleaver!"

Thrusting out her lower lip, Jocelyn pondered, then said, "You're just saying this to make me feel better . . . Keep going."

"And they don't run around trying to implicate innocent people just to cover their tracks . . . But what this all boils down to, Josh, is—and you have to pay attention now, okay?—you can play detective 'cause you're damn good at it, but you can't play God. Or judge and jury. You have to let the chips fall . . . and walk away."

"You're right. I know you're right, Phillip, and I wish I were more like you." But, as she stared out the window into the coal-black night, all she could see was that blur of stunned and stricken faces when Kowaleski's squad car had arrived that night, siren wailing, with the ambulance close behind; Hank's frozen in dread, Belinda's a study in mystification and dawning horror. And she didn't know how she could ever make those images go away.

Then a faint memory tugged at a corner of her mind. She knit her brow, trying to recall it, and asked, "Phillip, after they got me in the ambulance, I blacked out again, didn't I?"

He didn't answer at first, just gunned the engine and pulled away from the shoulder of the road. Frowning, he finally nodded and said, "Yeah, you were out for most of the ride to the hospital . . . You'd lost a lot of blood."

"But I came to once, didn't I? I said something to you, right?"

"Well, you said something, but not to me exactly," was his tight-lipped response.

"What did I say?"

Resisting that particular memory, he adopted the most matter-of-fact tone he could muster. "It was dark in that ambulance and you were close to shock, so we put a ton of blankets on you. But you did open your eyes once and look at me . . . And you said, 'Jack, how'd you get here?' Then you smiled and shut your eyes."

"Oh." Another long pause. The Percodan was starting to kick in now, making her feel woozy and light-headed, but she fought against it. "Like you said, I was in shock, Phillip. But I'm sorry if I—"

"Don't be sorry," he said too quickly. "Nothing to be sorry for. You'd been with him for the last—what?—almost six months. Only natural you'd want him by your side then."

"No. Look—I should've said something before, but I was just too—"

"Shit, Josh! You don't owe me an explanation or an apology. I know you were in a bad way and you conjured up the person who'd make you feel safest . . . And that's him, not me. Hell—I'd just let you walk into a fuckin' death trap!" He saw it again, in slow-motion replay, Jocelyn's body smashing against the glass as she blocked Miriam's suicidal leap. "And you've got the scars to show for it."

Now it was Jocelyn's turn to reach for the wheel. "Pull over, Phillip, please. Just pull over." After he heeded her command, she turned gingerly in her seat. "Now you're the one who has to listen—listen hard and fast 'cause the Percodan's gonna turn me into a pumpkin real soon. I was hurt and angry with you for a long time, for a lot of reasons. Mainly because you didn't trust me to handle the Burbage Theatre affair my own way. So I gave you grief when you showed up here."

"Oh? And I suppose my engagement to Trisha had nothing to do with it?"

"*No!* Not the way you think. Hell, Phillip, you wanted a wife and kids and you were entitled to that . . . Sure I was sad about it, but I was more upset by the way you'd tried to browbeat me into playing by your rules."

It was finally time to face the music and dance or change partners. Gerrard took a breath and admitted, "Yeah, I did. I couldn't see till later that you had your reasons—and then it seemed like it was too late, and saying 'Sorry' seemed like too little."

"I can see that. But you came up here and helped me out without putting any strings on it. Because you saw how I felt about Tessa —what I owed her. *And* you let me play it my way this time . . . I can't tell you how much that means to me."

"Well, it made the most sense, too," he admitted. "Miriam was watching me like a hawk. I was lucky to grab enough time to get Mike and Will alone and cook up that mock brawl. She never would've gone up to rifle the makeup case if I were in the house."

"Yeah, right, right," Josh chortled, giving in to the Percodan buzz. "Say what you will, Law Man, but you wouldn't have handled it that way a year ago. You knew I needed to confront Miriam myself."

Scratching his head in befuddlement, Phillip asked, "You mean you're giving me *points* for putting you in jeopardy, woman?!"

"No, dear. And, frankly, I would've loved it if you'd intercepted her before we hit the glass. But what I love more is that you had faith me."

"Uh, okay, I get it." He looked at her out of the corner of his eye and added carefully, "But, sweetheart, if I'd been on this case in a professional capacity, I don't know that I'd've let you—"

"Well, if wishes were fishes, we'd all be swimming upstream," she giggled.

"What the *hell* does that mean?!"

"It means leave it alone for now, Phillip," Josh cooed dreamily. "That's all. Let's not analyze it into oblivion . . . Just be glad we got our friendship back."

"*Friendship?* Is that what it's going to be?"

"For starters, yeah." She let her head sink against his shoulder, then added muzzily, "I just don't want to pull an Uncle Willy."

"Huh? Who's Uncle Willy?"

"Didn't I ever tell you about him? He's famous in my family. *Loves* to give presents—at birthdays, Christmas, whenever. Only trouble is, he always buys you something *he* wants. Every time."

"Uh-huh, so?" When she didn't answer, he jostled her head gently. "What does Uncle Willy have to do with *us?*"

Raising her head from his shoulder, Jocelyn exhaled heavily. "Well, it struck me a while back that sometimes people give love the way Willy gives gifts. We give the love we *want* to give, that makes us feel good about ourselves. Not necessarily the love the other person needs."

Phillip sucked in his cheeks and mulled this over for a bit. When he spoke, his voice was tight but controlled. "Is that what I did to you?"

"You?" O'Roarke blinked and shook her head to clear it. "No, I was talking about me. *I'm* Uncle Willy. You wanted a wife—I gave you a playmate. It wasn't enough, but I wouldn't see that."

"Don't make it sound so one-sided. I wouldn't see your side, either," he admitted. Then, disarmed by her candor, blurted out, "Truth is, Josh, I kidded myself for a long time. You were the one woman who never gave me a hard time about my job. Never bitched when I had to cancel a date or when I was tied up on a case and couldn't see you for weeks sometimes. Never cried or carried on when you knew I was on a dangerous assignment."

This last bit prompted her to confess, "Well, not around *you,* maybe. But I was a wreck when you were working on that drug lord homicide."

"Okay. But the point is, I saw that as proof of your absolute devotion. Your willingness to sacrifice all for yours truly," he said with a shamefaced smile. "I blocked out the fact that you could put up with it because you didn't *need* me there all the time. You had a full life independent of me, a life you *liked.* Hell, I was so blind, I didn't even propose to you—I gave an ultimatum. Then, when you wouldn't hop to, I walked out . . . I was a schmuck, Josh."

"Well, yes, you were, sort of. But we're all schmucks sometimes, sweets," O'Roarke soothed as she rubbed her cheek against the sleeve of his jacket. "I think the best any of us can hope for is to not be a schmuck twice . . . That's why I think we should go with the friendship thing."

"How come?! Damn it, Josh, I don't want to be your *pal!*" He spat the last word out with ferocious disdain as he gunned the engine and jerked the car back on the road. Phillip was a hell of a guy, but he was still a guy; a guy who clearly thought that such a heartfelt confession deserved a greater—warmer—reward.

In a sense, it did, but Jocelyn didn't feel that she was the lady to bestow it. Summoning up what was left of her reason and her reasons, she said gently, "Look, things didn't work out between you and Trisha, I know. But that doesn't mean you're going to stop wanting a wife and family, does it?"

"I—I don't know anymore. I haven't really given it much thought."

"It's not a thinking matter, Phil. It's a need people have . . . or they don't. That's all."

"And you just . . . *don't?*"

"That's right . . . but I'd hate myself if I kept you from having it." Squeezing his arm as she squeezed her eyes shut, Jocelyn whispered softly, " 'Cause I think you'd make a great dad, love."

The car was quiet now, save for the hum of the engine, and there were no other vehicles on the road. Phillip looked out at the broad expanse of night sky as his feelings for the woman beside him wrestled against hard sense. Then he saw a sudden spark in the sky, descending toward the horizon.

"Look, Josh. A falling star."

But she was asleep now, deaf to his call. Most of her face was buried in his sleeve, but he thought he saw a drop of moisture in the corner of her right eye and his heart sighed.

Then another star shot down from above and, smiling at his own folly, he made a wish.

FOR THE BEST IN PAPERBACKS, LOOK FOR THE

In every corner of the world, on every subject under the sun, Penguin represents quality and variety—the very best in publishing today.

For complete information about books available from Penguin—including Puffins, Penguin Classics, and Arkana—and how to order them, write to us at the appropriate address below. Please note that for copyright reasons the selection of books varies from country to country.

In the United Kingdom: Please write to *Dept. JC, Penguin Books Ltd, FREEPOST, West Drayton, Middlesex UB7 0BR.*

If you have any difficulty in obtaining a title, please send your order with the correct money, plus ten percent for postage and packaging, to *P.O. Box No. 11, West Drayton, Middlesex UB7 0BR*

In the United States: Please write to *Consumer Sales, Penguin USA, P.O. Box 999, Dept. 17109, Bergenfield, New Jersey 07621-0120.* VISA and MasterCard holders call 1-800-253-6476 to order all Penguin titles

In Canada: Please write to *Penguin Books Canada Ltd, 10 Alcorn Avenue, Suite 300, Toronto, Ontario M4V 3B2*

In Australia: Please write to *Penguin Books Australia Ltd, P.O. Box 257, Ringwood, Victoria 3134*

In New Zealand: Please write to *Penguin Books (NZ) Ltd, Private Bag 102902, North Shore Mail Centre, Auckland 10*

In India: Please write to *Penguin Books India Pvt Ltd, 706 Eros Apartments, 56 Nehru Place, New Delhi 110 019*

In the Netherlands: Please write to *Penguin Books Netherlands bv, Postbus 3507, NL-1001 AH Amsterdam*

In Germany: Please write to *Penguin Books Deutschland GmbH, Metzlerstrasse 26, 60594 Frankfurt am Main*

In Spain: Please write to *Penguin Books S.A., Bravo Murillo 19, 1° B, 28015 Madrid*

In Italy: Please write to *Penguin Italia s.r.l., Via Felice Casati 20, I-20124 Milano*

In France: Please write to *Penguin France S.A., 17 rue Lejeune, F-31000 Toulouse*

In Japan: Please write to *Penguin Books Japan, Ishikiribashi Building, 2-5-4, Suido, Bunkyo-ku, Tokyo 112*

In Greece: Please write to *Penguin Hellas Ltd, Dimocritou 3, GR-106 71 Athens*

In South Africa: Please write to *Longman Penguin Southern Africa (Pty) Ltd, Private Bag X08, Bertsham 2013*